BEST
LESBIAN
LOVE
STORIES
2003

BEST
LESBIAN
LOVE
STORIES

2003

Edited by
ANGELA BROWN

alyson books
los angeles | new york

© 2003 BY ALYSON PUBLICATIONS. ALL RIGHTS RESERVED.

MANUFACTURED IN THE UNITED STATES OF AMERICA.

THIS TRADE PAPERBACK ORIGINAL IS PUBLISHED BY ALYSON PUBLICATIONS,
P.O. BOX 4371, LOS ANGELES, CALIFORNIA 90078-4371.
DISTRIBUTION IN THE UNITED KINGDOM BY TURNAROUND PUBLISHER SERVICES LTD.,
UNIT 3, OLYMPIA TRADING ESTATE, COBURG ROAD, WOOD GREEN,
LONDON N22 6TZ ENGLAND.

FIRST EDITION: JANUARY 2003

03 04 05 06 07 a 10 9 8 7 6 5 4 3 2 1

ISBN 1-55583-765-4

LIBRARY OF CONGRESS CATALOGING-IN-PUBLICATION DATA
    BEST LESBIAN LOVE STORIES 2003 / EDITED BY ANGELA BROWN.—1ST ED.
        ISBN 1-55583-765-5
        1. LESBIANS—FICTION. 2. LOVE STORIES, AMERICAN. 3. AMERICAN FICTION—21ST
    CENTURY. I. BROWN, ANGELA, 1970–
    PS648.L47 B465 2003
    813'085089206643—DC21   2002028028

CREDITS
COVER PHOTOGRAPHY BY STONE.
COVER DESIGN BY MATT SAMS.

For my dear friend
Lisa E. Davis

—CONTENTS—

—INTRODUCTION—

"WHAT IS LOVE?" Most of us so casually toss this word around that the answer doesn't come easily or quickly. We all know saying "I love lobster" isn't the same as telling your girlfriend you love her. And certainly the lobster doesn't feel any of your love (unless you're keeping it as a pet).

All of the stories in this book, in some way or another, attempt to answer this age-old question. And the answers are complex, moving, real. Sometimes, however, there are no answers, only more questions.

In Sally Bellerose's "Portrait of an Artist," for example, love is something unconditional, private; it sets no requirements and makes no demands.

In "Kicks on Route 66," Sylvia Rose shows us that love is about finding out who you are and that sometimes the people we meet on life's path lead us down new and better—and often stranger—paths, even if things don't work out as we'd expected.

Love, in Vittoria repetto's "The Morning Prayer," means being flexible, taking actions you'd never thought you'd take, merely because your lover asks you with a wink and a smile.

In Abbe Ireland's "Soul Jumper," love demands that you not be afraid—afraid to take risks, afraid to be the person you were meant to be. Love is about fulfilling your potential.

Siobhàn Houston, in "Every Day Is a Good Day," equates love with trust.

Zsa Zsa Gershick, in "With You in Spirit," tells us love means being true to yourself.

In "Mrs. Houdini's Wife," Orly Brownstein echoes that sentiment: "That's the worst sin of all," she writes, "to keep your heart locked up, to not say the words you need to say, because you're too proud and maybe afraid."

But perhaps love is best summed up in Elana Dykewomon's "What Love Is":

> You look at the way women's cheeks turn red in the sunlight, the way the old women in the public pool shield themselves from the sun while the young ones splash in whatever covers their nipples and pubic bones. You notice two Chinese-American girls—they look like girls to you, but maybe they're twenty—who just introduced themselves at the beginning of the week, now coming hand in hand, splashing through the slow lane with kick boards and flippers, talking…. All this is love—the quotidian love you get used to in yourself, the kind that makes life tolerable.

So maybe that's what love is: what makes life tolerable. Now, some might say that's not terribly romantic, but in many ways it is. To be able to find love wherever you look? That's not just romantic: It's a gift.

As Elana goes on to explain, "what's interesting about love is the ability to keep loving." My hope is that this book, which is filled with passionate, imaginative, quirky, and heartfelt stories of lesbian love and desire, helps each and every one of you to keep loving. Certainly, *being* loved is a joy, but it's our *ability to love* that makes life worth living—and makes us who we are.

My heartfelt thanks go out to the people *I* love and who love me back: Lisa, Jane, Melissa, Alan, Jon, Becky, Harry, and Redsie. Thank you for your gifts; you make me a better person.

—Angela Brown

—TWO HOUSES, ONE HOME—

Renee Hawkins

"KEEP YOUR VOICE DOWN, WE IN CHURCH!"

"Church is over and I don't give a—"

"Don't you say it! Don't you *dare* say it!"

"God already knows what I was gonna say and so do you!"

Ermond Johnson and her friend Billie Jenkins walked out of the Wednesday service at Osuna Baptist Church. Ermond wondered why they had bothered to come at all. The pair hissed and spat at each other through the entire program. As they made their way to the car, they said hello and goodbye to their friends and argued some more.

"Good night, Sister Johnson, Sister Jenkins."

The two women turned to see the Reverend Charles Hightower walking toward his white Lincoln Navigator.

"Good night, Reverend," they said in unison.

Billie waited until he was out of earshot. "I think we should talk about it now, E!"

"Not now and not here!" Ermond raised her voice.

"Why you keep puttin' me off?"

"Why'd you have to make me clown in church?"

"I didn't make you do anything. Why can't—"

"Billie Jenkins, I said I won't discuss it anymore tonight!"

Billie was not only Ermond's best friend but also her lover. Although the pair looked nothing alike (Ermond was short and brown; Billie was lanky and much darker), they were often mistaken for sisters. Everyone who knew them said they fought like sisters—and this argument was a doozie.

The couple had always talked about living together when Ermond's children left home. After all these years, their plan of moving in "one day" would soon be a reality—maybe.

Billie never bore her own children, but she was there while Ermond took care of two sons and a daughter, along with Ermond's niece. One by one they raised their babies and watched them leave the nest. The last child, Elijah, would be moving out in just a few days, and Billie was anxious to finally "be in one dwelling," as she put it.

But which dwelling? Both women had the idea that hers would be the best place to live in. Both women assumed wrong. Where *exactly* they would settle had never seriously been discussed until now.

"You coming?" Ermond asked. She had already gotten in and started the car.

"Scoot over," said Billie. "I ain't puttin' my life in your hands when you this upset. I'll drive."

The two rode in silence all the way to Ermond's house. Billie pulled into the driveway and turned off the ignition. She looked at Ermond, who had not unfolded her arms since they'd left the church parking lot.

"Ain't no use trying to talk anymore tonight," Billie said, more to herself than Ermond.

"Nope."

Billie sighed. "To hell with it then." She got out of the car, slammed the door, and walked across the street to her house.

BY THE FOLLOWING AFTERNOON, the couple still had not spoken to each other. Ermond sat on the edge of Elijah's bed and watched him pack while she thought about their argument.

"Why aren't you with Aunt Billie today?" he asked her.

"We don't always have to be together."

"Well, it's Saturday and y'all are usually doin' something."

"I want to make sure your cousin makes it in okay."

"Yeah, NeeCee should get here pretty soon. I'm glad she's gonna make the party."

Ermond had planned a little get-together for her baby son. His friends, along with Ermond and Billie's, were invited, and NeeCee being in town would make things extra special. It was going to be a festive Saturday night...if Billie wasn't still acting up.

"What's wrong, Ma?" asked Elijah.

"Nothing. I'm just thinking about what I'm going to do with this room after you move out." Ermond didn't want Elijah to know any more than he had to.

"Why can't you leave my room the way it is? What if I need to move back home?"

"Boy, you'd better not! You're the last one out of my house, and I'm changing the locks. It's time I got a life too, you know."

"I was just playin'. NeeCee is going to take good care of me in D.C."

Ermond was glad Elijah would have some family nearby. His brother and sister had both settled on the West Coast—Isaac in San Francisco and Maya in San Diego.

Elijah had accepted a job at an accounting firm in Washington and would stay with NeeCee until he got squared away. She and her partner, Chantal, had insisted on coming down to help him move. They'd have an entire week together before Elijah would be out of the house for good. And then what? It was time for Ermond to begin a new phase of her life as well; she just didn't know what to do about Billie.

"Hey, Mom?"

"Yeah, baby?"

"We got any boxes in the basement?"

"I don't think so," she answered. Suddenly she had an idea.

"I'll go and see if your auntie has some." Ermond couldn't stand it any longer. She decided she would be the bigger person and go talk to Billie. She was also curious as to what Billie had been doing all day without her. She checked her salt-and-pepper hair in the mirror and walked outside.

It took exactly 137 steps to get to Billie's front door, and it pained Ermond to take every one of them. The situation had gotten ridiculous, and she wasn't up for any more fighting. It was time to settle things, and Billie needed to come around to her way of thinking *quickly*.

Billie's house sat on the corner and was much bigger than Ermond's. It was an old-style Victorian structure, and Billie kept the grounds immaculate, toiling in her garden every weekend. Although it was comfortable, Ermond argued that it would take a lot of work for them to try and keep up with.

Ermond let herself in and found Billie on the couch eating a sandwich. "Billie, you're sittin' there like we don't have anything to do today."

"What we got to do today is decide where we gonna be tomorrow. I say right here."

"Woman, it makes no sense to live here."

"Why not?" Billie asked.

"This house is a monstrosity and you know it!"

"And *you* know what I went through to hang onto this place!"

Billie hadn't had much of a marriage. Although she was a supervisor at the auto plant and dubbed a "fierce independent woman" by her coworkers, her husband had controlled her. He had seldom been at home and had stayed out all night when he wanted to. And when he had been with her, he was negative and abusive. He eventually took up with another woman, leaving Billie with all of their bills. Would she lose her independence if she sold her house and moved into Ermond's?

"You know you can make any changes you want," Ermond told her.

"Make changes. I wouldn't want to inconvenience you."

"That's not what I mean."

"Well, what do you mean?"

"I mean we should discuss this some more."

"What you really mean is you gonna keep on talkin' till you wear me down."

Ermond threw her hands in the air. "You're still bein' a smart aleck. We might as well not talk about this anymore today."

"Fine with me."

"Fine, then I'm going home. And you know NeeCee will be here any minute, and you know she's going to want to see you."

"When has she ever *not* wanted to see her favorite auntie?"

"I'm just lettin' you know."

"Fine."

Ermond retraced the 137 steps back to her house.

NEECEE AND HER GIRLFRIEND, CHANTAL, arrived just as the sun was going down. They were tired from the drive but excited to finally be there. Ermond hugged them both. She liked Chantal and was happy to see her niece.

NeeCee had come to live with Ermond when she was only fourteen. Ermond's sister Carolyn had kicked the child out of the house after NeeCee announced one day that she was a lesbian. Ermond simply did the right thing and took her in.

Ermond tried to talk to Carolyn about NeeCee, but it didn't change things. Their father was a reverend and they'd had a very strict upbringing. Ermond understood how her sister felt about homosexuality, she just didn't agree—and kicking out your own flesh and blood was unthinkable.

Ermond believed the Lord loved everybody, no matter who they had sex with. She and God were tight, and she was strong in the church, attending with Billie at least twice a week. They raised all her children in a way that they could make their own choices about religion.

NeeCee and Chantal came downstairs. "We're going over to Aunt Billie's," NeeCee announced.

Ermond wanted to go too, but she wasn't about to step foot across the street without Billie's personal invitation. "Y'all go ahead. I need to start a list for the party," she told them.

After they left, Ermond loaded the dishwasher and puttered around the kitchen. "I'm not trying to wear her down," she mumbled. Who did Billie think she was talking to?

Ermond went to the large walk-in closet she used as a pantry. It could hold everything under the sun, including several months' worth of groceries—and there was still room for a small army to sit inside and eat. She opened one of the accordion doors and peered inside, trying to remember why she had gone there in the first place. "That woman makes me so mad!" Ermond said. Kicking and cursing, she took her anger out on the door—and with no one else in the house, she made as much noise as she wanted to. Her tantrum, however, was cut short by voices on the front porch. The kids were already back home.

"Did you see your Aunt Billie?" she asked them.

"Yeah, but she wasn't feeling well, so we came home," replied Chantal.

"She didn't tell you to tell me anything?"

"She just said she'd see us tomorrow," Elijah told her.

"I guess I'm going to lie down myself," Ermond said. She went up to her room, slammed the door, and went to bed.

ON FRIDAY, ERMOND RAN ERRANDS with the girls and tried to stay busy. She kept checking her messages even though her cell phone never rang. When they got back to the house, Ermond finally picked up the phone and dialed Billie's number.

"Hello?"

"Were you going to call me today?" Ermond demanded.

Billie knew whatever she said was not going to be the right thing, so she didn't say anything.

"Well, don't you think I need help with the party tomorrow?"

Billie still didn't answer, so Ermond switched gears. "The kids and I are going to watch a movie. Why don't you come over?"

"I ain't coming over for another battle, I promise you that," Billie finally said.

"I didn't say anything about fighting! We're going to watch TV. You comin' or not?"

"If we don't fight, I will."

"I said there won't be any fighting."

"But we do need to talk."

"Look, woman, I'm not going to beg you. Come if you want." Ermond hung up the phone.

Billie came right over, and it was like the old days again. Chantal and NeeCee were home and so was Elijah for a change. He had his own life now and wasn't around much in the evenings. Billie couldn't remember the last time they had all watched TV together.

The couple drank quite a bit of wine, and Ermond was feeling no pain. She tried to convince the kids to stay for another movie, but they decided to visit one of Elijah's friends instead.

"Let's go in the kitchen and get us another 'little taste,' " Ermond suggested.

"You finally ready to talk?"

Ermond poured herself a glass of Alizé and took a healthy swallow. "Billie, I don't want to argue tonight. I don't want to argue anymore, period. So let's just call a truce until Elijah leaves. We'll work it out then. Deal?"

Billie was a little disappointed, but she didn't want to push things. They were having such a good time together, and Ermond looked so fine tonight. "Okay," Billie agreed. She leaned over and grazed Ermond's mouth with her own.

What started out as a light kiss turned into much more— and Ermond was in heaven. Billie put her in a state of suspended ecstasy for what seemed like hours. Every stitch of their clothing went on the floor and Ermond didn't care. Her skin was electrified by Billie's touch, her head swimming. She leaned back on the kitchen table and pushed Billie's head downward.

Suddenly they heard voices outside and a key turning in the front door. Billie and Ermond were trapped in the kitchen, and there was no time to get dressed.

"Quick! Get in the pantry!" Ermond told Billie. She grabbed their clothes and pushed her inside.

"Well, baby, we've never screwed in the food closet before," Billie said.

"And we ain't gonna now!" Ermond hissed. "Shut up and get dressed!"

"But we just got *undressed*," Billie protested.

Chantal and NeeCee came into the kitchen, and one of them opened the refrigerator door.

"I guess everybody's 'sleep," said Chantal.

"Are you hungry?" NeeCee asked.

"I'm too tired to eat. Maybe we should've gone with Elijah and his little girlfriend."

"Now, you know he didn't want us going to eat with them. I can heat you up something if you want."

Ermond was mortified. "If they come in here, what are we gonna say?" she asked Billie.

"Whose house is this? We ain't got to explain ourselves."

"Hush, Billie, and put your clothes back on!" Ermond commanded.

NeeCee walked across the kitchen to Chantal. "Well, I know what I'd like to eat."

Chantal moved away from NeeCee and stood right outside the pantry door. "I know where this is going, and I don't want to do anything down here."

"Girl, don't worry," NeeCee told her.

"No! Somebody might walk in on us."

"I can be quiet, Chantal, I promise."

"You're crazy, NeeCee...stop." Chantal giggled.

Ermond was beside herself. She didn't want to get caught in

the pantry, and she certainly didn't want to hear any more of what was going on in the kitchen. She held on to Billie and wished they were invisible.

The two women heard NeeCee say, "Uh-uh-uh *no-o-o,* baby, move your hand."

Billie almost laughed out loud at that one. Ermond put her hand over Billie's mouth just in case. "Quiet!" she told her.

Chantal finally came up for air. "NeeCee, I can't here. Let's go upstairs, okay?"

"Okay, baby."

When Ermond and Billie were sure the girls had gone upstairs, they came out of the pantry.

"I taught my NeeCee everything she knows," Billie said.

"And what did you tell her to do if she was ever found half-naked in the kitchen?"

"I told her to enjoy herself first, 'cause life's too short."

Ermond laughed despite the situation. "The next time NeeCee visits, we'll be living in one house." she said. "And soon we won't have to worry about what goes on here in the kitchen."

Billie suddenly became angry. "E, why does it have to be here?"

"It doesn't, honey. That's not what I meant."

"Yeah, I know what you meant. Here we go again." Billie walked toward the front door. "Damn, we might as well keep things the way they is."

Ermond started after Billie but then let her go. *Now, how did that happen?* Ermond asked herself.

ERMOND SAT ON HER FRONT PORCH and yawned. It was early Saturday morning and the sun was barely rising in the sky. She hardly noticed what a beautiful day it was going to be. She felt as if someone had unplugged her; she'd tossed and turned all night and finally got up and went outside. Ermond needed a place to sit and think; being on the swing usually soothed her.

She looked up and down the street and tried to enjoy the quiet. Clarkston, Georgia, was just far enough away from downtown Atlanta to have a small-town feel, and Ermond loved her neighborhood. The subdivisions that had sprung up around them offered nothing but cookie-cutter boxes built too close together. Ermond and Billie wanted to have nothing to do with a new house. It was the only thing they agreed on at that point.

Ermond thought she saw the curtains move across the street. No, not yet, it was too early. Billie slept late on Saturdays, slept late whenever she could. One thing Ermond knew for sure, Billie was able to snore through anything. She, on the other hand, slept light and could never rest when there was something on her mind. Last night was hard, especially after Billie had gotten her so worked up. They'd come so close to making up!

Ermond thought back to how it all started between them. She and Billie had been neighbors for many years, but they began to spend more time together after Ermond's divorce. Her husband, Albert, was a good man, but there was really no "juice" between them. They were so young when they started dating. He was the son of a church deacon, and that was the only reason her mother and father had let him come around at all. Deacon's son or not, he was still a teenager, and he and Ermond hadn't been careful. On her seventeenth birthday, Ermond found out that she was pregnant, which caused a scandal within the church and a hasty wedding.

Albert joined the military and supported his family, while Ermond kept up with her education and became a teacher. The couple had two more children and settled into a comfortable life—but not the life Ermond wanted. She asked Albert for a divorce and he obliged her. He remained a good father to his children and eventually remarried.

Ermond knew something was still missing; she just couldn't figure out what it was. She began spending more and more time with Billie until all at once she realized that was all she wanted to do.

The two women had gotten into the habit of renting movies on Fridays. They'd watch a PG video first, then something more adult after the kids went to bed. Ermond liked love stories, Billie liked scary movies, and they both enjoyed comedies. They'd order pizza or get takeout and have a ball. But Ermond could never sit through an entire movie. She'd often make them stop in the middle and go on the porch to have a smoke. Billie eventually helped her kick the habit, but in those days Ermond could puff through a pack in no time.

One night, after getting the kids off to bed, Ermond and Billie took a break outside. It was the middle of summer and the air was muggy. The pair turned off the porch light and watched the fireflies streak across the yard like shooting stars.

When Ermond realized she had forgotten about having a cigarette, she knew this was the time to let Billie know how she felt. On the porch, in the dark, on the swing, she told her. "I want to be with you the way I am with myself," she announced. She couldn't make out the expression on Billie's face, so she took a deep breath and continued. "I always wanted a companion who was also my friend. I feel like I can have that with you. And I know I want to spend the rest of my life with you—as a couple."

Billie shifted her weight on the swing but said nothing. Ermond knew—she just *knew*—Billie felt the same way she did. Finally, Billie reached over and took Ermond's hand.

They didn't watch a second movie that night. Instead they stayed on the porch and talked for hours. And just before the sun came up and Billie was about to go home, Ermond gave her the sweetest kiss. And so they began.

A MOVEMENT ACROSS THE STREET caught Ermond's eye. Billie had just opened her front door and had already pulled back the curtains in the living room. She was finally awake. Ermond wanted to talk to her, but she was too stubborn to go and make peace. Ermond reasoned that there was no sense in approaching her until Billie finished her yard work anyway; she'd be heading for the lawn mower any minute. Before the boys got older, she'd come over and do Ermond's grass too. Now there would be no need for all that trouble. Ermond's lot was just the right size for both of them. "That woman needs to come to her senses," she said out loud.

She didn't want Billie to see her but knew she already had. Ermond stood up and went into the kitchen for some caffeine. Billie had surprised her with a bag of Jamaican Blue Mountain a while back, and she had been thrilled. This morning it was just what the doctor ordered. Ermond ground some beans and poured water into the coffeemaker. It was too early to start breakfast for the kids, so she sat at the kitchen table in anticipation of her first cup of the morning and thought more about Billie.

Their relationship had blossomed over the years, and they stole moments together when they could. There were only a handful of times that the couple slept all night in the same bed, especially when the children got older. Billie usually went back across the street before anyone got up.

But once a year they'd drop off the kids at their grandparents' house and go out of town, just the two of them. Ermond and Billie had lived that way for more than twenty years. Even though they talked about having a home together at some point, they knew it wasn't going to be anytime soon. Suddenly, though, it seemed that time had crept up on them.

SATURDAY NIGHT CAME, and Ermond's house was full of people. Elijah, NeeCee, and their friends mixed it up with the older crowd. The music alternated between "old school" and the most current, and everyone seemed to be having a good time—except Ermond.

Billie didn't call all afternoon but had finally come over to help with the party. She kept her distance from Ermond, and they were never alone long enough to talk.

A serious game of bid whist was underway. There was a lot

of trash-talking, and cards were slammed down on the table for emphasis. Partners weren't supposed to talk to each other about what was in their hands, so elaborate codes were used to communicate. Those looking on were quite entertained as they awaited their turn to play.

A big-boned woman named Ruby Knight came to the card table with a plate piled high with food. "Could someone tell Sister Johnson and Sister Jenkins they *won't* be together tonight so things can be little more fair?" she asked.

Billie reached over and plucked a wing from the woman's hand. "Well, could someone tell Sister Knight she is a guest up in my camp and when she is in *her* house she can make up all the rules she wants?"

"Y'all know you can read each other's minds," Sister Knight retorted.

Ermond listened to the banter and had what she called a "lightbulb moment." No one seemed to notice that Billie had just announced that this was her house too. Ermond knew her well enough to know that was exactly what she meant. She wished she really could read Billie's mind right now.

Everyone was laughing at Billie, who hadn't let up on Sister Knight. "And if you paid half attention to your partner, you might have a chance to win a round." She paused for effect. "But I doubt it."

NeeCee entered the fray. "Don't worry, Miss Ruby. I'll sit in for Aunt Billie and give you a chance."

"I ain't buyin' that. You gals are 'The Sly, the Slick, and the Wicked.'"

NeeCee laughed, because it was true. She could play with Ermond or Billie and do quite well. She'd learned every trick in the book just by watching them.

Ermond was still thinking about what Billie had said. Had she really made up her mind? If only she could get Billie alone, she could talk to her. Maybe they could go upstairs for a few minutes.

Billie stood up, and Ermond thought this might be her chance.

"Whew, what a night! I think I'm gonna go home," Billie announced.

Elijah stood up too. "Why you got to leave so soon, Aunt Billie?"

"Baby, your Aunt Billie is tired. I'm going to bed." She said good night to everyone, casually touching Ermond's arm as she made her way to the front door. "I'll holler at you tomorrow, E" was all she said.

Ermond was hurt but couldn't let it show in front of everyone. She finished out the night fine, even winning a few rounds of bid whist with NeeCee, but her heart wasn't in it. She missed Billie and desperately wanted to talk to her.

After everyone left, Ermond started on the dishes. She could never go to bed with a messy house, and cleaning took her mind off Billie. She put the children to work too, and they laughed and talked while they got things back in order.

"So, Mrs. Johnson, how do you feel about having the place all to yourself?" Chantal asked. "Elijah will be out of here soon."

Ermond looked at her son. Elijah was the baby of the family, just a year younger than NeeCee. He came into the world weighing less than any of his siblings had when they were born, but he turned out just fine, shooting up taller than his dad or brother. Now he was all grown up, ready to take his place in the world.

"I've done a good job," she answered truthfully. She turned to Elijah. "Son, how do you feel about leaving your old mother alone?"

"I'm not leaving you completely alone, Ma. You have Aunt Billie."

"I won't have a man around the house to do my chores anymore."

"You have enough money to pay somebody," Elijah replied. "And you and Aunt Billie should be together now anyways."

Ermond froze. She looked at each of the faces of the children.

"It's not like we haven't known all these years, Mom." Elijah came over and hugged her. "It's okay with me—it's been okay with all of us."

"Chantal and I want the kind of relationship you and Aunt Billie have," NeeCee added.

Ermond was amazed. She never thought she'd see the day when she discussed her sex life with her kids. "Sometimes the obvious still needs to be said," she told them.

Ermond had always had two reasons not to live with Billie. She didn't care what other people thought, but she didn't want to bring any negativity on her children. She also felt that shackin' up with someone other than their father wasn't the right example to set while the kids were growing up. But were those just excuses? Had she cheated herself and Billie all these years? She was too old now to care about how anybody felt, although it was nice to have her family's blessing.

FIRST THING SUNDAY MORNING, Ermond tried to call Billie but got her answering machine. Disappointed, she hung up without leaving a message, and she and the kids went to church without Billie. But when Billie didn't show up at the service, it was all Ermond could do to stay and listen to Reverend Hightower's sermon on patience. God definitely had a sense of humor.

As soon as they got home, Ermond sent everyone inside, and she headed across the street. It was time to have a talk with Miss Billie Jenkins. She walked in the front door and found Billie in the kitchen, putting glaze on a fresh cake.

"Are you going to stop this foolishness?" Ermond asked.

"The only one who's being foolish is you."

"NeeCee came all this way to see you and you haven't even been around."

"NeeCee's gonna be here for a whole week, and we've had plenty of time together already," Billie replied. " 'Sides, who you think this pound cake is for?"

That stopped Ermond, who didn't know what to say next. She watched Billie slowly move about the kitchen.

Billie spoke as if she had just read Ermond's mind. "My back was actin' up this morning, so I didn't make it to church."

"You seem to be feeling better now. I tried to call you."

"I didn't hear the phone," Billie replied. "E, were you worried about NeeCee or did you think about me at all?"

"I miss you," Ermond admitted.

Billie put her arms around her. "I miss you too. I just don't wanna fuss no more."

"Are you going to eat Sunday dinner with us?"

"Of course."

Ermond picked up the cake and walked Billie across the street. The kids met the pair at the door.

"Pound cake! My favorite!" NeeCee squealed.

"Don't y'all ruin your dinner," Ermond scolded. "We're eating in a little while."

By then it was too late, because Elijah had already broken off a piece. "Aunt Billie, you put your whole foot in this cake!"

"Thank you, baby," Billie replied.

Ermond rolled her eyes. "Oh, never mind. You kids eat dinner when you're ready—we're going upstairs for a while."

"Yeah, you two need to talk," said Elijah.

Billie looked at him. "Don't talk with your mouth full. And watch yourself, now—you don't need to be in my Kool-Aid."

"Enough," Ermond interrupted the pair. "I'm going to make your auntie go soak in the tub."

The couple went upstairs to the bathroom, and Ermond started the water. That tub had always been good to her. It was an oversize cast-iron monster, and Ermond was shocked when she had recently priced a fake one at the bath and tile store. Whoever made that thing must have had her in mind. After a hard day at school, Ermond would lock herself in her bedroom and soak in her big, beautiful bathtub.

Ermond got out of her church clothes and put on her housecoat.

She pulled out Billie's robe too and took it into the bathroom for her. Before she placed it on the commode, Ermond did something she hadn't done in a while. She put the robe to her face and inhaled Billie's scent.

Billie watched as she lowered herself into the water. "I've never seen you do that before."

"You weren't ever supposed to see me do that," Ermond replied.

"It's been a while since we both been in here, huh?"

"Mm-hmm."

Ermond thought about all the times they'd had in that tub. She remembered giving Billie a bath after she'd hurt her back at work. She remembered getting bathed when she'd been in the car accident last year. And there were other memories that made her tingle.

"I told you it would do you some good," Ermond said.

"Yeah, I know." Billie turned up the hot water with her big toe.

Ermond leaned against the sink and watched a wave of pleasure roll across Billie's face as the bathwater got warmer. She walked over and studied Billie's hair. "I need to trim this mess on your neck," she told her. She fingered the new growth, then began massaging Billie's back. She wanted to pull the tension out of her skin and rub away the brick wall between them. She took the washcloth out of Billie's hand and turned off the faucet.

"Guess I overdid it in the yard yesterday," Billie said.

"You don't have to do everything, you know."

"I know."

Ermond kissed Billie's shoulder. "You don't need all that house now, you really don't."

"You had to say that."

"Honey, I know you love your yard, but it's gotten too big for you, don't you think?"

Billie would not concede the point but turned so that Ermond could wash more of her skin. Ermond gently made broad, soapy circles; she moved the cloth over Billie's breasts, then down into the water between her legs.

Billie protested, but Ermond cleared her throat and said, "Uh-uh-uh *no-o-o*, baby, move your hand." The two women laughed at Ermond's impression of NeeCee.

With one hand, Ermond continued to use the washcloth, and with the other hand, she unbuttoned her housecoat. Her body ached with desire as she climbed into the tub with Billie.

Ermond knew Billie's body well and took her time as she led her on a familiar journey. They splashed water all over the walls and floor and never thought about how the sound in the bathroom carried. At one point, Ermond thought about making use of the shower wand, but she didn't want to stop even for a minute—things were too delicious.

There was no one else in the world but Billie and Ermond. And when Billie climaxed, she raised up all the way out of the water, just like Ermond knew she would. Ermond gave herself to Billie and came soon afterward.

"If we could be in this tub more, I wouldn't put up such a fight," Billie said.

"No more fighting. I just want you with me," Ermond whispered. She hugged Billie. Their lovemaking had been so good, she didn't mind that she had just sweated out all the curls in her fresh perm.

"We've been arguing a lot lately," Billie told her.

"We're going to have disagreements...we always have," Ermond murmured.

"You right about that."

Ermond felt wonderful. If she had her way, she would stay cocooned in the bathtub with Billie all day. She turned so that she could look directly into her eyes. "I know I don't say it much anymore, but I love you, Billie Jenkins, I really do. And I love what we just did."

"E, honestly, you still want me, don't you?"

"After all this time you still have to wonder? Woman, we're stuck with each other."

"Then my vote is we live here," Billie said.

"Here?"

"Yup."

Ermond looked at her in surprise. "You'd already decided, hadn't you?"

"Yeah, Saturday morning. You looked so miserable on the porch with your chin on the floor." Billie laughed.

Ermond giggled and pinched her. "You should've come across the street and talked to me."

"You're the one who wanted to wait to talk, remember?"

"And what made you decide?"

"I thought about it, E. What good would it be if I had my big ol' house and not you? And then my back started talkin' to me after I did the yard." Billie smiled. "The answer was obvious."

"So you really mean it? You want to live here?"

"I really do," Billie said.

"Then welcome home, woman." And with that Ermond gave Billie the sweetest kiss.

—MARTIN BEBARTIN—

Carol Guess

KATE IS CURLED UP IN THE BIG CHAIR in the bookstore's back room, a pile of children's books stacked beside her, Martin's blond head just visible above the armrest. She's reading to him in her soft, expressive voice, and he's yawning, as Leigh slips in the back door. It's Leigh's turn to work—she volunteers at WomanSpark Books on Saturday afternoons—and she's nine minutes late for her shift. She doesn't see Kate or Martin as she makes her way to the front of the store, still panting from her hurried bike ride, clutching a bag that smells of butter and chocolate.

"Jeez, I'm sorry, Alicia," Leigh says to the gray-eyed woman behind the register. "I meant to be on time, but then I smelled the scones at The Bake Off and had to stop. But I got you one." She ruffles inside the bag. "Here you go."

"Thanks, kid. Can you take over the register now? I need to pick up Lindy."

"Sure. It's my shift, isn't it? I'm all set." Leigh settles into the chair behind the desk and begins straightening the pens and bookmarks. "Take off. Fly and be free."

Alicia smiles; once she's shut the door behind her, Leigh flips off Alicia's tape—*Sounds of the Forest (With Hoot Owls)*—and puts on k.d. lang. She turns up the volume a notch for good measure, then rummages for the feather duster and attacks the Women's Spirituality section. Dust flies as she hums, occasionally conducting.

After a few minutes of frenzied cleaning, Leigh gets bored and settles behind the desk with *The Joy of Lesbian Sex*. She reads for about half an hour, until she hears a noise—a small cough, like a little kid's. Weird. Has someone come in the store unnoticed? She gets up to explore and finds her answer in the far room: a dark-haired woman in a dark-blue shirt, her mouth open as she sleeps in the big green chair, and a boy, no more than five or six, curled crossways in her arms, also sleeping, but nodding his head fitfully.

Leigh stands still for a moment. She can hear the music a little, even here, and tiptoes back to turn it off, but by the time she's reached the desk she hears slow waking sounds: a woman's voice to a child, a child's drawling reply. A few minutes more, and the boy emerges, tugging on his yellow-and-white YMCA T-shirt, his hair sticking straight up. He looks gravely at Leigh and frowns; Leigh looks gravely back. She likes the *idea* of kids, but in reality she feels awkward around them.

"Where's Alicia?" His tone is indignant; Leigh senses he'll be hard to placate. She holds out her hand.

"Hi, I'm Leigh. What's your name?"

He looks down at the carpet and tugs harder on his shirt.

Leigh tries again. Holding out a paper bag: "Do you like chocolate?" A slow smile; without looking up, he puts his hand in and pulls out a chocolate-chip scone. Leigh feels relieved, but as he eats she begins to wonder: Should she have asked his mother first? What if he's allergic to chocolate?

"How kind of you."

Leigh looks up to see the dark-haired woman in the doorway; she's startled by how young the woman looks. Not more than twenty-five, thinks Leigh, not much older than her. Her eyes are extremely blue, and there's a gap between her front teeth. She has overalls on, and yellow sneakers.

"I'm Kate, and this is Martin. It was super of you to give him a goodie. Marty, can you say thanks to…"

"My name's Leigh."

"Say, 'Thanks, Leigh,' " Kate prompts, but Martin wraps his arms around his mother's legs and turns his face away. "I'm sorry." Kate smiles at Leigh. "He's terribly shy." She tousles his hair, and he makes a small sound, like a sigh. He turns his attention back to his scone.

"Has Alicia taken off, then?"

Leigh nods. "Yeah, I work the rest of the Saturday shift."

"Ah, you must be new, then, since we've never met. We come in almost every Saturday." Kate looks down at her son, who's busy picking chocolate chips out of his scone. "This is Martin's favorite store. Right, Marty?"

Martin drops his chin to his chest. "Can I color?"

"Sure, hon."

He hops on one foot over to the coloring books by the window. Both women laugh.

"So, are you new?"

"Not really. I mean, what counts as new, right? I've been working here five or six weeks."

"That's new." Kate smiles. "But that also explains why we haven't met. We've been coming during story hour on Saturdays the last two months."

"Oh, so that's how you know Alicia," Leigh begins, as the phone rings. She picks up: "Hello, WomanSpark Books…yes, till six…certainly. Thanks for calling." Turning again to Kate: "I know Alicia runs the storytelling program."

"Oh, yes. And Martin hates to miss a Saturday. But that's not how I…that's not how…well, Alicia is my ex-partner. That's how I…that's how we know her."

Leigh stands quietly for a moment, still holding the phone. She feels surprised, and angry at herself for feeling surprised. "Wow," she says, aware of sounding stupid but unsure what else to say.

"Mom, I did a picture of Samuel." Martin waves a crayoned sheet of paper at Kate's knees.

"Wow, Marty. You've really captured his spirit." Kate hands the paper to Leigh, who takes in several yellow circles and a horizontal orange slash.

"No!" Martin grabs at the paper. "No! She's got it all upside down!"

Leigh tilts the paper. "Who's Samuel?"

"Alicia's cat," Kate says, as the door rattles and several women enter.

"Let me know if I can help you with anything." Leigh smiles in their direction; one of the women nods. Kate glances at her watch.

"It's almost five. Marty, we'd better get a move on if we're going to stop by the library." She puts two books on the counter. "I'll take these."

From behind the register, Leigh watches as Kate kneels beside Martin and helps him with his jacket. She rings up the first book, a slim kids' story with a watercolor of a turtle on the cover. The cover of the book underneath gleams red and gold: Above the head of a naked woman shown from the back is the title, *The Erotic Naiad*. Leigh finds herself blushing. She places a yellow WomanSpark bookmark inside the turtle book.

Kate stands up, rummaging in her purse for her checkbook. As she leans over the counter to write, without looking up, she says, "I'm glad we met. Maybe we'll run into each other again next Saturday." It sounds very much like a question. She tears off a check and hands it to Leigh, still looking down at her checkbook. Leigh forgets for a moment to give Kate the books she's just bought. They're both still.

Then Martin is at Kate's side, wanting to go, whining a little. Kate faces Leigh. "Well, you know, Marty will be staying with his dad next weekend. So maybe if...I mean, maybe if you wanted, we could...have coffee after your shift. I mean, if you're not too busy." She puts the books under her arm and chews on her bottom lip.

23

"That'd be great. I get off at six."

"Should I just meet you here before closing?" Kate's tone is casual now; she looks Leigh in the eye steadily.

"Sure." Leigh looks away.

"Well, see you next Saturday." Leigh watches through the glass door, and then through the window, as Kate and Martin head for a small blue Honda.

BACK HOME, LEIGH SLIPS INTO her pajamas and opens a box of Oreos. She could go to the bar with Kim and Amy, but she doesn't feel up to it. Besides, she wants to think. She needs to understand what's just happened, who Kate is, what she wants.

Leigh is nibbling on a cookie and searching under her bed for her journal when the phone rings. It's Cassie, her best friend. Cassie lives in North Carolina and works as a cashier in a health food store. She left the history department three months ago with a master's: "No more theory," she said, and took off, leaving Leigh to mourn and run up extravagant phone bills. Leigh always says to anyone who'll listen that if Cassie weren't straight—if only she weren't straight! Of course, she never says this to Cassie. It's the only thing she never says to Cassie.

"Hey, Cass, what's up?" Cassie is embroiled in a turbulent long-distance affair with a man ten years her senior, who's seeing another woman simultaneously. The other woman's name is Mary Christmas. The man's name is Joe Smith.

"Joe and I are through." Cassie's voice is resolute, hardened; Leigh sits back to listen. Cassie and Joe are forever breaking up, getting together again, then slowly drifting apart.

"Cass. Tell me about it," and she does, breathlessly speeding through days' worth of minute thoughts, only to stop abruptly.

"But wait, Leigh, tell me what's happening with you."

Leigh is thinking of Kate's face when she first saw her, sleeping in the back room. She's trying to remember how her eyes looked when they were shut: if the lids were translucent, if her lashes fluttered slightly.

"Well, Cass, I met this woman today..."

Cassie breaks through with a roar. "That's fabulous! Tell me about her."

Twisting the phone cord around her wrist, Leigh describes Kate: her slow way of talking, words interspersed with long silences, the way her hair just brushes her shoulders, her bright overalls.

"Is she gay?" Cassie's twin sisters are both gay, and sometimes Leigh feels as if Cassie knows more about lesbians than she does.

"She mentioned something about Alicia being her ex-partner."

"Sounds like she wanted you to know that."

"Well, maybe."

"Will you see her again, do you think?"

Leigh swallows a bite of cookie. "Umm...I mean, that's the thing, Cassie. She sort of...she said we could...well, we're going to have coffee next Saturday."

"She asked you out?"

"Oh, no, she just wants to have coffee." Leigh wants Cassie to understand the difference.

"Leigh Ann Nicholson. Don't you know a line when you hear it? She wants to go out with you. It's your first dyke date!" Cassie begins whistling the wedding march.

Leigh closes her eyes. "Shut up."

"Leigh, my God. What's wrong? You should be excited. She sounds nice, she's cute, she's interested in you. You've been wanting this for how long now? How long have you been out?"

Cipher, Leigh's cat, begins clawing at her thigh. She puts him in her lap and rubs his chin. "Five months." She remembers sitting on Cassie's back porch that evening in June, watching shadows blend into nightfall, sipping beer, trying to make the hard words come. They stayed up till four because, as it turned out, Cassie was also keeping back words. They sat in the dark for hours, talking about nothing, each trying in her own way to broach the subject, each wishing the other would read her mind. Finally, around one-thirty, Cassie turned to Leigh.

"Put your hand on my stomach," she said, and Leigh froze, wondering whether Cassie had indeed read her mind. Leigh sat like a stone, so Cassie took her left hand and placed it on her belly. "I'm pregnant."

"Aren't you excited, Leigh? Isn't this what you've wanted?"

Cipher rolls over, paws straight up in the air like a dead thing, and Leigh rubs his belly. She can't explain what she's feeling to Cassie. She can't figure it out in her head, much less put it into words. But she knows what she's feeling has something to do with Martin. She imagines his small, chicken-yellow hair; she sees again Kate fixing his jacket.

"She's a mother, Cass." Leigh feels the impact of the words—they seem to carry colors with them, little pennants.

"So?"

"What do you mean, 'So?' "

"What do you mean, 'She's a mother?' "

"You know what I mean!" Leigh hopes Cassie will indeed know and can explain it to Leigh, who's not at all sure why she's said what she's said, who's lost in her feelings, muddy inside.

"I don't do mind-reading." Leigh can tell Cassie is on the brink of becoming angry. She holds the phone cord over her head so Cipher will stop batting at it.

"Shit, Cass...I don't know what I mean. It's like...well, she was in WomanSpark with her son, whose name is Martin. He must be five or six..."

"How old is she?"

"I think probably twenty-five. Yeah, so anyway, she was in there, and when I first saw them, I thought for sure she was straight."

Cassie whistles. "Oh, I get it. You figured if she had a kid, she couldn't be queer, right? And now you're feeling weirded out and stupid because your first impression of her was wrong?"

Why not be more blunt, thinks Leigh. "Sort of."

"If I'm wrong, don't humor me. Explain yourself."

Leigh takes a deep breath; Cipher jumps off her lap and begins clawing the curtains. "I don't know...I just feel strange. I mean, she's around my age, but she has a child. It feels...incestuous or something."

"Leigh, she's not *your* mother."

"It's just not what I was expecting."

"Do you like her? Does she seem cool? Are you attracted to her?"

"Yeah. Yeah, I am."

"Well, it sounds like you need to get over your big problem. Sounds like you've got motheraphobia, and it's got to go."

THAT NIGHT, LEIGH STRETCHES out on her bed, staring at the ceiling and listening to Cipher lick his paws. After a while, he purrs, and Leigh relaxes a little. His purr is odd—it's what made her choose him from among the cuter and younger kittens at the shelter. He always sounds like he's humming; sometimes she tries to put a tune to it. Tonight she decides it sounds like "Layla."

She looks over at the clock: four minutes after twelve. She wishes she could fall asleep the way Cassie does, swiftly, curved into a C, with always a little smile on her mouth. She remembers lying on the futon across from Cassie's bed that night in June, watching Cassie breathe, wondering about the baby. She knew even then that Cassie would have an abortion, although Cassie hadn't said anything about it that night.

Now, imagining Cassie sleeping, Leigh puts one hand under the covers. The cat's purr vanishes, and she closes her eyes, picturing a strange woman's face, a woman's body above her body, a woman's eyes looking into her eyes, over her breasts, over and above her thighs. Leigh feels the way she often feels at night now: full of wanting, ready with pictures. But she always stops herself quickly. She'll sit up, biting her lip, snap on the light, drink from the glass of water beside her bed. It's as if there's something keeping her from dreaming. She doesn't know what she's afraid of. She doesn't know what she would see if she let herself keep going.

ON SATURDAY, LEIGH PUTS ON her favorite Two Nice Girls T-shirt, the one with the fist. She wears her brown hiking boots and her oldest jeans. Her shift drags and drags; she makes small talk with customers but keeps drifting off mid conversation, saying inane things. At exactly five forty-five, Leigh spots Kate through the glass door. She turns her head away quickly, pretends to be absorbed in conversation with Millie, who's trying to enlighten Leigh about ecofeminism.

"Yeah," Leigh says, nodding intently, not listening at all. Millie has on a big, chunky necklace made of some sort of bone. The bone is wrapped with several brightly colored feathers. She's wearing a blue T-shirt with a picture of the earth that says LOVE YOUR MOTHER. The picture reminds Leigh of a TV show she watched as a kid: *Big Blue Marble*. Is that still going? she wonders. Does Martin watch it? She nods again at Millie. "Yeah, that's right."

Kate disappears into the back. Later, when they're settled into a booth at Java Corner, Leigh will tease Kate, asking why she didn't stop at the register to say hi first. And Kate will say, logically, "You seemed pretty busy with Millie." And Leigh will think to herself, why do I do these things, why do I pretend I care when I don't, why do I pretend I don't care when I do, why am I so shy and awkward. But then their waitress will come, and Leigh will stop to watch her pour their coffee and to giggle afterward when Kate says, "Gads, she is sexy, isn't she? I think we're going to need several refills." It's funny to Leigh because Kate seems so prim, beautiful but in an untouchable sort of way, like an icon. It's funny because it's hard for Leigh to imagine her having sex, all sweaty and messy, or crying out in pleasure, her careful, lovely voice gone high and frantic.

But Leigh notices Kate watching her as they drink their coffee, and there's something in Kate's expression that's different from the expression she had on her face when she was buttoning Martin's coat, or holding him as they both slept. Kate doesn't look like a mother now, Leigh decides. She looks hungry. She looks more like me.

"THE WOMAN WANTS YOU," Cassie says to Leigh over the phone Sunday night.

Kate and Leigh had talked a long while at the coffee shop; after, as they said goodbye in the parking lot, Kate had offhandedly suggested they get together at her house for dinner during the week.

"Cass, you've got it all wrong."

"I don't understand why you refuse to acknowledge her interest in you. What do you think she's after, a baby-sitter?"

Leigh is not amused. But on Tuesday night, as she drives into Valley Homes, Kate's apartment complex, she thinks again about the way Kate looked at her while they were drinking coffee. She thinks about last night, lying in bed imagining Kate touching her, imagining her own hands exploring Kate's body. As she pulls into the driveway, Leigh begins to worry. What if, while she and Kate are kissing, Martin bangs his head on the table and gets knocked unconscious and they don't hear him fall? Will Kate think it's Leigh's fault? Leigh is vaguely aware that she's being silly, but she can't shake her anxiety. What if, what if—the catastrophic possibilities seem endless.

But when she sees Kate's face through the window, when Kate opens the door for her and hugs her, Leigh calms down, at first a little, and then a lot. Kate smells like basil, and as they hug, Leigh can feel Kate's breasts pressed against her own. It's an amazing feeling; she's a little dazed when Kate lets go of her, and she's quiet as Kate takes the bread she's brought, as Kate leads her into the kitchen, where vegetables lie scattered about the wooden table.

"I'm not a vegetarian," Kate says, "but I thought you might be.

Here's a cutting board—I'm putting you to work. After we finish chopping these it'll go in to bake, then we can sit and talk a while and I'll show you around."

Leigh takes the wooden board and a tiny knife and begins chopping carrots. There's music playing, but she can't identify it. Something classical, delicate and fluid. Then she thinks to ask, "Where's Martin?"

"He's playing at his friend Tim's house. We have to pick him up at eight. He's eating there, so we'll have some time to ourselves." Kate takes a step toward Leigh, touches her shoulder. "We can talk, get to know each other a little better."

Sitting on the sofa, her feet tucked up beneath her, Kate looks different yet again. She's very quiet; her confident hustle-and-bustle is gone. She seems to be waiting for Leigh to speak.

"So tell me about your job," Leigh prompts her, and Kate begins: She works as a secretary in a doctor's office uptown. While Kate talks, Leigh watches her hands; they move rapidly as she speaks, accenting each change in tone. When the lasagna is ready, Kate pulls it from the oven with mitts shaped like toothy crocodiles. She serves each of them a tiny portion. Leigh gobbles hers up, then sits awkwardly as Kate nibbles pieces of onion and spinach.

They pick up Martin at eight. Tim has an older brother and a baby sister; he lives with his parents and grandfather in a double-wide trailer. His mother, Maureen, gives Kate and Leigh two chunky oatmeal cookies wrapped in tinfoil to take home with them. Leigh bites into hers; it's incredibly sweet, with little clumps of sugar still intact. As Kate starts the car, Leigh asks quietly, "Does Maureen know you're gay?"

Laughter. "Oh, no. I'd never tell her...I mean, she's always so kind to us. She might be accepting, but you never know. I can't risk it." She glances at Leigh as they wait for the light to change. "Martin's father lives in town." There's a pause and then she raises her voice: "Martin Richards, how many times have I told you never, ever unbuckle your seat belt!" Leigh looks behind her: Martin is scrunched up on the floor of the backseat, running his car across a ridge in the upholstery.

"Aw, Mom."

When they get back, Kate gives Martin a huge tablet of paper to draw on, and the two women sit with him, watching him color, printing letters and words for him to copy, sometimes doodling on the margins of the paper. Kate gets into it, but Leigh has to fight to keep from yawning. She doesn't like coloring—she didn't even like coloring when she was a kid. But Martin and Kate are happy, talking among themselves, almost speaking another language: phrases Leigh doesn't recognize, little jokes, names of people she doesn't know. She wonders if Kate would mind if she turned on the TV, but instead she draws the same shape over and over, her sky-blue crayon gliding lightly over the surface of the page.

At nine, Kate sends Martin into his room to get ready for bed. He emerges a few minutes later, fully decked in pajamas, the bottoms of which are on backwards, so that the flannel feet stick out from his heels.

"Ma, I want you to read to me now."

"Sleepy Marty." Kate picks him up, sits him in her lap. "Sleepy Marty." She tousles his hair. "Martin," she says, turning name to song, over and over, two syllables drawn out, at first distinct, black-and-white, then blurring into something gray, and at last to gray-gone-silver, something fine and gleaming, her mouth at his ear, his face resting against her chest. Only when his eyes are drooping does she break the spell: "Martin Bebartin," she teases, and his eyes snap almost awake again, "Martin Bebartin, Martin Bebartin," and he laughs, nuzzling his face into her belly.

"What do you want to read, Marty?" Kate smiles at Leigh and winks: Martin has refused to read anything but *Where's Waldo?* for two weeks now.

"*Where's Waldo?*" Martin says, and Kate shakes her head, laughing.

"Are you sure you don't want to try something else? *Old Turtle? Heather Has Two Mommies?* How about the Berenstain Bears?" But Martin shakes his head adamantly, so Kate gets up, leaving him beside Leigh on the sofa. "I'll go find it. You sit with Leigh for a moment, okay?"

Kate vanishes into his bedroom. Martin curls into a ball and radiates hostile vibes toward Leigh. She's at a loss. Should she try singing to him like Kate? She watches as he inches farther away, until he's practically falling off the edge of the couch. She clears her throat, hums softly. Kate's rummaging in the bedroom. Hurry up, she thinks, just hurry up. Martin looks over at her, and Leigh stops humming.

"Why do you like *Where's Waldo?* so much, Martin?" she asks. He's sucking on his thumb, something she's never seen him do before.

"Shut up."

Leigh is shocked. Shut up? Where did he learn shut up? She doesn't get it. She's just trying to be nice. From the bedroom she can hear Kate opening drawers. "Martin Bebartin," Leigh says. "What a great nickname." She reaches over to pat one of his floppy pajama toes.

Martin responds by stumbling off the sofa. "Shut up! You can't call me that. That's what my mom calls me. You didn't make that up. My mom made that up. You have to call me Martin Richards." He turns toward Leigh when he reaches the door to his bedroom. "That's what my mom calls me. You're not my mom. Shut up!" He slams the door behind him.

Leigh runs her hand across the nubby sofa upholstery: beige, with brown stripes. She takes one of the throw pillows and puts it behind her head, rubbing her temples. Just then Kate emerges from the bedroom with *Where's Waldo?* but without Martin. She walks over to the couch and sits down, puts one hand on Leigh's shoulder.

"Leigh."

It sounds like a question, a very complicated question, one

Leigh isn't sure she can answer now or anytime in the near future. "Leigh," Kate says again, and then she's bending over her, and her mouth is on Leigh's mouth. Leigh closes her eyes, runs her tongue over Kate's lips. She feels Kate's fingers in her hair, and for a moment she wants to grab Kate and pull her into her, to be closer than even this close, to be inside her. She reaches around Kate and presses her hands along her back. Kisses Kate's neck, beneath her ears, then finds her mouth again, and kisses that.

"Ma!" Martin calls out from the bedroom, and Kate sits up quickly, keeping one hand on Leigh's thigh.

"Do you want to read to him with me?"

Leigh thinks for a second—maybe too long, because Kate gets up, smiles a short smile, and says, "It's okay. Wait here. I'll be back in a few minutes." As Kate heads for the bedroom, she snaps on the TV. "Make yourself comfortable. There's some ice cream in the freezer."

Leigh nods. Just then, Martin peers out from the bedroom door. Kate notices at almost the same moment, and goes to him, scoops him up in her arms. "Martin Bebartin," she says, and her face softens. Leigh watches. For an instant it's as if there's a glass pane stretched across the door frame, separating them, but leaving all three visible. Kate and Martin disappear into the bedroom. "I'll be back in a few minutes," Kate calls over her shoulder, as Leigh heads for the sofa, where she will sit for seventeen minutes while Kate reads *Where's Waldo?* aloud for the forty-second time, where she will close her eyes and listen to Debussy, because that's what's playing, because that's what she's been listening to all along.

—A RECKONING IN LABRADOR—

Shelly Rafferty

MOIRA KEARNEY CAUGHT MY EYE in a tumbledown restaurant on a dark Labrador night in June. She was wrestling a lobster with a hammer and nutcracker, as a bad pennywhistler and decent fiddle backed up the local noise with some of their own.

Me, I was eating chowder at the bar. Watching. Watching her.

"Come on, Kearney," chided the barkeep, a husky, one-armed fellow named O'Fallon. He set a small glass of Scotch next to her plate and leaned in close. He had the ruddy cheeks of a dog musher, and the strawberry fuzz of his hair exhaled a dusty light of its own. He gestured toward the lobster. "Give him a shot of this. That'll put him out."

"The damned fish is rugged, all right," Kearney responded, unfazed. She gave the red monster another whack with the hammer. The shell shattered and sent splinters upward, planting a small scarlet shard on her cheek. "But I believe I've found his weak spot!"

"Not like he wasn't already killed once, Moira," said Jimmy Dunn, as he dropped his steaming plate of mussels across from hers.

O'Fallon laughed and turned for the bar. "Look out for that

one, lads," he shouted to the other fishermen. "Even after you're
dead, you'll have to pay up."

Kearney raised an eyebrow at Jimmy, and they both grinned.
The Scotch glass tinked against the side of Jimmy's beer, and the
two knocked back a quick splash.

I mopped up my chowder with a crust of oat bread and signaled O'Fallon for another beer. "Do you want to make my
business known?" I asked him. "Or what's the best protocol?"

O'Fallon wiped up under my soup bowl. "Now's as good a
time as any, I suppose. I'll clear you a space in a second. Here,
try a few of these"—he pushed some crab bites and lemon
toward me—"while the band finishes up. You can't be putting
off Paddy and Mike during these bleedin' shanties, as if we were
all headed out tomorrow with our eye patches and peg legs. Let
'em sing the chorus and I'll get you their attention."

I couldn't take my eyes off her, truth be told.

It wasn't that she was so beautiful, but that she ignored the
din around her. She'd doffed her funny hat on the table beside
her, revealing a wavy walnut haircut, pushed back behind the
ears and curling at the collar of her dark turtleneck. Her straight
teeth flashed the white of fresh apple, and the Black Irish glint of
mischief flickered in her eye. An inch-long scar in the shadow of
her right wind-burned cheekbone pointed away to an unseen
horizon. Her hands looked strong and quick.

The men around her didn't so much dismiss her as not notice
her. She wasn't for any of them, that's for sure. Moira Kearney
hadn't seen me yet, but I could read the code of her lesbian identity in the cut of her shirt and in the disdain for the attention one
persistent drunk was trying to pay her. She waved him off with
a nautical estimate of his likelihood of getting laid, and he
laughed and tottered away, unoffended.

It had been a long time since I'd indulged the impulse to stare.
In the six years I was with Jenny, I had never so much as turned
my head. After she left me, I'd spent months trying to figure out
why I'd never even seen her departure coming. I simply hadn't

believed her capable of the deceit her infidelity had demanded.

"Open your eyes, Wren," Jenny had told me wearily. "No matter how many times you place me on some stupid pedestal, there really isn't one there."

Looking at Moira Kearney, I suddenly remembered that. There are no pedestals, no perfect worlds, no sublime romances, no moral absolutes, no humans without faults. I cautioned myself not to idealize her, even in my few moments of staring, when my sense of intrigue and attraction had unexpectedly been aroused.

I turned my attention back to my notes.

SUCH AS IT WAS, O'FALLON'S little bar constituted the only real social space in Kentry Leg, a tiny fishing hamlet of 400 residents, tucked in a deep crevasse on the central coast of the Canadian north. Innu natives and the descendants of Moravian immigrants made up the minority; the rest were Scotch-Irish or Anglo-French.

I had a list of all the residents, supplied by the Provincial Census Board. The men outnumbered the women ten to one. "Who's Moira Kearney?" I'd asked O'Fallon earlier in the day, as I reviewed my clipboard. He'd met me at the supply ship *Osprey* when I'd landed.

He scratched at his temple and cocked an eyebrow. "Now, what would you be wanting with her?"

"Just curious," I answered honestly. "According to my list, she appears to be the only unmarried woman in town."

"She's a fisher, runs her father's old boat. She'll be in tonight."

O'Fallon and I started the short trudge to his place. He'd somehow managed to shoulder my valise; I huffed under the weight of my backpack and black bag. "In?" I asked.

"She's out after redfish and cod, I think. All the fellas come in on Thursday night for the drink. She'll be there too, with Jimmy Dunn."

I looked over my list again. Dunn and Kearney shared the same address. *Living in sin,* I thought.

"She's not the only unmarried one, though," O'Fallon continued.

I quickly scanned my pages again, puzzled. "There's someone I've missed?"

"Well," smiled O'Fallon kindly, "there's you."

AS IT TURNED OUT, JIMMY DUNN was neither Kearney's paramour nor her illegitimate son, but a local half-wit she'd inherited from her father's crew. Rumors abounded about where he'd come from, as if he were feral and dangerous, but the truth was that his mother and father lived upcoast another thirty miles or so.

O'Fallon moved the musicians off their stools and motioned me into their dimly lit alcove. He tipped over a milk crate for me to stand on and rapped a pewter mug on the side of a nearby table to muster attention. As I made my way forward I caught Kearney's eye. She straightened in her chair and tilted her head just slightly, sizing me up. I brushed by her table with a lift of my eyebrows and felt her gaze follow me. A little applause and a few catcalls reminded me that whatever novelty my gender offered was appreciated. I felt the slightest bit intrigued that Kearney was clapping too.

"All right, settle down, lads," O'Fallon started. "You've all no doubt noticed we've an unaccompanied woman among us, but this lady's not here for your entertainment. She's on a mission of mercy." I must have looked rather serious, because the clatter of cheap silver and glassware began to settle. "But I'll let her tell it."

I set my half-full beer glass on a stool and stepped up on the milk crate. "I'm Wren Connolly and I'm from the National Health Service. As many of you know, last week Scott Ritchie's trawler *Azimuth*—out of Great Derry—radioed in that his crew was sick. By the time a rescue could be effected, Ritchie and two of his crew had died, and two more were deathly sick.

What we're seeing is Glasgow flu, a strain that's come across the North Atlantic. I'm here to inoculate you."

"You a doctor?" someone shouted from the crowd.

I shaded my eyes and tried to discern the asker, to no avail. "Yes, I'm a doctor." I paused. "This is a serious outbreak, folks. I'll start giving shots in the morning in the church. The shots might make you a little sore for a day or two, but we think it's an effective deterrent."

"What happened to the rest of Ritchie's men?"

"They've recovered, but they're still in hospital." The room was quiet now, with just a few forks tinkling against the dusky china plates. "But don't let their survival give you a false sense of security. Glasgow flu killed 1,800 people in that fair city in 1949. We don't want to see it here.

"So, in the morning," I continued, "bring your wives and children, your brothers and grannies. I start vaccinating at eight o'clock. If you've got a neighbor who isn't here tonight, gather him in with the rest of your kin. I can't force you to be immunized, but we know what this flu can do. I'd appreciate your cooperation."

A hand held high in the air was meant for me.

It was Jimmy Dunn.

"Yes, sir? A question?"

"Tomorrow's our trapping day. We can't come tomorrow." He looked at Moira Kearney with uncertainty. "Do we have to go?" he whispered to her.

A few men chuckled, and Kearney reached for Jimmy's wrist. There was a strange tenderness in her tone, a protectiveness that seemed to escape out of her and reach across the space between them. "Don't worry, Jimmy. I'll take care of the traps." She spoke matter-of-factly but firmly. She silenced the unkind murmur among the men behind her with a sober glance.

Then she slowly stood, took her glass from the table, and held it up over her head. She stared right at me, just a moment too long.

"To Scott Ritchie!" she shouted.

Like everyone else in the bar, I emptied my glass.

O'FALLON'S BOY, ERIC, a gangly but literate curly-headed high schooler, kept the records while I parsed the vaccine among the residents for the next day and a half. Fortified with hazelnut oatmeal and strong coffee, I kept up through the second morning with a steady stream of Kentry Leggers draped in oilskin jackets and woolen scarves.

At eleven or so, we took a break so I could suture up the toe of a fellow who'd dropped his boning knife on his foot—he got a tetanus shot as well as the vaccine. I sent Eric after some sandwiches. I made a quick sign for the church door and was just about to hang it.

"Dr. Connolly?"

I recognized the slow man's sad face. He clutched his soft watch cap and waited for me to answer.

"Mr. Dunn."

He looked nervous. I pulled the door wide open and beckoned him inside. I glanced up the road behind him but found it deserted. Only the alders riffled with life in the late morning wind. "You're alone."

"Moira said I had to come," he said sluggishly. "But she ain't comin'. Moira don't care much for shots and medicine."

"What about you, Mr. Dunn? Do you care for shots and medicine?"

"She dunna want me to get sick and carried off."

I smiled, recognizing the lilt of his hometown in his voice. "She's watching out for you, then, Jimmy." I pulled the chair out next to the desk. "We'll be done in a second."

He unbuttoned the wool pea coat and settled himself gently in the ladder-back chair. "I dunna want Moira to get sick either," he said abruptly.

"Roll up your sleeve, Jimmy." As he did, I checked his name off my list, then washed his upper arm with some alcohol. I pricked the vial of vaccine and filled my needle, then jabbed him. He didn't flinch. I swabbed a blood drop with a small piece of gauze.

"You can make her take the medicine, Dr. Connolly," Jimmy said. He was struggling with the button at the cuff of his sleeve, and I knelt beside him and fastened it.

"I can't, Jimmy."

"Please. Come up to our house. Please."

I looked at my watch. It would be close to sundown before I could get there.

"Moira's all I got," Jimmy said, his soft voice weighted with defeat. "She won't come."

The anguish in his face was too much to bear. "All right," I said. "Will you be making the supper?" He didn't understand, I could see. "Never mind. Where do you live?"

He told me.

BY LATE AFTERNOON I'd inoculated everyone on my list but Moira Kearney. I wearily packed up my bag and bundled myself into my coat. I left the litter of vaccine boxes stacked on the table in the church. Eric would clean them up later.

In my room over O'Fallon's bar, I ditched the equipment case. The *Osprey* would return to get me—and several tons of fish—in thirty-six hours, and I was glad to put aside the trappings of my responsibilities for the evening. Still, I put on my hiking boots and loaded my stethoscope, cuff, thermometer, syringe, and a vial of vaccine into my shoulder bag. Thinking ahead, I added a flashlight and scarf, and stuck my leather gloves in my pocket.

O'Fallon's bar was empty but unlocked. I snagged a small bottle of Scotch and made my way out into the fading daylight. The narrow, bare patch of muck and stone that passed for a road ran up the shoreline and disappeared into the trees. I kept a healthy pace to ward off the late-spring cold. I could see my breath.

Three-quarters of a mile up the way I found Moira splitting wood on a tree stump in her yard. She'd removed her lined denim jacket, and she swung the Hudson Bay ax with the grace of a base hitter. Her spine curved in a gentle sweep of muscle and tendons as she raised the ax over her head. Each strike split a length of ash with a satisfying *ccchhhkk*. "Jimmy said you were coming," she began, straightening up for a rest. "But you're wasting your time, pretty girl."

Her tone betrayed a knowing familiarity, a signal that she'd recognized me too. "Flattery won't get you out of it," I said, patting the shoulder bag. "Where's Jimmy?"

She put her ax aside and began to gather up the splits. I shouldered my bag again and extended my arms. Without missing a beat, she loaded me up. "He spends his Saturday night in town. Eats pizza with Eric. Gets a bath. Goes to church in the morning."

"He's worried about you."

Moira nodded and wiped at a trickle of sweat from her temple. "You want a beer?"

"Sure," I said.

She gestured for me to follow her inside, and I did.

She handed me a cold longneck. "What's your name? Wren? I'm not sure I've heard that one before." Her attempt at obfuscation was obvious, but I let it pass.

"It's a family name. Not very common." I looked around the room and she nodded at me to sit down. "You need to be immunized."

This idea seemed to amuse her. "I don't like needles. I'm sure Jimmy told you."

"He asked me to come up. He's worried you might get sick and die."

"Oh, it's not that serious, is it?" Kearney said gently. She'd set her beer bottle down and taken up a small broom at the edge of the fireplace. She dusted a bit in the brickwork, then gathered up some kindling and started to lay it out methodically in the center of the grate. "This damn thing will probably burn itself out before a single Kentry Legger has a chance to catch a cold. I hardly think I'm a good candidate for dyin' of the flu."

"Did you think Scott Ritchie was?"

She thought about that for a minute. "I didn't know him well," she answered, as she continued her fire-building. She struck a match, and the piney crackle in the tinder sent a raft of sparks up the flue. "But I drunk some whiskey with him in Great Derry once. He seemed a hail-fella-well-met. Not sure why he got sick. I'm sure he didn't see it coming."

"That's my point. Why take chances?"

Moira drank from her beer bottle again. "You know, every day I go out in my boat and I don't know what I'll catch. Mostly I get what I expect, but I can't tell you I've never found a stray swordfish or crazy sharklet dug in among the cod. It's not what I go out for, but sometimes you catch it anyway. That's what comes from casting your net wide, I guess."

The frown on my forehead belied the disdain I held for such a simple rationalization. "I'm not talking about something random, though. Once you catch it, you can't throw Glasgow flu back into the sea."

She shook her head. "I told you, I don't like needles."

"That's all I've got."

"You're not going to talk me into it, Wren."

"You're set in your ways."

"More or less."

I didn't understand her stubbornness. I looked around for a photograph, a keepsake, some sign of her attachments. "You're alone here."

"I've got Jimmy," she answered as she got to her feet. "Come on, I'll fix us some supper. You look hungry."

LATER, AFTER SOME CRABS, boiled potatoes, and spicy pickled beans someone had carefully put up in a Mason jar, she made coffee and I got out the Scotch. She said she didn't want any. "Only on Thursdays," she said with a grin. "But you go ahead."

I took the top off the little bottle and poured the amber into a short glass, and followed her back to the couch. She threw some more wood on the fire. There was a quarter-cord stacked inside the door. It wouldn't last a week; that's what I figured. Life here was brutal, unforgiving, and lonely. "Don't you ever get sick?" I asked.

"We keep penicillin in the cupboard. Jimmy gets a good cough once a year."

"When's the last time you saw a doctor?"

"A doctor comes by every September and gives us all a check-up. Otherwise, Harry Fletcher has a helicopter. If someone is deathly ill, he flies him into Goose Bay, or we set down on a close-by cruise ship. We dropped Liam McGregor on the *Atlantic Empress* last October. Damn Liam had a heart attack. Lived his whole life in the most abject poverty you can imagine: illiterate, unskilled, always hacking up half a lung with stupid cigarette smoke. Then one day he keeled over in O'Fallon's bar. Harry and I loaded him onto the copter and flew him ten miles out to a Caribbean registry carrying a load of honeymooners from Quebec City. He died in the lap of luxury, right on deck, next to the pool."

"It could happen to you."

"It could," she replied slowly. "Or I could get swept over-board, or struck by lightning, or scuttled by pirates."

"You know what I mean."

"Is Glasgow flu coming to get me?"

"Let me give you a shot. Think of it as a small measure of protection."

"I told you, I don't like needles."

"What do you like, then?"

Moira shrugged. "I like this, this quiet. This fire. I like going out in my boat and bringing in my catch." She knelt and pokered through the embers of the fire, stirring up little tongues of flame. "I suppose I am being silly." She shook her head slowly. "I've always had an irrational fear of needles. It's not the pain. It's the magic I don't trust, I guess."

I reached for my shoulder bag and unbuckled it, then pulled out my stethoscope and slipped it around my neck. I went to stand beside her. "Come on, then," I said, reaching for her hand. "Get up. At least let me examine you."

The deliberateness with which she came to her feet was full of challenge. Her dark eyes dared me. The scar on her right cheekbone was crooked. It hadn't been sewn. "Unbutton your shirt, please," I said.

She smiled wryly and slowly slipped one button from its slit, then the next, and the next. She was wearing nothing underneath. She stared at me with a strange intensity and I stared back. I opened my stethoscope and set it in my ears, then grasped her shoulder and pressed the instrument on her sternum and listened. Her heartbeat was strong and regular, if a little fast. I moved the diaphragm close to her right breast.

Her hands were at my ears then, removing the stethoscope. Slowly she covered my hand with her own and pulled the instrument out. It dangled uselessly from her left hand.

"Is Glasgow flu coming for me?" she repeated. "Or are you?"

My hands paused at the open placket of her shirt, and I found myself studying the weave of the fabric, the delicate crosshatch of color in the tattersall, immediately stricken with the way each ridge imprinted itself on my finger. A shimmery, invisible heat drifted up between us, but I didn't let go and I wanted to tell her that I wanted to kiss her, but in an instant our lips brushed with questions, then a tentative kiss, all the time checking, staring, trying to think and not to think. She reached for my waist. It was just a moment. Then her mouth was on mine, insistent and rough, and I liked it. Her tongue found a spot in my palate and behind an eyetooth, and she tasted of balsam and beer, of fresh air and wind. I moved my hands up to her jaw, and broke away, and pulled her down to the couch.

I felt the color of arousal warm in my face. Moira's hair was mussed, but she was smiling, her eyes almost bright with excitement. "I shouldn't—" I started, but she was shaking her head, up on one knee, then straddling my lap.

"You're not going to call out the code of ethics, are you now?" Her fingers were at work at my collar buttons. "Don't try telling yourself this is some kind of house call." She began to trace down my throat.

"I saw you in the bar the other night," I whispered.

"I saw you too." She leaned over me and kissed my neck, behind my ear. "I saw you too," she repeated, her mouth hot against my throat. "You have beautiful shoulders." She'd opened my shirt far enough to reveal the bony juncture of my collarbone and shoulder, and I felt her teeth measuring.

I extracted her shirttail from her jeans and finished unbuttoning her. My hands found their way to her lower back. What was I doing? I didn't know her beyond her name. My mouth savored a nipple, taut and eager.

She rocked evenly on my pelvis, gaining rhythm, and my hands gripped her ass. Her nipple was sweet, rolling in my mouth, and I wanted to stay there, tasting and mindless, but after a minute she pulled away. She was breathing hard. I shifted back a few inches. "I don't want you to stop," she said.

I knew she was giving me permission to do just that. "I know I can," I said slowly. The confusion of the moment, the tatters of guilt that remained from Jenny, the assault of her fragrance that buzzed like static in the air paralyzed me. "I don't know what to make of you."

"Do you have someone?"

"No," I whispered. "Not for a long time." I knew she saw the sadness in my eyes.

She smiled. Her hands moved slowly over the chamois of my shirt, her thumbs lingering at the edges of my nipples, and she threw a long, shallow shadow over me as she leaned down to my mouth again.

HER BED WAS DEEP AND SIMPLE, swathed in cotton, wool, and down. It was dark, after midnight, when I awoke. I hadn't been asleep long.

I pulled myself up to an elbow and turned up the low lamp next to the bed, throwing a pale copper light over us. Moira slept on beside me, her bare shoulders turned in my direction, her face calm. The scar under her right eye glistened in the firelight.

The fucking had been fierce and wordless, thrilling and slow. In the darkness I remembered the strength of her resistance, the tightness inside her, the pulse of her orgasm in my mouth. She hadn't called my name or tried to romance me; she'd simply come hard, her exhalations rapid, her hands tearing in my hair, then she fell away for a few moments, drawing her legs up under her and holding me off when I tried to take her in my arms. "Jesus," she'd breathed. "Just give me a minute."

My own patience had surprised me. We lay side by side then, wet and spent, eyeing each other. After a minute, I reached out for her face and touched the edge of her scar with my fingertip. *Swordfish,* she'd said. *Nicked me in the catch when I wasn't looking.*

The unexpected one, I'd replied.

Like I said, I take my chances, she'd answered.

I WAS SUDDENLY CHILLED, and I dug carefully among the bedclothes for my chamois shirt, but I couldn't find it. I leaned over the bed and discovered it hanging over my canvas bag. I pulled the bag and shirt up from the floor, and set the bag between my knees, and slipped my arms into my shirt.

Moira was still sleeping. Quietly, I unbuckled the straps of my bag and fumbled around inside for the little vial of vaccine. I turned it over in my hand and studied the label, the white stickered paper with the indecipherable writing, and the transparent liquid sloshing against the sturdy glass. It would be easy to stick her now, but I hesitated.

What did I want to save her from? She was right about the flu, she wasn't likely to catch it. Even if she did, she had such little contact with others that she'd most likely be dead before she'd have the occasion to pass it on. Hers would be an isolated case.

I looked at her again. In the moonlight, the little scar on her cheekbone smiled back with imperfection and vulnerability. What was I thinking? Why was I rationalizing her, as if she were impervious to disease, faultless, and unflawed? Really, her arrogance was selfish. What would Jimmy Dunn do without her? She *could* get sick.

What if someone loved her?

I uncapped the syringe, pierced the vial with the sharp needle, and slowly drew back the plunger. I snapped my finger against the shaft of the syringe, releasing the breath of dangerous oxygen trapped inside, then nudged the plunger forward. The needle spit a few tears of medicine.

The roundness of Moira's left shoulder peeked above the quilt edge. I didn't have her consent, but I didn't care. She wasn't Jenny. I turned and shifted my hip against her waist, and quietly reached under the blanket to grasp her wrist.

"Open your eyes," I whispered, forgave myself, and stuck Moira Kearney in the arm.

—WITH YOU IN SPIRIT—

Zsa Zsa Gershick

"I felt the whole room vibrate sensibly; and at the far end there rose, as from the floor, sparks or globules like bubbles of light, many-coloured—green, yellow, fire-red, azure…. Suddenly, as forth from the chair, there grew a shape—a woman's shape."

—"The Haunted and the Haunters,"
Sir Edward Bulwer-Lytton, 1921

ANNA RUHL HAD BEEN ANIMATED on the flight from Los Angeles to Austin. The seating in the airplane's last rows had been train-like, the four final seats facing each other, making for easy conversation. The man beside her, a techie from IBM, had been fascinated by her project, he said, a study of Texas ranch women, but had been equally taken by her cleavage, which his gaze gently dropped to during the pauses in their conversation. She felt strong and sexy and didn't deny him. And when the pilot announced their descent, they exchanged numbers.

Anna liked the attention. Her husband wasn't interested, she reasoned, why not put it up for grabs? But Anna had never cheated beyond the flirting and the imagined indiscretions. It was true enough that she didn't love Bill anymore, couldn't remember why she ever had. After eight years, they were long past the fighting phase: No longer relating, but unwilling to move on, they had merely retreated to their respective corners of the ring. They were pleasant, in a tight-lipped sort of way, filed taxes together, attended each other's faculty get-togethers, but neither had any idea what the other was thinking or feeling. Anna knew intimate details about her husband: what pleased him sexually, his dreams and stories, but they were hard facts now, tucked away in the cold storage of her head, annexed to a remote part of herself without emotional resonance.

She thought of her friends sitting around Westside cafés, lamenting the absence of men in their lives.

"They're all geeks or skanks or perennial children," said Margaret, Anna's oldest friend, who cut hair for a living and bore a striking resemblance to a blond Edith Head. "There's something wrong with a thirty-eight-year-old who wears Spider-Man T-shirts and drinks milk out of a Welch's Flintstone jelly-jar glass," she said, referring to her last boyfriend. "Face it: You have to be married or a lesbian to find the desirable men."

And it was true. Anna, a married woman, always found attractive, intelligent men flirting with her. There was no dearth in her world. And her sister, Kay, gay as they come, ran into date-worthy men wherever she went. Unavailability enhanced desirability.

The late-afternoon air at the Austin Municipal Airport was still and warm, tinged with the smell of jet fuel and automobile exhaust. Anna threw her bags into the trunk of a waiting taxi. She'd packed light: boots, jeans, laptop. A few of Bill's worn oxford shirts. Nothing fancy, just enough for a summer's worth of research. She hadn't brought as much as a lipstick and welcomed the liberation of it.

Springtime in the Hill Country was green and lush, with bluebonnets bursting everywhere along the roadsides. They drove out beyond the Austin city limits, passing peach and honey vendors, veered off the highway beyond a battered mail-box with the word HIGHGATE painted crudely on the side, then bumped along a dirt road for some time before coming to a large turn-of-the-century ranch house. It needed a coat of paint, but the tall glass windows were sparkling and intact, and the buff flagstone gave the house an impenetrable aura. She paid the driver as he pulled her luggage from the trunk, and left the techie's crumpled card on the backseat.

"Anybody home?" Anna called, opening the front door. Inside, the house was cool and clean, *freshly* cleaned for her arrival, she noted. The scent of Pine-Sol barely covered the mustiness. She heard footsteps on the front-porch planking.

"Señora Ruhl?" said a slight Texican, removing his hat. "*Bienvenidos.* Welcome to HighGate. I'm Eduardo Garcia, the caretaker. My wife Graciela and I live in the cottage behind here."

The sun was hot and bright; Eduardo squinted in its glare and reached for Anna's meager bags and, disappearing, placed them in one of the first-floor bedrooms. He was small but strong, she noted, watching the man's smooth, golden arm muscles go taut like cable as he lifted.

"There's a truck in the shed for you, all gassed up," he said, returning. "We go into town every Monday for groceries. Just leave us a list and some cash, and we'll pick up your supplies. If you need anything else—you find a scorpion *en el baño*, that kind of thing—just holler."

"What about keys and locking up?" asked Anna.

The man smiled. "The Hill Country is not Los Angeles, *señora.* Just close the door when you want to go."

SITTING ON THE PORCH that night, Anna was not prepared for the quiet. And the sky was so big and so full of stars that she could hardly believe it. She felt tense, not yet in sync with her surroundings. She longed to collapse into the dark stillness but remained on urban alert. The Bullock Foundation had thought of everything, she mused. The house was perfect, a quirky mixture of comfortable old leather ranch furniture and crystal chandeliers hinting at an earlier, more elegant incarnation. HighGate's original owner had been a lady rancher who'd lived into her nineties and left the place to the University of Texas to establish as a residence for visiting female scholars—wouldn't bequeath it unless that provision was strictly adhered to: women only.

At ten P.M., Anna went to bed, her short dark hair damp from the bath. The white cotton sheets felt cool against her skin, and the old wooden ceiling fan gently moved the warm night air around the room. A book was opened on her chest, and the bedside lamp was on. She'd leave it on, she thought, because she was alone and the surroundings were new. She began to read, wide-eyed in the hush, but faded out after only a page.

ANNA AWOKE AT DAWN to the cheerful squealing of baby raccoons reluctantly allowing their mother to put them to bed beneath the floorboards of the house. They sounded like human children, she thought: giggling, irrepressibly happy. The morning air was alive with cicadas and the rat-a-tat-tatting of a woodpecker in a nearby tree, which she would not have known had she not peered out the window and seen the creature attached to a limb, pecking away. It was almost unbelievable: She'd seen such a thing only in cartoons.

She padded to the kitchen, made some coffee, and began her rounds of the house, looking for the perfect workroom. She found it upstairs, in a nearly empty bed-sitting room with a sweeping view of the hills, already brown from the summer sun and dotted with clusters of scrub oak. It was, in fact, the only room on the second floor, at the top of a steep staircase with a faded oriental rug running down the middle. Inside the room were the essentials: writing table, chair, and sofa.

Anna stood back and imagined herself at work there.

It is perfect, isn't it? said a voice inside her head, which startled Anna because she knew it was not her own.

She swiveled around, spilling a gulp of coffee from her mug, and caught a faint scent of lavender. It reminded her of her grandmother, the crepe of her dress, the wrinkled but welcoming bosom, like a big, pillowy shelf to rest her head upon and forget the little humiliations of each day.

"Christ, it's too quiet here," Anna muttered, blotting the polished oak floor with a wadded paper towel that earlier had held her toast. She padded back downstairs for her laptop, notebook, and pencils. She'd start work right away.

THAT WEEK ANNA VENTURED out into the Hill Country in search of her first lady ranchers. She'd called the sheriff's office, the editors of the local newspapers, and the managers of feed stores to find her women: They roped, they rode, they worked with their husbands from sunup to sundown and typically had a whole passel of kids. They were tough women without frills, women who might be mistaken for dykes in an urban setting, women with rough hands and hard bodies that could take whatever life threw at them. Their husbands, the ones Anna met, were wiry cowboys with tight little asses and skinny legs sheathed in Wrangler jeans. Clearly, they loved the strength of their women.

"Well, hell," Tom "Blackjack" Jackman had said of his wife, MaryBeth, "there's nothin' I can do around here that she cain't do 'bout a million times better. Beth and me's a team, and by God, she's the better half of it."

Anna tried to imagine any of these women treadmilling in a spandex thong and snorted to herself on the ride home. She was tired, fully tired, and ready for a quiet dinner and a good night's rest.

ANNA'S HUSBAND CALLED four weeks after she'd arrived, wondering what was going on and making the small talk that had become the hallmark of their relationship. The solicitation of trivial facts had long passed for intimate conversation, and she answered his queries with reportorial efficiency. It wasn't as if she herself were dying to be intimate. There were a million things she could have said that would have drawn him into her world, but she refused to offer him admittance.

It was about that same time that the woman appeared to her.

Anna had been transcribing interview tapes. Every part of her strained to hear each word and nuance; her back and neck ached from arching over the computer screen. Her collar and under-arms were wet, and she stank from the intensity of her effort. She had looked up, wanting to rest her eyes on the rolling hills, as framed by the tall, narrow ranch-house windows.

And then she saw her, faintly, sitting on the sofa, a fine china cup raised to her lips.

The woman was young, no more than thirty, with lustrous auburn hair loosely drawn back and wrapped in a chignon. She wore a high-collared blue silk dress with swatches of black velvet at the collar and cuffs. Her waist was amazingly small, her body angular, and on her feet were dainty black leather button-up boots.

Lips gently pursed, she met Anna's astonished gaze with a good-humored wink.

Anna squinted and rose, and so did the woman, placing the cup and saucer soundlessly on the sofa, whose worn red cushions seemed oddly restored, even lustrous. The woman went over to the window—Anna couldn't say she had "walked"—stared a moment at the hills, then simply faded out.

At least that's what she recounted, long distance, to her buddy Margaret, who wondered if the twin thrill of oxygen-rich air and husbandlessness wasn't having a hallucinatory effect.

"Were you hungover, Annie?"

"Please! I was just sitting there working. I looked up to give my eyes a rest, and there she was. She looked at me and winked."

"Wow. You know, my mother took me to a funeral once when I was about six. The guy in the coffin had been in a motorcycle accident, so his head was all bandaged up. She told me not to look, but I did, and I swore I saw his chest rise. I mean, don't take me coffin-side and ask me not to look, you know?" Margaret was running off on one of her characteristic tangents.

Anna knew her friend would link the two experiences at some point and waited patiently for the payoff.

"What I mean is, you can't always believe what you see."

"Yeah, I guess," said Anna. She blew Margaret some kisses into the phone and said good night. In the morning she'd talk to Eduardo.

EDUARDO ALWAYS BRUSHED and fed the horses at seven A.M., Anna noted, and when he got to the barn the next morning, Anna was leaning over the weathered gate, waiting for him. There were only two mares left, gluepot nags long past their prime, and they neighed excitedly when they caught sight of him. Apples and oats were the high point of their day.

"*Buenos días, señora,*" Eduardo said brightly.

She handed him a cup of coffee.

"Very kind of you." He set the steaming mug on a post. "*Muchas gracias.* I'll have it right after *mijas* here have their *desayuno.* Wouldn't be fair for me to have mine before they've had theirs, eh?"

As Eduardo brushed his girls, after they'd eaten and were content, Anna began. "Frances Bullock, the owner of this place. Did you know her well?"

"*Si y no,*" said Eduardo, pausing to choose the right word. "She was a very quiet lady. *Calma, pero muy determinada...* determined. She always got what she wanted. When Graciela and I arrived, she was already very old. Almost never had visitors."

"She died here?"

"Oh, *si. Aquí.*"

"In the second-floor room?"

"The dining room. She could barely walk. We made her

bedroom downstairs, to make it easier for her. She missed her sitting room, but the stairs were *muy difícil*."

Anna toed the dirt, pretending to find it fascinating. Her voice was a whisper. "Eduardo, have you ever..." She paused. "Have you—"

"Seen her?" he interrupted. "*Su espectra?*"

Anna's eyebrows furled.

"Her ghost?" Eduardo laughed good-naturedly and took his mug from the post. "Not me, but my wife. She swears she's seen her. Graciela's *abuela* was *una hechicera*, a seer, a witch, eh? So I say maybe that's why. Sometimes I know I've closed the blinds, and then I find them open. Sometimes I hear the door upstairs close when there's no breeze. *Señora* Bullock was good to me in life, and so *en muerto* what do I have to fear? Maybe she sees I'm still taking care of the place. You've seen her?"

"I think so—in the room. But young, sipping from a cup."

"*Café con miel,*" said Eduardo, regarding his cup. "She liked it just like this." He looked at Anna, head craned in interest, wanting more. The sun was climbing and already harsh. He could take a minute, he thought, feel the A/C on his hot, leathery face. "There are photos," he said. "*Mira*, let me show you."

Inside the house, Eduardo went to a hulking, rough-hewn armoire and pulled out a cracked black-leather volume that smelled like hide.

There was Frances Bullock as a baby in the 1880s, then as a teenage traveler in a middy blouse standing, hands on hips, beside the stone head of Ramses II.

"There, that's who I saw," said Anna, pointing to a photo of Frances astride a great, muscular mare. The picture was dated 1910. "Who's that?" She pointed to a handsome woman in chaps standing beside the pair.

"*No sé,*" said Eduardo, shrugging. "A neighbor, maybe. *La Señora* had no brothers or sisters." He stood up, his labors calling, as Anna lingered over the book. "*Muchas gracias, señora*, I thank you," he said, raising the cup almost in a toast. "I'll wash this and bring it back."

IT WAS DAYS BEFORE FRANCES appeared again. And when she did, she said simply, "You."

Anna had been sitting at the writing table for a week, staring at the sofa, squinting, wondering whether she would see anything more, *had* seen anything in the first place.

First the face: The dark hair, full mouth, vaguely cleft chin and sparkling eyes faded in. Then the torso with its straight shoulders and wasp-like waist. And the full skirt and black kid button-up boots. And finally the silver coffeepot and delicate china appeared on the table.

"Blond and sweet, I'd imagine." The woman extended a cup and saucer to Anna. "As far as the java."

Anna could only stare.

"Gracious sakes, I won't bite," said the woman.

"You're not real," said Anna, rising from her chair.

"Hmm. If that's so, the coffee's going to be a terrible disappointment, and you look like you could use a cup."

Anna took four halting steps forward and stood before her.

"That's a better view, isn't it?" said the specter.

Anna touched the cup gingerly, rim first, then ran her finger down to the saucer. It was solid. Finally, she grasped the handle and drank.

"Ah!" said the woman. "You see? A bracing cup of joe is a foursquare reality anywhere! You have no idea how long a lady has to wait for attractive company, Anna. May I call you Anna?"

Anna nodded, dumbstruck.

"That's fine," said the specter. "Why stand on ceremony, since you are sleeping in my bed and all?" She paused to sip and went on. "Last year's scholar, God bless her, had twin hairs growing from a mole on her left cheek. I do what I can to influence the selection, an intuitive thought planted in the administrator's mind, such as it is, but it's damn hard to get a clear channel. I blame that largely on consumer electronics."

THAT WAS HOW IT BEGAN. And an odd thing happened. As the days wore on and their conversations continued, the room, once bleak, grew warm and full and bright. It happened gradually, like a hard, tight bud that takes forever to blossom then bursts out, all pillowy, in electric magenta. First the rich red-velvet draperies and the paintings faded in, and then the walls took on a buttery hue. The sofa's soft silk was restored, and the crystal, suddenly dustless, sparkled once again. And when Anna left the room, she felt Frances with her, wanted her to see the stars, feel the sun, hear the cicadas as she heard them.

Eduardo was the first to notice the spring in Anna's step and the way she warbled in the morning as she made her coffee. "*Pues, que pasa allá?*" he said to Graciela one morning over his usual *huevos* and toast. "*Está enamorada?* Is she in love?"

And Anna had dreams. At first disturbing, then longed for as she fell asleep: They were in opposite corners of a white room. Meeting soundlessly in the middle, Anna leaned in and kissed Frances, at first tentatively, then deeply, pressing against her, their bodies at once taut and relaxed. She felt the fullness of Frances's breasts, the roundness of her hips, the firmness of her long legs. She inhaled the lavender and something else, something not present in the sitting room: sweet cunt and sweat and breath.

Anna always awoke with desire.

During the next month, the phone calls to L.A. became more desultory, then stopped altogether. And the interviews grew less and less interesting, until Anna barely left the house.

And then Eduardo called Bill.

" 'THAT NIGHT SHE STARED at herself in the glass; and even as she did so, she hated her body with its muscular shoulders, its small compact breasts, and its slender flanks of an athlete,' "

Anna read aloud. "'All her life she must drag this body of hers like a monstrous fetter imposed upon her spirit. This strangely ardent yet sterile body that must worship but never be worshiped in return by the creature of its adoration.'"

"Sweet Jesus! I cannot hear another word!" said Frances, seated on the edge of the desk. "If she thinks she has problems, that dull Stephen Gordon ought to try being dead! It has one deleterious effect on matters of intimacy."

Anna, lying on the sofa, her boots dangling over a thickly padded bolster, placed the book on her chest and scowled playfully. "You asked me to read it."

"Yes, but it's giving me a headache. There were plenty of ladies who would have enjoyed a girl in a suit—even then. Her Stephen just didn't look hard enough. As they say: Half measures avail us nothing."

Anna took a short, tight breath. "Frances?"

"Just a minute, darlin'," said the specter, flipping through the pages. "I'm looking for the good part."

"Who was the woman in the photograph, the one in the chaps?"

Anna could almost hear the click of the lady's gaze as it snapped up from the page.

"Emily Sawyer Johnston," said Frances. "Her people owned the land adjacent to ours—all the way to the horizon and ten miles beyond." The specter now looked past Anna, out on to the rolling brown hills, and closed her eyes. "God, but Em was fine. The deepest brown eyes, and golden hair all piled up on her head. When she cut it in that Rudy Valentino way, her mother liked to have calved. Her lips were like an angel's bow, full and deep red, without a lick of pout. Just looking at her made my heart race."

Frances opened her eyes. Anna shifted uncomfortably in her seat and fingered the gold rim of her cup.

"What happened?"

"I waited for her my whole life," said Frances, the corners of her mouth downturning. "Her father married her to a cattle-man from Colorado. Sent her off like a Christmas goose, with 200 head as her dowry. In her letters she'd write, 'I'm coming to you. I can't stand another day outside your embrace.'" Frances bowed her head as if reading from the letter. "She had an elegant hand." She looked at Anna. "And *hands*—strong but graceful, like yours."

"She never came back?"

"No." Frances snapped from her reverie. "Not to me or to herself. She took to the sherry after her firstborn."

"I'm sorry," said Anna, making a feeble attempt at sympathy. It wasn't her strong suit: She was much better at mowing through uncomfortable feelings, trampling them until she'd convinced herself they'd never existed.

"No, I'm sorry," said Frances. "There's nothing more tiresome than anybody—dead or alive—who can't stop discussing the past."

Anna laughed.

"But that's what we represent, don't we?"

Anna stopped.

"Missed opportunities? People and places that will never come again?" She leveled her gaze at Anna. "I'm wondering what your excuse is."

"I'm thirty-five," Anna said, a crease of disappointment deepening between her eyebrows. "I've made my deal, and I'm living with it. Bill and I do our own thing. It works."

"Huh," said Frances sharply, one short, dismissive round released from the chamber. "Seems on the arid side."

She moved soundlessly to Anna.

"I..." said Anna.

"Yes, my love..." Frances bent over Anna, who lifted herself the rest of the way. As their lips met, Anna all at once felt heat and cold, darkness and light, softness and steel. The room began to shift and the ceiling spin, as though she were on a turntable.

"My God, Anna. What are you doing?"

It was a man's voice. And somewhere a plug was pulled, a needle ripped back across vinyl, and the room, its curtains, its crystal, its luster and sheen, and Frances faded, like fast-moving water down a drain. The lavender, too, disappeared, and a funk hung in the air.

"My God! Look at yourself: You're a mess! When was the last time you showered? And who are you talking to?"

Bill pulled Anna to him, a big, awkward bear's embrace.

Eduardo and Graciela, her hands pressed against her mouth as if holding back some horror, stood in the doorway.

"What do you mean?" She blinked. "I'm talking to"—Anna thought fast—"to myself. That's how writers work, Bill. They talk things through, act them out." She paused and pushed him away. "What are you doing here?"

He grabbed her hard by the arm. "You're scaring me," he said. "I'm not leaving until you tell me what's going on. You've stopped working. You're not bathing. You barely leave the house, and nobody's heard from you in weeks."

"Suddenly we're interested in each other?" She twisted out of his grip and pushed past the caretakers, into the hallway. "Whatever I do here, it's my business."

"*Ay, Díos mío,*" said Graciela, crossing herself as Anna headed for the stairs.

Bill scrambled after her and caught her pajama top. One by one, the buttons popped from the strain and fell like flat, round teeth to the floor. He grabbed her hair.

"Goddamn you, goddamn you! Get off me!" She flailed and grabbed his tie as she kicked him hard in the shin, trying to knee him, trying to free herself. The shrill yelping of the cornered rose up from the tangle of arms and legs, snot and tears.

And then she fell, back and down.

And Bill receded fast at an odd angle. And she felt a rush, the wind. And, at the bottom of the staircase, heard the snap and thud.

Later, when the police arrived, no one could quite say how it happened.

ANNA FELT HERSELF SPEEDING along a corridor. She heard laughter. And a Victrola. And found herself standing in the doorway of the sitting room, wearing a suit of soft, black wool with a string tie.

In her hand was a black Stetson.

"It's bad business to keep a lady waiting," said Frances, kicking one of her high-buttoned shoes ever so slightly in the air. "But at least you're properly attired."

She rose from her perch and walked across to Anna, taking her hat and tossing it square in the middle of the mission desk's green felt blotter. Frances grabbed the lapels of Anna's coat and drew her near.

Anna smelled the woman's hair, felt the whalebone in her corset, and knew she was home.

—KICKS ON ROUTE 66—

Sylvia Rose

"KICK—HER NAME WAS KICK, which is weird enough, but do you know what I really can't help thinking about?" she told the little wheat-haired hitchhiker. "Her eyes. Isn't that silly?"

The girl, not more than seventeen, not under fifteen, nodded, looking shy and nervous, expecting Julia to ask for—or maybe disappointed that Julia wasn't asking for—gas, ass, or grass, and that, yeah, really, the ride was free.

"I mean, shouldn't it be like the color of her hair—romantic shit and all—or the sound of her voice? Eyes...it's just too damned obvious, you know? But that's what I think about the most. She has these eyes, like marbles: blue and gray mixed together, with a little bit of gold."

The girl, chin resting on the top of her thin, bony chest, smiled. Not a deep smile, just the hint of one: a few muscles, not a lot. She wanted to giggle at the tension dropping away from her, the free ride sinking in.

"But it isn't just her eyes—though they're really special and all—but what she does with them. She can see the most wonderful things: stuff that's there, but not, you know? Like, look out there. Those birds—crows, I think...I don't know birds—on those wires. She'd look at them and start to whistle...get it?

62

Notes, musical notes: That's what she'd see when she looked at birds on a wire. She'd call a wheat field at sunset 'burning,' and you know, that's all I'd think of when I saw one like that: sun going down behind it, the wheat all brown and glowing—"

The girl looked out the window, not wanting the nice young woman giving her a ride to see the snickering grin on her tiny face. Out the window, the fields were raw copper, the sun nowhere near setting—but then they started to burn in her mind, to glow like embers at a nice summer weenie roast.

"Or like the road—this road—with the dotted line down the center, she'd talk about how it looked like a place where some giant would write his name or cut the county in two with big-ass scissors. Know what I mean?"

The girl scooted down in her seat, mumbling something like "Yeah, I know." Low, she looked up and saw the wires, then the birds, and began to plink out a stupid little tune in her head: a crow or blackbird, a low or a high note, depending on the bird or the wire.

"She'd see stuff—stuff you never would have thought of in a million years. She's great—oh, man, she's terrific. There's a lot of great things about her, but what she sees, that's really something."

The girl got off at Bark's Lake, a rock's toss from absolutely nowhere, waving goodbye as Julia drove away. Walking down the dusty road toward the cheap-jewelry neon MOM'S DINER, she couldn't help look down the road and wonder if she'd recognize God's name, scrawled on the asphalt, if she saw it.

A LONG DAY LATER: Julia was driving mostly by night, the hard Arizona sun too damned hot, burning her hands on the wheel. Long stretches of dark highway, only the stars and the quarter—then almost full—moon for company and light. Driving, she dreamed, trying to put herself at the end of the road: Boston, with its baked beans and "Boid on the wattah" accents (she'd never been before). Finding the little bookshop, walking in, smiling, having Kick smile back, offering coffee and a place to talk; Kick smiling more and suggesting a great little place nearby. The kiss, then more kisses; then that night, then the morning: back to the way things had been between them, but better.

Kick's absence was an ache, high and to the left—in that part of her body that broke so badly and too damned easily.

"You got too much bad crap," Kick would have said about an ache like that. "Got to get it out, got to pour it out, babe."

Julia, behind the wheel, sighed deep and long, feeling tears make her eyes heavy, the stars and the partial moon blur in the sky.

"Got to ask someone to take it away, get it out of you. Can't ask your mom for that. Can't ask anyone else for that. Too much to heap on someone you love, too much for a stranger. You got to offer it up, you see? Got to give it to the big sky, the universe up there. It's a big place, more than enough room for all your hurt."

Julia pulled over and took a few deep, quavering breaths. Ahead, the road was long and dark, vanishing instantly behind the reach of her headlights. Behind, the soft black was even closer. She was alone in the middle of the desert.

At first she didn't think about taking her clothes off, stripping down, but then Kick was again in her mind, and she knew she wouldn't have had it any other way—can't make a sacrifice with your clothes on, right? She didn't go far into the desert, just a dozen or so steps. With her car behind her, the interior hovering in the night from the feeble dome light, and the stars high above— a billion, billion, billion bright, bright, bright stars—she spread her hands wide and cried until the tears wouldn't come anymore.

When she was done she felt like Kick was standing next to her, a warm hand on Julia's chilly shoulder. "Better?" she'd say, with a special, kindly smile on her face.

Even though she knew she was alone out there in the desert, she nodded, feeling warm, and walked back to the car. It was what Kick would have done, what she would have advised—and it felt good. In fact, it felt so good, she did it a lot as she drove— each time she felt the heaviness, giving it all to the night sky, which was big enough, and empty enough, to take it all—with room enough for stars.

FOUR DOLLARS FOR A CHEESE SANDWICH, a can of Pepsi, and a slice of gooey pecan pie. Except for Julia, a mysterious cook hidden behind steam in the kitchen, and a tiny, bent old woman, the place was empty. Watching the old lady shuffle from one end of the tiny diner to the other, carefully tidying crusty and cracked sugar dispensers or swirling a once-white, now-yellow dishcloth over the red-and-white checked vinyl tablecloths, Julia could easily imagine Kick saying something like "Be right back" and wordlessly adding her own elbows and grease, her own composition style with flatware and tiny steel pots full of warm cream.

Just like when they were together—even though they were apart—Julia got up and added her own hands. The road was very long that night, and very dark, and it felt good to be home—if only a kind of home—for an hour or two. The old woman never spoke and neither did Julia: They went from table to table, filling salt shakers, wiping away stains, straightening little packets of jam, in warm silence.

Finally, when it was ten o'clock by the angrily buzzing beer sign behind the register, the old woman flipped OPEN to CLOSED. When it happened before, when Kick helped someone without asking, Julia had felt dragged along, pulled into Samaritanship by her lover's wake, but that night the inertia wasn't there. It felt good, very good. She knew why Kick had done it.

When she went out into the cold darkness, the woman held the door for her, a sweet smile on her dried-apple face—and Julia felt warm and good without having Kick to follow. She thanked Kick, though, as she stood by her car under the stars and the gaze of the still-smiling woman in the little diner.

"SHE'S JUST SO…IMPULSIVE—but that's not the right word. She isn't fickle; she just likes to do the unexpected, follow the twists of the world. Like when she got this offer to run a bookstore in

Boston, she just went for it, you know? Dove off and started swimming. I wish I could be like that."

She said her name was Mary. Julia had spotted her standing on the side of the road, her sixteen-wheeler now fifteen, one tire black curls scattered along the highway. Without thinking, Julia had pulled over: "Need a lift?"

"I just couldn't do it," Julia said. "I mean, toss everything away and hit the road, without a guarantee of what would be on the other end. I just couldn't. I wish I could, you know? Just get behind the wheel and head out for something like a job. It's not in me."

Mary was strong and broad, but her eyes, peeking out from under a gimme cap, were surprisingly warm and soft. She wore grease like a heavenly mother wears butter and flour. As Julia drove, the truck driver calmly reached into a denim pocket and brought out a packet of tobacco and a sheaf of rolling papers. As Julia talked, Mary calmly rolled a cigarette, nodding and lowly answering when there was a long enough pause to do so. "Like you," she said when Julia was quiet for a moment, distracted by a particularly complex road sign.

"It isn't like she was rash or anything—just like, well…like she sees everyone like they could be a friend. She doesn't see serial killers everywhere, but rather strangers who could be good pals. She isn't really scared of anything. Not foolish, just not so worried about people being bad."

The highway was a dark line pointing to where a too-blue sky met bright green trees. It was a strong pull—so strong that Julia found it hard to tear her eyes away from the vanishing point, but when she did she smiled at the big woman next to her, now leisurely smoking her hand-rolled cigarette. "Like with you, she'd pull right over, open the door, and say 'Want a lift?' She's like that, you know—like the world's just full of friends she hasn't met yet."

"Like you," mumbled Mary around her cigarette, smiling so slight and sly that Julia didn't notice.

"She's like that everywhere—places to eat, movies to see,

books to read: She'd walk down the street till something just got her." Julia's laugh rolled in the small car's interior. "Got a lot of crap—oh, man, this place she found in Oakland—the roaches wouldn't even eat there. But sometimes…sometimes she'd touch something really special, something you'd never have noticed otherwise."

Signs flickered past their windows. Mary's window was down, and each passing buffeted them—even with just a low roll of deep sound. Mary took a long drag on her cigarette and blew the smoke, carefully, out the side window—the gray instantly vanishing. "You can let me off up there," she said, gesturing with the dry end at a sprawling truck stop, big machines swarming around islands of diesel.

Julia pulled over, the highway background moan fading as she slowed. Maneuvering through the labyrinth of trucks, she cruised up to the frantic coffee shop.

"I miss her, I guess," Julia said, turning to Mary. "I miss that sense of adventure she had. It took me a while to figure that out, I guess. That's why I'm driving all this way to be with her again."

Mary put her large hand on the door, popping it open but not swinging it out yet. "Thanks for the lift. You in San Antone, you come and look me—"

Julia leaned across and kissed her, quick (but not too quick) and hard (but not too hard). "Just miss that, you know—miss that kind of thing about her."

Mary got out, smiling, and carefully closed the door—feeling loose, lifted, and buoyant. She waved like a little kid as Julia pulled away, her grin growing wider as Julia waved back. But before going in for a cup of coffee, before trying to track down a tow for her rig, she looked out at the highway and said, "Just like you."

THE COLD BRICKS OF BOSTON: gray sky above, hard looks from people on the street, people in other cars. Her heart should have been pounding, but instead she was cool and quiet. The city seemed held back, locked down by something: money, history, a faith packed with martyrs—she didn't know. The air was chilly, but Julia had the feeling that even if the sun had been out, the steel overcast gone, the people of the city would have put something up equally dull and oppressive.

She should have been light, flying with anticipation—or at least more of it. A tingling giddiness made her head swim, her body lighter, but not as much as she'd thought it would. On the road, between where she'd come from and where she—and Kick—was, she dreamed of laughing, singing, cheering as she drove into the city. Instead she smiled. She just smiled.

It wasn't hard to find the bookstore, surprisingly; for a big city, it felt like a brick-fortified neighborhood. Tucked off a street of dull cement, cracked asphalt, and faded brick, a sign on a bright blue awning read: SHE SPACE: BOOKS FOR WOMEN. Parking was easy, though she wished she'd had more time to circle and get even more. Getting out of the car, she looked down the street, the looming dark sky like a great steel lid keeping the city cool and low.

A short distance away she saw a woman step out of her car, walk up to her house, one arm full of groceries, the other fumbling for keys. Without thinking, Julia stepped up, offered to help. The woman looked at her slightly askance, but as a plastic bottle of soda thumped onto the sidewalk and started to roll away, she said "sure" with an embarrassed little smile.

After helping the woman with her bags—Susan, as she learned the woman's name was—Julia stepped toward the bookstore again, and again saw delightful, hidden things: the way the leafless trees made shadows like cracks on the sidewalk, the rust on an old car like metal acne, a headline cut to "Fall Lead" by a newspaper rack, and then—completely on the spur of the moment, she leaped up and grabbed a low, thick branch. Hanging there, she listened to the little noises of the tree, then she let go—landing lightly, like a cat, on the balls of her feet. Taking a step forward, she noticed something tickling her hand. She looked down and saw a chubby eyebrow of a caterpillar, working its way from one knuckle to the next. She held her hand out to the tree, encouraging the creature's slow progress with a gentle laugh.

Then she was in front of the store and then her hand was on the knob. It was hot inside, like a sauna. It was full of mad colors, like a forest in autumn: too many bold titles, too many bright covers. She turned to the counter, spoke to the stern young woman meticulously writing in a ledger. "Excuse me, I'm looking for someone who works here. Her name is Kick."

The woman looked up, shock in her cloudy-gray eyes. "Julia?" Kick said.

KICK DID KNOW A PLACE, not that far away. A hand-painted mural of a mermaid on one wall, with old Christmas glitter for braided-seaweed hair. The tables were roughly handled spools for heavy cable; no two chairs—or place settings—were alike. On a whim, Julia ordered the "sprout surprise," and Kick ordered "the usual."

As they'd walked, Julia had kept her eyes cast at her old lover—or, to be more precise, had looked for her old lover in this woman. The eyes were the same, the face was exact, the body—as far as she could tell under the brown wool suit—was similar, but nothing else was.

"How's your job?" was one of the first things Kick asked her.

Looking comically sideways at the "special" on her plate, Julia said, "Quit."

"Quit? Just like that?"

"Sure. I can always find another job." *But there's only one you* was left unsaid. "I've missed you," she finished in a low voice.

"That's nice," Kick said, looking for a long moment out the window.

"How's the job? You were so excited about it. Is it everything you'd hoped it'd be?"

Kick looked down at her special-blend tea. "I guess

so...there's just a lot of emotions at play, you know. Like this girl, Alice, she's nice enough, but sometimes she just sort of stands on process—like she has to make sure we don't turn into a dreaded patriarchy or something. Just the other day, in fact, I wanted to order this new book *Angel Falling* by Dorthea Lamont, and she got all upset that the publisher recently refused to publish this collection of Virginia Woolf essays because it wasn't 'commercially viable.' She said this proved we shouldn't support this kind of 'machismo economics.' And then Betty got involved—she works in our shipping and receiving department, but only part-time because she's also a massage therapist—and she said we shouldn't keep good work out of people's hands because the publisher was being a fascist..."

"Uh-huh," said Julia, noticing the way the mermaid's scaled tail reflected in the curve of her spoon, making the naiad appear to be swimming in a sea of mercury.

"Which was definitely not the case, and besides, I've read those old essays—Virginia Woolf, I mean—and they are definitely not worth losing a publisher over, or even pissing off a distributor. I mean, they're good, but there's some better stuff out there, and it's too reactionary to cut off all these new people for something that's been in print before and probably will be again, but Alice is just like that..."

Julia smiled, holding up a hand. "Just a minute, hold that thought." She got up quickly and helped a delivery girl with her wobbly hand truck. When she'd given her a hand getting some boxes into the kitchen, she sat back down. "Had to help out with that. Please go on."

"Anyway, then there's Diana—she's nice and all, but she really has issues about stripping books, so I have to make sure she's not around or she goes on this trip about 'destroying the trees of our mother' kind of thing, which I agree with of course, but if we don't strip the books then we have to pay for them, and we just don't have that kind of income, not with the tax reevaluation the city hit us with last quarter."

Julia mumbled a fourth—or was it fifth...or more like a tenth?—"uh-huh" and picked at her special, deciding with a wry smile that there was a lot that was special about it, taste not being one of them. Then there was a long silence and she looked up, suddenly realizing Kick had fallen silent.

"I said, 'What have you been up to?'" Kick said, a tiny burn of acid in her voice.

Julia looked at her, thinking: I've stood naked under the stars and offered my pain to the sky. I've seen birds write symphonies on telephone wires and driven down the dotted line of a highway contract with God. I've cleaned diners and cafés, hauled boxes up stairs, and once helped paint a VFW hall. On a lark, a whim, I've driven hundreds of miles to see the World's Largest Nail, the World's Smallest Church, and the World's Shortest Horse. I sometimes haven't had the world's best time, but sometimes it's come damned close. I've kissed a truck driver who had great motherly arms. I've cried with a young punk kid who wanted to go home but was also scared to. I've driven clear across the country to see you and...

"Not much," Julia said after a long time, "just driving...just finding stuff out about myself, you know. That kinda thing."

Kick asked if she had a place to stay, her tone hinting that if Julia didn't then Kick might possibly have room for two, but Julia slowly shook her head. "Got to get going," she said.

"Where to?" Kick replied, sounding concerned, implying that any trip had to have a destination.

"No idea," Julia said, smiling. "Absolutely no idea. Maybe nowhere—I'll send you a postcard when I get there."

So Julia left, heading—with the flip of a coin—north, waving to Kick as she pulled into the light traffic, saying goodbye to what was behind her and excited at what she'd find out next.

NOT THE END, NOT QUITE. Because for a long time—a cold winter and a very hot summer and then some—certain people...people like a hitchhiker not more than seventeen, not under fifteen; an old woman who cleaned a tiny diner's tables each and every night; a trucker named Mary; and many others would look out onto the highway and think about the girl with the special eyes (and what she saw with them), the girl who helped people who needed it, who was wonderfully impulsive and caring, and smile, saying, "I think her name was Kick."

—BREATHE—

Gina Ranalli

PICTURE THIS:

It's a hot August night, and I'm stuck in the backseat of my mother's Saab while she drives and chats all comfy-cozy girl-chat with my sister, who's seated beside her. They're both enjoying the pleasant A/C breeze flowing out of the dash. (My mother refuses to turn it up enough to reach me, says cranking it up to high is a waste of air-conditioning fluid.) So I'm pretty much panting out the window. The *closed* window, that is. Mom screeches every time I attempt to crack it, just like she did when I was a kid and the three of us were in these exact same positions.

It feels like a time warp, like I'm nine instead of twenty-nine. If this isn't my version of hell, it's at least within blistering distance of it. I sigh, gaze out at all the passing vehicles, and wonder why I agreed to go to dinner with them in the first place.

Then I remember.

Mom's birthday. Right. The gravity of guilt is a mighty force.

"I wish Jeffery and the boys were able to join us," my mother was saying, referring to my brother-in-law and two monster nephews.

"No, you don't," Michelle told her. "Jeff had them out all

day doing God only knows what. All I know is that when they got home, all three of them were bouncing off the walls."

"You shouldn't let them eat so much sugar," Mom said.

My sister ignored her, rolled down her window, and lit a cigarette. I waited for my mother to scold her, and when it didn't happen I growled under my breath. Michelle is the prized daughter, three years younger and living her life the way it's supposed to be lived, with a family and a "sensible" career as a nurse.

I, on the other hand, have been nothing but disappointment. A single lesbian working as a freelance writer, or as Mom likes to call it, "bum work." Much to their astonishment, however, I had been relatively happy in both my job and my love life. True, I could easily have stood to make a little more money, and there were nights when I felt a longing to fill the vacancy in my bed with something more than indifference, but all in all I felt I was doing pretty good.

"Oh, girls," my mother raised her voice slightly in an attempt to make sure I knew I was being addressed as well. "Before we go to the restaurant, I need to make a quick stop at the Winslow Street house."

Without hesitation, her good daughter replied, "Sure, Mom, no problem."

Her bad daughter resisted the urge to groan and asked, "How come?"

Eyeballing me in the rearview mirror, Mom said, "I need to check on Fin."

"Who?"

She gave me an irritated look. "Fin Abraham." I stared back at her blankly, prompting her to say, "Good Lord, Dyan, the girl's lived there her whole life, practically."

My brain quickly buzzed through its memory files and finally recalled the tenants in the two-family rental my mom owned. "Oh, right," I said. "Fin."

A moment of silence passed before my mother challenged: "You don't remember her, do you?"

"Of course I do!" I neglected to add the word *vaguely*.

"Well, her father, James, died last week," Mom said.

"Really? That's awful." And suddenly I clearly remembered James Abraham. A recent widower, he and his tiny, oddly named daughter had moved into my parents' property when I was still in high school. "Fin was just a baby when they moved in, right?"

"I think she was six," Michelle said, chugging out smoke that blew back into my face. "Which would make her…seventeen, I guess. What a shame." She shook her head for emphasis, and Mom mimicked the motion, watching Michelle with a pleased expression.

"How did it happen?" I asked.

"Heart attack," Mom replied. "And only forty-six. Can you imagine?" She made a sad clucking sound with her tongue. "That poor child. An orphan at seventeen."

I nodded my agreement. My own dad had passed away shortly before my twentieth birthday, but at least we'd had our mother. "So, Fin is still at the house?"

Stopping at a traffic light, Mom said, "She made more money than God last year when they published that poetry book of hers."

A book of *poetry* made money? I almost laughed out loud but thought better of it and simply said, "Oh?"

"Apparently," she continued, "people are calling her a wunderkind and that sort of thing. You said you'd heard of her in your little writers' circles when I mentioned it a while back. Said you'd even read one of her poems, if I recall correctly."

"'Transgressor,'" I said suddenly. "That's right." Glancing out the window, I added, "I'll be damned."

"That's it," she agreed, making her turn. " 'Transgressor.' She even won some awards for it, I understand. Her father was so proud, and I can't say I blame him. She's overcome many obstacles, not the least of which was being born with a name like Affinity. My lord, who but a hippie would call his child that?"

Ignoring the hippie-bashing, I said, "Yeah, it's a great poem.

Amazing it was written by a kid." What was even more amazing was that I'd been so self-involved, I hadn't even realized this local phenom was actually living in my mom's house. Small world, I thought, waving smoke out of my face.

A COUPLE OF MINUTES LATER, Mom parked her Saab in the driveway at 84 Winslow Street, a somewhat shabby house painted an ugly hospital-green. She insisted we both accompany her to the door, which I didn't mind, but Michelle was disgruntled because she wanted to have another cigarette.

"You can wait another five minutes to continue giving yourself heart disease, Michelle," Mom told her acidly.

I blinked in surprise but said nothing, and together the three of us climbed up the peeling porch steps and waited for someone to answer Mom's knock.

The girl who opened the door looked older than seventeen and didn't smile when she saw us. Mom explained how she just wanted to see that everything was okay and asked if we could come in.

Fin hesitated and I thought she was going to tell us no, but then, without a word, she stepped aside and held the door open.

As we shuffled inside, she eyed all of us—but for some reason, especially me—with undisguised suspicion. Mom was already yapping away, giving the girl her classic I've-been-so-worried pitch, which she's practiced to perfection.

Fin Abraham was tall and thin. Baby-fine long blond hair hung down to her shoulder blades as she led the way down a narrow hall into a sparsely decorated living room.

There was almost no furniture in the place, with the exception of a single couch, several bookcases, and a battle-scarred mahogany coffee table. Every available surface—the floor included—was buried beneath deep drifts of books and magazines, and any space that *wasn't* filled with reading material was occupied by a wide variety of plants. The apartment was like a primitive garden, allowed to grow wild and tangled, the hanging plants weaving together in creative loops and braids. I felt like I'd stepped into a sacred rainforest and wouldn't have been surprised to hear the distant call of a tropical bird.

Fin flopped herself down on the couch and watched us with enormous faded-blue eyes, her full lips set grimly. Wearing a white sleeveless blouse and tattered cutoffs, she tucked her bare feet beneath her butt and sat cross-legged and silent, listening to my mother rattle on about "the shame of it all."

My writer's attention to detail kicked in, and I noticed Fin had on what appeared to be a pewter Earth Goddess pendant on a chocolate-brown shoelace around her neck. Several strands of colored twine decorated each of her slender wrists, and many of her fingers were adorned with shiny silver and turquoise rings. I also noticed she had a nail-biting habit, and I wondered if this was a recent quirk, acquired since her father's death, or if she'd always chewed them.

"Well," Mom was saying, "we just came by to see if you needed anything."

"I'm fine," Fin said, her voice startlingly husky. She glanced at me, and I gave her what I hoped looked like a friendly smile.

Mom noticed the exchange. "Oh, damn. I'm sorry, Fin," she blurted. "You haven't met my oldest daughter, have you? This is Dyan. She's a writer too."

Somewhat embarrassed, I stepped forward and extended my hand, which Fin accepted limply and without comment. "You're a phenomenal poet," I told her. "Really brilliant."

Fin cocked her head to one side, eyeing me with interest. Ignoring the compliment, she asked, "What do you write?"

"Mostly freelance stuff. Little things no one reads, really."

"Oh." She was clearly unimpressed and there was an awkward moment of silence.

Mom eventually came to the rescue by asking Fin what her plans were, perhaps there were some relatives somewhere?

"Why? Are you throwing me out?" Fin frowned.

"God, no. Of course not!" Mom gasped as if the girl had

asked her if she condoned bestiality. "I just assumed...well, you're so *young*..." She trailed off, obviously uncomfortable. Fin stared at her expectantly and actually so did I.

"Er...well..." My mother continued to stammer, struggling to find words that wouldn't offend the girl. Finally she managed, "I presumed a girl your age wouldn't want to live alone."

"Why not?" Fin asked seriously. "Who else would be better company for me than me?"

I couldn't help smiling at that. Apparently, the girl and I had more in common than writing.

"People drive me nuts," Fin added, then abruptly rose from the couch and left the room, bumping into Michelle along the way.

Mom stood slack-jawed as we listened to a door slam. I released a loud sigh and looked at Michelle, who shrugged, her expression mild.

"What the hell was that?" Mom demanded.

I thought about it for a second. "Artists are so temperamental, aren't they?"

Mom didn't laugh. "What did I say?"

"Whatever it was," Michelle said, "it pissed her off."

"But *why*? I only wanted to know what her plans were. My lord!"

My sister shrugged again. "Well, I'm hungry. Let's go."

"But..." Mom continued to looked flustered, gazing at me with uncertainty.

I placed a hand on her shoulder. "Don't worry about it. I'm sure she's just had a crappy week. You can call her tomorrow or something."

She appeared to mull this over for a few seconds, then said, "Dyan, why don't you go talk to her?"

"What?" I cried. "I don't even know her!"

"Mom, I'm hungry," Michelle whined.

"Come on, Dyan," Mom said. "You're the closest thing we have to a teenager. And you're a writer!"

I gaped at her. "The closest thing to a...what the hell is that supposed to mean?"

"If anyone could relate to her, you could."

I lowered my voice to a whisper. "Are you suggesting I might be inclined to wear twine as a bracelet?"

"We can't just go," Mom said. "I wouldn't feel right."

I started to argue with her, but Michelle interrupted. "Dyan, go talk to the girl. I told Jeffery I'd be home by ten and it's almost eight now."

Shifting my weight from one foot to the other, I glanced back and forth between them and finally held my hands up in surrender. "Okay, fine," I told my mom, sighing. "I'll talk to her, but you're coming with me."

Evidently she knew it was the best deal she was going to get and immediately agreed. Michelle informed us she'd be waiting in the car while Mom and I went in search of Fin.

"This is insane," I muttered, peering into vacant rooms off the hallway.

"She's in here," my mother hissed, pointing to the closed door she had her ear pressed against.

I leaned against the wall beside the door. "Good job, Nancy Drew."

"I hear movement." She straightened up and looked at me. "Knock."

I shook my head. "*You* knock."

Mom furrowed her brow in disgust and rapped on the door, which instantly swung open and—surprisingly—*outward,* trapping me between it and the wall.

"Hello again," Mom said. I couldn't see her face, but I could tell by the sound of her voice that she was giving the girl the same phony, humoring smile she gave me when she thought I was behaving childishly. "We wanted to be sure you didn't need anything before we get going."

"We?" Fin sounded confused, so I stepped out from behind the door and flashed my best stepping-out-from-behind-a-door smile. At the sight of me, Fin's first expression was bewilderment, which quickly morphed into annoyance. I gave her an apologetic shrug, and her pale ancient eyes shifted from me back to my mom. "Thanks," she said. "But I don't need anything. I'm completely fine."

"Really?" Mom gave me a quick, desperate glance before looking back at Fin and announcing, "Dyan was wondering if she could have an autographed copy of your book."

I glared at her, coming dangerously close to blurting expletives. Aware that Fin was watching us curiously, I managed to hold my tongue in check and turned to her, wearing what I'm sure appeared to be an insane grin. Through clenched teeth, I confirmed the claim that I wanted an autographed book, though I knew, as I'm sure Fin knew, that the usual custom is to *already have* a copy of the book for the author to sign.

Fin leaned against the doorjamb and appeared to be considering the possibility that we might actually be stalkers, so I was stunned when she said, "Okay, let me find a copy." She whirled on her feet and rummaged around what turned out to be her bedroom, sifting through more stacks of books strewn all about. The room, like the rest of the place, looked as if a library had fallen out of the sky and landed with an explosion in a wild green jungle.

Taking a step into the room, I said, "It's okay if you don't have one. I can drop by another time."

Her back to me, Fin said, "I know I have one here someplace. It's just a matter of..." She trailed off, bending over a precarious tower of books that nearly reached her thighs.

Innocently, my eyes wandered from the littered floor and up her legs, marveling at their amazing length and beauty. *Youth,* I thought, with more than a little envy. And then my gaze, of its own accord, traveled farther upward and settled on her perfectly curved ass, the way the faded cutoffs hugged it, almost seemed to caress it...

With a panicky sense of alarm, I tore my eyes from her body

and forced myself to study a woven tapestry above the bed, my cheeks burning.

"Found one," Fin said, straightening up and facing me, waving a thin paperback in the air. The smile she wore was so unexpected and stunningly radiant, it caused my heart to thud painfully against my ribcage. Suddenly, and without rational explanation, I felt the need to sit down.

"Great!" my mother exclaimed from where she still stood in the hallway.

"Now the trick is to find a pen," Fin said, glancing around the room until her eyes found mine. "You wouldn't happen to have one, would you?"

I shook my head. "Mom?"

She was already pawing through her purse. "Here's one."

Fin accepted the pen with a nod and turned back to me. "Want me to say anything in particular?"

Once again my gaze was roving over her body, and once again I felt myself blush furiously, positive I'd been busted and in the next second Fin would be screaming for the old-lady perv police. Instead, though, I was surprised to see her smile once more, her eyes holding mine, sharp and steady.

"Anything in particular?" she repeated.

I took a deep breath. "Anything you want is fine."

She arched an eyebrow at me, her smile growing more amused. "Turn around."

I blinked stupidly. "Beg your pardon?"

"I'll use your back," she explained. "To brace the book."

"Oh. Right." I obliged, and a moment later she had the book pressed against me, asking me to spell my name. I listened to the sound of the pen scratching across the page and tried to ignore her dark, rainy-woods scent. When she finished, I turned and she passed me the slender volume.

"Ever been to Linear Books?" she asked suddenly.

It took me a second to register that she'd asked a real question. "Uh...yeah. I've been there a few times."

"Well, tomorrow night is poetry jam night. A bunch of people show up to read or listen or whatever. If you're not doing anything, you should drop by."

"Um..." I could only stare at her.

"It's all ages. All everything, really. Published, unpublished, boy, girl. Any variation of the two." Her eyes flashed mischievously as she said that last bit.

"That sounds fabulous!" Mom piped in from the doorway, reminding me of her presence. "You should go, Dyan. Get out of that stuffy apartment of yours!"

My mind raced. Was this girl asking me out? This precocious seventeen-year-old waif with her seventeen-year-old body and ageless, endless eyes? And if so, what do I say? How do I respond? I instantly knew how I *should* respond, but I also knew how I *wanted* to respond, and the two didn't mesh at all.

Not at all.

I cleared my throat. "I'm not sure what I have planned for tomorrow night. Can I give you a 'maybe'?"

"That's cool. It starts around seven and goes till eleven or so. It's all very loose, laid-back, free and easy." She smiled her heart-slaying smile again. "You'll have fun."

"Dyan, we really should get going. Your sister is probably ready to have one of her hissy fits."

"Okay, Mom," I said.

Fin and I stood a few feet apart, our gazes locked for I don't know how long, and there was an instant, a single blip of time when I almost told my mother to go on without me. Then I blinked and moved past Fin, back out to the hallway and toward the front door.

"Hope I'll see you tomorrow," Fin called.

Practically sprinting across the lawn to the car, I waved without turning, wanting to get away from her as fast as my feet would allow.

All through dinner I tried to concentrate on the conversations about the latest Hollywood blockbusters and Revlon's newest lipstick line. But despite my best efforts, my thoughts returned to images of a certain willowy poet with huge faded eyes.

It wasn't until much later, just before going to bed, that I thought to check the inscription Fin had written inside my book. I grabbed it off my kitchen table and opened it to the title page. When I read it, the book slipped from my fingers and clattered to the floor. It was nearly a full minute before I could pick it up and read the message again.

Written in small curling letters, the inscription read:

> *Dyan,*
> *Every woman I've ever kissed*
> *in a dream was you.*
> *—Fin*

Wide awake after that, I read her poetry while lying in bed. The girl was undeniably mature and gifted. I was particularly impressed with a long poem entitled "Antithesis," in which she raged ferociously against stereotyping people based on surface impressions. Putting the book aside, I lay back against the pillows and stared at the ceiling, twisting strands of hair around my finger. It was a long time before I was able to sleep.

I SPENT THE FOLLOWING MORNING drinking coffee while working on a story about a group of lesbian students wreaking havoc at a New Hampshire college. Although I hadn't slept particularly well, by noon I'd almost completely forgotten about the flirtatious yet forbidden Fin. Deep into the guts of the article, I wasn't aware of anything else until the phone rang. Usually if I'm working, I let the machine take it, and this time was no exception. That is, until I heard my friend Kim's voice. She sounded impatient, so I stopped typing and grabbed the cordless.

"Hey, I'm here."

"I knew it." Her voice was slightly muffled, and it took me a second to realize she was eating something. "I'm bored," she said between munches.

"I'm working," I told her. "Can't you be bored for someone else?"

"I love you too, babycakes. But you need to hear what happened to me last night!" And before I could respond, Kim was off and running, telling me the intricate details of her latest sexploit. I listened politely for a while, and then my mind began wandering, meandering delicately in a land filled with books and plants and poetry.

"If your night can beat that," Kim said, "our next Mexican dinner is on me."

I tapped gibberish across my computer screen, thinking.

"Hello? Dyan?"

Bravely plunging in, I asked, "Kim, what do you think about someone our age dating a seventeen-year-old woman?"

There was a moment of silence during which I considered crawling under my desk. Finally, she said, "Baby, that's not a question, that's a felony." She paused. "Why do you ask?"

I slumped in my chair. "I just wondered about...uh...your opinion."

"Hmm. Well, first I'd beat some sense into the bitch, even if I didn't know the child."

"Oh." I was beginning to feel nauseous.

She must have sensed something was amiss. "Why are you asking me this? Are you messing around with someone you shouldn't be?"

"No! Don't be ridiculous!" I hesitated, then quickly added, "I'm working on a story, that's all."

Kim sighed. "It's not worth it, Dy. Remember, perky tits are fun for only so long, until you start craving an adult conversation to go along with them."

That gave me a chuckle. "Oh, you mean, like the conversations *we* have?"

"You and I," she said, "are not bumping uglies."

"Good grief," I muttered. "All right, I have to get back to work."

"Okay, fine, be that way. I'll talk to you in a few days. Oh, and Dy?"

"Yeah?"

"Feel free to call if you need bail money."

"Very funny. I'm hanging up now, Ms. DeGeneres."

She started to say something—another wiseass comment, I'm sure—but I cut her off with a punch of the "end" button.

I stared at the computer screen for a while, stewing. Eventually, I began drumming my fingers against the desk, just for variety. When that got boring, I got up, made myself another cup of coffee, and returned, ready to tackle the article again.

It took a few minutes to get back into the groove, but once I did, I was cooking with gas. It was maybe half an hour later that the phone rang again, but this time I was determined to ignore it. Even if it had been the voice of Gillian Anderson, dripping slow and sweet like honey out of the answering machine, I would have kept on typing. I'm a professional and I had a deadline, after all. But as it turned out, the second caller hung up without leaving a message and I didn't miss a beat.

The rest of the afternoon flew by with barely a nod of acknowledgment from me, and by the time evening rolled around, I knew I wouldn't be attending Fin's reading. How could I? She was a kid, for crying out loud. A smart, attractive, wise-well-beyond-her-years kid, but still a kid, and it would be wrong to lead her on. I remembered what it was like to be seventeen and have a crush on an older woman. Of course, *that* older woman had actually slept with me, and I didn't appear to have suffered any damage from the experience, but still. Kim was right. I would do the intelligent thing and not even pick up the matches, therefore thwarting any temptation to play with them. For once I'd be the adult.

When the decision was made, I was able to relax and, like a good little American, spend a couple of mindless hours drooling before my twenty-four-inch alien transmitter. Seven o'clock came and went without my noticing.

Honest.

THAT NIGHT, I DREAMED OF HER.

We were sitting on her crowded green sofa, going at it like…well, like teenagers. Distantly, an old ABBA song could be heard, as if someone had left a stereo on in another part of the house. She pressed her slender body hard into mine, murmuring unintelligible phrases against my mouth, her breath hot and minty. Her hair flowed smoothly down her back like a sparkling river of sunshine, and just as I sank my hands into it she pulled back from me and announced, "ABBA is the greatest band ever. Every song is a golden nugget of wisdom."

Unspeakably excited, I could only think to say the cold hard fact: "ABBA sucks." And with that, I reached for her, anxious to resume our makeout session.

Without protest, Fin met me halfway, but just before our lips touched, a set of false teeth spilled out of my mouth and into her lap.

We both screamed in horror and disgust.

I woke with a start, my hair damp and plastered to my fore-head. Mortified, I buried my face in the pillow and tried to quell the ache in my chest. But even after several minutes of controlled deep breathing, my heart continued to race, as if that stupid muscle had a Morse code of its own and with every beat thumped out the letters of her name.

IT WAS WHILE I WAS TRYING TO SCOOP a dead Molly out of the fish tank the following afternoon that the knock came. I knew before I even put down the net that it would be her. Somehow I knew.

A quick peep through the peephole confirmed my premonition. I stood before the door without opening it, chewing my lower lip. How did she know where I lived? The answer was obvious. My mother had told her. How else?

I debated pretending I wasn't home, but then the knock came again, more insistent than the first time, and so, with suddenly moist palms, I opened it.

The sight of her nearly smacked me sideways. Wearing nothing more extraordinary than jeans, a sleeveless black T-shirt, and sandals, she was breathtaking. A lone thin braid hung along the right side of her face, tied off with bright blue string, while the rest of her hair remained long and loose.

"Hi," she said, regarding me with an expression I couldn't read.

"You didn't show up last night," she said, as if this were news to me. She watched my face expectantly, then looked at her feet and asked, "Can I come in for a minute?"

Knowing the answer should be no, I found myself stepping aside to let her enter. I closed the door and led her into the living room, where neither of us apparently felt like sitting. Instead we stood in the center of the room, facing each other. She glanced around, taking in the place before turning her attention back to me. Then, looking directly into my eyes, she asked, "Why didn't you show?"

I released the breath I didn't know I'd been holding and finally found my voice. "I couldn't come, Fin. I'm sorry. I shouldn't have said I would."

Her face remained neutral. "You didn't answer my question."

I dropped my gaze, remained silent.

"What are you doing right now?" she asked.

"Huh?" I braved a peek at her.

"We could get a cup of coffee or something." I must have looked completely baffled, because she added, "You know, go *out*. You do go out, don't you?"

I shifted my weight and muttered, "Not with kids."

Which was evidently the wrong thing to say. "Excuse me?" she said sharply. "Kids?"

"You're..." I sighed again. "You're just a..."

"Just a what? A kid?"

I ran a hand through my hair. "Seventeen is very young, Fin."

She raised her chin defiantly. "You're attracted to me."

I could only gape at her, my heart thudding.

"Tell me you're not," she said. "Look me in the eye and tell me you're not."

How could I argue with that? Which was somewhat beside the point anyway, because I didn't feel like arguing; I felt more like crying.

"You can't," Fin said, almost soothingly. "You can't because you are. And *I'm* attracted to *you,* so what's the big deal? We can just hang out, can't we? Get to know each other? See where things go?"

"No." My voice was quiet, almost a whisper.

Fin abruptly took a step forward and snatched my hand. I tried to yank it back, but her grip was surprisingly strong, almost painful. "Feel this?" she asked, lacing her fingers through mine. Her pale blue eyes pierced mine and seemed to penetrate my very core. I shivered. "Do you know what this is?" she went on, raising both our hands to eye level and squeezing. "This is electricity. This is magnetism. And for all we know, it could be fate. Things happen for a reason. Don't you believe that?"

"Yes," I croaked, then pulled my hand away. "But it's not always an obvious reason."

Her face changed then, became almost wounded, and she looked down at her feet once more. "You know," she said softly, "you can't change destiny with pettiness."

I nearly laughed at that but stifled the urge. "You're right," I told her.

"Age is relative."

"Sometimes."

"And sometimes people just know...you know...when it's right."

I said nothing, wanting desperately to agree with her and at the same time wanting to scramble under the nearest rock just for *wanting* to agree with her.

She cleared her throat and looked up into my face. "I've been an emancipated minor since I was fifteen. I know it sounds lame, but everyone's always said I was...an old soul." She smiled slightly, rolling her eyes in embarrassment, and for the first time since meeting her I thought she actually looked seventeen. Beautiful and profoundly clever, but still seventeen. "*And,*" she continued, "I'm critically acclaimed." Her smile blossomed into a big grin, and I, seeing she was making a final, silly effort to woo me, smiled too.

"That's a hard one to resist," I conceded. "But..." I shook my head, unable to say the actual words.

Fin nodded, her smile wilting. We looked at each other for a long time, just as we had in her bedroom two days before. Then she shrugged, seemed to regain some of her humor. "Well, I guess I should go, huh?"

"Yeah." I swallowed hard, not wanting her to, but suddenly afraid if she didn't leave right then, things could happen.

Minds could change.

"Well...see ya, I guess." She gave a little wave and started for the front door, me trailing behind her like a sad puppy. Opening the door, she stepped outside into a bright-blue day. Then, without warning, she turned back to me and smiled. Tucking a lock of blond hair behind an ear, she said, "I have a birthday in two months."

My heart kicking hard, I tried to return her smile. "I hope it's a good one."

"It will be." She winked and turned away, strolling briskly up the walkway and out to the sidewalk.

I clutched the doorjamb and watched until she rounded the corner and disappeared from sight. Then I closed the door and leaned against it, reminding myself to breathe.

Just breathe.

—SUZANNE'S—

Sarah Pemberton Strong

IT'S STRANGE BEING AT SUZANNE'S without her. Her presence in the apartment is much stronger than when she's actually here; a faint electrical current seems to be running through the room. I stand in the doorway of her tiny garden apartment, her extra set of keys in my hand, and survey the furniture and posters and books I've seen a thousand times, checking for evidence of the girlfriend.

I feel a surge of electricity flow through my body, as if I'm trespassing, and I remind myself that's stupid: Actually, I'm doing Suzanne a favor. I said I'd come on Wednesday to feed the dog, and here I am.

In the old days Suzanne would never have had a dog, but if she had, I would have offered for the whole week, maybe stayed here even. Now that Suzanne has a girlfriend, I'm only needed on Wednesday: On Wednesday the girlfriend, Vonne, has to work late.

On Suzanne's bed there's a leather jacket, flung casually across the quilt as if it were the first arrival at a party. I sit beside it. It's really good leather, expensive and soft and touchable, and way out of range of Suzanne's thrift-store budget. I wonder if it's a gift from the girlfriend. I touch the steel teeth of the zipper, the dark folds of the lapels. The cut is much too butch for Suzanne; Vonne obviously doesn't know her taste at all. If I were Suzanne I'd have told her straight out: Sorry, this just isn't me. You should have asked Margie. She'd have known what to get.

If Vonne had asked me, I would have explained buttons, not zipper, and tailored, not motorcycle. Thinking this, I realize Vonne, who owns a motorcycle, is probably also the owner of this jacket and it's not Suzanne's at all; Vonne just threw it across Suzanne's bed as if she owned that too. I think of dogs peeing on turf they want to mark as theirs. Which reminds me why I'm here: I should let the dog in. But first I lift Vonne's expensive butch jacket off the bed and drop it gently on the floor.

I've slept in this bed too, once. I mean one time. I hadn't known Suzanne very long—maybe six months that already seemed like years and years because we spent so much time together. Even if all we were doing was something like Saturday morning laundry, we were doing it together, and then come Sunday night we'd still be hanging out. We'd be in her kitchen eating ice cream out of the box, or lying on her bed talking, and then the next day, Monday, we'd have to call each other at work, just to catch up. And one Sunday night we were lying on her bed and Suzanne had her back to the alarm clock. Every so often I'd glance at the glowing red numbers, advancing blink by blink: 10:49, 11:16, but Suzanne kept laughing at things I said and saying, "Oh, Margie," and wiping her eyes from laughing so hard.

11:56, 12:01, and Suzanne never yawned or looked at the clock or said "I'll walk you out," and so I stayed. Finally, when she did yawn and said Jesus, what time is it, it was 1:23. I got up to go, but Suzanne said, "Just stay here, Margie," as if it were no big deal. Which for her it wasn't: I learned that Suzanne always falls asleep right away. Her hand was stretched out through the space between us so that her fingertips grazed my shoulder. She sleeps with her mouth open. I woke up with a stiff neck.

When I call Suzanne on Saturday mornings now her machine picks up. Either they're still in bed or they're out walking the dog. Suzanne was never a dog person before.

I go into Suzanne's kitchen to let the dog—Rocket, a Doberman-shepherd mix—in from the yard. I'm not a dog person either. I suspect Vonne is a dog person. Vonne picked him out from the pound. If I were Suzanne I would have told Vonne this apartment is way too small for a dog that size, even if I do have a yard.

The bolt on the back door sticks, and my jiggling it brings Rocket bounding across the yard to the door. I hear him whine eagerly, his toenails scraping against the door. It sounds as if he's up on his hind legs, trying to push the door open from his side, which is not helpful. He's scratching and whining himself into a frenzy; I hear his tail thumping against the garbage cans. But when I finally get the door open and he sees me, he suddenly goes silent. Then he starts to bark.

"Hey, Rocket, good dog," I say shakily, backing away. He'd been expecting Suzanne, or Vonne, I suppose, not me. I'm an intruder. The dog advances a few steps, still barking. I try to remember what I know about dogs. You have to let them smell you, is all I can think of. But offering my hand to the muzzle of a barking Doberman-shepherd mix seems like a bad idea. Dogs can smell fear—I remember that too—and I'm thinking that I'm not really scared, it's just the noise of the barking. But I back up some more, out of the kitchen and into the other room, the dog advancing as I retreat through the apartment.

Then I can't go any farther; I've backed up against the far wall, and it's not the wall with the front door in it. It's the wall with the walk-in closet.

"Good Rocket," I say, trying to make my voice sound like Suzanne's, and for one fabulous second the dog stops barking. "Good Rocket," I say again in Suzanne's voice, and instead of barking he starts to growl, which turns out to be worse. A low, snarling growl with his lips curled back around his teeth. I slide my hand along the wall and Suzanne's closet door. Then, kind of fast, I'm inside.

It's totally dark in here, and my back is smack up against the dresser. I feel around for the overhead pull chain and finally yank on the light. Her closet is a mess, dirty clothes everywhere, smelling faintly of coconut and cotton and sweat, a Suzanne smell, which gives me an idea. I pick up a wadded camisole from the overflowing laundry basket and inhale the satin, the smell of Suzanne as certain as if she were hugging me the way she will when she comes back from the conference, the smell I'll smell when I breathe into her hair. I take off my own shirt and bra and slide Suzanne's camisole over my head. I look around for something else and notice I'm standing on a pair of green tights. I kick off my shoes and wiggle out of my jeans and underwear and pull on Suzanne's tights. I look at the clothes on hangers. There's a short black skirt I recognize. I've always liked that skirt on Suzanne. I slide it over my thighs and zip it up. It fits perfectly.

Suzanne wears hats. I take a purple felt hat she bought last year at the Salvation Army and breathe into its crown. Suzanne's hair. I mash the hat down over my ears. I take a pair of Suzanne's dirty underwear from the laundry basket and rub it between my hands. Then, very slowly, I open the closet door.

The dog is lying on the bed now. He raises his head and looks at me, and I hold out my hand and let him sniff. His ears twitch. He doesn't bite me. He sniffs a couple of times and drops his head back onto his paws.

"Good dog," I say with relief. I notice the feeling of trespassing has disappeared.

I snap my fingers and point to the floor, something I've seen Suzanne do. "Rocket. Off the bed," I say, and miraculously the dog raises himself up on his big haunches and lumbers onto the floor. "Good dog," I say, mimicking Suzanne. "You're my good boy." The dog thumps his tail on the floor.

I wander back into the kitchen. "This is my kitchen," I say aloud. I open the refrigerator door. *I bought this food,* I think. I take a swig of orange juice from the carton and shut the door, go back into the other room. The dog is still lying on the floor. I lie down on the bed. "This is my bed," I tell him. I rest my cheek on the pillow that smells like her hair and play with the lace trimming on her camisole. I slide my hand around the bodice, and my fingers catch on a nipple, already stiff beneath the satiny drag of fabric moving under my hand. "So this is how your breasts feel," I say softly. "They're fuller than they look through your clothes." I take the hem of Suzanne's camisole between my fingers and slowly peel it back, look at the smooth skin of belly underneath, dusted with fine pale hairs. I lift the satin farther back and contemplate those breasts. I notice two small freckles above the nipple of the left one. "I didn't know you had those," I say softly. I tweak the nipples and watch them tighten and flush, then I slip my other hand down the waistband of Suzanne's skirt and inside her tights.

"I've always wanted to do this," I whisper.

Suddenly, the door to the apartment is opening. I yank my hand free and jump up, horrified, but it's too late: Vonne is staring at me from the doorway with a set of keys in her hand.

The dog jumps up and begins to bark again.

"I didn't expect you to be here. I was just lying down for a while," I stammer over the noise of the barking. "I'm just about to take him for a walk."

"Rocket, be quiet," Vonne says sharply. The dog obeys at once.

"I was just lying down for a minute," I go on, "but now I'm going to take him for a walk. I'm just looking for the leash so I can walk him."

She raises an eyebrow. I stop talking, it's futile—she's seen me lying on the bed with my hand in Suzanne's skirt; there is no such thing as an explanation.

I look at the floor. "I didn't expect you here," I mumble.

"I see that," says Vonne coolly. She doesn't sound mad. She sounds almost—amused, I realize—and I raise my head and look up at her from under the brim of the hat. I've never really looked at Vonne before. The fact of her being Suzanne's girlfriend enveloped her like a cloak and made her into the featureless outline of a body, a body with one arm around Suzanne. Now she looks back at me, crosses her arms over her chest and doesn't say anything. She's got this little almost-smile on her lips, and I notice her lips are full and pale and slightly parted, revealing a row of small straight teeth.

"Suzanne—" Vonne says, and lets the word hang there, not yet attached to anything.

"Yes," I say. I take a step toward her and feel the buzz in my throat, the sudden slippery flush in my tights. *This is what I see when I look at my girlfriend,* I think. She's sexy, my girlfriend, she's turning me on. She reaches out and hooks her index finger under the strap of her girlfriend's camisole.

"You look good in those clothes," she says playfully.

I shrug so that her finger slips off my shoulder and down over my arm. She takes her hand away.

"Suzanne—" she starts to say again, and I cut her off.

"Yes," I say again. Vonne's eyes are blue.

"The hat's not right," she says after a moment. "The angle's wrong."

"Fix it for me," I say, and she does, taking the brim in both hands and tilting it back on my head so that more of my face is exposed. She's right, this is the way it's supposed to be. I take her hand and put it over my breast, let her feel the hard pebble of my nipple against her palm. Her short black hair has streaks of gray in it; her eyes are blue, flecked with brown.

"I missed you," I say.

Vonne doesn't take her hand away. She slides it across my chest and under the satin and takes my other nipple between her fingers. This is how she touches her girlfriend. Just like this. "We don't usually do this in the afternoon," Vonne says haltingly.

I look at the clock. Its red numbers glow 5:15.

"It's after five," I say.

"I left work early," says Vonne, and then I close my eyes.

The dog stands up and begins to bark.

"Lie down, Rocket," Vonne says, and he does.

"Lie down, Suzanne," she says to me, and I do. I lie down on our bed, my eyes closed, waiting for her to be ready to kiss me, and then she does, leaning over me, first with soft dry lips and then with the wetness of her mouth, and then her body is alongside me and then pressed against me, into me, part of me, all of me until I can no longer think, I'm nobody, she loves me; and one of us is saying, over and over, *Suzanne, Suzanne, Suzanne.*

—FINGERS: 10 x LOVE—

Ruthann Robson

(1)

BECCA TOOK A DEEP BREATH of the lucky air. A cold beer, a stunning view, a companion—what else could she desire? The reclaimed wood planks under her sport-sandaled feet looked pristine, especially compared with the wooden walkways and stairs she'd been scrubbing all day. The hemp roof of the pavilion might seem skimpy, but it obviously provided some protection for the wood. Becca knew this was something she should note in her journal, since she was here to explore "environmental sensitivity" as she had stated in her application.

But for the moment she contented herself at a pavilion table with Jayne, one of her coworkers, watching as Jayne's sensuality waxed with the beers. The Caribbean glistened below, as tantalizing as a postcard, while the sun pulsated into hues of orange. Becca tried not to think that this perfect romantic setting was marred by the fact that Jayne was presumably straight, no matter how many beers Jayne might drink. And that Becca should be doing something other than thinking about her supervisor, Gretchen, who was suspected of not being straight but was definitely older. Becca tamped down the thought that she should have learned her lesson by now.

Becca found Gretchen tinged with mystery, but she wasn't alone. No one was quite sure where Gretchen was from, which was the way she preferred it. Before Gretchen was twenty, she'd realized both the importance of accents and the fact that she could not merely erase the ugly echo of her parents. So she'd worked on obscuring her English by accretion, piling one accent atop another by moving across continents and between them, until her cadences were now unfamiliar even to herself.

Becca liked to speculate about the older woman's origins; it gave her something that seemed safe to talk about with Jayne and it gave her something that seemed safe to think about Gretchen.

"Australia," Becca said to Jayne as their beer bottles touched on the plastic table overlooking the Caribbean. The sunset, the blue water, the volcanic mountains in the distance made Becca feel extravagantly privileged. But on her first day at the eco-tourist camp Harmony, she'd learned that the "workers" didn't admire the views lest they sink into the category of tourists. Despite her pleasure in arranging what she thought of as a vacation, even if she had to paint stairs and sweep leaves for five hours a day, Becca quickly joined the chorus of complaints about the heat, the humidity, the work, and her supervisor, Gretchen.

"I dunno," Jayne replied, trying to mimic an accent she recalled from some commercial—for a car, or beer, or a restaurant.

Becca giggled in appreciation, if not sincerity. Jayne sounded silly even through the mist of Becca's fourth non-Australian beer, but Becca wanted to keep Jayne at the table. Not only because she wanted to be with Jayne, but because she hoped Gretchen would make her usual appearance in the pavilion as the darkness descended. Gretchen, in her usual baggy khaki camp shorts that made her legs look long and strong. Gretchen, with eyes blue as her faded denim work shirt, and face tanned and lined as a cowboy. Or so Becca had described Gretchen in her journal.

Becca had also tried to capture the sunsets, with a series of descriptions: *huge, orange as an orange, brilliant with incredible majesty, unbelievable, almost like an orgasm.* Becca never wrote: *lonely.* She didn't wonder whether coming to Harmony for the summer had been the right thing to do, since it had seemed the only thing possible. To get out of the town that now thought of her as another one of Professor Quinto's conquests.

"There she is," Jayne nodded, her head tilting in the opposite direction of the sun sliding into the sea.

As Becca turned to look, she saw Gretchen striding over to them, her own beer bottle in hand. Pulling up a plastic chair, Gretchen asked if she could join them, though she was already sitting down.

"Beautiful sunset, eh?" Gretchen asked the two younger women.

Jayne gushed in agreement. Becca felt her face flush; at least Gretchen wasn't so self-conscious that she was afraid to be thought a tourist.

Becca listened while Jayne and Gretchen talked more easily than Becca had imagined they would, although Becca was beginning to understand how Jayne's moods were calibrated to the beers. Jayne chatted about the progress on the Goat Trail steps, the planned excursion to Coral Bay for Saturday morning snorkeling, the likelihood that the volcano on Montserrat would continue to erupt. In the midst of the casual conversation, Jayne scouted for information by mentioning a sunset she'd once seen in Australia.

"In Auckland, I think it was. Have you ever been there?" Jayne asked boldly.

Gretchen's answer was that Auckland was in New Zealand, also known by its Maori name of Aotearoa.

Becca was humiliated enough for both of them, but Jayne didn't seem chagrined. In fact, Jayne merely seemed drunk, and

Becca started to worry that next Jayne would be asking whether Gretchen had a lover. Though from the small smile on Gretchen's face, Becca assumed that Gretchen would be able to sidestep anything that Jayne, or anyone else, might ask.

Becca kept sipping from her empty beer bottle, letting her fingers touch Jayne's unfinished bottle, beaded with sweat. She licked the moisture off her fingers, hoping Jayne would notice, hoping Gretchen would notice, hoping they wouldn't.

(2)

THEY WERE FIGHTING ABOUT JOMO AGAIN.

Fighting the way they always fought, without words, with cold stares, with polite inquiries about groceries or petrol. The kiss goodbye electrified the air with the terrorism of obligation.

After Rose went to work, Gretchen slammed around the small house. Rose's small house in Rose's stupid suburb in Rose's dangerous city in Rose's godforsaken country. Everything belonged to Rose. Especially Jomo. Rose's son. No matter how much mothering Gretchen had done, Jomo was always and only Rose's son.

The son who refused to grow up, according to Gretchen. The boy was twenty years old. When she'd been twenty, she'd been long gone from her parents, she'd been on another continent, living in Bolinas, California, and trying to learn to be a car mechanic. Sure, mostly she was surfing, but she was on her own, that was the main thing. Not like Jomo, content to eat his mother's food and "borrow" her money. And argue politics with Gretchen.

Yeah, now Gretchen was the white woman, the Afrikaner who'd been run out of her own country, the bourgeois dilettante who'd charmed her way into a United States passport. Sometimes he called her "Great White Hunter" or "Safari Lady," because she worked for Bushbuck Ltd., conveniently forgetting that her work booking game drives at Bushbuck partially supported him. Well, at least he didn't call her a dyke.

She figured he only resisted that because of what that would say about his mother.

Though she'd heard him say other things about his mother. He'd been on the phone, not realizing she could overhear or not caring, comparing his mother to a superstitious Maasai, ignorant as a giraffe. She hadn't been able to forgive him, no matter how she twisted Jomo's words into pop-psychology explanations that stressed his self-loathing. Rose Thuku was her lover, but even when Gretchen was trying to be objective, it could be nothing less than obvious that Rose was special. A head nurse at Agha Khan hospital, an adviser to other women in their Parkland suburb, descendant of Harry Thuku, the leader of post–World War I rallies for black independence, a political woman who'd named her son after Jomo Kenyatta, Kenya's first president. Why wasn't he proud of her? Why didn't he realize her sophistication, her stature, her power? Why did he treat her like a dishrag when she worked her fingers to the bone for him?

And why the hell didn't she see it?

This was what frustrated Gretchen most. Frustrated her so much that after a few months, she finally told Rose what Jomo had said on the phone that day, Gretchen's voice squeaking in anger when she reached the second syllable of *giraffe*.

Rose had only laughed. "He's just being macho. Finding his manhood. And besides, giraffes are so beautiful, don't you think? Don't the tourists always remark on their *soulful* eyes?"

Gretchen turned away from Rose's mocking, but later that week as the long rains continued and Gretchen's boss fretted about making payroll, Gretchen heard about the Harmony job. It seemed a sort of solution. A summer stint in the Caribbean to compensate for the slow safari season in Kenya; a way to make Rose realize the importance of their relationship.

She told Rose about it, expecting her to protest.

When Rose closed her face like a mask, Gretchen pouted for a few days but then resorted to the argument of the body.

Making love with Rose was like finger painting, Gretchen

thought, as she traced the bones of Rose's chest until they disappeared under Rose's breasts. Gretchen could almost see the colors fluorescent where she had touched, flaring like a high sensitive film being exposed to the light, then fading as her fingers lingered on other portions of Rose's body. Sometimes Gretchen drew. The sun. The mountains. The ocean in the distance. A fish under the water of the world, exploring the coral that was Rose and taking refuge in its caverns. Sometimes Gretchen spelled out words, in English and in Swahili. Forever. Love. *Ningojee.* *Ningojee.* Wait for me. *Sisi.* Us. Ask me not to go. Goddamn you, Rose, just ask me not to go and I won't.

(3)

BECCA WANTED THE PAGES of her journal to be filled with lyrical honesty. Yet she observed that as she became more lyrical, she was becoming less honest. On rereading, she judged her descriptions overwrought and smothering. The simple sword palmetto outside her tent seemed buried in the volcanic ash of her adjectives, only a bit of its green sharpness protruding.

As she sat in her tent and held the pen and pressed it against the pages of her notebook, sweat from her hand moistening the paper, she hesitated. She convinced herself that she was searching for a bon mot, but really she was searching for the opposite. Some expression that wasn't quite right, that didn't capture the complexity of emotions or events. She craved the evasive phrase that might remind her later of what had happened, but that didn't deign to describe anything in a more than vaguely intelligible manner. It wasn't that she thought someone might read her notebook (no one here cared enough to spy on her) or that she was worried what might happen when she left the island (that seemed very far in the future), but that even with herself as the only witness, she was embarrassed.

She'd brought the yellow notebook to Harmony to write about Professor Quinto. Maria. But what was there to say that wasn't a cliché? College student goes gaga over teacher and within a semester gets thrown over for another student. Another student who was cuter, smarter, and was once Becca's roommate, once a woman Becca had considered as a possible lover. Yes, she hated Professor Quinto, but she loathed herself more.

And here she was, at least 3,000 miles away from the University of California campus, making the same mistake. Tongue hanging out for another older woman, her supervisor, Gretchen. Maybe she should switch her major from environmental studies to psychology so she could figure out her subconscious. Or start writing in her journal about her mother and her sister.

Instead, Becca wrote about the sounds of the island. The frogs playing jazz at midnight. The donkey braying accompaniment in the distance. It was noisy and not as scary as silence. It was like nirvana, like a Zen parable, like the promise that the moon was always there singing, even in the daylight when it was invisible.

She did not write that she heard those sounds walking back from town with Jayne. Goddamn Jayne. Not even an older woman, but a college student, just like she was—and both of them from New York, what a coincidence!—and still things were fucked. The canopied taxi had left them off on the road near Harmony so that they could take the shortcut back to the workers' tents, forgetting that this part of the campground was unlighted, forgetting that they hadn't brought their flashlights. As they started on the dark path, Jayne had seemed scared, Becca had thought, so Becca had reached for Jayne's hand, lacing her fingers through her friend's as if they were children.

But Jayne was no child. And Jayne had had only two of the expensive beers in town. It didn't take a second before Jayne slapped hard at Becca's fingers, probably much harder than she'd meant, or so Becca had thought at first.

"What's the matter with you? You want people to think we're gay?"

"What people? It's pitch-black," Becca had said, but not until later, after Jayne had found the path to her own tent, leaving Becca to continue her trek, the frogs singing loudly and maybe menacingly.

(4)

WHEN BECCA REGISTERED for classes her first year at the University of California, Santa Cruz, she wanted not only the courses in ecology that she had been lusting after when she'd been in high school taking stupid courses mandated by the New York Regents, but also something that would prove to herself that she'd been brave enough to leave New York and was really at Santa Cruz. So she enrolled in Introduction to Women's Studies and a course called Zen Thinking. She'd seen the women's studies professor, Maria Quinto, at a table during registration: *hot*. As for Zen Thinking, she couldn't wait to write her friends about that.

On the first day of classes, Professor Quinto handed out an eleven-page syllabus that made the students gasp, but Becca found it chatty, almost like a love letter. The Zen Thinking professor did not distribute anything, but made them sit in a circle while he read them what he called "the finger parable":

> *Whenever anyone asked him about Zen, the great master Gutei would quietly raise one finger into the air. A boy in the village began to imitate this behavior. Whenever he heard people talking about Gutei's teachings, he would interrupt the discussion and raise his finger. Gutei heard about the boy's mischief. When he saw him in the street, he seized him and cut off his finger. The boy cried and began to run off, but Gutei called out to him. When the boy turned to look, Gutei raised his finger into the air. At that moment the boy became enlightened.*

During the discussion, many of Becca's classmates voiced concerns about the cruelty of the Zen master's actions, which led to accusations of child abuse. Other students argued that child abuse was a cultural construct and it was imperialist to make such judgments. Becca waited for the professor to intercede, but he seemed content to ask questions, settling on Becca at the end of the class:

"Would you lose a finger for enlightenment?"

"It depends on which finger," Becca had answered, thinking that she was being both witty and erudite.

After that, she garnered various nicknames, most of them plays on fingers and dyke. Her roommate called her Dutchgirl, and then simply Dutch, so that Becca felt white, or even blond, although she was neither.

Having a nickname had seemed almost affectionate, at least until the rumors about Dutchgirl and Professor Maria started to circulate, at which point Becca's roommate devised names for Becca that grew progressively nastier.

(5)

JAYNE SEEMED TO HAVE FORGOTTEN about the attempted hand-holding, and Becca certainly wasn't going to mention it. Becca hadn't made many other friends at Harmony Bay—probably none if she excluded her supervisor, Gretchen—and the pickings were pretty slim since men at the eco-camp outnumbered the women by a ratio she estimated at five to one.

Yes, Jayne was racist and homophobic, even if she was from New York, although Becca was starting to understand that Jayne wasn't from the same New York that Becca had inhabited. Jayne was what Becca's high school friends would have called "rich white bitch," the kind of woman they'd told her she'd meet when she went to college in California. Well, she hadn't met any there, or if she had, they'd learned to camouflage themselves. The students at Santa Cruz would never admit to taking a corporate job with their fathers after graduation, as Jayne had bragged over beer the other evening. Becca had thought she'd seen a small smirk gather at the sides of Gretchen's mouth, but then Gretchen had wiped the spot with her index finger, as if there had been a droplet of foam there.

Whatever the undercurrents, Gretchen assigned Becca and Jayne to work together, and today they had to paint white reflective strips on the boardwalk steps near the Harmony snorkel shop. After they'd finished their five-hour stint in the hottest part of the day, they'd gone to the camp store and splurged on ice cream bars, which cost twice as much as they did on the mainland but which tasted three times as good. Then they'd gone back down to the snorkel shop, gotten some gear, and headed down the steps into Harmony Bay.

Even in the late afternoon, the ocean water remained clear. When Becca had first arrived, she'd been less than enthused about trying snorkeling, but Jayne had persisted, not accepting Becca's explanations of her childhood asthma. And whatever else Becca thought about Jayne, she was grateful for this gift. Jayne had sympathetically supported her with the tips of her fingers while Becca had floated facedown, gradually losing her fear of suffocating and finally opening her eyes.

Now Becca could keep her face in the water for as long as she wanted, listening to her breathing through the tube, flapping her fins lackadaisically, looking for the brightly colored fish and watching the finger coral wave at her. In the clear Caribbean, she forgot about Jayne floating not far from her; forgot about Gretchen back on land inspecting the wooden stairs; forgot about Professor Maria Quinto.

Becca even forgot about Becca; she felt more like a figurine in an aquarium than like herself. She vaguely wondered if other people felt the same, but she knew such a question was beneath even the tourists, at least the adult ones. It was so uncool she didn't even pose it in her journal.

What she did write was an annotated list, using the Caribbean

Underwater Guidebook she'd purchased in town. She taught herself to identify what she was seeing: queen angelfish, iridescently spotted juvenile yellowtail damselfish, schools of French grunts, the solitary red grouper, and an amberjack so huge she found it slightly scary. She also studied the pictures in the little book, noting the specimens she had yet to glimpse, and then feeling successful when she spotted one and could silently recite the name.

As much as she liked the fish and coral, though, she fell in love with the turtles. She searched until she found one, then imagined herself a cloud following it as its strong flippers with the beginnings of fingers propelled it through its world. Outside of the water, she used her time on the "cyberhut" computer to research the turtles, and she was considering writing one of her fall semester papers on the hawksbill, once killed for tortoiseshell eyeglasses but now protected under the Endangered Species Act.

Her passion for the turtles made the plumbing system of the eco-conscious campground that she had come here to study seem dull by comparison. When she felt unfaithful to her original project, she reminded herself that it was nature, after all, that had drawn her to want to study ecology. Though *nature* sounded so abstract. And superficial, in a New Age self-indulgent sort of way. She'd always known that what she felt was difficult to explain, but she'd always felt it. Even as a kid in Yonkers, she went out in the back lots near her apartment building and found beautiful red berries in what her mother had called the dead of winter. Picking them off the sticker bushes, she'd slit them open with her nail and use the juice as a kind of paint for her fingernails. She'd made designs with the tiny pale seeds, placing them in a pattern on her knuckles and trying to walk home with her unmittened fingers outstretched in the cold so that she could show the design to her mother, a woman in need of some beauty if ever there was one.

But even if her mother never understood her fascination with dead leaves or the sky, at least she seemed to indulge her. Hadn't even complained too much when Becca had applied to UC Santa Cruz and Evergreen in Washington State, although her mother honestly hadn't thought she'd be admitted, never mind be awarded the necessary scholarship.

Becca's guidance counselor had been more difficult. He'd practically told her that black people didn't pursue ecology, perhaps thinking that because he was also African-American he was entitled to condition his certification of her high school records on a "more even distribution of college applications." Becca had also dutifully applied to the state university system, selecting the most competitive campuses and submitting the same essay, which stressed, as her guidance counselor phrased it, her "tree-hugging qualities." When the UC Santa Cruz acceptance, complete with scholarship, had arrived, she'd tried to feign equanimity. But inside she'd been ecstatic. It was as if loving the world—the worldness of the world—were no longer some private quirk.

Perhaps if she'd known that Professor Maria Quinto was waiting for her—like a shark, she thought now—she'd have chosen Evergreen College in Washington.

(6)

THE WIND IS DESULTORY and sultry. Which means that if the place were Johannesburg it would have been January and if it were New York it would have been August and if it were the Kenyan flatlands bisecting the equator it could have been almost any time.

The little girl is getting ready for bed. Her hair is blond or it is not. But her nightgown, undoubtedly, is pink, and it has a ruffle near the neck that scratches her when she sleeps. With one hand, she tugs on her collar.

With the other, she moves her nightgown away from her thighs.

She pulls her fingers through the river of herself. Wet and

slippery, her fingers slide while the heat outside her body seems to cool, then fade. Her fingers are like vividly complected tropical fish, flashing through the stream, then turning and diving deep into the caverns, leaving tingling sensations that must be the traces of their lights. Drinking in the water from which they derived their oxygen, as she'd recently learned in school, with bubbles coming from their bodies, tickling her so that she wanted to laugh.

And maybe she did laugh, standing there at the bottom of her bed, with her hand up her pink nightgown, when her mother found her.

Her mother shouting that she is a bad girl, a disgusting creature, who will destroy herself for marriage.

Her mother slapping her hand, then spanking her rear end, then pushing her into bed with a shove and a open-handed slap across the face so that her ring catches the girl's nose and makes it bleed.

Later, the mother would have come into her daughter's bedroom to make sure she hadn't left a bruise. She would have said: Gretchen, Becca, Jayne, Rose, I only do these things because I love you.

Later, the girl will snuggle in bed and suck the fingers of her naughty hand, a taste like nothing she could recall swirling into her mouth, acrid and sweet at the same time, maybe like the ocean, but at night with some of the moon slipped into it.

(7)

THREE HOURS AFTER GRETCHEN'S plane left Nairobi, Rose Thulu regretted the stubbornness that had prevented her from giving Gretchen any signal to stay. Rose had known she would miss talking to her lover as they made dinner or took a walk through Parkland. She knew she would miss Gretchen's stories about Bushbuck Ltd. and the pale people who were paying great sums of money because they believed their lives would be complete if they could see a lion through a rifle scope, even though hunting was rarely allowed anymore. She knew she'd feel the loss of Gretchen as Jomo's other mother, as brittle as it had been for the last few years. Yet she was not prepared for the physical grief that overtook her as she found herself sobbing over a strand of Gretchen's hair left behind in their bed. Rose Thulu thought of herself as a person inured to the claims of the body— she was by profession a nurse, after all—and so the stabbing physical absence of the woman she had been living with for the past fifteen years shocked her.

She blamed herself and she blamed Jomo, the only person with whom she'd ever been so carnally connected. Hadn't she suckled him? Hadn't she carried him strapped to her body before he learned to walk and even afterward, when he was tired? Hadn't he lived inside her very skin?

But now he was separate, larger and stronger than she was, and seemingly bent on obliterating any union between them. He was an adult and she was proud of that, grateful that he'd lived to manhood when many boys did not, but damn him, he was still acting like a spoiled suburban child rather than a grownup. Gretchen had been right. And she was left alone to remedy it.

When Rose told Jomo she was going to charge him room and board, 7,000 Kenyan shillings, and that he would find a job or move out, she'd hadn't expected an easy acquiescence. Maybe he missed Gretchen too; he probably couldn't remember his life without her. Or maybe he just wanted to be spiteful. Within a week he'd found a position as a "courier," delivering "documents" downtown, or so he described it to Rose, and pointedly told her that's how she should describe it to Gretchen when she wrote her. A glorified errand boy, Rose thought, but at least it was something. And soon she was laughing at his adventures negotiating Haile Selassie Avenue in his blue uniform, flirting in the elevators of the Cooperative Bank House, or stopping at the French Embassy to visit a friend. Jomo boasted he knew the streets and wasn't one to be robbed and told Rose he was thinking of starting his own service once he learned "the ropes." *He wants to be an entrepreneur,* she wrote Gretchen, imagining that her lover would smirk at the word.

Imagining that her lover would be ready to come home at the end of the season. Rose carefully crafted her letters so that they displayed expectation but never invitation. *You will laugh when you see Jomo in his uniform. We will have to paint the house soon. Wait until you see the new garage being built by the Kalandis on the corner.* Never: *Come home. I need to touch you.*

When Gretchen left Harmony Bay in August, rushing and barely packed, climbing first into the taxi, then taking a boat, then a bus to the airport, then by plane to London, then another plane to Nairobi, it was too late. Rose was surrounded by women and seemed to barely recognize her.

It was true. It couldn't be true. It was true.

Jomo had been in the Ufundi Cooperative Building, wearing his blue uniform and carrying his pouch of documents, when the United States Embassy had been bombed.

We don't know he was really there. You know how Jomo is; he's probably helping someone and will be back soon. We won't give up hope until he's home. Home.

"They've found Jomo," Rose announced after a long day downtown, arguing and weeping and dealing with the government and foreign bureaucrats. "Or at least his finger."

(8)

IF GRETCHEN KNEW ANYTHING, she knew sharks. She'd been born in South Africa, moved to California, toured Europe, made a life in Nairobi, and come to work in the Caribbean—had an adventuresome life that people envied—but everywhere there were sharks. Here, she was worried not about the small sharks of the clear Caribbean Sea that might occasionally nick a snorkeler, but the more dangerous type. The ones that hunted in the thick air of the resort, looking for the brightly colored young women and men who initially saw the sharks as harmless, even ridiculous. The way the young often viewed the middle-aged.

He was hanging around Becca and Jayne. Coming to their plastic table in the pavilion at sunset, joined by his wife and their daughter, buying beers and acting sociable. When the sky darkened and the child tired, the shark stayed at the pavilion while his wife went back to their tent with the toddler. He bought the young women beers and moved his chair closer.

Gretchen tried to join the table whenever she could, asking the shark questions about his wife and daughter and what they had done that day. Had they gone to see the ruins of the sugar plantation? Had they snorkeled at the bay to the west, where the sea grasses attracted the hawksbill turtles? Had they eaten in town at the restaurant known for its blackened grouper? How long were they staying?

The crescent moon had replaced the sunset by the time Gretchen got to the pavilion that night. Becca sat at the table alone, pulling the label from her beer bottle, looking distracted and somewhat forlorn. Gretchen immediately surmised that the shark had made off with Jayne. Perhaps another person would have assumed that Becca was disappointed by the shark's choice of prey, but Gretchen's inference was different.

"Hey, you." Gretchen sat down next to Becca. "You did a great job painting the stairs."

"Like anyone couldn't paint a white strip on a step," Becca replied, looking into her beer bottle.

"You'd be surprised." Gretchen laughed. "Or maybe you wouldn't."

Becca did not respond, and Gretchen found herself noticing that under the pavilion lights Becca's fingers looked stained not with white paint, but with red.

"What happened to your hand?" Gretchen asked, almost taking the woman's hand in her own. "Did you cut yourself today?"

"Oh, that? No, no. That's ink. I had a pen explode." Becca didn't mention the huge red splotch across her notebook.

Satisfactorily like blood, she'd thought at the time, though she'd removed the rest of her pens from the little leather pouch that had been a gift from Maria Quinto.

"Heat and humidity will do that. Hope you have other pens. Are you writing letters? You should tell them what a good worker you are. It isn't unnoticed, you know. I was doing the weekly evaluations today, and you've done a good job. I sometimes forget to actually tell people that, thinking that since I've written it on a little form, they somehow know."

"How long have you been working here?"

"Oh, this is my third summer. After the first one I thought I wouldn't come back..."

"It was that bad?" Becca smiled.

"No. No, it was nice really. But while I was away something awful happened at home."

"Where's home?" Becca asked bravely. Oh, she couldn't wait to tell Jayne the answer, if she ever talked to Jayne again.

"Nairobi."

"You grew up there?"

"No, I grew up in South Africa."

Becca had never felt more black. Here she was, sitting in the Caribbean at a white eco-resort carved from a mountain that had once been a sugar plantation for slaves, talking to a white woman who'd been part of apartheid. Jesus. Becca realized she'd said it aloud.

"Not a very pretty picture, I can tell you that. Even for some of the Afrikaners. I left as soon as I could. Went to California."

"That's where I'm going to school. I just had to get out of New York."

"Do you think you'll go back?"

"I don't know. Why did you go back to Africa?"

"Well, Nairobi is very different than Johannesburg. Though, even Johannesburg is different from Johannesburg now. But truthfully, I met a woman and she had a son and that's where she lives."

Becca had known. Just knew Gretchen was a dyke and now Gretchen was sitting here talking about her lover. She wasn't going to tell Jayne this, that was for sure.

"You leave them every summer?"

"That wasn't the plan. But, well, that's the way things have turned out. My job is slow in the summer. And my lover hasn't been working since…since my first summer here. Since our son died. Things have gotten a bit tough, let's leave it at that."

The women sat there silently, listening to the frogs start their nightly symphony as the other inhabitants of Harmony Bay left the pavilion. When they were the last ones, Becca started to feel awkward, unsure how they would ever leave.

"How about a swim?" Gretchen suggested.

"Sounds great," Becca replied. God, she couldn't believe this. She was going to go down to the beach with Gretchen in the dark.

Becca thought that Gretchen might reach for her hand, but Becca's fingers dangled in the dark. Finally, she let them slide along the railings, reaching out across the narrow boardwalk of 110 stairs that led to the Caribbean.

Gretchen slid into the water before Becca even had her shorts off. She wondered whether Gretchen had been prepared with a swimsuit under her clothes. Becca left on her sports bra and her skivvy shorts, knowing that later she'd wish she had a towel.

The moon by now was high in the sky, behind them as they looked back at the eco-camp's small lights, flashlights and lanterns at many of the tents, and the large safety lamp near the taxipark north of the pavilion. Becca floated on her back, trying to identify constellations.

Gretchen, then Becca, saw the flashlight coming toward the beach, on what must have been the boardwalk stairs. Some distance back, another flashlight beamed, larger and more shakily.

Becca shivered. Shit. Now she'd be the talk of Harmony Bay the way she'd been the talk of the campus. And this time she wasn't even doing anything with the older woman.

"Shhh…" Gretchen needlessly warned.

When the two flashlights became parallel and then close, the voices carried over the water to the invisible swimmers. Becca and Gretchen both recognized the modulated tone of the shark, punctuating the shrill rant about promises broken that could only be coming from his wife. First Becca, then Gretchen, recognized Jayne's slurring protests that she was not a slut and who the hell did these people think they were and that they were both crazy and he was just some soft-bellied old man and she wasn't going to ruin their stupid marriage and people got divorced all the time so it was nothing to get so fucking upset about.

After the splash, Gretchen paddled toward the sound, hoping Jayne wasn't as drunk as she sounded. The two flashlights receded, any voices covered by the cacophonous frogs.

"That prick. He knows she's drunk and he leaves her in the ocean alone at night."

"We're here."

"Yeah, but he doesn't know that."

"But we do."

"Now I know you're here too," Jayne whispered.

"I won't even tell you how dumb you are!" Becca responded.

"Well, I guess you know that at least I'm not a fucking dyke."

"At least," Gretchen laughed. And then Becca laughed too. And finally, Jayne.

The three women stayed in the salty water that was warmer than the night air, until long after the flashlights disappeared, until Becca thought their fingers would become webbed if they stayed in the ocean much longer.

(9)

JAYNE TRIED TO FEEL LUCKY. Lucky to have graduated college. Lucky to have a job at an impressive address in the most important city in the world, even if she was now beholden to her father, and even if she'd imagined something better than being cooped up with two other women in a small office separated from the main floors of the corporation. Lucky to have traveled so that she could say she had been here or there, although she admitted most places sounded better as stories than in her memories. Lucky because she was straight, though of course she didn't hold any grudges against those who weren't, not even her mother. Or those women at Harmony Bay this past summer, including, unbelievably, the supervisor Gretchen who turned out to be queer, which Jayne should have known, looking like that, but who would have thought sweet Becca would be one also, though with black women it could be hard to tell.

At least she knew her black coworker wasn't gay. Maybe Pentecostal wasn't much better, but Jayne didn't need to worry about the woman grabbing her hand or even worse. Gail was harsh, but the only personal threat she posed was her sharp comments when Jayne wore slacks. Apparently, Deuteronomy had something to say about women wearing "garments that pertaineth to men," and Gail could quote chapter and verse.

Jayne wasn't so sure about the other woman in her office, a white woman with dyed and spiked hair, who wore tight pants and spent her nights at what she boasted was the "East Village theater scene." Or maybe Clarice was taunting Gail rather than boasting, because Gail always pursed her lips and issued some sound between a sigh and a whistle, which then caused Clarice to say something like, "Lo, I hear the winds of hell doth whisper."

Sequestered in the small room with Gail and Clarice, Jayne sometimes felt like she was back living at home, back before her parents separated, when her mom was "coming out" although Jayne didn't know that then, and probably her father didn't know it either, and maybe her mother just thought the world was coming to an end. The way Gail and Clarice bickered, passionate over some column of numbers that Jayne only vaguely understood. Yet Jayne couldn't help notice the way the women leaned their heads together toward the computer screen and laughed in harmony when the outcome was good; or the way the women seemed to bond against her at first, obviously knowing the precise height of Jayne's father in the corporate chain but pretending they didn't.

Jayne was sipping coffee when she heard the sound—the blast of it—but she continued to hold the cup at her mouth until she heard Gail scream. Clarice was next to Gail in a moment, pulling the larger woman away from the windows and down to the floor. "Sit the fuck down," Clarice commanded, so Jayne did the same. The phones started ringing and Jayne unfolded her legs to stand, but Clarice tugged at her arm and patted the floor beside her. "Stay under the table," Clarice instructed.

The women heard sirens far below.

"We need to find out what's going on." Gail was calm now.

"Answer the phone." Clarice made no move to do so herself, so Gail pulled the phone's cord toward her, but when she lifted the receiver of the still-ringing phone, there was no voice to be heard.

"We need to figure out which stairway."

"Let's try the closest," Clarice said as she was crawling toward her desk, looking in the bottom drawer for her bag.

"What the fuck are you doing? This is no time to be concerned for your worldly possessions."

"Water," Clarice said simply.

"Damn good idea," Gail answered. "C'mon, Jayne. We need to get out of here. God helps them that help themselves. And sure as shit no Daddy ain't coming to rescue us."

In the corridor the lights still flickered, but the stairwell was dark, crowded with people from the upper floors, coughing and crying.

The three women joined the procession, holding hands, Jayne in the middle, walking blindly in what seemed to be the direction of down, though after a while Jayne couldn't be sure. At one point, Gail had tugged her to the side of a landing, and Jayne heard the ripping of what must have been Gail's skirt, then the gurgle of water being poured, and Gail's sharp instruction, "Tie this over your mouth and nose." Jayne heard Clarice's voice, "Got it" and then her own "Yes" and the women again descended.

Jayne felt her throat closing and her eyes stinging. She heard the murmurs of counting and from far away, some singing. She tried to figure out how many stairs were left, but she had no idea—she'd never been in anything but the elevator before; shouldn't someone have told her about the emergency stairwells during her orientation? She wondered why the stairs weren't painted with a white strip, like the wooden stairs at Harmony Bay, the stairs she had scrubbed with Gail—no, Becca—so long ago—was it only last month?—or maybe the stairs were painted but it was too dark and too smoky to see and there were too many feet rubbing off any paint that was left.

When the piece of Gail's skirt slipped off Jayne's mouth, she let go of Clarice's hand—or was it Gail's hand?—to adjust it. And then Jayne's fingers sought out those of the woman who would be closer than any lover for the rest of her life, no matter how long that might be.

(10)

IN MY JOURNALS, EVERYTHING is present, flattened into words or invisible in the spaces between the words, but *there*. Sometimes I worry the ink will fade into the dampening paper here in the soggy Northwest and I will lose the evidence of my existence, but mostly I think that such a tragedy will not happen, or if it does, I will cope.

Today was a good workday. I made a lot of progress on my orca research for my Evergreen independent project and think that soon I will be able to do a first draft. Professor Lung's suggestion that I do a comprehensive research paper and submit it *before* I do any fieldwork next semester is a good one, I think, though at first I just wanted to get out into the Pacific and start looking and listening for whales! This way, as she says, I'll know more about what I'm looking for. She's helping me get an intern position on an orca-watch boat that takes tourists around the San Juan Islands. That will be pretty different from Harmony Bay, but she says the contrast will be interesting. I'm thinking of doing graduate work in marine science—wouldn't that be wild? When I get a job, I'm going to write my old guidance counselor. Maybe I'll even write the famous heartthrob Professor Maria—no, I don't think so. I'll just let her hear of my huge success. Though she was nice enough to write me a good recommendation so I could leave Santa Cruz and get admitted to Evergreen. She probably didn't want to see me around anymore.

I have written Gretchen, who seems to think the orca study is cool. She only writes back postcards, so I'm not sending her any more of my really, really long letters. But I'm pretty sure she's not much of a writer, so I don't really mind. And I do get these rad postcards from Nairobi, which seem to impress Caitlin and Doris, my roommates, especially when I mentioned Gretchen is a safari guide. I did ask Gretchen if she had heard anything from Jayne or even remembered her last name, since I'm worried about her after what happened in New York. My mother's friend's son was almost killed—he's a carpet installer and had a job there that day, but decided to stop somewhere for a big breakfast since he wasn't feeling all that well. But New York is a big city, and I'm not even sure Jayne went back there.

This morning I had a really intense dream. I was underwater and there were all these tropical fish swimming around me—I must have been at Harmony Bay. Only the fish were people too. People from here and people from there and my mother and some people I'd never even met, like Gretchen's lover, who she introduced me to, and I recognized her as a big French angelfish and in my dream I realized I'd never imagined her as black, but there she was, only the smallest taints of yellow on each scale. There was also this juvenile French angelfish, smaller and with more yellow, and Gretchen told me that was their dead son. Creepy.

But in the dream I was happy. Swimming, a smooth under-water breaststroke propelling me like I was a turtle. Or an orca. I could breath underwater, asthma or no asthma. And I was looking at my fingers, spread so wide, and they looked daring, like they were tinted with iridescent ink. They looked childlike and really innocent. And they didn't look like mine.

—THE MORNING PRAYER—

Vittoria repetto

SEVEN TWENTY-FIVE—SATURDAY MORNING. The night had been another New Yorker, hot and muggy, and though we had the two fans angled at the bed so that the air crisscrossed over our bodies, last night's lovemaking had soaked both the bed and us. The sheet was turned down so that the air from the fans hit us directly. The evaporation from the bed cooled us off as we lay next to each other, face-up. My left hand was on Esther's thigh, her right hand on mine.

Our bodies were still new to each other; we had met two months ago, in the beginning of May, on the dance floor at a friend's party. And it seemed that we danced around each other for a while, meeting again by chance at a poetry reading and again at the Rubyfruit Bar till I finally got up the nerve to ask her out for coffee.

We spent hours talking on the sofa at the Big Cup, oblivious to the swirl of gay boys around us. The guys behind the counter finally had to kick us out so they could close. Esther was a Chelsea girl, so I walked her to her apartment. As I kissed her at the lobby door, my knees felt like they would buckle under any second. She asked me if I wanted to come upstairs; I declined, saying I was sort of an old-fashioned girl and I wanted our relationship to build slowly, steadily. Knowing full well as I said this that the anticipation leading up to that first time would only serve to fan the fire of our desire.

And so now, in mid July, it was a little less than a week since we had begun to fulfill those desires that had taken root in May with the late-night kisses, the long walks, the reading of poetry to each other. We'd make love for hours, and in the morning our bodies would be exhausted from the lack of sleep. At work, my colleagues would question me when they saw me staring off into the distance, smiling a mysterious, mischievous smile.

Seven-thirty. Bong!! The bells from the Transfiguration Church down the block started ringing.

"What the hell is that?" asked Esther.

"Oh!" I said. "That's the bell for the Angelus Dei."

"The what?"

Without saying a word, I rolled out of bed and headed for the living room and my bookcases. Returning with my St. Joseph's Daily Missal open in my hand, I said, "The Angelus Dei. It's one of the prayers you can say in the morning, for indulgences, so you spend less time in purgatory burning off minor sins so you can get into heaven faster. Indulgences are sort of like...religious coupons."

Esther stared at me, her eyes wide in disbelief, giving me that look I had seen before on the faces of other Jewish lovers.

"What! Alessandra, how would you like it if—"

"If I were Jewish and someone was constantly pushing their religion, their Christian holidays down my throat," I said, completing her sentence. That stopped her cold; she wasn't expecting the speed or accuracy of my acknowledgment.

"Trust me," I said. "Lie down, close your eyes. Come on, do it! Please!"

With an exasperated sigh, she lay back down and shut her eyes.

"I adore you with the most profound humility."

With my fingertips, I traced the outline of her breastbone, the articulation and slope of her ribs, the fanning out of the fifth and sixth ribs, leading to creamy white soft breasts, circled the brown-pink areolae surrounding her nipples, the skin of the areolae puckered and her nipples erect.

"I praise you and give you thanks with all my heart for the favors you have bestowed on me."

With my tongue, I licked what my fingertips had explored. I sucked and gently bit her nipples, till she let out a deep guttural moan.

"Your goodness has brought me safely to the beginning of this day."

I brushed and nuzzled her pubic hair and her upper thigh with the side of my head like a grateful cat. This made Esther relax her muscles, her thighs parting like the Red Sea. And then cupping her clit with my lips, I blew a warm gush of air that perfumed the bedroom with the smell of her.

"I offer you my whole being and in particular all my thoughts, words, and actions."

I kissed her now-parted lips, our tongues entwined. I gently lay on top of her, her body now pure submission as she whispered, "Amen."

—BLIND DATE CITY—

Anne Seale

I'M IN LOVE WITH KIM. We're very close, inseparable in fact, except for the time she spends with her lover, Penny. I don't like it, of course, the fact that she spends so much time with Penny, but I try not to let it get to me. I figure their relationship is temporary, like all Kim's relationships, and someday Kim will realize that, I, Frankie, am the woman she really wants. Anyway, as long as Kim and Penny aren't living together, I don't worry.

Meanwhile, I'm happy to hang with Kim, listening patiently to her venting of Penny-problems and giving helpful advice—more helpful to me than to Penny. "You don't have to put up with this aggravation," I tell Kim. "Send her to Deep-Six City!"

She never follows my advice. She just goes back for more. It's very frustrating.

I myself do not date, even though I'm easy to look at. Every once in a while some woman tries to pick me up, but I always say, "Thanks, but no thanks." It would be a waste of both of our time, feeling as I do about Kim.

Therefore, I have a real problem when Kim wants me to have dinner Saturday evening at Casper's Grill with her and Penny and Penny's cousin Barbara who just moved to town and wants to meet people. "Is this a blind date?" I ask warily.

"Not really," Kim says, but she's not looking me in the eye.

"C'mon, Kim, don't be putting me on," I say.

"Okay, it's a blind date," she says, "but look at it this way, Frankie, you'll be doing me a real favor, and I'll even pay for your dinner."

Wee-bob, does this woman know how to please me or what?

She senses I'm weakening. "Here, Penny said to show you this." She takes a photo from her shirt pocket and hands it to me. It's a three-by-five of a young woman sitting in a lawn chair in somebody's backyard. Part of her face is blocked by an elbow, so all I can see is that she has dark hair and at least one eye.

I hand it back. "Not my type."

"Frankie, I'm begging you. Just meet the girl. If you don't like her," Kim says, "you can eat and leave."

"You won't be mad?"

"Of course not."

I think about it for a while. It would be an evening spent in Kim's company, always a delight. I'd also be one up on her, favor-wise. The clincher, of course, is the free meal. "Okay, but I'm not picking her up."

Saturday afternoon I look through my closet, trying to find something worthy of Casper's Grill, but all my shirts are stained and/or torn, so I go to Kmart and buy a new blue sweater. Blue is Kim's favorite color. Then I look for the black slacks I was wearing the day Kim said, "Nice ass!" I finally find them under the bed, soiled and full of dust bunnies, so I have to make a quick trip to the Laundromat.

Kim is waiting in the restaurant foyer when I get there. "You're late. I was afraid you chickened out," she says. "Great sweater."

"This old thing?" I say happily.

Penny is sitting at a table, chatting with a dark-haired woman who looks better in person than in the snapshot. They look up as we approach. "Good to see you, Frankie," Penny says.

My greeting to her is cool. I try to keep an emotional distance between us so I won't have to feel bad when Kim leaves her for me.

She introduces Barbara, who extends her hand. I shake it briefly and ask how she likes Chicago.

"I love it," she answers. "Everyone here seems so friendly."

"Huh!" is all I say, because that says it all. I sit down and open my menu.

We eat without incident. Barbara orders charbroiled ribs and picks at them—most end up in a doggie bag. I, however, devour with gusto a heaping pile of Casper's famous liver, bacon, and onions. Most places serve liver and bacon *or* liver and onions, so it's a real treat to get all three on the same plate.

During dessert, Kim turns to me. "Frankie, why don't you take Barbara on a tour of women's bars after dinner? Unfortunately, Penny and I have to be up early, so we can't come with you."

Barbara turns to me, hope written all over her face. I nearly choke on a bite of Death by Chocolate. Whatever happened to *You can eat and leave?* This is all Penny's fault, I think. She probably thinks that if she can get me to fall for her dumb cousin, I won't be a threat to her and Kim anymore.

I almost say, "Oh, too bad. I have to be up early too," but then I get a great idea. I'll get all cozy with Barbara just to make Kim jealous. When she sees me with somebody else, she'll see how much she wants me for herself, and it'll be Backfire City for Penny. It's hard to keep from chuckling as I say, "Sure, why not?"

After saying good night to Kim and Penny, Barbara and I hit a few bars, dance a little, and play some pool. She wins the first three games easily, but then I guess she gets tired or something, because she starts messing up, and I win the last three.

After dropping her off at her apartment, I notice her doggie bag is still on the passenger seat, so I do a U-turn and take it back because I hate ribs. She apologizes for forgetting it and invites me in for coffee. I say okay, unless all she's got is that dumb flavored kind. She says it's plain old Folger's, so I stay. We listen to music and talk. I don't get home until two-thirty.

The next morning I call Kim at nine. She's still in bed, which proves the "getting up early" story was a big crock of you-know-what. I enthusiastically thank her for introducing me to Barbara and tell her what a great time the two of us had after leaving them.

"That's great," she says. "Are you going to see her again?"

"You bet I am!" I say, wondering how enthusiastic I have to get before her jealousy kicks in.

Then I call Barbara and ask if she'd like to go to a movie tonight. She says she'd love to, and why don't I come by for supper first. I fret all day, wondering if she'll serve something I don't like, which includes all meat besides hamburger, liver, and bacon, and most veggies. My worries are for nothing, however. She's cooked up a big pot of spaghetti with meatballs in a sauce that's the best I've ever tasted. She says she's Italian on her maternal grandmother's side, which explains it.

Later, when we're in the theater, she takes my hand and holds it. This really scares me, so I don't accept her invitation for a nightcap. Who knows where that kind of stuff could lead?

It's still early after I drop her off, so I drive by Kim's place. She doesn't answer the door until I've given my secret knock five times, then I see that her eyes are red and swollen. "What's wrong?" I ask.

"Penny and I broke up," she says, sobbing wildly. I lead her to the couch and hold her close, assuring her that everything will turn out all right, and as always, she's got me. Déjà Vu City.

I told Barbara I'd call her sometime during the week, but I don't. I'm spending my time with Kim doing bachelorly things—bowling, working on her truck, etc. Friday evening we're playing Upwords when the doorbell rings, and there's Barbara.

"Hey, Barb," I say. "How'd you know where I live?"

"Penny told me." She's wringing her hands, but when she sees me looking at them she puts them behind her back.

"What's up?"

"Are you busy?" she asks.

"Actually, I am."

"How about later? We could get a pizza."

"Kim and I are grilling tonight."

"Tomorrow?"

"Nope. Kim and I are going to the demolition derby. Wait, no, that's Sunday." I scratch my head. "We're doing something tomorrow, anyway."

Her cheeks turn red like I've slapped her. "I see," she says softly. "Sorry for bothering you." She runs to her car and peels off before I can say, "No problem."

Kim has a hard time getting over the breakup. I try to cheer her up by telling jokes and stuff, but she's just not her pre-Penny self. One evening I'm waiting for her to come over to watch *Thelma and Louise* for the seventeenth time—we're memorizing it—when the phone rings.

"Frankie?" Kim says, before I can even say hello. "I'm so happy! I got together with Penny today and we made up."

"Oh?" is the best I can do.

"And guess what! I've asked her to come live with me."

"You did?" My worst nightmare.

"Yes. That's why I'm calling. Can you help move her things over to my place next weekend?"

"You know what, Kim? I can't." It's still hard to say no to her, but it's hard enough seeing my dream die without putting in heavy labor too.

After a few days I phone Barbara. She doesn't seem happy to hear my voice and tells me up front that she's seeing a woman named Rae whom she likes very much. Yes, she actually says "whom." What a classy gal. I feel my heart go pitty-pat.

"I was just hoping we could be friends," I say.

"Friends?" I can tell this is the last thing she expected to hear.

"Yeah. You know, hang together, go shopping, stuff like that."

"I don't know." She's quiet for a minute, then says, "Well,

I don't have many friends in Chicago yet, so I guess we could give it a try."

"Great," I say, and we make plans to play pee-wee golf sometime soon.

I can hardly wait, because, you see, I'm in love with Barbara. We're going to be very close, inseparable, in fact, except for the time she'll have to spend with her lover, Rae. I won't like it much, the time she spends with Rae, but I'll try not to let it get to me...

—WHAT LOVE IS—

Elana Dykewomon

EVERYONE ASKS FOR LOVE STORIES. Solicitations in the mail, on the computer, from friends. What do they expect? Patent intimacy, encouragement, vindication? You used to get away with telling adventure stories—the lesbian separatist Fourth of July canoe disaster, the time an alligator nearly chomped you in the Everglades, or how dyke patrol trashed an abusive man's car at three A.M., spray-painting RAPIST all over it in his suburban neighborhood. You used to say romantic love was a heterosexual plot, created to drive women to distraction and submission. Remember that?

Now you're over fifty, distracted, and—submissive? Cultures swing back and forth, everyone knows that. Smart folks get out of the way of the pendulum before they get clocked. Okay, so it's not funny. But *clocked* and *plot* have an off-rhyme that ties the first two paragraphs together. Writers think about these things, even if they rarely talk about it. Today you want to expose the gears, the mechanisms, underlying pattern. And you can tell love stories, if that's what fashion dictates. You don't mean to brag, but you actually know what love is.

You look at the way women's cheeks turn red in the sunlight, the way the old women in the public pool shield themselves from the sun while the young ones splash in whatever covers their nipples and pubic bones. You notice two Chinese-American girls—they look like girls to you, but maybe they're twenty—who just introduced themselves at the beginning of the week, now coming hand in hand, splashing through the slow lane with kick boards and flippers, talking. One of them shows off long sleek black hair; the other's is cropped, dyed orange. In the pool shower, you offer soap to the old woman who wears a straw hat and leotards under her bathing suit. All this is love—the quotidian love you get used to in yourself, the kind that makes life tolerable.

Once, driving through the redwoods, you stopped at a popular tree. Americans choose trees the same way they choose prom queens—by their awesome measurements: If you're going to look at any of them at all, make sure to check out this one. You used to drive through the redwoods often, because you lived in Oregon for five years and had a long-distance lover in Oakland for two of them. Sometimes love is a good excuse for a ride. It's eight or nine hours from the southern Oregon coast, where you lived, to the Bay, and those hours, driving with your dog, singing show music as the road dipped out of forest to cup the ocean in its asphalt hands, were a meditational ecstasy. Simple, singular truths would shrug off the great redwood branches with the morning mist; joy would flop along into the mouth of a pelican scooping up dinner; bitterness would be ameliorated on the ride home by reaching into the lunch your lover packed and finding a purple sequined star.

You stopped at most of the short trails and wayside nature attractions at least once. At the most popular tree it was easy to notice how many hiking boots dug into the grass, flattened whole patches—the price of being singled out. And yet the grass came back. Maybe the forest service replanted it every month or season, but you doubt it. Things with roots have tenacity. Living things hold on because life is dear—dear to the grass, dear to the women you watch at the city pool, dear without premeditation. That resiliency—now that you're fifty, what's interesting about love is the ability to keep loving. After your long-distance nonmonogamous love affair fizzled out, you moved down to Oakland and after a month got a job printing for a ritzy department store, I. Magnin, gone out of business now, that had its operation center on the eastern edge of San Francisco, facing the Bay.

It was your first—actually only—foray into corporate life. In Oregon you learned how to print in a historical society, on an old letterpress—the kind of machine that uses lead type set in lines, one letter at a time. Eventually you convinced the historical society to buy an offset press, a very dinky version of the press this book was printed on. When I. Magnin hired you, it wasn't just to print, but to be the thirty-four-year-old head of the sign shop for the whole twenty-two store chain.

The best part of working in the sign shop was the view—the windows looked out onto China Basin, where the Giants' stadium is now. Then it was only a room in back of the mail room, which is about as isolated as you can get in a department store chain. Out of sight and thrown the bone of meager authority, you hired another butch—Lois, a fat African-American dyke with a beard and a low voice. She had no experience, but it was just the two of you in that cramped office looking out at the boats and herons. Sometimes you saw seals, and once, a guy swerve off the tiny bridge and burrow nose-down into the water—heart attack, the police said.

Many kinds of power separated you and Lois, but it was easy to recognize how power separated both of you from everyone else in the building, so you talked, carefully at first. Things you talked about—Buddhism, Judaism, your girlfriends—you never would have talked about with the head of the advertising department, whom you taught how to figure out a schedule. (You were standing in her office, kind of loving her—all that straight skinny middle-class white girl power she didn't own up to having—and she'd gotten this great San Francisco job—how? She didn't even have the natural insight to count backward from an event date and figure out if X was needed on Y, then it had to be ordered by Q. Either you were enlightening her or she was putting you on, probably dead serious, and not too ashamed to ask the printer if no one overheard her.) You noticed that even though the ad staff considered you a fashion disaster so extreme as to be an alien from outer space in their midst, you didn't balk about going to the cafeteria to eat lunch at the company-subsidized price, sitting alone at a table with a book. Lois wouldn't subject herself to any gaze she didn't have to—she ate in the office, food she brought, takeout from the night before.

Love for Lois made you quiver, hesitate, fall over your assumptions, and struggle to get up. You hired her because an acquaintance who taught a vocational printing class couldn't place her. When she appeared, no one thought Lois was out of place in the back of the mail room, which was staffed entirely by people of color except for you. The operation center was on the other side of town from the main store in Union Square, and while the buyers and ad people were always shuttling back and forth, it was rare for mail room staff to shop there, even with the twenty percent discount. What were you going to do, blow your paychecks on Gucci scarves? You did buy socks sometimes—the only thing in the store that fit you. And when you could, you'd get those little perfume sample bottles in pretty shapes from the cosmetic staff for your mother and your lover's mother—they always appreciated them.

No one but you knew that Lois could barely print or spell. The sign shop had a big flatbed proof press, on which you laid three-inch plastic letters on metal bars, holding them in place with magnets, and rolled out twenty, fifty signs—for special events or big sales—changing the dates or the prices depending on the store. You ran the small signs (20% OFF ALL COTTON SHEETS) on the offset, which was cranky, and gave Lois the big signs to do—they were heavier work, but easier to get right.

Lois couldn't proofread them, though, and sometimes you'd have to scrap a whole afternoon's production and start over because the "e" in Bob Mackie's name was upside down, or the "i" was missing. You thought it was because you grew up reading *The New Yorker* that you could do the job, a middle-class recovering East Coaster who had an attitude about the classes above you. You took to writing "Help—I'm a prisoner in the evil empire of fashion" on the bathroom walls. But having always taken pride in being efficient, organized, and reliable, you did the job you were paid for. Lois was your only subversion.

You were also supposed to supervise the calligrapher, Connie, who had worked for the store for twenty years and hand-lettered twenty or thirty—or more—signs a day. She had a separate office over on the advertising side of the hall, away from the noises of the printing presses and mail sorters. Once she told you she was going to a family reunion of all her mother's sisters who had been in the Japanese internment camp at Tule Lake during the war. "I was just a child then," she said.

"You remember it?"

"Not much."

"Well, have a good time," you said, not knowing what else to say.

"I will." She smiled—indulgently, you thought. You hoped.

You were protective toward Connie, and deferential. She worked, she took care of her mother. Your job was to make sure no one bothered her—the store managers would've had her write every sign if they could, and often you had to turn back five or six times the amount of requests she could reasonably do. The older guys in advertising knew Connie was exploitatively underpaid—"Every sign is a piece of art," they'd whisper, admiringly. You decided that love might also be running interference. But then, you've always been big on distant love.

Loving Connie was easy, though—all you had to do was back off, not make assumptions, and keep her workload as light as possible. Being in the same room with Lois, five days a week, nine to five, love was harder. Lois started having trouble, physical trouble, printing. She'd come in late, and her feet hurt, and she'd botch a batch or two and sit down and groan. "Maybe," you suggested one afternoon, "you should think about different work than printing." Your words twisted in the air and took on a bad smell. Lois stared. You shrugged and went back to work.

Maybe this was after the conversation about Oakland neighborhoods, in which you said "colored kids," meaning kids of color, different kinds, regretting it as soon as it was in the air, even before it was clear you had slapped her in the face. "What did you say?" You could only apologize, completely baffled by the racism you'd soaked up and leaked over her, the sticky underground substance your country pumps into the water and denies, no matter how often you complain about being poisoned. What reason could Lois have to trust you?

Listen, your feet hurt; you were thinking about different work, yourself. You developed plantar fasciitis, which made the soles of your feet cramp, from standing on concrete, and had to have physical therapy, whirlpool baths, and massages, three times a week for a couple months. Damned if you were going to let those hotshot ad people see you wince and groan—it was force of will, not physical ability, that got you up the stairs of the building every morning. You didn't tell Lois much about this either—maybe a little, to explain why you did all the sitting work you could when it was just you two butches in the press room. You meant the suggestion to be that of a comrade in suffering, but that's not what Lois heard. From the shadow that passed over her face and congealed into thunderclouds in her shoulders, you believe she heard, "You shiftless people can't get anything right," but you're guessing.

Lois complained to personnel. She thought they'd be fair, somehow, take her being offended into account, do something for her. What? You didn't have to say anything for personnel to take your side. You were the manager, and no union protected Lois. When you got called upstairs, what they explained was how to arrange her file so you could justify firing her. This shouldn't have surprised you, but it did. "I don't want to fire her," you said. "We'll work it out."

How could you? You were castoffs in the back reaches of the upper class, its servants. You had a fair sense of identity, though you were often self-deluded. Fat, Jewish, smart, competent—they hired you because your résumé was grammatically correct and not ink-stained, you could pretend to understand the importance of Anne Klein, and you weren't in a union. They actually told you so. You were making more money at thirty-three than you'd ever imagined, but it turned out you had very low expectations for a middle-class kid. Ten dollars an hour seemed like wealth, and you took advantage of the possibilities of being a manager, signing up for printing conferences and bringing in Macintoshes for the print shop and ad room.

But how could you imagine Lois? She came from the nearby Black neighborhood that had been a shipyard during World War II—now among the poorest dumping grounds in the city. She was roughly your size but taller, and everyone who got her on the phone assumed she was a man, from the register of her voice. Jheri curls were popular, and she wore her hair that way, shoulder-length, curly, and greased. She had a little mustache and went to Buddhist meetings as an alternative to A.A.—you could be a Buddhist and still drink, but you had to do it mindfully. Sometimes she worked at night as a bouncer for gay clubs. She had an active social life and was often worn-out at work. Later—after you left the job—you found out she had kidney problems so severe she had to be hospitalized, and you went to visit her in the hospital, clearly surprising her parents.

But that was after you worked it out. Did you work it out? Your lover at that time, Dora, was chronically unemployed, and during busy season—pre-Christmas and the two weeks after—you had money to hire temporary assistants, so you'd drag her into the city to help. She worked hard and smart, and was always after Lois to knock off when you weren't around (resist authority!)—meeting with Connie or the advertising people, going to the store to deliver opera show signs, or talking to your immediate supervisor, a gay man who had absolutely no use in the world for you and was grateful you had none for him, although you did have to consult once in a while about store promotions or your job review. Dora told Lois she should rebel against capitalism, she should embrace anarchism on the job. You wanted to throw Dora out the window, into the murky slough your building bordered, let her talk anarchism to the harbor seals. Subterfuge was not going to help you and Lois get through.

You were her boss. No two ways around it. You had never been anyone's boss. Lesbians talk about power in relationships as if the category of lover is different from other ways we negotiate how to get along. It's easier to write how you betrayed your lover or were transformed by letting yourself feel loved than it is to write about finding a way to work it out at work.

When crosses were popular as jewelry, she came in one day with a large crucifix swinging from her left ear. "Lois," you said, trying to figure out how to say *Get that thing out of here*, "I thought you were a Buddhist."

"You mean the earring? It's good, isn't it?"

"Well—"

"You don't like it?"

"It's just that the cross is a powerful symbol."

Lois regarded you warily. "My folks are Baptists."

"I know how important the Black church has been in keeping people together, in helping people have faith—"

"So?"

"Christianity, though—it's the dominant religion. The religion of the government."

Lois started to fiddle with the plastic letters on the rack. "You know I didn't mean anything about your people."

"I know. But it's not just about being Jewish. It's about how Christians have used Christianity to assimilate people— like in Hawaii, how they made the native Hawaiians ashamed of how they dressed and of their own language, and that made it easier for the big sugar companies to exploit them. And how Christians justified everything they did in Africa by saying they had to convert the heathens and that there were slaves in the Bible."

Lois fingered the cross. "I wasn't thinking of it like that."

Would you make the same argument to Cornel West? To anyone? Maybe. You've never been anyone's boss the same way since then, and you do like to give these little lectures, even when the power is closer to equal. More than once you've harangued your best friend for wearing lipstick, telling her the story of the tortured rabbits, as if she didn't know.

So you and Lois began conversations about the limits of organized religion, but you had to admit that Buddhism wasn't the same, that chanting didn't hurt anyone, that maybe it helped. You'd admit that.

When you showed your mother around the print shop, and introduced to her to Lois, she kept saying what a great thing you'd done for Lois, and this embarrassed you, because you were trying so hard to be a great thing for her without having to admit to a moment of condescension. Some days you could taste Lois's resentment, a metallic taste, as if you were swallowing ink. You developed a theory about the ability to conceptualize abstractly, filling in particulars as they were needed—as if a language had the coherency of a visual field and your signs were a series of examples. In this theory, you speculated that Lois couldn't see the whole, only learning case by case, which made it so much harder to remember specifics, to pull up the memory she needed in a particular situation.

Lois navigated the world and she navigated your silent speculations too—an expert in her own contexts. You made it through about two and a half years together, the length of an average lesbian love affair.

After you handed in your resignation, sometime in the last week, you took Lois to an upscale chain restaurant on Fisherman's Wharf that she wanted to try. It was a pleasure, sitting back, two big dykes, looking out at Alcatraz and the Golden Gate. "I want to confess something," Lois said. You waited. "I've got dyslexia—you know what that is?"

"Why didn't you tell me?"

"I was afraid you'd fire me."

"I'm sorry if you thought so. I would have tried to help you in a different way."

"Yeah, I guess you would've."

You couldn't tell if that was exactly what she didn't want, or if she was being wistful for a second chance.

"You know what? You taught me to take pride in my work."

"Yeah?"

"Yeah, thanks."

After that you had a couple dates—going to eat at the soul food restaurant way down 14th Street, with great candied yams. You heard she went into a detox program, or to a Buddhist retreat. You ran into her a couple times at street fairs, but it's been years.

You remember now the self-satisfaction of that meal on Fisherman's Wharf. How you let her thank you and never said thanks back.

—THIS GIRL—

Emily Chávez

I MET THIS GIRL TODAY. They call her Tasha. I see her sittin'
outside in the field at lunch. Sometimes she eat with these girls I
don't really know. Sometimes she sit by herself. This one time I
was goin to see Mr. Donahue bout tutoring cause my math
teacher called my momma and told her I need help with it. I told
her I don't need no help, I got a check on my last homework, but
she says I gotta go anyway. So Tasha come up to me askin where
do you go if you gotta have someone call your momma cause
you sick. I said, right there in back of you, silly, in Ms. Brown's
office, and she put her hand up to scratch her forehead, and then
I noticed she got a gold ring, so I was like, what, girl, you married or something? Naw, she said, I don't mess around with no
boys. We laugh cause she made such a funny face when she say
it, all scrunched up with her lips stickin out. Naw, I don't mess
around with no boys. So that's how we met. I notice that gold
ring every time I cross by her in the halls.

Yesterday I went to the store over there on the corner 'cross
from school with Antoine. He got Momma to give him some
money, so we wanna buy candy. We went over there with these
boys Antoine hang with sometime. Antoine say they "his boys"
or whatever, but I don't know nothin bout that. So we walkin to
the store, the one with the big painted rainbow in the window

that's peelin. One of them boys starts walkin all next to me sayin, what's up, Lorena, what you be doin after dinner, you be watchin TV? I just said, yeah or whatever, cause I was tryin to catch up with Antoine, he walk so damn fast. And this boy say, you got pretty eyes. I don't say nothin to him, just keep walkin, then he say it again. I still don't say nothin, and Antoine's up there walkin quick like he always do and I'm noticin this woman gettin offa her bus. She kinda big and her dress gets stuck on somethin inside the door. She carryin all these bags and I wanna go help her cause ain't nobody else helpin her, but I know Antoine'll yell at me, right in fronta all these boys too. He might even say he ain't gonna give me no money for candy. So I just look down at the sidewalk with all them wads of people's bubble gum and think about nothin. And this boy still tryin to talk to me and I don't even know what he been sayin. When I look up he talkin bout hey, girl, maybe I walk down your house sometime and we can chill. I don't wanna chill with no boys, I know that much. Momma done told me lotsa times she don't wanna see no boys comin around until I'm at least sixteen years old. Momma smart, and boy, she yell so loud you can't hear for three days afterward, so I for sure ain't about to be havin no boys comin down my house to chill. So I just look at this boy and say, I ain't allowed. He say, sure you is, then he walk over and put his arm around my neck and look at me, sorta half smile, half somethin else. So I look down again. But by now we standin outside the store. Antoine gone on in and I say, I'ma get me some candy, but this boy got a hold on me and he ain't lettin go. Girl, he say, why you want candy so bad? Only little kids want candy that bad. I look up after he say it and then he swings his arm that's around my shoulders toward him, so I can't go nowhere, and he presses his dry lips right against mine. I'm shakin my head, but he won't lift his mouth from mine and then I feel his wet tongue and his hand reachin down the front of my shirt. I throw my head back and scream. Boy, you is one dirty, nasty boy, I wanna tell him, your momma should wash your mouth out with soap a hundred times—a hundred million times—cause you is unconsiderate and nasty and you ain't even cute. But I just look at him. Go on, girl, go on and get your candy, he says, and I go inside.

I SEEN TASHA AGAIN TODAY. I mean, I talked to her again. She was walkin out the door to go to the field and I said, hi, Tasha, who you sit with out here? She said, nobody, usually. So I said, you wanna sit with me, my friend Sarah gone today, I think she sick. And she said, awright. So we sittin there, and boy, has that girl got a lot to say. She got all these stories bout livin in Kentucky and how the girls used to tease her bout bein poor and then her daddy got a good job workin for this company and that's how come she moved up to Cincinnati. I told her bout how my daddy moved out when we was little, but he moved back in last year and how Antoine tries to wrestle with him sometime after dinner. She ask me questions bout Antoine and at first I'm thinkin she like him. Lotsa them girls do, even my friend Sonya did for a while, till she slept over my house and seen what a goofball he is. But then she say, I always wanted a brother, all I got is five sisters, which change my mind. Brothers is nice sometime, I tell her. But sometime they try to boss you around and make you do stuff like they grown even though they ain't. She say, yeah, my sisters do that too.

When the bell rings I ask her if she wanna go skatin with me Friday cause Sarah and Sonya can't go and I already told my momma I was goin. She say yes right away and tell me she ain't gone out nowhere with nobody but her sisters since she got here, so she can't wait. I smile at her and she smile back, half squinting cause the sun be so bright.

SARAH COME INTO SCHOOL today with her hair done. Now I known Sarah since way back and she ain't never got her hair done, and today she come walkin in like she eighteen years old with her hair stiff and straight and fallin all over her face. She say her momma let her for her twelfth birthday. Well, shoot, I told her, I turned twelve seven months ago and my momma never took me nowhere to get my hair done.

Today at lunch she all talkin bout let's go downtown after school and go to the mall. I told her, girl, what you talkin bout, we ain't never go downtown, 'cept that one time last winter. Now just cause you got your hair done you wanna prance it all over downtown. I know the only reason you wanna go to the mall is so you can meet some boys with your hair all done up, yep, I know what you tryin to do, Sarah. Um-hmm, you ain't foolin nobody. And she say, so what if I wanna meet some boys. Well, I tell her, I just don't wanna come with you, that's all, I don't need to be talkin to no boys. Awright then, she say, I'll just ask Sonya. Fine with me, I say.

TASHA TOLD ME SHE ONLY been skatin once before in her whole life. I told her, damn, girl, I been skatin so many times I can't even count em—what you do with your friends in Kentucky? She say she only got one friend where she from ('sides her sisters) and they be climbin trees and playin jump rope and in the summer they be swimmin. Oh, I say, I don't know how to swim. She say, I'll teach you.

So there we was, skatin, and Tasha go real fast even though she say she can't. I guess she learn quick. I see some girls I know from school, but I don't talk to them. Man, we musta been skatin for two hours straight before we took a break. So we sittin on the side but then my song come on, so I say, aw, now we gotta go skate for this one. It's the backwards skate, too, which I can do real good cause Antoine taught me when I was about seven and I practice every time we go skatin. So we start skatin and Tasha say, wow, you can even go backwards and I say, yeah, girl, here, look, I'll teach you. So I hold onto her hands and she go slow at first, I think cause she scared of fallin, which she already did three times. But then she get the hang of it, and I say, see, it ain't so hard. But don't let go, she say, I don't wanna fall.

So I don't let go, and we skate around and around for the whole song and part of the next (which just happened to be my other song), and she start to laugh. So I'm like, girl, what you laughin at, and she say, nothin, just the way all the lights go across your face, the blue and yellow and the orange and all them, they make your face look different with all them different shadows. And then I notice how them lights go all over her face too, makin her dark skin turn every color in the rainbow while she skate backwards without fallin.

ANTOINE DIDN'T COME HOME with me today cause he goin over his friend Jay's house. So I come home, and Momma and Daddy, neither of them was there. So then I go lookin in my backpack for my key, but it ain't there nowhere. So I think maybe I can climb in a window, but Momma done locked all of em. So I just sit out on the back porch waitin for somebody to come. And I'm waitin for a long time. Then I feel this little somethin. Like…well, I don't know what it's like. It's a little somethin in between my legs, like I'm havin an accident, even though I ain't wet myself since I was eight years old and anyway I don't even have to pee. So I feel this thing and I'm just sittin there thinkin, what is it? So finally, since ain't nobody came home yet to let me in, I go back behind the bushes in the backyard cause I gotta know what it is, and I look at my underwear and I see this maroon color stuff on it. Lots of it, and I say, Momma! even though she can't hear me. I know what it is, and I also know I need Momma. I go back to the back porch to wait for her some more, and I start prayin to God, cause I heard this can hurt.

When Momma come home finally, she all in a rush cause she need to make dinner and Antoine ain't home yet like he supposed to be. I don't wanna bother her, I know how she can yell, so I go upstairs to lay on my bed and stare at the sky, which be the prettiest colors in fall. I haven't even taken off my shoes and somehow I fall asleep. When I wake up Momma's callin us for dinner. I stand up and see a circle of red where I been layin, like a little dark sea in between the blue and white flowers on the sheets. Later on when Momma sees my sheets she screams. Girl, what you do, she ask me, and I tell her what done happened. You shoulda told me earlier, she say, and I look at her face, and I think how it be the color of brown sugar. I know, Momma, I say, but I prayed to God so it wouldn't hurt. Well, she say, I don't know how much God's gonna help you when he a man hisself.

TASHA ASKED DO I WANNA spend the night on Saturday and I said yes, so that's what I did. Her momma real nice. She let us rent a movie and bought us some candy, and when we was done watchin the movie she let us turn on some music and dance too. Tasha dance good. She told me her sisters was teachin her to dance since she was little. She was like, where'd you learn to dance, Lorena? And I told her I teach myself offa them music videos. And she said, oh. So we dancin for like a hour and then her momma say it's time for bed. And I'm thinkin, ah, shoot, I don't never go to bed this early at my house. But I lay down anyway, and Tasha say, Momma don't like us to stay up late cause we keep her up, but it's okay if we whisper. So I say, okay, and we whisper. She tells me a story bout ridin her bike into a tree where she used to live. I don't got no stories bout bikes, but I tell her bout this time we went skatin, me and Antoine and my cousins and all these girls was tryin to kiss Antoine. I got her laughin good about that one too. Then she start to tell me another one but I don't even know what it's about. I'm so tired I just close my eyes and then I guess I go and fell asleep. Cause then I hear Tasha voice and I'm wakin up. But it ain't morning, it's still nighttime. I can just hardly make out her eyes cause it be real dark in the room. She say, you fell asleep, and I say, I know I did. Then she don't say nothin for a while and I close my eyes again. When I open them she still wide awake. Lorena, she say, you really pretty. What you mean, I ask her. She say it again. Then she reach over and kiss me right on my cheek. I don't know what to say to her. I heard girls talkin before bout girls who kiss other girls and like other girls. They say they nasty. They call em names and say they ain't got no friends. I tell Tasha, look, I ain't no dyke. She say, me neither.

So we just lyin there and I'm lookin at her black eyes and thinkin how she pretty too, so I say it to her. She grab my hand with both of hers and hold it. Her hands are warm and she got soft skin, like she be wearin lotion. Then I do somethin too. I slide my head till it's right by hers and I'm lookin right in her eyes and then I kiss her. Right there on the mouth. She say, have you ever kissed a boy before, and I say, I don't think so, have you? Naw, she say, and then she puts her lips on mine and leaves them there for a long time. Her lips are soft and warm like her hands, and I think I could just keep mine next to them forever, but then I start to laugh, so I can't. She ask me why I'm laughin, and I say, girl, you just be makin me happy, that's all.

When I wake up in the mornin she still holdin my hand in hers.

ANTOINE START HANGIN with this boy in the eleventh grade name Robert, and all a sudden he think he grown for sure. I remind him every day that he ain't, but the boy don't listen. And he done got hisself in trouble for it too. This one day he decide he ain't gone come home and he ain't gone tell Momma or Daddy neither. I told him, boy, Momma gonna get you for that, but it don't make no difference to him. I see him hangin out the window of Robert's car while they ridin by my bus stop. Me and Sonya just shakin our heads, cause Sonya know how loud my momma yell when she mad.

It bout dinner time and Antoine still ain't home yet. Momma already worked up bout it cause I told her I seen him drivin right by me goin right in the opposite direction of our house. So she pretty mad. It be like 8 o'clock, and the phone rings. Momma answer it and suddenly she talkin to the person and gettin all worried, almost sad, it sound like. She hang up and say Antoine in the hospital.

When we get there he asleep. Robert down the hall. Momma wake Antoine up and Daddy ask is he okay. He a little confused, and then he say, oh, yeah, I'm awright. What happened, Momma ask, and then he tell us bout how he was ridin in this car and then all a sudden they was havin to swerve off the road and they hit a pole. His leg broken and his head swollen in a couple places. He be in the hospital till tomorrow.

We don't stay long. Momma kiss his forehead even though I know she mad at him. Daddy touch his shoulder and I'm the last to say goodbye. I don't know why you gotta act like you grown, I tell him. He for once don't say nothin smart back to me. Antoine, I say, I'm glad you ain't kill yourself. You do some stupid things, but I'm glad you ain't dead. He smile and pat my head. You ain't so bad neither, he say. I hear Momma callin me from the hallway and I hug Antoine real quick before I run outside.

TASHA TAUGHT ME TO SWIM at the Y. Her momma let her go every Saturday with her sisters and one time I get to go too. I ain't no good, even though I swear she taught me each kinda different way to swim ten times. I just splash around and make her laugh with all the funny faces I be makin when water get in my nose. We swim the whole afternoon and then take a shower and put on our regular clothes to wait for Tasha momma to come pick us up. In the locker room Tasha kiss me real quick on the lips while we puttin on our clothes and I kiss her back and then we start laughin. Her sisters come over askin what's so funny, and Tasha say I'm tellin her this funny thing I seen on TV. They walk back over to where they was, and I can't stop smilin.

I ASKED TASHA TODAY if she wanna jump rope with me and Sarah and Sonya and she said she do. So I say, Sarah and Sonya, this Tasha, she wanna jump with us; Tasha, this is Sarah and Sonya. We start playin, me and Sonya turnin and Sarah and Tasha takin turns jumpin. Everything just fine, then I start noticin

Sonya and Sarah snickerin every time Tasha jumpin. When it's time to switch, I go up to em and say, why you snickerin, Tasha jumpin awright. Sarah roll her eyes and puff out her lips and I say, girl, why you actin like that. Cause, Sonya say, she a lesbian. No she ain't, I yell back, why you say that? You ain't got no proof—you triflin, tryin to judge my friend. Well, Sonya say, I ain't judgin nobody, that's just what people be sayin. Why they be sayin that, I say. All a sudden I got this heavy feelin in my stomach and I feel hot. Cause, Sonya say, she dress like a boy and she act like one too. No she ain't! I tell her, but Sarah and Sonya just standin there actin like nothin wrong at all. Why you get all mad, Lorena, you one too, Sarah ask me, and I put my hands on my hips and walk right up to her. Hell, naw, I ain't, I say. Then why you hang with her? Cause she my friend. And I thought y'all was too. Sarah drop the jump rope and say, I'm goin inside. Awright, then, I say as they walkin toward the door.

My face feel like it burnin as I turn back toward Tasha. My eyes feel wet. But Tasha smilin. Why you smilin, I tell her, you know what they just called you? She say, yeah, I do, and then she say, let's go sit in the field. We walk to the middle of the field and then she lay down. I lay down next to her and we starin at the clouds. The bell's gonna ring soon, I tell her, and she say, I know. I start wonderin bout what people is gonna think seein us layin here in the middle of the field together. I look over at Tasha and she look so calm, like she could just fall asleep right here. What are you thinkin bout, she ask me, and I open my mouth like I'm bout to say somethin, but then I shut it. I grab her hand, which is warm like always, and hold it real tight, right in between us, where no one can see it 'less they standin over us. I'm thinkin bout the sky, I say. She smile like she just seen God and say, me too.

—THE MIDWIFE—

Julie Auer

MAVIS IS A WISPY LITTLE WOMAN with wild curly hair—gray, though splashed in the stubborn red tones of her youth. All her features smile even when her spirits are low, which is rare. Words and notions spill out of her chattering mouth as soon as they enter her head, and any stranger standing within earshot is soon acquainted with whatever is on her mind.

She came to my law office in Prescott, Tennessee, two years ago with a doctor's diagnosis of acute muscle spasms brought about by an automobile accident. I was sorry for her misfortune, but glad for the business. The truck driver whose improper lane change had inflicted on Mavis personal injury, pain and suffering, and permanent disability—Mavis could no longer perform her duties as a licensed practical nurse—worked for a national trucking corporation. I got Mavis a handsome settlement, of which I pocketed a third. I was very fond of Mavis by that time, though not altogether on account of her successful case.

One April day, a few weeks after her case had settled, she paid me a social call. A woman I had always wanted to meet followed Mavis into my office. Her name was Libby, and I had learned a lot about her during the course of my representation of Mavis. I invited them to sit down.

"Oh, you should sit down too, Len," Mavis beamed. "I came by to share the good news, special just for you."

I savored the possibility that a dollar sign could be affixed to this good news.

"Libby has been saved!" Mavis cried.

I looked at Libby, a lanky, square-jawed woman who sat quietly next to Mavis and returned my curious stare with a shrug. She looked uncomfortable in an outmoded black pantsuit, preserved, I surmised, for the rare occasions when she had to dress up. Her thick salt-and-pepper hair was cropped at the ears, and her mouth—no doubt used to being shut after years of living with Mavis—turned up slightly in a timid smile.

"Congratulations," I said.

Libby averted her eyes to Mavis, who told her, "Len knows all about my walk with God." Then to me she added, "I've always been weak to Libby's advances, the way she is. But now that we're both with the Lord, I asked Preacher what he thought God would say about us sleeping in the same bed from here on out."

"Mavis," I said, "it's really none of my business."

"Preacher said it was our business where and how we slept, as long as our passions don't get a hold of us. I said, 'Preacher, we've shared that same bed through thick and thin.' Well, Len, I don't have to tell you that after a while it gets pretty thin, if you know what I mean. Still, by the grace of God almighty alone we shall overcome temptation. Praise the Lord. Isn't that right, Libby?"

Libby's lips parted long enough to pass a deep sigh.

"Of course, right," Mavis said, and patted Libby on the thigh.

For a Southern woman in her early sixties, Mavis had been peculiarly frank about her lifelong partnership with Libby, so much so that by the time I met Libby I felt we were already well acquainted. Libby came from a long line of horse breeders in the countryside outside of Prescott, but as soon as she reached adulthood she had moved to Memphis to find a woman. She found Mavis and brought her back to Prescott. With money saved from Libby's shoeing horses and Mavis's nursing, they bought a few acres along the Tennessee River on which they eventually built a farm.

Like Libby, I had left Prescott after high school, though with every intention of coming back. I went to college in Chicago and law school in Atlanta. I returned home and opened a small private practice. I was elected to the town council. I aspired to become mayor. So I went to the office by day and lived openly as a lawyer. I went home at night to a woman named Iris. We drew the curtains, locked the doors, and stole a few hours in our own skins before another day of posing as mere roommates. Nobody knew a thing about us, or more important, me.

But Mavis had me figured out. Right after her joyful announcement of Libby's conversion, she asked, "Who's that little girl you run around with?"

I cleared my throat. "I beg your pardon?"

"That cute little girl I saw you with down at the greenhouse last Saturday."

"She's not a girl. She's twenty-eight." I glared at Libby, who took my cue and turned to Mavis, shook her head, and seemed on the verge of speaking.

She wasn't fast enough. Mavis chirped, "Well, she's a little doll. I could tell you were more than friends. I've got a good eye for that kind of thing. Always have. Isn't that right, Libby? It's all in the eyes, the way people look at each other. I can spot it a mile away. I bet y'all live together, don't you, Len? Does your family know that?"

"Mavis," I said gently but firmly, "that's not your business."

"They're fine people, your family." She turned to Libby. "The Russells. Fine people. Len, do you go up to St. Cloud Episcopal, like the rest of the Russells?"

I frowned. "No. Well, on holidays. Anyway, it doesn't matter."

"Family always matters, Len. What's her name?" Mavis and Libby were both staring at me.

"Iris."

I GOT HOME LATE THAT NIGHT and found Iris asleep on the couch. We lived in the house she had picked out when I brought her to Prescott, a turreted work of timber and stucco propped up amid rose bushes and hollyhocks, now tended by Iris's patient hands. She worked at the greenhouse where Mavis had spotted us, and every evening she came home with seeds and cuttings, spending lonesome hours in our little plot of earth, giving to it what I denied her: liveliness and nurturing.

I sat on the edge of the couch and leaned over her. I meditated on her sleeping-doll features, illuminated in the blue glow of the TV, and marked their sadness. I brushed a stray lock of curly black hair from her cheek and stooped to kiss her. She awoke.

"Work late?" she asked.

"Yeah. Sorry."

"You didn't call."

"The council meeting ran late. Lots of officials around. You know."

"Oh," she yawned. "Yeah. Why would you call your roommate to tell her you'll have to miss supper?" She forced a chuckle and gazed into the TV.

IRIS WAS STOLEN. She had been the lover of another woman when I met her in Atlanta, and I made off with her like a bandit in the night, celebrating my spoils with the trip to San Francisco that Iris had always dreamed about. We had flirted with openness there, had lazed in the radiance of newfound love in a city that didn't stare.

But I belonged to Prescott. I was directly descended from the founding Prescotts, I had plenty of inheritance to look forward to, and I understood the place. It was small and Southern and full of values that descended from practical custom and solemn religion. I lived somewhere between those values and the truth, but Mavis lived rather naturally in the company of both. The next time I saw her, she had reconsidered her commitment to chastity.

"You would think," she reckoned loudly as she sat in my office for what had turned into a regular Friday afternoon visit, "that the passions of a woman my age would have lost their power by now. But Lord, have mercy. Libby's a devil of a temptress." She nudged Libby, whose complexion went scarlet. "Len, did I ever tell you the story about how ol' Libby here seduced me the first time?"

"Mavis, for chrissake," I said, "give her a break."

"She took me on a riverboat ride down the Mississippi. Wined and dined me, stealthy as a cat on a baby bird. We were standing alone on the starboard side looking up at the moon, and she leaned over and kissed me flat on the neck. I thought a lightning bolt had run through me. Before I knew it, we were molded together at the mouth, her hands running up and down my leg and up under my skirt—"

I let go a nervous laugh. "I get the picture, Mavis. Please."

Mavis smiled sweetly at Libby. "When I recall that night, I just can't say no forever. Isn't that right, sugar plum?" She kissed Libby's plum-colored cheek. "You're the love of my life." Libby's bashful grin stayed with me even after they had gone.

I lingered at my desk and spied the street through slats of Venetian blinds. People lolled along the sidewalks, idly and in no hurry, as the late-afternoon sun warmed their shoulders and slowed their steps to home. I suddenly looked forward to home and Iris. I arrived in time for supper, the sacred first rite of Iris and Len's Friday night ritual lineup of food, wine, conversation, entertainment, and with any luck, lovemaking and/or deviant sex. After four years, our lovemaking had lost its spontaneity— no more lunchtime trysts, shower-stall shakedowns, or passion amid spent champagne flutes in front of the fireplace. About all I hoped for lately was a sober bit of heavy petting before turning off the lamp on the bedside table. The mechanics of sex had displaced its intimacy with routine, yet I longed for the nights not so long ago when Iris had warmed to my caresses, let her nightshirt fall open in my embrace, and given over the voluptuous properties of her body and soul.

Iris's sensuality braided itself around her natural wholesomeness, and in her kitchen these dual aspects were absorbed. She grew her own vegetables and herbs, collected sundries in bulk from the farmer's market, and conjured in a simple meal pleasures for all the senses. But when I got home that Friday night, I found the kitchen empty. No steam arose from a pot of boiling pasta. There was no familiar clattering of pans and dishes, no aroma of chopped rosemary and cardamom, no taste of sweet garlic on Iris's fingertips. She was gone.

MAVIS CAME BY WITHOUT LIBBY the next Friday afternoon, explaining that she was down in her knee again. "Here I am, still ailing from that truck wreck, still on painkillers, and she gets a little cramp in the knee and you would think she was paralyzed for life. She gets all hangdog and grumpy, no fun at all when that rheumatism sets in. So I said, well, fine then, Libby, I'll just go on to town and visit with Len by myself. What do you think of that?"

I forced a smile.

"I said, what do you think of that, Len?"

"Oh, you mean me? I thought you were talking to Libby."

"Libby isn't here, Len."

"I know. I meant, I thought you were telling me what you told Libby."

"Huh? What's got into you? You're even more down in the dumps than Libby. I might as well be back home for all your sour company."

I rolled my shoulders. "Nothing's got into me."

"You look like you haven't been sleeping, but it ain't that good-time tired look. It's mournful. Come on, sugar. Tell Mavis what ails you."

I stared at her for a moment, suspended in vanity, determined not to show weakness. Then the words rather mechanically rolled over my tongue, almost against my will, and I found myself disclosing secrets that had tortured me all week long. I told her how I had arrived home last Friday to find Iris missing, how by nightfall I'd become worried that she had been in an accident. No, it wasn't like Iris to just leave without a word; she was too sensitive for that. I drove to the farmer's market and asked if she had been seen there that day—they knew Iris—but she hadn't been by there on Friday. I called the greenhouse, but it was closed. I called all the personal numbers listed in Iris's greenhouse address book, and all her friends, to no avail.

"Then I panicked," I told Mavis. "When she still hadn't come home by midnight, I imagined the worst. She had been abducted by some sick predator...or predators."

"What in the world made you think that?" Mavis asked sharply.

"I handle criminal cases too. I've read case studies of terrible things happening to women who live or travel alone. Iris is always by herself, and I was morbidly afraid. I called the sheriff and reported her missing."

"What did he do?"

"He said it was too soon to file a report. He asked a lot of personal questions, and I gave honest answers, a full confession. He said she was probably just mad at me and told me not to worry. She'd come back. It didn't dawn on me until I got off the phone that I had just utterly outed myself to the sheriff of Prescott County."

"Out of worry over your poor sweet girlfriend. Aw, that's sweet, Len."

"Sweet?" I nearly shouted. "More like stupid. It's one thing to come out by accident, but to do it in some irrational fit of panic! I miss Iris for three hours, and I'm calling the sheriff, a political powerhouse in these parts, begging him to find my girlfriend, not having considered that she could actually leave me. I mean, it never once entered my mind that she had left me. Me! No, clearly she had been kidnapped by thugs. So not only am I a town dyke, I'm the village idiot too!"

"I take it you found out she's all right."

I took a deep breath and reached for a bottle of ibuprofen I kept in my desk. "She called me ten minutes after I got off the phone with the sheriff."

Mavis let go a musical gush of laughter.

"It isn't funny, Mavis," I snapped. I felt my eyes go hot with tears. "She's left me. She picked up the rest of her stuff yesterday." I groped an empty box whose tissue I had used up before lunchtime. My weeping embarrassed me, so I swiveled my chair around to escape Mavis's direct line of pity.

"Aw, poor baby," I heard her coo. Suddenly she was beside me, pulling me out of the chair and over to the sofa, where I laid my head in her lap, crying like a fool.

It dawned on me that I had not yet let my loss sink in and that I had nobody in whom to confide my sorrow other than Mavis. My few friends were really Iris's friends, granola types whom I had always kept at a careful distance. I had lost touch with my Atlanta friends, having taken special care to sever ties with old girlfriends. My family wouldn't want to hear it; they had taught me everything I practiced about propriety and self-censorship. Mavis was, at that moment, all the family I had.

"I know it's my fault. I'm a terrible person," I sobbed. "I'm a selfish, conceited bitch. I wish I were dead."

"Oh, hush," Mavis said soothingly. "Lord, have mercy. Here I sit, petting my lawyer's head. What's the world coming to?"

IRIS TOLD ME THERE WAS no one thing that set her off and made her want to leave me. I asked her why she chose that particular Friday. She gave a bitter account. "I got off early on Friday and was on my way to the market when I decided that another routine Friday would make me hate you. I already hate your lawyer friends, all those political jerks. I felt like ramming the car into the goddamned courthouse steps and getting out and yelling at every suit that walked by, 'Lenora Russell is my lover! Give her back!'" Iris pulled away when I tried to touch her. "I'm leaving you while I still love you, rather than waiting until I grow to despise you, Len."

We were sitting on her futon, in her new apartment on the sunny second floor of a Queen Anne on Gable Street, not two blocks from my office. "You could have given me some notice," I said sullenly.

"It just hit me that day," she said, and began to cry softly. "There was no point in waiting for you to get home and pretend we have a good life. I was tired of being treated like a roommate. I deserve the same dignity as a spouse. I deserve a phone call when you're running late, Len. I want a stupid kiss when we bump into each other on the street, instead of some lame wave or 'hi.' I want to sit next to you at dinner parties and those dumb-ass bar association banquets."

"You would hate them," I said, noticing that her otherwise modest cotton shirt was unbuttoned down to the cleft of her bosom.

"I know! But I'd appreciate the chance to decide that for myself."

Iris had called me hopeless during one of our countless phone conversations, and I felt it now more than ever. I would have done anything to persuade her to come back to me. I had a thought. "I want you to meet Mavis," I said.

Iris looked at me scathingly. "Who the hell is Mavis?"

"Just a friend."

She smirked. "You have a friend?"

"Be nice," I said. "Yes, I have a friend. Her name is Mavis." I started to say more but was distracted by the sudden, upward movement of Iris's hand. She scratched the back of her neck, and the backward motion of her collar caused the deep V of her cleavage to widen, exposing the swell of her left breast. I moved closer to her. "You'd like Mavis. I really want you to meet her. I really want you to."

She smiled like a vamp. "I can hear fine, you know."

"Yeah, but I have to whisper this next part."

"You're up to no good."

I nuzzled against her ink-black curls. "I really want you," I kissed her neck, "to meet Mavis."

"Maybe," she breathed. She pulled me into a protracted and promising kiss, a real grope-and-wallow. We tumbled onto the floor, rolling over on top of each other, clumsily yanking off clothing, caught up in the kind of passion that grips only the newly enamored, with rare and fortunate exceptions like ours.

SHE THREW ME OUT around eleven that night, after we had dressed and shared a few glasses of wine. "Will you come home with me?" I asked, though I knew better.

She grinned. "Why? We have better sex here."

I blushed. "So you're asking me to move in, huh?"

She said gently, "It's too small. Besides, an upstanding citizen like you needs a proper house."

"I bought it because you loved it. You called it witchy, remember?"

"Yeah, I remember," she smiled. "But I'm gonna stay here."

"How long?"

"As long as it takes." She kissed me and bid me good night, telling me she loved me. Then I, loopy from excesses of wine and passion, walked with a slightly springing gait along sleepy sidewalks, all the way home.

MY PHONE RANG at the crack of dawn. Only one woman ever called me that early. Whenever Mavis called me at home, there was at first a pretense of business. Her nephew wanted to sue his landlord, or Buck at the feed store was finally going to divorce his faithless wife. None of it ever amounted to more than an opportunity for Mavis to lay siege on my privacy for up to an hour.

"What is it, Mavis?" I grumbled.

"Oh. You want Mavis?" a low voice inquired.

I sat upright in bed. "Is this Libby?" Before that moment, she had never uttered a word to me.

There was a bit of a pause, then one terse, husky line. "My brother Frank got the stable girl pregnant."

"Huh? What did you say?"

"Ruthie down at the stable. She's pregnant. Says Frank done it. She's got too big for work, and I need a stable hand."

"Libby, what can I do for you?"

"She says I owe her. Wants six months time off, paid in advance."

"And if you don't pay her?"

"Says she'll sue me for child support."

"Libby, Ruthie can't collect child support from you. You didn't get her pregnant."

"Why, hell, I never even looked twice at her!"

"Now, on the other hand, Frank may have a problem."

She said disgustedly, "He's always had a problem. Ol' jack rabbit."

"How old is he?"

"Fifty-two. Too old for tomcattin'."

"And Ruthie is...?"

"Old enough to keep her legs crossed against Frank's prying hands."

"For Frank's sake, she'd better be over eighteen."

She sounded irritated, even insulted. "Of course she's over eighteen! Been working for me six years. Takes a real horse-woman to work for me."

"Well, this horsewoman's baby sounds like Frank's problem, not yours."

"What about her time off?"

"Is she full-time or part-time?"

"Part-time. I got no use for a full-time hand."

"Then she's out of luck. But you know, Libby, you ought to help her."

There was a brief, stubborn silence, followed by a dramatic sigh, one fraught with desperation, detectable even over telephone lines. "I suppose so. Ain't right casting out a woman with child, especially it being my own niece or, God forbid, nephew."

"What are you willing to do?"

"I don't know how to help her. I got barely enough money to pay for regular work, let alone time off. But she's mad as a wet hornet. Don't blame her. Frank's a varmint. He won't pay. Got nine younguns by four different women already. Only married two of 'em. He cheated on 'em both! Ol' jack rabbit."

It was her way of asking for my intercession. I gave in. "I'll talk to Ruthie. We'll work something out, Libby. Don't worry."

WE SETTLED ON A SATURDAY afternoon meeting with Ruthie, with whom I would negotiate on Libby's behalf an arrangement for Ruthie's maternity leave and some form of financial assistance until she was able to return to work. It would be simple and informal, with no legal enforceability, so there would be no fee. It was a favor for my friends, and a means of offering security to a scared young pregnant woman.

I was aloft in peace and goodwill, already calculating the positive effects my mediation would have on my budding political life. I knew my offer of help would please Mavis. I expected the invitation to supper and got it, for Mavis had the old-fashioned grace of rewarding the promise of a favor even before it was done. She even planned on including Ruthie at supper, since, she explained, Ruthie often lunched with them anyway on the days that she worked.

I called Iris at work to brag about my big heart. "Of course," I made sure to tell her, "I wouldn't dare quote them a fee. That's why Mavis is cooking supper for me. That's what I love about this town, when it's all said and done. We treat each other like humans, like family. That would never have happened in Atlanta. Urbanism and humility can't coexist." I waited for Iris's approval.

"I'm thinking of going back," she said.

"Where?" I asked weakly, though I knew.

"Atlanta. Where else?"

"Soon?"

"I don't know. You just reminded me of what I've already been thinking about. Going home."

"You said you were going to stay here, remember? You said for as long as it takes. That's what you said." In the instant I realized how petulant and childish my tone was, I snapped, "By the way, what did you mean by 'as long as it takes?' As long as *what* takes?"

"I guess I meant as long I can stand it," she said.

Grasping for anything, I reminded her, "You also said you would meet Mavis."

"I have to go, Len. It's getting busy."

"Anyway, will you go with me on Saturday?"

"It's not my party. It's for you. You'll be there on business, and then the supper is for you. I wasn't invited."

"Yes, you were," I lied. "Mavis specifically asked me to tell you. Why do you think I called you?" She wanted to get off the phone, nearly hung up on me, but I begged relentlessly until she, impatient and exasperated, agreed. I was a braggart, a beggar, and a liar, but I was in love.

I TURNED OFF THE HIGHWAY onto the narrow country lane that wound around a barren hill to the farmhouse where Mavis and Libby lived. It was an old two-story log house with two chimneys festooned in ivy and casement windows bedecked in showy arrays of flora spilling out of window boxes. The air was redolent of wisteria and honeysuckle, while a May breeze rippled lazily along peach tree branches. Iris remarked on the beauty of the place just about the time I recognized the figure waiting on the porch.

Ruthie, that poor, spurned stable hand, the spawn of a jack rabbit curled in her womb, sat primly on an inert porch swing, anchored by the weight of her hugely pregnant form. I had seen her before, at civic events, town meetings, political rallies. I had never known her name, because the sheriff had only ever introduced her to me as his daughter.

"Daddy told me I should have my own lawyer," she said glumly when I introduced myself. "But when I told him who was coming, which was you, he said no mind, that you could be trusted."

"Is that so?" I said with bated breath. "How nice." Iris jabbed me. "Oh. This is Iris," I announced vaguely.

"Is she your girlfriend?" Ruthie asked. "Daddy said you called him about a missing girlfriend. I'll tell him you found her." She looked reflective and added, "He don't have the means to care for me and the child, what with him being a widower."

Mavis bounced onto the porch in the nick of time. "Len, honey! Aw, is this your sweet little Iris? She's a doll. A *doll*."

My smile frozen, I more or less thought out loud, "Ruthie is the sheriff's daughter."

Mavis grabbed Ruthie's wrists and rocked twice before heaving her forward off the swing. "Didn't Libby tell you about her pa?" she panted. "Lord, Ruthie, you're big as an ox. I believe you're nigh of birthing that baby!"

"Anytime now," Ruthie mumbled, her mouth drooping amid large, sullen features. She had been a big girl even before pregnancy had inflated her.

"Libby didn't mention Ruthie's father," I said.

"Well, she ain't much for words."

We convened to the parlor, where in the course of a couple of hours we discussed Ruthie's needs, in respect of Libby's ability to provide. The negotiations concluded easily. Ruthie would live with Mavis and Libby, who would provide food and necessities for both her and the baby until Ruthie was strong enough to start work again. In the meantime, Libby would manage the horses by herself. She considered that with warmer weather ahead, a few months of grooming, feeding, and stable tending wouldn't be too laborious for a woman her age. Frank would be banned from the farm, what with his being a useless, no-account jack rabbit.

Libby served us supper—pork roast, sweet potatoes, fried okra, and turnip greens—and we all retired to the porch at sunset. Ruthie and Iris sat on the porch swing opposite me. Mavis sat in a chair next to mine, while Libby leaned serenely against the porch railing. The twilight was best enjoyed in silence, and we all cast our eyes on the hilltop's orange halo.

Suddenly, Ruthie lurched forward. She gave a hideous growl, followed by a sharp cry that caused birds to burst forth from the treetops. "Oh, my God!" she wailed. "My insides are afire!"

"Aw, she's having that baby," Mavis cooed. "Praise Jesus."

"Wait a minute," I said. "All of a sudden? Don't contractions come first?"

"I've had 'em," Ruthie grunted. She collapsed into Iris's arms. "All day long."

"Why the hell didn't you say something?" I shouted.

"Len!" Iris snapped. "Call a doctor."

"Mavis is a nurse. Mavis," I commanded, "nurse!"

"Ruthie, sugar," Mavis asked calmly, "how far apart have these contractions been?"

"I had my last one in the bathroom during supper," Ruthie said miserably. "I hid back there when I felt it coming on, and didn't come out till it passed. I think the okra's what done me in."

"Law," Mavis marveled. "That weren't twenty minutes ago. We best get her in the bed. Len, you come on back and help me."

"Iris is more maternal," I said.

"That's why she's gonna hold poor Ruthie's sweet shoulders while you and I catch her youngun. Now do as I say." She eyed Libby. "Meanwhile, Libby, you go fetch the sheriff."

The next half-hour was a frenzy of shouts, commands, screaming, cajoling, weeping, cursing, laughter, a baby's indignant wail, and finally, peace. Ruthie lay mesmerized with her son in her arms, a nephew for Libby and Mavis. Iris giddily hugged and kissed everyone in the room, laying a powerful smooch on me. She called me brave, but I didn't believe that.

Then the sheriff arrived. His delight at the sight of his grandson absolved all misgivings he might have had for his daughter's predicament. He slapped Libby's back and shouted for laughter, shook Mavis's hands, and then spotted me. He gave Iris a courtly nod, and said to me, "Don't worry, Ms. Russell. You know I'm no gossip. I appreciate what you've done here."

"What gossip?" I asked automatically. "You mean Iris? Oh, I don't want gossip, either. The truth is, Iris left me that night I called you about her, and I'm not sure if she wants to come home yet, or ever. But I sure to God hope she does, because I love her just as much as you ever loved your wife. And you can take that clear to the mayor's office." I fell backward into an armchair. Gazing over the foot of the bed where Ruthie lay, I caught her baby in a tiny yawn that crinkled his ruddy newborn face, causing one bright eye to shut against his mother's breast. From where I sat, I could have sworn he was winking.

"COUNCILWOMAN DELIVERS SHERIFF'S GRANDSON," the *Prescott Banner*'s headline read the next day. Asked for a comment, the sheriff gave credit for the successful birth to Ruthie's employers and "prominent Prescott lawyer Lenora Russell and her special friend, Iris Perry." My family has invited me to explain the significance of the word "special." I will tell them what I have just told my fellows on the town council, that Mavis brought more than one baby at the farm that day.

In the meantime, I tell them I have to get home. Iris needs help taking down the curtains, and tomorrow we clean the windows. May's good weather for airing things out.

—SOUL JUMPER—

Abbe Ireland

IT WAS THE LAST DAMN THING you'd expect walking into a bar: someone who could jump outside the body, then move around, just the Being free and clear where you could see it, and I know people have their Realities about this sort of thing, but I know what I saw. I know what I can see. Only it was so damn unexpected I stayed until last call watching the perpetrator of this wildness, who was so goddamn pretty it wasn't a hardship watching anyway.

I'd already spent half the night noticing, since it was the first thing my eye caught as I walked through blinking neon lights to a long bar where I ordered tequila in a snifter. Actually, I noticed her butt first, but it only took a minute to travel the slender body to the pretty face, a damn nice place to end up.

The Phenomenon happened later when I decided to test myself saying something besides another drink order.

"Excuse me."

I must have startled her good. Spinning from the register, she jumped out the right side of her head and back two feet, simultaneously hurling a Stopping Wall that hit my forehead. Stopped me cold. Like I'd walked into a window I didn't see. I barely managed to ask my dumb question about after-hours clubs, thinking the whole time: Whoa, girl, relax! Calm down! I'm not going to slam you across the bar and lay a Big One on you. Not that the thought hadn't crossed my mind, but women don't do that to other women. Especially cowards like me.

Especially being old enough to be her mother. I never once imagined myself doing May-December. Never expected it anymore than I expected to run into a bona fide soul jumper that night...

I only meant to release a little back tension from hunching over a keyboard all day. I worked as a freelance writer in every sense of the word—moving by whim, settling temporarily to work when ideas hit—until I walked into a bar with a soul-jumping bartender too goddamn stunning to blink at once, then leave.

Next night, I returned to the same barroom lights, loud music, dull chatter, and jokes. Probably the same clientele, if I'd noticed anyone but the bartender the night before. I ordered tequila and settled down to more watching, getting a good eyeful of that tall cocky lovely, wondering if I'd hallucinated the psychic circus.

I didn't think so, and no. Past midnight, when the music and talking had cranked to a giddy roar, I stood up too quickly. Startled again, she jumped again to watch. I mean, *really* watch—the Being, Spirit, Soul seeing—in the rapid time/no time this stuff takes.

Damn! An undeniable marvel of the universe! I'd never seen anyone leave the body so easily. Next time she brings a drink, I thought, I have to ask.

"So...how long you been psychic?"

She stopped, stared at me hard with the darkest damn eyes I'd ever seen, finished pouring, set the glass down, didn't move.

"Psychic?"

"Yeah. Psychic. Do you know? Is it conscious?"

"Why? Are you?"

She was staring so hard I was having trouble breathing, but this kind of conversation I could handle. Seeing this stuff is normal and easy as seeing my thumbnail, although I'd never seen anybody do what she did.

"Yeah, but I'm mostly receptive. Not busy like you... You're the busiest I've ever seen."

This almost got a smile.

"You leave your body," I continued. "You move, too, and throw energy around like Zeus. I'd say you're damn near telekinetic. Probably wouldn't take much to learn."

That brought a flat-out smile before she took off to fill another drink order, but I had her hooked. When she finished, she came back for more.

"You can see all that?"

"As easy as I can see this." I waved my hand in the air.

"Telekinetic, huh?" she laughed.

"You almost knocked my head off last night. That's a novel way to sober up drunks at the end of an evening."

We were both smiling now. She took a long beat before answering.

"I don't like being surprised."

This time I laughed.

"Obviously. It was like running into a glass wall. Do that, you'll never need Mace, that's for sure."

Another laugh. More drinks to fix.

"So what do *you* do...being receptive and all?" she asked when she returned.

"Me? I see energy. Feel it really. Kind of a baby Betazoid. Can't read minds, though. Nothing like that."

"But you can see me? Outside my body?"

"Yup. It's a little alarming. You're pretty mild in your body, but outside...you're *very* intense."

Another smile.

"In a game of war, " I went on, "you'd have a big advantage. You'd be outside your body watching an enemy looking for you in the wrong place."

Another laugh.

"Like I said. I don't like surprises."

We met after the bar closed at a tacky, all-night restaurant—Howard Johnson's secret life as a dive. Yellow plastic booths were crowded with early-morning revelers exuding sexual innuendo of either appetite or repletion under fluorescent lights. Hunger of one kind or another charged the large, noisy room. Steaming hot coffee served by Amy, my transgendering Jane Wyatt wanna-be waitress, tasted good after tequila.

I sat waiting in a daze with a good dose of stomach jitters plus creeping embarrassment that she'd only agreed to meet to get rid of me. But damned if she didn't show up right when I was thinking it would be a relief if she didn't. I had no need for distractions, major or minor, in my life, and—oh, shit—I was smiling like a geek, not prepared to handle the Reality walking my way.

"So...did you order me cottage cheese and milk?" she asked, smiling as she slid into the booth, looking damn fresh in a crisp, white cotton shirt and tight jeans after tending bar all night.

"Uh...no." I smiled back.

"Guess you can't read minds, huh?"

"Not yet."

"Too bad."

"Maybe. Maybe not."

She ordered food from dear Amy, who hovered over us in white-blouse, black-slack, black-apron, waitress drag and spoke in a Texas drawl heavy with fey sibilance and wry, catty comments about other diners. They obviously knew each other. After Amy left, she asked, "So what do you do when you're not almost reading minds?"

"Write," I said, making it sound like a job, which it was, only more mobile and independent than most.

"So you're traveling? Just passing through?"

"Not entirely. I've rented an apartment. Furnished. I need some stability or I'd never get anything done."

"How long do you stay in one place?"

"Depends."

"Depends? That's vague enough."

"Not by the time I leave. It's gotten pretty solid and concrete by then."

"Oh. That mean heavy?"

I didn't know what to say. I didn't want to sound flighty. I'd worked hard to live the way I wanted but didn't know how to say that without sounding like a horse's ass. But whatever I did say had to be right. She was studying me with those dark eyes so hard I expected her to pop outside her head for a Real Look before she decided. She was definitely measuring, deciding something. I felt it like a radar beam aimed straight at me and didn't want to blow it.

"I mean complete," I said finally.

"Ah...so you stick around until everything's complete. Which you decide, no doubt."

There was a cool irony in her voice that made it feel like we'd had a fight, sitting in tense silence while Amy served cottage cheese and milk. It was a damned peculiar way to feel so soon.

"How *old* are you?" she asked after Amy sylphed away.

Great. Like I needed reminding, since I wasn't feeling anywhere near my chronological age at the moment.

"Forty-four."

"Huh."

It didn't seem to impress her one way or the other. I asked the same question. She was twenty-seven and local, born and raised. Did she like bartending? Sure. It was easy, money was good, life was fine...at the moment.

At the moment, I had to agree. Life was damn fine. For once I hardly noticed my surroundings, an unusual state for a professional people-watcher. But I was too busy watching this young woman, young enough to be my daughter, whose youngness totally disappeared in the calm stare of eyes so sure of themselves I had a hard time meeting them. Me? I never blink when someone plays that game. I also usually don't feel so jumpy, out of control, silly, stupid, and enjoying every minute of it.

"You never answered," I finally said, wanting to end the tense silence and hear myself sound normal, back in control. "How long have you been psychic?"

"You really like that stuff, huh? It's interesting to you?"

"Very."

"Why?"

"People talk about it, but you never see anyone do it. When they do, it's interesting. Especially the stuff you do."

"So you can see energy, right?"

"Sometimes."

"What's mine look like?"

I smiled, glancing at both hands clutching my coffee cup.

"Uhhh, don't know... Afraid I've been paying more attention to your butt than your aura."

I managed to hang in there, holding my breath through another intense staring exchange that said where the whole thing was going, causing every cell in my body to go nuts.

"At least you're honest," she said finally, snapping off the look, leaning back, smiling, hands folded in her lap. "My butt...that's original."

I shrugged. "It was right there. Eye-level. Couldn't help it."

"Well, if I ate more than this at night, you'd see way too much of it, that's for sure."

We chatted, flirted, stared more before she reached for her coat, saying she had to go.

"Thanks for the food." She stood up. "It was nice meeting you."

It sounded kind of final, surprising me. I felt a sharp pang of disappointment but adjusted quickly—oh, well, that's life—as she stuck out her hand to shake.

"Bye," I said, smiling wanly, more than a little forlorn.

The handshake was surprisingly firm. So was the eye contact. Then bam! She did it. Popped out the right side of her head, tugged toward me, reentered her body, turned, and walked away.

I sat there paralyzed, mouth mentally agape, realizing she'd avoided answering questions about being psychic until she shot the answer right at me. Willed. Intentional. Controlled.

Son of a—

I sat back hard and let go a whistle. People don't do that! People have Realities about such things! Regular normal realities. Regular normal communication. People don't—people can't—damn! I'd never seen anyone play that way!

I marveled over this amazing fact the whole way home, a short drive since my new apartment was downtown, near the restaurant. By the time I unlocked my door, I realized I was hooked. Big-time.

So I waited a day to return to the bar. Very important. One day...

She didn't look surprised to see me. I slid onto my patched vinyl bar stool, took a sip of tequila, and settled in for a woozy evening. I figured the pleasant, queasy feeling in the pit of my stomach had something to do with an imminent collision between me and a Reality I hadn't planned on visiting for a long, long time. I asked if she wanted to meet later. She said yes, did I have cottage cheese and milk at home? I did, so we went to my apartment after closing, instead of the ever-busy Ho-Mo's.

My new "home" was a generic, upstairs rental in an older, two-story building with a porch, fireplace, high ceilings, tall windows, and wavy wooden floors. The furnishings were generic too—almost-antique tables and chairs, an armoire with glass doors, a four-poster bed, and a huge oak desk. A massive couch and matching overstuffed chair occupied much of the living room. I'd added hanging plants, potted trees, and an indoor herb garden in the kitchen. Framed O'Keeffe posters and Ansel Adams landscapes added needed color to tall white walls in all four rooms.

"Not bad. This is nice," she observed, looking around. "For someone just passing through."

"I'm not passing through," I objected, dishing out cottage cheese, pouring milk, then a glass of water for myself. "I don't move that fast. I'm not on the run or anything." I laughed, more than a little self-consciously.

"Oh" was all she said, walking into the kitchen, taking the milk, and staring at me over the glass lip as she drank.

I was having a hard time standing so close in such a small space, so I asked what kind of music she liked, as I headed back into the living room.

"What station do you have your radio on?"

"Classical."

"Turn it on."

Something by Dvořák filled the room. A gorgeous cello concerto.

She brought her snack into the living room and sat in the middle of the couch. Either end I picked I'd be sitting close unless I took the chair, which seemed totally stupid and chickenshit, considering.

Deciding to be brave, I sat sideways against an armrest, sipping water before placing my glass on a butler table cluttered with books, magazines, and notebooks. I let my side sink into the couch and sat there watching her eat...slowly...the whole time watching me. Finally finished, she washed it down with milk.

"So where do you write?"

"In the second bedroom."

"*What* do you write?"

"Fiction. Nonfiction. Whatever pops into my head. Whatever I feel like. It's nice. That kind of freedom."

"Freedom. You like that word, don't you? As much as you like psychic stuff?"

It didn't sound like a question the way she said it, so I didn't know what to answer. I really didn't think about it much, since freedom's a good thing, right? Besides, I didn't know what she wanted to hear, so I sipped more water instead.

A long silence passed, feeling like another fight, when the whole thing hadn't started yet. Well, actually it had. She was just trying to get an idea of what it was. If I were smarter, I'd find out myself—only I never do.

"Do you have anything you've published here?"

"Some of it."

"Show me."

We walked into my study, where I pulled a novel and two short-story collections off a built-in bookshelf. She looked through each one briefly before handing them back. We were standing very close. *Uh-oh. All hell's about to break loose,* I thought. Of course it was only a kiss coming, and I'd been through more than a few of those, even toe-curlers where I forgot to breathe, so I figured I could handle it no problem. Only this time I forgot to breathe, my hands rang like Christmas bells, and my knees felt like rubber bands.

Then something like all hell did break loose. Only it happened in breathless slow-mo, the way making love does sometimes when mutual attention slooooows it way down 'cause there's so much to absorb, no matter how hot, fast, and passionate it is. Or maybe mind and body get so overwhelmed processing so much richness, the movie *has* to run in slow motion. Or maybe you just don't want all the bumpity-bump sucking stroking fucking hot goodness to stop ever, so you slow the whole thing down to freeze-frame by freeze-frame. And wasn't it Einstein anyway who said if you put a clock in a rocket and drive it at the speed of light, no time will have passed when it returns to Earth? So maybe he wasn't just talking physics. Maybe he was talking about making love when no time seems to pass, and isn't it a grand, old, quark-quantum-charmed particle universe when that kind of love-lust happens.

And if he didn't say it, he should've.

I woke up after that first night with my cheeks sore from

smiling in my sleep. For two months I floated in a daze wait-ing for phone calls, which kept happening (much to my sur-prise), and long talks without generational friction (much to my surprise), and laughing a lot (much to my surprise), plus long dinners, long nights, more Einsteinian moments. Waiting gave me plenty of time to work, but I didn't. I kept drifting off daydreaming about this new Reality, thinking it's the only time Reality is any good—when it's new—only it can't last, nature of the beast and all. And then what? It just couldn't last, that was the only certainty. It was too weird, too unexpected, the whole damn thing.

I still should've been happier than a pig in shit—at least temporarily—and I was, but I wasn't. It had been a long time since I'd been so distracted. I liked it and I didn't like it. My self-control and discipline had vanished after one night. I knew, of course, that the fascination would lessen eventually—it had to, it always does—but I grew more and more anxious for the decline to start, so life could move on, settle down, return to normal.

Finally, I couldn't stand it. I took control. There was an upcom-ing writer's conference I'd never attended but suddenly thought I should...at least once...professionally speaking, of course. And maybe I'd stay in New England afterward for a while.

I presented this plan in the most nonchalant manner possible one night during a candlelit dinner. Apparently it wasn't non-chalant enough. After I'd delivered news of my imminent depar-ture, she stopped eating and stared at me.

"What?" I pleaded innocence, practically squirming in my seat, "knowing" I was telling the truth. It was no big deal, I wasn't "planning" anything, I'd be back in a few weeks...or a month...or two. So what? It's a trip.

Finally, I stopped blathering and stuffed my face inside my wineglass, hiding, an old habit when I see trouble coming—and Trouble was on its way by the look I was getting. I half expected a Zeus thunderbolt to sprawl me back in my chair.

"So this is your idea of complete?"

"No! Of course not! Not at all! I'm coming back. I won't be gone long…really…and I'm coming back *right here.*"

I pointed at the table. She continued to stare.

"And I'll write…call…keep in touch. It's a trip, that's all."

Those dark eyes.

"Really. It's no big deal. It's a professional thing."

I don't know why I bothered rambling, knowing perfectly well you can't lie to people who can really "see," even when you're covering your ass by lying to yourself. I waited for her to jump outside her head to check it out, check me out, but apparently she didn't need to see anything on that level. No need for anything that subtle or penetrating.

The meal was almost over; we finished in silence.

"So are you okay?" I asked finally, trying to sound light and cheery over something resembling a lump rising in my throat.

She picked up her plate and headed for the kitchen.

"I have to go."

"What? So soon?"

Like I didn't know this would ruin the evening.

"You're not mad, are you? Why don't we talk about it more?"

She didn't answer until she had her coat on and hit the door. She opened it, then stopped.

"I'm not mad."

Staring one last time, then walking away.

"Hey! I'm not leaving till next week," I called after, feeling more adolescent than I cared to admit. It's so nice being the "older" one.

"Good. You'll have plenty of time to pack." That back over her shoulder, not turning around.

I'll call, I almost shouted, then felt too stupid. I shut the door, not feeling well.

Hey. It'll be fine. You know what you're doing.

Of course I did. I was master of my own destiny again.

I didn't call before leaving. I did, however, attend the conference, not ready to make that much of a liar of myself. It was definitely a high-water mark in my career too. I spent the entire time picking places in New England I wanted to see.

I did send a postcard from Cape Cod, giving the address and phone number of where I stayed finally, but the remaining contents were glib and generically stupid. I didn't hear from her at all.

IT WAS ALMOST TWO MONTHS to the day when I made it back. I don't know what I expected to find when I returned. I guess maybe I figured two months was plenty of time for her to find a new girlfriend, boyfriend, whatever. Hell, maybe she was married and had two kids. I was resigned to accept anything. I really was.

Except I also found myself running scenes of romantic, off-the-chart sexual renewal through my head. I tried to stop but couldn't. During my two-month flight, I'd missed her far more than I cared to admit. For two months I'd fought the truth, writing two stories in record time. Good stories. Delirious with creativity, I'd tried burning her from my mind but failed, the main reason I then tried like hell to convince myself it was a good thing, an inevitable thing if she were seeing someone else already. Or maybe she wouldn't want to see me at all again, not wanting to deal with someone who could, would, up and run away whenever the mood struck. I couldn't blame her for that.

What I got when I walked up to the bar was another dead stop, soul jump, and look: hot, cold, fierce, angry, and distant. I knew right away what I was up against. Big time. Again, I couldn't blame her.

She served me tequila without saying a word. I kept my mouth shut, swallowing every cute greeting that raced through my mind.

"Can I talk to you?" I finally managed to spit out when she served my second drink, setting it down hard in front of me.

She glared at me. "No."

I waited outside until she finished for the night. Seeing me in the parking lot, she walked to her car, climbed in, and drove away.

Next night, I waited outside again. This time she stopped at her car door, turned, and asked, "So when are you leaving again?"

"I'm not."

"Really?"

"Really."

"Never?"

Shit. Never. Who knows about never?

"Never is a—can't we talk about now?" I sighed with exasperation. "Or the time between now and never?"

She drove off without answering.

We played this game for a week. Nothing changed, except any lingering confusion I'd had vanished like fog in a hurricane. I was in love, I was an idiot, and I was miserable. If I'd thought being distracted was inconvenient, being miserable made me utterly worthless. A basset hound looked like Skippy the Canine Clown compared to me when I decided it was hopeless and took up couch-dwelling in blue pajamas, sipping goblets of red wine, listening to Billie Holiday croon her own love misery, all lights off except an open porch door and candles flickering in lumpy wax mountains along the mantel, taking lost love morbidity to new artistic heights.

I'd found Ray Milland's "lost weekend" and turned it into two full weeks when she knocked on my door at three in the morning, moving quickly past me into the heavily shadowed apartment with the same crackling energy as the jagged heat lightning flashing silently outside. I followed wide-eyed and hopeful into the living room. My stomach was located somewhere in the back of my throat.

"This place is a wreck," she declared, spinning around to face me after surveying tangled sheets on the couch, empty wine glasses, crumpled Kleenexes, books, notebooks, newspapers strewn everywhere across the butler's table and floor. "At least you have the door open, so it doesn't *smell* like a dump."

She was wearing a black sleeveless mock T-neck stretched tight into white jeans that were secured by a silver belt. An assortment of silver rings highlighted slender fingers. She stood with her thumbs hooked inside the belt loops and glared at me. It was a stunning pose: sexy, provocative, inviting, and prohibitively angry at once. I stared and gulped.

"So," she demanded, "talk."

"Uhh, sure. Can we sit...down?" I asked weakly, feeling a sharp this-isn't-going-to-be-easy stab in my chest, inhaling deeply, wishing the hard stuff would handle itself because I handled it so poorly on my own.

Moving to the couch first, I tossed the sheets in the chair so she couldn't sit too far away. She stopped, glared at me, then sat in the opposite couch corner, a seething mass of sexy fury I had only moments to tame...

So why is it so damned difficult bringing up the *L* word first? As if saying it is a declaration of a fatal disease or acute character weakness? Why does it always feel like falling off some dizzying height? And finally, why does spilling one's guts always feel like throwing up for real?

I knew this stuff was racing through my mind because I didn't want to open my mouth. But if I didn't, I'd be an even bigger idiot than I'd already been.

I swallowed my stomach and bit the bullet. It was damned hard looking into those dark, angry eyes, but it wouldn't have meant anything if I didn't. She wouldn't have let me get away with it anyway.

"Look. I'm really sorry," I began softly. "Really sorry, really stupid. I can't believe *how* stupid! I just thought I was done with this."

"With me?" she interrupted sharply.

"No! Not you!" I practically shouted, turning quickly on the couch to sit cross-legged facing her. "With just...with this kind of intensity."

Her eyes narrowed ominously.

"And what *kind* of intensity is this?"

I was hedging—she knew it—I knew she knew. Oh, shit! Throat constricting, stomach churning, I got ready to dive off the cliff. I let it out in a big rush, free-falling, scarcely breathing.

"This is—I never thought—" I stopped, feeling tears that had flowed for weeks push at the back of my eyes. "I just never thought I'd be in love again. Not like this. Not ever again... And I freaked and I'm sorry and I really hope...*really* hope...we can try it again."

I practically wheezed the last part, having run out of breath halfway through. My face burned. My body was numb with dread. I sat watching her, totally helpless.

Some anger left her eyes, but not all.

"You're not playing games, are you?"

"No." My voice was barely audible.

"And you won't pull another bullshit disappearing act?"

"Never."

She glanced sideways at me. A faint smile played briefly on her lips, but the eyes were still cautious as she grabbed a pillow before turning to gaze at the flickering candles.

"Okay," she finally said, turning her head to stare at me, no trace of a smile. This was it. No more second chances.

Nausea and tension drained from my body, replaced by the most searing desire I'd ever felt. My crotch, gut, chest, hands, tits—all registered electric heat instantly.

But the huge gulf I'd idiotically created yawned much wider than three feet of couch. I was thinking I had no idea how to close it when she suddenly flung the pillow sideways hard against my chest.

"I'm still mad at you! You know that, I hope!"

I knew. But nowhere near as angry as she'd been.

"I know...I'm sorry," I said, wanting to smile, not daring, returning the pillow to the couch.

Some distance had disappeared.

She grabbed the pillow again, stared at it, then flung it again. I defended myself and laughed. She yanked the pillow back and turned toward me, demanding, "You think this is funny?"

I held up my hands, ready for the next attack, still grinning. "No."

"Then why are you laughing?"

She'd moved onto her knees.

"Because."

"Because why?"

Still waiting for the attack, I held up my arms. "Because," I said, "I think you're going to let me touch you again."

"Oh, you do, do you?"

She inched closer, towering over me, trying to look serious.

"Yes, I do."

"Yeah, right! In your dreams!"

She let go with the pillow again, whipping it harder with her right hand. I deflected it with my forearm then ducked under my arms, laughing while she flailed away, tiny white feathers and blue expletives flying everywhere.

"You son of a—you have no...idea...how goddamn angry... I...have...been...sooooo angry at you!"

She whaled on and on, puffing, grunting, growling, swearing while I laughed, protecting my head, until she collapsed, flushed, sweaty, chest heaving, one hand on my knee, the other clutching a seriously depleted pillow. She looked at its limp form, then at me, grinned, then suddenly started laughing.

"Damn! That felt good!"

I put my hands down and smiled.

"Feel better?"

She nodded, still panting. "Way better! You okay?"

"Yup."

Unable to wait any longer, I slid my hand slowly up her arm, gently stroking the soft inner flesh of forearm up to her elbow. The whole time up and back, she watched my hand. When I returned to her wrist, she slowly looked up, anger finally gone, soft again, inviting.

Finally. The green light!

Next trip with my fingers, I tickled inside her elbow before sliding higher over her shoulder, leaning forward as fingertips of both hands caressed her neck, jaw, face, cheekbones, ending with a kiss. Sweetly, breathlessly—it had been so long!

Eyes closed, I inhaled the smell of skin, warm breath from her nostrils, perfume, shampoo—an intoxicating mix of sweet, salty, tangy, pleasant—then tasted her mouth, hot tongue and lips growing more urgent.

Still kissing, I straddled her on my knees, feeling rough jeans and copper buttons through the thin cotton of my pajama crotch. Hot juice gushed between my legs in anticipation.

It was almost too rich. I leaned back, hands still cradling her face. It was a gorgeous sight, smell, touch, moment. I wanted to say thank you, but choked, heart pounding. Thunder roaring in my ears accompanied the lightning outside.

She held my gaze for a chest-tearing eternity, causing tears to push behind my eyes again, thinking about what I'd almost lost.

"Oh, you're not going mushy on me, are you?" she whispered, gently running fingers along my chin, eyes watering too.

I shook my head. I couldn't answer.

"Wait. I know what'll distract you."

She slipped both hands under my top, stroking my stomach before gliding to my breasts, cupping them, massaging, tickling both hard nipples with the palms of her hands.

I inhaled sharply.

"You're right! That's distracting!" I gasped, brushing away a tear before covering her hands with mine as she massaged my breasts. "Damn, that feels good!" I groaned. A surge of electricity hot-wired my crotch. Pulling, tugging, tossing clothes everywhere, we ended up naked in feather down, nibbling, sucking, stroking, thighs rocking into soaked crotches, fingers into hot achy holes, hungry horny humping finally, urgent, fire heat on heat, dancing the ultimate dance: Love Fucking!

Resting after our initial fever, we lay listening to light rain finally falling, making quiet love, whispering small talk, sucking it all in through sight, smell, touch until fingertips tingled again, a sure sign renewed desire was ready to surge again.

Rain had lowered the temperature, evaporating our sweat to pleasant coolness. A slight breeze through the open porch door ruffled a pillow feather against my right areola causing the nipple to respond instantly, gorging, puckering.

"Ooooo, naughty wind," I said, laughing. "It's playing with me. It wants to play too."

She leaned onto an elbow and smiled at me.

"It wasn't the wind."

"Ah! You're the wind. You blew it over my nipple. Nice. Subtle, but definitely effective. Lovely. Let's see…light touch here…"

I picked up a tiny white feather and twirled it between my fingers, touching her nipple with the spinning end.

"…achy spasm…"

Trailing it down her stomach, I stopped to twirl inside her navel.

"…down here."

I moved again to tease her soft inner thighs.

"I didn't blow it," she replied, eyelids drooping as her legs eased apart.

"What?"

I was too busy playing, touching the twirling feather to her swollen clit, making my own throb in response.

"I said…" she repeated, inhaling sharply, "I didn't blow it."

"Then what did you do?" I asked innocently.

"Watch."

She closed her eyes. A moment passed before another feather moved, swirling around my other nipple. I frowned, puzzled. I hadn't felt a breeze or breath, yet the feather had definitely moved. Popping open her eyes, she cocked her head, waiting for me to figure it out. Finally, it hit me.

"Oh, shit! You didn't!"

She grinned. "You said you liked that stuff. Cool, huh?"

Cool wasn't the word for it; *sensational* was the word.

"Have you ever done that before?"

"No. Never tried."

"Whoa! Do it again!"

She closed her eyes and made the feather dance again. Unbelievable!

"Parapsychology labs would love to get you!" I said, still incredulous.

"Hang on. I want to try something," she said, sitting up, straddling me, bare ass resting on my thighs and soaked bush.

She picked up the pillow, grabbed the torn seam, and asked, "Can I?"

"For the sake of science, sure."

"Fuck science. I want to play."

She ripped the seam open, dumping the remaining feathers onto my stomach.

"What're you going to do?"

"Wait and see."

She spread the downy feathers with both hands over my bare skin, covering both breasts, squeezing each nipple between thumb and forefinger in the process. I grunted my approval, closed my eyes and arched my back, pushing my thighs against her ass, rocking her forward making the wet tangles of our pubic mounds almost kiss, whispering heat back and forth.

"Hold still," she commanded. "I have to concentrate."

I lay back and watched as she sat, eyes closed. Kneeling, naked, she sat back on her heels, hands resting on her thighs. Soft flickering candlelight cast elegant shadows over the sexy, sensual curves of her body.

"You're really gorgeous, you know that?" I whispered.

She smiled quickly, then frowned, scolding, "Don't distract me."

This time long moments passed with nothing happening. Then it started. Slowly one feather barely moved, then another trembled, lay still, trembled again, before more and more moved, fluttering until each one came alive, dancing! The lightest, softest, most incredible down tickling swirled over my bare tits, stomach, armpits, shoulders, neck!

I gazed at the amazing display before closing my eyes, giving in to the feeling, grinning, giggling—it was so delightful—until I burst out laughing at the utter deliciousness of the sensation.

"How does it feel?"

"A-mazing! It's heavenly! I wish I could do this, so you could feel it!"

"There's some on my thighs. I have a good idea."

"It's so light, the touch. Soooo stimulating! Whoa! Less is definitely more!"

I was practically breathless when she finally stopped, leaning forward to kiss me, easing her body on top of mine.

"What else can you do?"

"Lots of things."

She nibbled my right earlobe before flicking her tongue inside.

"That's not psychic," I laughed. "That's reptilian."

"I know," she said, moving her mouth to one tit, lip-sucking the nipple, teasing with her tongue then pulling hard between teeth. "And that's mammalian."

"But what about psychic?" I gasped, giving in completely to the electric current rocking my body.

"Stick around," she whispered provocatively, tongue rimming my belly button. "You just might find out."

My whole body shivered, thrilled by the prospect, feeling feathers flutter then dance, suddenly swirling, ready to fly, as her head and tongue sloooooowly migrated south...

—LIFELONG—

Terry Wolverton

AFTER FRAN DIED, Carolyn's friends all told her to get Fran's things cleared out of the house as quickly as she could. They'd barely been home from the cemetery an hour, had scarcely finished setting out the platters of cold chicken and sliced roast beef, bowls of carrot-raisin and potato salads, loaves of bread and tins of brownies on the dining room table, the one Fran had spent all winter building twenty years ago, before the assembled intimates began giving Carolyn advice.

"I'll come over early next week and help you box things up and take them over to the thrift shop," Irene announced. She looked funny, bustling around the kitchen in a wool skirt that stretched tight over her broad girth. Her legs seemed naked in nylon stockings in a way they never did in shorts. Somehow she'd been delegated the task of making the coffee, though everyone knew Irene always brewed it thick as mud.

"That's a good idea," Jean affirmed in the Southern drawl she'd never managed to shake. She was busy dabbing at a spot of mustard that had slid from her sandwich onto the front of her good white shirt. "Better to do it fast and get it over with."

"You've got to make a new life for yourself," Peg declared in a tone at once bossy and solicitous. She tossed her sleek blond pageboy. "That's what Fran would want."

Carolyn believed, but did not say, that what Fran would want was to still be here with Carolyn in the old life they had shared for thirty-two-and-a-half years. She could imagine Fran circling the dining room table, piling her plate high with her friends' cooking, the way she always did, at Peg's annual Fourth of July barbecue, at Lois's traditional New Year's Eve bash. Fran would have easily dispensed with their unsolicited wisdom, saying, "Now, don't poke your nose in where it doesn't belong," firmly, but without a trace of rancor.

Carolyn wasn't quite able to manage that; instead she'd ducked beneath her friends' well-meaning words, neither agreeing nor protesting, as if the swell of counsel were a giant wave breaking over her. She hoped that, when she surfaced, the women would all be gone and she could go lie down alone in the bed where she and Fran had slept since they were both young women, the bed in which Fran had died only three days ago. Carolyn wanted to lie there in the dark, smelling whatever traces of Fran remained, drawing them deep inside where they could not be taken away.

It wasn't that Carolyn didn't love their friends, women she and Fran had known for decades, had in fact grown up and grown old with. She owed them debts she could never begin to repay. Lois had come every day to read to Fran during the long, awful siege of chemotherapy, her voice patient and melodious. Jean was the one who'd driven them home the day the doctor had told Fran, "There's nothing more we can do," and had stoically held back her own tears in order to comfort Carolyn.

Peg had sat with Fran for hours going over bank statements and legal documents, taking care of unresolved business. Irene had been the one to call the others, the night she'd heard from Carolyn that Fran was gone. Without their devoted attention, their resolve and practicality, Carolyn couldn't imagine how she would have gotten through these last ten months. Even now her house was cleaned, her refrigerator bursting with food, due to the ministrations of these women.

Still, it was pure relief to close the door on the last of them, finicky Evelyn, whom Carolyn found scouring the stove top with a copper Chore Boy. Evelyn had always gotten on Fran's nerves, and Carolyn knew Fran would not have had any qualms about saying, "Evelyn, just stop that. It's time to go home." Carolyn had never been blunt with people; it was not her way. She was the kind of woman who would rather be put out herself than inconvenience another. She gently approached Evelyn and said bashfully, "I think it's clean enough."

Evelyn, who always took even the gentlest correction as a severe rebuke, grew flustered. "Oh, I'm sorry, I just thought I'd help out." Her wheedling tone made Carolyn feel guilty to have spoken, but, remembering Fran, she said, "Thanks so much. I'm just a little tired now," and Evelyn scuttled away.

Tired she was. Carolyn had taken to sitting up beside Fran at night for the last few weeks, dozing but alert to every shift in Fran's breathing, every moan or movement. The last two nights, ever since Fran had been bundled into a plastic bag and carried away, Carolyn had simply wandered the house, a stranger to the rooms they'd occupied for nearly three decades.

She felt suddenly as if every ounce of energy had been sucked from her sixty-year-old body, a gas tank drained of even the fumes, nothing left to fuel her. Fran had always followed an elaborate ritual of closing up the house for the night, checking the locks on the doors and windows, shutting off the lamps and switching on nightlights. Even at her sickest she'd pestered Carolyn to follow the routine, rasping from her bed, "Don't forget to check the basement latch," and Carolyn had faithfully obliged. Tonight, though, Carolyn hadn't the stamina. She couldn't quite recall if she'd locked the front door behind Evelyn, but neither could she bring herself to check it.

Guiltily, she collapsed onto the bed without even removing her clothes. Lois had tried yesterday to change the sheets, but Carolyn had diverted her by asking her to drive to the airport to pick up the cousin of Fran's who'd flown in for the service. "You can't leave those on there," Lois objected, waving her delicate hands. "She was so ill." But Carolyn had retorted, "It was cancer, Lois, I'm not going to catch it." The sickness and the drugs and the process of dying had all changed Fran's scent, from salty and robust into something softer, sweet and pungent, the aroma of decay, but even this now was dear to Carolyn. She hugged Fran's pillow to her chest and inhaled. It was not like having Fran there with her, but it was like having a memory.

ON MONDAY MORNING of the following week, Irene arrived at eight in her van; Peg was right behind her in her BMW convertible. Both vehicles were laden with empty cartons, carefully preserved in closets and attics for just such an occasion. Watching them confer in her driveway, Carolyn was transported back years to when Irene had helped Fran and Carolyn move into this house, back when they were young. Irene had owned a truck then, a Ford, a red one, in which she took a lot of pride. Then as now, she was a big woman, athletic, and she was always being called upon to help move the women in their circle.

It had been a hot day, September; they'd started early in the morning and by mid afternoon were sitting around with cold beers in what had then been the scruffy, untended backyard. Jean had come over later to help unpack, her nurse's uniform exchanged for dungarees, and had immediately begun instructing Carolyn in what she ought to do to fix up the yard ("I'd pull out those ratty-looking shrubs and get a flowerbed going along the garage. And if you plant a citrus tree there in the back, in a few years you'll have fruit *and* shade!"). To this day, Carolyn enjoyed the Meyer lemons she plucked from that tree.

Peg was the agent who'd sold them the house, and when she stopped by later that night with a casserole dish and a bottle of wine to check on how they were settling in, she'd been only too happy to pour a glass and join the other women, her high heels making little holes in the dirt of the backyard. They hadn't even known Lois then, Carolyn recalled, but met her not too long after that.

Now Carolyn waited until the doorbell rang to open the door, less happy than she wanted to be to see their kind, determined faces. Irene had retired from teaching high school geometry two years earlier, and was dressed as she now was most days, in a relaxed pair of cotton slacks and a tidy, oversize T-shirt that hugged an ample torso. Today's T-shirt bore the logo of the senior women's softball team for which she pitched. Although she scarcely needed the money, Peg still kept her hand in real estate, and her tailored linen suit signaled that she had clients scheduled for later that day. Carolyn greeted them with hugs, assuring the two that she'd been sleeping just fine, waving away Peg's offer of a few Xanax.

"I've got the van cleared out and we're ready to haul," Irene announced, but Carolyn balked.

"I'm don't think I'm quite ready to do that," she said meekly, looking away from them at the view outside the kitchen window.

"I don't think you oughta drag your feet on this," Peg protested, dropping her trim leather handbag onto the kitchen counter. "The longer you put it off, the more painful it's going to be."

Ordinarily this group could bully Carolyn into almost anything. Not that they were cruel or mean-spirited; they were simply women with forcefully held opinions, and they certainly seemed to know more of the world than she did. Over the years they'd persuaded her to go camping in the High Sierras (where she'd gotten altitude sickness and had to be carried down the mountain on the back of a mule), to drink margaritas in Oaxaca (and she *had* gotten violently ill, just as she'd predicted), to invest in a mutual fund (which had turned a handsome profit), and to sell her 1966 Mustang, something she still regretted having done.

Carolyn would often look to Fran for counsel in these circumstances. Fran always seemed able to make up her own mind, and once she had, nothing anyone could say would sway her. Only Peg had the temerity to really contradict her, but Fran had a way of holding her ground and making it look effortless. Fran had never tried to influence Carolyn in her decisions, though. Always, when asked for her opinion, she would declare, "Whatever you want to do is okay by me."

Carolyn raised her chin in that stubborn way Fran used to. This time she met their eyes and said again, "I'm not ready. I appreciate all your help, but I have to take this at my own pace."

Peg and Irene exchanged glances. "It's not going to do you any good to put this off..." Peg started to argue, but Irene cut her off.

"That's okay, honey," Irene soothed in a jocular tone, running a meaty hand through her wild gray hair. "You just take your time. We don't mean to come in here like gangbusters and tell you what to do. Just let us know when you're ready, and we'll be here to help."

As the two women backed out of the door, Carolyn knew that within the hour everyone in their small circle would be informed of this development. Peg would no more than have backed out the driveway before she'd be on her cellular phone to Lois and then perhaps to Evelyn. Irene would drop by Jean's condo on the way home and pry her attention from the soaps. Amongst the five of them, plans would be suggested and discarded, strategies outlined and refined, all aimed at tackling the problem of Carolyn.

Once they were gone, it seemed more possible to hold on to the feeling of Fran. Carolyn ambled into the living room and sank onto the flowered couch. She was unaccustomed to having nothing to do; she'd only taken her retirement from the phone company once Fran started getting sick, and since that time she'd had her hands full with Fran's treatments and finally, with her dying. Although both Lois and Evelyn had lectured Carolyn about the importance of keeping busy, at this moment she was grateful for her leisure, grateful to have nothing more to do than to sit in her living room and listen to the birdsong beyond the window.

Her eyes strayed over the familiar objects in the living room, the worn recliner draped with a plaid blanket, a basket of shells collected from some long-ago Florida vacation. On the mantle above the fireplace was a framed photograph of herself and Fran, taken thirty-two years before. Carolyn rose to retrieve the photo, carrying it back to the couch. She studied the young faces that stared up at her, so fearless and unknowing. In the snapshot, Fran sported a short thatch of hair that had not changed substantially in style from that time to a few days ago, only its carroty color, which had first dimmed, then paled to white over the progression of years. Carolyn's own hair had been long then, an unimpressive shade of brown, but she had cut it no more than a year after this photo was taken and worn it short ever since.

When she met Fran she'd been twenty-eight and already destined, seemingly, to be an old maid. Most of her friends had married right out of high school, but boys had never shown much interest in Carolyn. This would not have seemed cataclysmic to her had it not been so distressing to her mother, who regularly predicted that Carolyn would end up alone and bitter. At the age of twenty, Carolyn had taken a job at the phone company, where she'd received regular promotions until she was making enough to move out of her mother's home and get her own apartment. She liked living on her own, but it did get lonely, so when some of the women in her department started a bowling team, she'd gratefully agreed to join.

The married women on the team were eager to have a night away from their husbands, and the single ones were hoping to meet men. Only Carolyn was genuinely interested in bowling, and she grew impatient with the way the game lagged while her teammates flirted or gossiped about the men they'd left at home.

Fran had been on a team that bowled on the same night as Carolyn's. Carolyn had noticed her, and admired the little shake of the head she always gave when she bowled a strike, as if to deny any pride in her accomplishment. Although Carolyn didn't remember it when she was introduced to them later, both Irene and Jean were on that team with Fran as well.

They'd only met because one of Carolyn's teammates, a peroxide blond whose name Carolyn could no longer remember, had gone off with a man she'd met in the bar and stranded Carolyn without a ride home.

"You don't mind, do ya, hon? Something real important just came up!" The woman had given a lopsided wink from beneath her white bangs, as if, of course, Carolyn would understand and share her priorities.

Carolyn was asking the man behind the counter about bus schedules when Fran walked up. "I couldn't help but overhear that you got stuck here. If you want, I could give you a ride home."

Something about the even gaze of Fran's blue eyes, the straightforward way in which she spoke, made Carolyn forget to be shy, and she was glad to accept the offer. Just before Fran had dropped her off at the apartment, she'd asked Carolyn if she'd like to go to dinner the following night, and again Carolyn had said yes. She had no words in her vocabulary for the kind of woman Fran was—indeed, the kind of woman Carolyn was herself—but she had felt a sense of comfort and trust in Fran's presence that she never thought to question.

Years later she would ask Fran how she could have known about Carolyn, what trait or sign had clued her that Carolyn could be approached. Fran would shrug, insist there was no signal, no set of characteristics. She'd point to Peg, who had her blond hair done every week and always wore skirts and high heels, or to Evelyn, who'd been married and raised two children. "I saw you watching me," she finally explained, "and just thought I'd take a chance."

Carolyn knew there must have been some gossip at work when she started seeing Fran regularly, but nobody said anything to her face. The office bowling team disbanded after just one season, but by then she'd met Irene and Jean and others, a tightly knit network of friends who played sports, went to the movies, took vacations, and shot pool together in a tiny, dark bar on a side street in Hollywood. Her mother had been glad to see she finally had a "friend" but had never relented in her disappointment that her daughter had remained unwed.

The photo she now held in her hands had been taken by Jean at a picnic, perhaps a month after Fran drove Carolyn home from the bowling alley. It was a Sunday afternoon, one of those glorious February days in Southern California where the temperature soars to bring a foretaste of summer. What she remembered most about the day was that it was the first time Fran had kissed her.

"Come take a walk with me," Fran had encouraged, almost as soon as the group has pitched their blankets and arranged their baskets and coolers.

"Hey, where're you going with my first basewoman?" Irene hollered after them. She was trying to organize a little softball, but Fran advised her to start without them.

Fran had a sure, confident stride that on a man might be called a swagger, but she never appeared cocky or boastful. She seemed to know the trail that led them deeper into a stand of trees, and there she kissed Carolyn without apology. All of Carolyn's mother's predictions of a lonely future melted away in those prolonged kisses.

A while later they made their way back, where the women greeted them with knowing grins and Jean had snapped the picture. There was gentle teasing, which made Carolyn blush and Fran say, "Don't you women have anything better to do?" Still, no one on that day, not even Fran and Carolyn, could have predicted that their bond would be lifelong.

It was a couple of months after the picnic when Carolyn learned that Fran and Jean had once been in love. They were out on a Friday night, shooting pool, drinking a couple of beers. Fran was showing Carolyn how to bank, her arms around

Carolyn as she guided the cue. From the other end of the table Jean drawled, "I remember when you gave me that lesson!" She gave a broad wink to the others, and the unflappable Fran had actually blushed.

"It was five years ago, it doesn't mean anything," Fran had insisted in the bar's tiny bathroom, while Carolyn had sobbed from inside the stall, "But you see her all the time. Isn't that because you're still in love with her?" Only the passage of time had convinced Carolyn that the bond between Fran and Jean was one of deep friendship, almost familial, rooted certainly in their history of intimacy but transmuted into something different.

It had happened to others within their circle of friends. They'd first met Lois when Peg started going out with her. Lois was a dance instructor, and perhaps they'd all fallen a little in love with the dark hair she piled atop her head, her dark eyes and fluid gestures. Like all of Peg's affairs, it lasted only a few months, but Lois had remained part of the group, bonded to them.

Evelyn had lived with Irene for seven years; Irene had helped her raise her children, two boys who were a handful. They'd fought almost the whole time, and Carolyn could remember nights Irene had spent drinking beer with Fran in their kitchen, unable to go home because Evelyn had thrown her out. Irene and Evelyn's breakup had been no less dramatic, full of accusation and blame, but somehow Evelyn too had been retained, held within the circle. Others came and went, passions cooling not into friendship but bitter animosity or worse, indifference.

Only she and Fran had lasted, all these years.

For all her drive and glamour, Peg had had nothing steady, nothing that lasted beyond six or nine months, a year at most. For the past decade she'd been drawn to a parade of ever-younger women, women who wanted to go dancing at late-night clubs, women with tattoos, women who found nothing more tiresome than talking with a group of women nearly old enough to be their grandmothers. Jean haunted a series of self-help groups, with names like "True Love After Fifty" and

"Overcoming Fears of Intimacy," but still managed to disapprove of everyone to whom she was introduced.

Fifteen years ago, Lois had fallen in love with a woman who lived in Mexico; since neither would give up her homeland for the other, they saw each other once or twice a year, exchanged increasingly infrequent letters and phone calls. After Irene, Evelyn claimed to have given up, insisting that she was most contented when she was alone, making an art of solitude, yet in private she was always asking, "Isn't there someone you could introduce me to?" Irene was currently courting a widow from the softball team, who seemed definitely flattered but who, Irene's friends had decided, hadn't a clue about the nature of Irene's overtures.

Over the years, their friends had marveled at the couple's longevity. They'd been frequently asked—by a friend in the throes of heartbreak or by her stricken ex—to what they owed their constancy. These desperate women were looking for a formula, some magic, and they always seemed a little let down by Fran's terse reply, "It's hard work."

For Carolyn, it never seemed like work, or at least, not the onerous kind. It was work like raking leaves on a bright October morning, when the sky is a crisp blue and the sun warms your back but not too much, and you feel thankful for the task. It was work like slicing apples for a pie, stealing a tart wedge to munch on and the smell of cinnamon flooding your mouth. She never knew what to say to the red-eyed women that pressed for her secret. They always seemed to be wanting something different than whatever they had, while she had never wanted anything but Fran.

A swell of tears now threatened to overwhelm her. To escape it, Carolyn hoisted her body from the hold of the couch and made her way outside to the garage Fran had used as a tool shed. She pushed open the door, spilling warmth and daylight into the dark, cool space. A swarm of scents engulfed her—sawdust and solvents, dried leaves and gasoline. Fran had not been able to come out here the last couple of months, and a fine layer of dust covered the woodworking benches, but the rows of tools still hung in orderly progression, everything in top repair. Fran had once told her, "I'm happiest when I know I've made something with my own hands," and Carolyn had envied the wood, transformed beneath Fran's careful, determined fingers. Carolyn ran her palm lightly over the ragged teeth of a saw blade. How could Irene and Peg and the rest really think she would want to give these things away?

Carolyn sat in the middle of the cement floor, feeling its cool dampness seep into her hips and legs. Tonight they would ache, she knew, with no one there to rub them till she fell asleep, but for the moment she didn't care. Surrounded by planks of planed wood, she had a feeling like she used to get in church when she was a little girl, a sense of wonder and vastness. As when she'd been a child, awe made her turn her face in the direction of the sky. She stared up into the rough grain of the wood ceiling, eyes tracing the patterns she found.

It was then she noticed a brown cardboard carton poised on the rafters, and without even needing to investigate, she suddenly remembered what it was. As if it were yesterday, Carolyn recalled the morning years ago when Peg had zoomed into their driveway, this box poking out the top of her little red MG. "I can't have this stuff in my house anymore," Peg had insisted, referring to the contents of the carton, things that Lois had left behind when their relationship ended. This was in the first few weeks of their separation, when activities had to be planned with care so as not to include both women. Fran had patiently agreed to take the carton off Peg's hands, intending to give the items over to a rummage sale, but she must have forgotten all about it.

Carolyn rose from the floor to drag the wooden stepladder into the center of the room. She opened it up, making sure to place the stops in a locked position. Slowly, she climbed, coming to precarious balance on the top step to reach the carton. "Easy does it, now," she heard Fran say, and it steadied her.

The carton was coated with dust and left a trail of grime across her sweater as she hugged it to her chest to carry it down. Thorough, wanting to leave this room as Fran had left it, she returned the ladder to its place against the wall before resettling herself on the cement floor and turning her attention to the box.

On the lid, still visible through the accumulated layers of soot, the word LOIS was slashed in Peg's impatient hand. Carolyn slit the tape that held the lid in place and opened it. Despite the tape, a few generations of spiders had nested in the top of the carton, leaving behind the woolly circles of abandoned egg sacs, but the contents seemed undisturbed. The items inside were commonplace: some novels, a few vinyl record albums, an old pair of suede boots, a silk shirt the shade of periwinkle—Lois's favorite color—and a still-new-looking porcelain-faced doll that Carolyn suspected had been a gift to Lois from Peg. For Carolyn, they were simply objects, yet for Peg they'd held the power to keep her locked in the past.

The women in their circle had always helped each other this way, moving one's possessions to a new home after a traumatic breakup, pitching in to paint rooms or lay new carpet in the effort to blot out memory. They'd grown accustomed to starting over, trying again, believing that just around the corner would be perfect love, enduring companionship. It was the same for them at sixty as it had been at thirty: With the demise of each relationship, they cleaned out their closets, sweeping away the evidence of failure, of dashed hope, and resolved to start over, to get on with their lives.

Though not unkind, she and Fran had always felt a little smug, observing the repeated drama in the lives of their friends. Perhaps the two of them had even quietly mocked these efforts to begin anew, the eternal optimism, but on this morning it seemed to Carolyn that these women had an awesome bravery. She could not help marveling at it, this skill they'd used to survive the disappointments of the years, this secret they were trying to share with her now.

And understanding this, she could finally be grateful, humbled in fact by their generosity. They, of course, had lost Fran too, but they marshaled themselves to come to Carolyn's aid with all the knowledge they possessed.

Still, she knew she did not share their courage. She was not like the widows on Irene's softball team, seeking out new hobbies, keeping busy; not like her friends, embracing the future, picking up the pieces to try to fashion a new life. Her life had been with Fran and she resolved to not give up one more bit of it without a fight.

She gathered herself up off the floor once more, clutching the box, feeling the creak of her bones as she stood, giving the workbench a last loving stroke with her hand before she left the garage. Her friends would be disappointed in her, she knew, but they would come to accept it, even if they never understood. That was how they were with each other.

—PORTRAIT OF THE ARTIST—

Sally Bellerose

I'M AN EXOTIC DANCER. I strut my stuff under hot lights on a stage raised above a bar. For money. For men. It's a job. When I'm feeling uppity I call it a profession.

The Top of the Hill, the club where I work, has a group photo of the dancers posted outside the back entrance. It's a big glossy studio portrait in one of those deep wooden frames with a glass front and a lock on the side to protect it from weather and the sticky paws of some small-time thief. A five-by-seven of the same shot is for sale inside for $1.75. Half dressed, we're a female version of the Village People. Except we don't get to sing, travel, or be on TV. And we only make $500 a week. Not that I'm complaining. We work hard for our money, but it's only four hours a night. Try standing on your feet eight hours a day, five days in a row for $350 at the Super Stop and Shop and you'll see what I like about this job.

None of the girls have agents or publicists or financial managers, but we do have our own personal themes. In the photo each girl's name and theme is written over her head in gold letters. Under the picture in the same gold ink are the words "A Portrait of the Artists."

I'm Rita, "The Athlete." Some guys get off watching the strong, take-charge type prance across the stage. All the girls are athletic, but on me it shows. Thick legs, Popeye biceps, round muscular butt. My costume is bicycle shorts cropped off halfway up my glutes and the lowest-cut, least supportive sports bra that the "Title Nine Clothes for a New Generation" catalog offers. If I were really true to type I'd wear sweatpants and bind the jiggle out of my breasts with a "frog top." But like I say, I'm not complaining. It's a cheap, comfortable getup as far as sleazy dancing costumes go.

Dumbbells are my main prop. I have a kick-boxing routine that drives them crazy. After the iron woman routine I'm usually dripping with sweat. When I'm lathered up like that all I have to do is put on a little extra tough-girl attitude and *act* like I could keep it up all night and everybody's happy.

The gig has worked out pretty well for eight years, but now my persona is undergoing some changes. I guess it's a thirty-something crisis. "The Athlete" and I are getting older, the makeup is getting heavier, and I'm embarrassed to admit this, but I take some pride in the integrity of my theme. I know the whole shtick is corny. Still, "The Athlete" is a natural type, not meant to perform in pancake makeup.

This is the only club I've worked. The other girls tell me the bosses at some of these places treat the girls real bad. Jack, my boss, is a peach. If there's trouble, which rarely happens, he stands behind us a hundred percent. When I talk about quitting, he slaps the bar and says, "People should use the gifts God gave them. Rita, you can dance."

I know a lot of people claim to be good at what they do. But I tell you, Jack knows his business: I can dance. Which is why it's time to go. I like being someone who's good at what she does. I want to leave while the music's still hot. Most of our customers are second-shift mill workers who come in to relax with a beer before going home to their sleeping wives. I like these guys. It's the occasional jerk who has to prove his manhood that I *don't* like. I'm no dummy, I know part of "The Athlete's" appeal is that her strength is confined to a two-foot runway. I also realize that most of the guys with the stained fingernails understand all too well about the demands and constraints of the workplace. They respect that the dancers have a job to do, and they leave us alone to do it.

My lover, Lisa, will talk your ear off about how patriarchy and heterosexism have messed up the planet. She teaches queer theory at the university. Did I mention I'm a dyke? I didn't want to bring it up too early. I figure, let them get over the exotic-dancer piece first. People won't listen to your story if they don't like certain things about you. If you want to get a fair hearing, or any hearing at all, reel out one socially unacceptable fact at a time.

Anyway, what I'm really sick to death of at the club is the ignorant questions the occasional jerk lays on me. Like, "Aren't you afraid of disease?" What disease do you get from listening to stupid questions? Secondhand smoke and high-heeled sneakers are my biggest health risks. "What's a nice girl like you doing in a place like this?" I swear some guys still pull that one. Then they smirk as if they personally invented irony. My all-time most hated line is, "Does it bother your boyfriend that you dance?" It's not that I mind the guy assuming I'm heterosexual. Most women are heterosexual—not most of the girls I work with, but still, it's a reasonable error. I only have a tenth-grade education. I'm not working my way through graduate school like the girl wonder in *Flashdance,* but I'm smart enough to know that if there's something to feel humiliated about, these guys get a piece of it too. At least I'm getting paid and the beer is free. Why do people you barely know think they can root around in your personal life just because you're a dancer? If a guy is trying to find out if I have a boyfriend, I'd think more of him if he asked that nosy question directly and didn't try to belittle me in the bargain.

Lisa, my girlfriend, is studying the "culture" of exotic dancing, fieldwork for her Ph.D. She writes and writes. Sometimes she reads her writing to me. I like the sound of her voice. I like the way she strokes my hair as she reads. I don't remember much of it because my head is usually on her shoulder and I fall asleep. I don't know what "postmodern" means exactly, but it comes up when she reads, and when I call her my "postmodern pussy bumper" she smiles. Before we met I didn't know the Top of the Hill had culture to study. I'm the native she fell in love with.

Sex with women, sex with men—physically I can be happy either way. I've got a little button. Press it just right, it turns me on. Some people say that makes me bisexual. I say I'm a lesbian because when I hooked up with Lisa, I found a keeper. If I'm going to slap a label on myself, it's going to advertise who I actually sleep with, not announce who I might sleep with if we break up. Lisa and her friends can spend hours talking about the meaning of a loaded word like *lesbian*. When they get together, I like to hang around and read whatever is new from the Quality Paperback Book Club or flip through *Marie Claire*. I like the passion in their voices. I like to hear their cups clink on the coffee table. I like to see Lisa's cheeks flush when she argues. Most of the conversation itself bores me. Lesbian. Bisexual. If I cared what people called me, I wouldn't be an exotic dancer. Lisa says I'm a concrete thinker. Maybe. I don't spend much time thinking about how I think about things.

Anyway, she couldn't care less what I call myself as long as I take her dancing somewhere besides the Top of the Hill once in a while. She likes to watch me dance when it's not a canned routine she's seen fifty times.

The American Legion is the only place in our small town where dykes can dance with one another in peace. The fact that lesbians are only allowed to rent the hall on the third Tuesday of the month drives Lisa crazy. Any other group who gives up $175 plus a $500 security deposit is welcome to the hall whenever it's available. I've got my own selfish reasons for being glad that the club only welcomes us once a month. I dance Thursday through Sunday, so a "Ladies Only" night every thirty days is enough for me. Tuesday is the middle of the weekend as far I'm concerned.

The third Tuesday of last month was one of those muggy spring nights. The scent of sweaty lesbians saturated the air in the American Legion Hall. As soon as we walk in the door Lisa says, "Dance for me, honey?" Which I'm happy to do. She bellies up to the bar, orders a beer, and settles in to watch me and the rest of the girls on the dance floor. There's plenty to watch.

It feels good to dance without makeup and Spandex. I'm laughing, bumping hips, part of the tangle of bodies, when an acquaintance of Lisa's, a communications professor who's spent time in deep conversation on our couch—and by the looks of her moves, has spent an equal amount of time on the dance floor—leans in to speak to me. "Can I ask you a question?" she says. "Would you consider being interviewed for a study I'm working on?"

I cock my head, confused as to why she's talking about this in the middle of "Livin' la Vida Loca." She takes my expression as an invitation to go on.

"It's about class and lesbian relationships. I know Lisa is studying your workplace, and I'm hoping you'll talk to me about how that informs and influences your life as a couple."

I point to my ear, pretending I can't hear over the music. I spot my friend Alyson's red miniskirt and give her a look that says, *Rescue me.* She's a pal, so she wiggles her way over. Her small, competent hands steer my hips from behind, away from the Professor, leaving me free to watch Lisa, who's now sitting with a bunch of our friends at one of the long Formica-topped tables that skirt the room.

Lisa waves to me, tips a beer bottle to her lips, throws her head back, and laughs. She's in her glory. Lesbians have taken over the long buffet tables that have serviced generations of baby showers, First Communion celebrations, and football banquets. Her big breasts bounce joyously under the low-cut neck of her pink jumpsuit, making me very happy. Alyson continues to press her hands into my hips, touring us in a wide circle around the floor. By the time we make a complete 360-degree turn, my girl-friend is leaning against the wall, talking to a woman with a shaved head. Their necks bend and their heads bob.

It's a kick to look out from the dance floor as Alyson steers me in a wide easy arc. What happens off the floor is as much fun to watch as the bump and grind going on in the middle of the room. You can talk and talk about sexuality. Analyze what it means to be attracted to the same sex till the cows come home, and all I'll have to say on the subject is that being in the middle of these girls feels right to me. I could suck up the whole scene in one slurp, even the part that ripples out into the parking lot, where rowdy laughter pierces through Aretha's "Chain, chain, chain..." I con-sider thanking Alyson and excusing myself to answer the call of the loud-mouthed girls in the street, but I love being in the middle of the dance floor too much to leave the American Legion Hall.

It's Alyson who moves away, claimed by her girlfriend, led herself now into a slow grind that makes me think of naked skin between clean sheets. They curve and sway to Marvin Gaye's "What's Goin' On?" Pinned together, billowing apart, like fresh laundry in a breeze.

I travel around the floor alone, but I feel like I'm in the mid-dle of some carefully choreographed routine that involves every other woman in the room. Eventually, I end up shaking my booty across from the Professor again. The DJ must like the Artist Formerly Known As because she plays three Prince songs in a row. When the third song starts, The Professor and I grin at each other to beat the band, united by the fact that we both know the lyrics to "Kiss." We spin around a few times. She's good. I've never been able to master this move. I'm used to danc-ing alone, so a complicated tandem twirl is hard for me. I'm real-ly getting into it when she starts again. "I didn't mean to be intrusive earlier," she says. "I'm interested in how we, as les-bians, negotiate the culture and subculture, especially how we interface class and sexuality. You and Lisa have a fascinating dynamic that dovetails perfectly with my area of interest."

"Lisa's educated and comes from money. I got a GED and dance in a dive. How do we make it together? Is that what you're asking?" I study her face. Her expression matters to me. It's an open face. She nods. I realize the Professor and the Doctor are the only women here I identify only by profession. "What's your name?" I ask.

"Jackie." She smiles attentively.

I decide to show her the same respect I would if I hadn't written her off because of the way she talks and what she does for a living. She reminds me of Lisa in a way, so greedy to understand everybody and everything. Lust for knowledge: It's as legitimate as any other kind of lust, as long as all parties are consenting. I lean in. "Jackie," I say, in a voice made breathy by all this dancing, "I barely know you. My relationship with my girlfriend is private."

"Sorry," she says sincerely, and offers her hand. I take it and she twirls me around on my heels.

When "Kiss" ends we bow to each other and Jackie disappears into the crowd.

I stand alone, thinking that there's a different pecking order on the dance floor, no more or less fair than anywhere else, just different. Education, which side of the tracks you're from, that kind of stuff doesn't matter in the same way. The hierarchy breaks down or at least gets mixed up. Me, I'm stronger, more in control—even if I'm not in character as "The Athlete"—when I dance. Inside the beat I don't feel so inclined to answer other people's questions. I have my own questions—like should I drag my ass over to the Women in Transition Program at the community college and try to get into the RN program? I bet that work would be confining in its own way. No two-foot runways, but plenty of supervisors, doctors, and a whole medical system to reign you in. Still, I think there's an art to nursing that I'd be good at. I could use some of the skills I've learned at the club, like endurance, patience, and dependability. But I'll think about this stuff later.

I came to dance. Annie Lennox is moaning, "Take me to the river." A slow swish-and-sway number. I search the big room for Lisa. Lucky me, she's headed straight for me with that look of fierce tenderness and possession. Wrapped in the sexy comfort of her arms, I feel as if I've taken a seat in the La-Z-Boy after a long night's work. After five years there's a groove to our sex. It's worn, tried and true like the corners of the pages of our favorite passages in *Vixen Love*. We comment on the women at the dance, what they're wearing, who came with who. A group of very young women moves in a sexy slow snake dance, slithering against one another, making as much of a scene, with as much noise and body contact, as possible.

I rub my belly and breasts against Lisa and ask, "Does it ever bother you that I dance at the club? Should we be talking about it? I mean, not just, you know, as some kind of cultural phenomenon?"

"Bother me?" She ponders my question, then grins. "It bothers me just fine."

—EXORCISING—

Jill Dolan

PATSY DARE JOINED OUR HIGH SCHOOL later than the rest of us, came to us from some far-flung Southern place we'd barely heard of. She was a non-Jew in a public school that seemed to us half African-American and half Jewish, although those percentages were probably skewed. Growing up as we did in middle-class, half-double tract houses in an inner-city Pittsburgh neighborhood that segregated neatly into blacks and Jews, the occasional white non-Jew intrigued us—or at least me, always on the lookout for some hint of how to reconcile my own dawning differences with a world that seemed relentlessly the same. So far, taking acting classes at the Pittsburgh Playhouse was my only escape—into other lives through characters in plays and away from my friends and their new, insistent heterosexuality, which I already found myself avoiding without quite knowing why.

To me, Patsy Dare plopped down in our midst to highlight what we were and what the rest of the world wasn't. She lived with her mother in an apartment. Her parents were divorced, which, along with her non-Jewishness, made her highly exotic and vaguely tragic and deeply attractive to me. Here was a girl from a broken home, when all of ours were still intact. I can imagine now the vigor with which the couples in our neighborhood must have

plastered over the cracks in the surfaces of their lives, the res-
olutely wholesome and handsome and normal fronts they presented to people who shared their small half-houses, who saw
their comings and goings and could hear, if they fought, through
the thin walls that joined our separate homes. As a child, though,
I didn't see beyond the surfaces. I thought families stayed together, that children of divorce needed special care, because their lives
were fragmented and fragile, compared to ours.

Patsy wasn't as smart as the rest of us, all the good Jewish
children who'd been raised to strive for high grades and to plan
on sensible majors in the colleges we'd inevitably attend. But
Patsy was a singer and she too liked theater, which bonded us
outside the conventional interests of the rest of my friends. We
took singing lessons together on Saturdays at the Center for the
Musically Talented, an embarrassing name for a school program
that described Patsy better than it did me. She sang well, seemed
to be able to wrap her fearless vocal cords around any musical
genre. She cut a striking figure as a singer; she was tall and had
strawberry-blond hair that I learned only later, when her dark
roots began to show like a runway down either side of her part,
was dyed. She laughed loudly, with a drawling inflection that
made people turn around to see who'd made that peculiar, foreign sound. She was physical and incautious; she liked to poke
you when she talked. I was captivated by her lack of restraint,
by her largeness of self and the way she flung it at you with every
part of her body. "Hey, let's go for burgers," she'd yell at me
after our Saturday classes. We'd eat in a nearby Arby's, where
she'd peer at me across the bolted-down table and say, "You
really should pluck your eyebrows, ya know." I was flattered by
her attention, and embarrassed by my deficiencies as a girl, but
I had no intention of following her suggestions for beauty
makeovers.

Patsy was my first illicit relationship, not because we ever did
anything untoward like having sex or even kissing, but because
I knew I wanted her, that I longed for time alone with her, that I

wanted her to fling her arm around me in that casual, horsey way she had and just draw me into a world so utterly different from my own. I liked being close to her, even though outside of music and theater we had little in common and I rarely knew what to say. I only occasionally talked to any of the girls I had crushes on in high school. I peered out at them through the heavy lids of my desire, looking at them for signs of reciprocity, turning a studied face in their direction, hiding the signs of my own want and need. I'm sure that to Patsy I was a friend, since she was new in town and the castoffs and strangers were always my bailiwick. But to me she was a place I wanted to go, she was a territory I wanted to cover, and I spent hours scheming how to chart my course.

Her mother left town one weekend, and Patsy invited me to spend the night. We went to see *The Exorcist,* both of us terrified beyond words at the movie's horrors. I hoped that our fearful experience of the film might draw us closer together, that our anxiety and trauma would make us turn to each other in the night for comfort and surety. I never planned these scenarios consciously; they were all managed by fantasy and desire, all pictured as hopeful images to which I barely even gave words. That night we'd be sharing her mother's bed, which made me tremble with expectation, although I didn't know what I expected or even wanted. I knew too that the last time I'd slept beside a non-Jewish girl, at an arts camp reunion a year or two before, she'd awakened me in the middle of the night, staring at me in the light that filtered through the motel's plastic curtains. Startled, I'd asked her what was wrong, and she said, "I was looking for your horns. All Jews have horns in their heads, don't they?" I hoped that despite Patsy's charmingly rustic Southernisms, we'd only spend the night talking about Linda Blair's horns and I wouldn't find her combing through my hair for mine.

When we got back from the movie, Patsy's mom's basement apartment felt cramped instead of intimate. Its low ceilings and crowded furniture made us both seem like giants who would

bounce off each other's gawky, awkward angles instead of settling warmly into what I'd imagined as some soothing, soulful
softness. Right away, in that small dark space, I began to doubt
my own fantasies—if I could barely navigate the furniture without banging stupidly about, how could I begin to enact the suave
seduction I'd tried in vain to keep myself from imagining?

Patsy, obviously, was accustomed to fitting her even larger
self around the odd assortment of furniture and moved easily
from the kitchenette/living room into her mother's bedroom. She
dropped her coat and bags everywhere, littering the small room
so that it became an even more impossible maze. I stepped
around her things, guessing at the most appropriate place to
store my own belongings for the evening, trying not to look too
obviously around this small home to figure out why it felt so different from mine. The furniture seemed assembled, rather than
chosen, taken without a fight in the division of marital property
than had landed Patsy and her mother here. The apartment
looked temporary, a place to move through rather than to move
into to stay. Although eventually I lived in more places around
the country than most people I know, the transience of Patsy's
apartment made me nervous then, as though it foreshadowed a
future I wasn't ready to embrace.

Patsy changed her clothes, dropping everything in a heap on
the floor, and hopped happily into the small double bed, enjoying the tremors of fear *The Exorcist* inspired. "Can you believe
her head turned all the way around like that? How'd they
make her rise so far above the bed like that? Wasn't it just disgusting when she spit up all that green shit?" I murmured little
agreements as I stood at the foot of the bed by her mother's
cheap bedroom set, starting to sweat as I tried to figure out
how to change my clothes in front of her without revealing my
body or my shyness. I'd tried hard to be bold all night, talking
as loudly as she did, overstating my reactions to the film,
agreeing with her observations, trying to pretend we were alike
as a way to get close to the difference I craved. But stuck in

front of a dresser mirror that reflected back at the oblivious Patsy all my awkward attempts to hide myself, my utter inability to be casual caught me and began to pull me toward what I would only later recognize as shame.

"D'ya think she'll have to get exorcised again? D'ya think there'll be a sequel?" Lounging against the bed pillows, Patsy's words just tumbled out, unedited, unrehearsed, unimpeded from her brain to her mouth, while I suffered, humiliating myself with my overextended undressing ritual. Time seemed to stretch inexorably through what was probably only a moment.

"I don't know about a sequel," I mumbled, as I debated whether to take off my shirt and then my bra, or to take my bra off under my shirt and then my shirt, as I calculated what I'd reveal and how embarrassed I'd be by choosing any of the available options. I also kicked myself for not getting to this more quickly, for now being forced to put on a show for her because she'd been so blithe and fast, as though she undressed in front of someone everyday. I tried to cover the moment with chat, but my tongue got as tied as my bra straps and my loud red face broadcast my mortification.

My body-shyness was paralyzing to me, not, I think, because I was self-conscious about being seen by someone, but because I was afraid my body would reveal other things, because I worried that written on my skin was the truth about my difference. I stayed locked in that panicked fear for years, every time I had to undress in a girls' locker room, or change my clothes for movement classes in the women's bathroom as a theater major in college or be anything but fully dressed anywhere, anytime. I was afraid my skin would tell my story, that I'd be uncovered as a spy, an infiltrator, as someone who didn't belong among other women, because she wanted them too much, because she didn't know how to be casual with herself or with others, like them, because she was afraid her desire made her male.

That moment with Patsy dragged on forever, although it was probably just seconds for her, while she waited for me to get to

bed. "What are you doing over there?" she asked, finally noticing she was talking to my back or to my reflection in the mirror instead of to me. Somehow I accomplished the awful task
and crawled in between her mother's sheets, longing for and terrified of this moment of proximity, determined not to be the
first one to make contact. We did cling to each other, for a
moment, convincing each other of how scared we were. Then
she quickly drifted off to sleep, leaving me alone with my
thwarted anticipation for something I couldn't even describe. I
only knew it wasn't enough, that I needed more, that I was tortured just lying beside her, taut with my own awareness of how
close her body was to mine, yet how removed she was from me,
how alone I was in a night that seemed interminable, once she
left me in it by myself.

I SPENT MANY NIGHTS like that after Patsy, with women beside
me whose sleep made them inaccessible, removed, as though they
weren't there, except for the necessity they inspired for me to be
quiet and still, when my mind raced and my senses quickened and
I lay, watchful and awake, as though it were the middle of a very
strange day. I lost many nights beside straight women, waiting for
them to wake up and be with me, to realize my need, my alone-
ness, to roll over and see me caught in it, to rescue me from it and
chase away the demons that found me, always in the night.
Always it was desire, taunting me, challenging me, mocking me,
daring me to do something about it, to recognize it, to go where
I could sate it, say it, be everything it tempted me toward. Those
beds were prisons, where I stood guard against myself, terrified
I'd slip up and move toward someone in my sleep, say something
that revealed what I really was, what I really wanted, that uncovered this repugnancy that *was* my desire, for which I was sure I'd
be stoned, tarred, feathered, and exiled. When I saw *Ryan's
Daughter*, not many years after *The Exorcist*, I was haunted by
Sarah Miles's face, twisted with longing for her inappropriate
lover, caught finally by the townspeople who'd learned her secret,

exposed on the streets, surrounded, her hair shorn, her body covered with tar and feathers, shamed. I had internalized my own damnation so thoroughly, I didn't even need this to happen. I was already doing it to myself. Those nights of watchfulness beside girls I wanted to love were just a taste of the torment I was capable of putting myself through, that I'd somehow consigned myself to, for as long as it took, I supposed, to draw this thing inside me out so that I could squash it, silence it, dissolve the terror it caused me, exorcise it, and put it and myself finally to rest.

Patsy Dare and I drifted apart, soon after our sleepover. I gave up the illusion that I could sing and quit going to the Center for the Musically Talented; our class schedules stopped overlapping; and I committed myself more and more to theater, where my new crushes on women were just as elusive, but because of the pretend intimacy of the stage, more fulfilling. Patsy didn't come to our tenth high school reunion, or our twentieth, to which I brought my by then longtime lesbian partner. I stopped looking out for Patsy, stopped wondering what color her hair would be now or if her irrepressible, flailing, insistent self had ever been subdued or tamed. And I never saw the sequel to *The Exorcist*.

—A FEW SMALL THINGS OUT OF PLACE—

Katherine Granfield

WE ALL CAME TOGETHER for lunch. Nan and Rhonda came from high school, and I came from work. If you hadn't known better, you might have thought we met on purpose, but that wasn't true. We dodged each other in the kitchen and ended up on the same couch watching TV, not because of our affection for each other but because of our disaffection with the alternatives. I owned my own store, but after ten years it didn't make any difference: I still snuck out for lunch like—well, a schoolchild playing hooky. Home was ham sandwiches and chips and soda and a soft couch and the dog on the floor and no one to tell us what to do or demand service.

Nan was my near namesake and daughter. Rhonda was her best friend. Nan wore a letter jacket, though her affair with athletics was long over; Rhonda wore a dung-black leather jacket and storm trooper boots, and no matter how fastidiously she went outside to smoke and tipped the ashes into an empty soda can and crushed the butts out on the cement and took them to the garbage, still she brought the exotic aura of char and nicotine back into the house with her. Rhonda was a year older than Nan. She was not the friend I would have chosen for my daughter, but she was the friend Nan had chosen for me, or in spite of me.

"How's business, Nancy?" Rhonda would inevitably ask whenever we met in front of the refrigerator. She liked to use my name and accost me with her eyes.

"Business is fine," I'd inevitably reply. I sold cameras, but we never got to that level of specificity. I suspected Rhonda had no knowledge of cameras and no real interest in the well-being of my business. The encounters were simply a running provocation, a piece of performance art or guerrilla theater.

I didn't mind if Rhonda wanted to be Nan's fist, Nan's champion, and go tilting against my business success. It was the standard complaint of the dependent and preresponsible against the responsible, and I was perfectly comfortable with my solvency. I did mind her saying it as if we were talking about something else, though, about something deeply personal—implying an intimate knowledge that transcended even the voluminous intelligence she no doubt had from Nan, a knowledge that she placed before me, with her insinuating phrase, like blackmail. *What do you mean?* I wanted to say. *How do you know? What is your price?* But I didn't. We never got to that level of specificity.

One day in the kitchen I was standing in front of the magnet-studded refrigerator, dreaming, when a pair of foreign hands suddenly fastened about my waist and seized me from behind. It was noon and one of our lunches, and I was holding a mayonnaise jar. As I spun, the jar flew from my fingers and tumbled to the floor. I cringed at the sound of its impact. Naturally my assailant was Rhonda; I registered that recognition even as my body was overtaken by waves of chemical terror.

As we stared at each other, though, I discovered one more thing to be amazed about: We *both* seemed surprised to be there. Rhonda didn't look like a provocateur at all, but like a startled motorist facing me, the startled deer. She seemed as unable to recall her inappropriate hands as I was unable to recall my blush. I forced myself to look down past her fingers to the floor. Miraculously, the jar was unbroken.

I became convinced we were having an extraordinary experience. While nature held its breath and suspended its laws, a palpable sympathy passed between us through our contact. It was our standard kitchen encounter, but elevated: with the possibility of true knowledge suddenly, dizzyingly open before us. I put a hand on her arm. She looked open-mouthed and quizzical at me, ready for conversion.

And then Nan stirred on the couch. The marvelous fled. Rhonda was simply Rhonda again, and I was in the way. She smiled ironically, slid me aside, and reached into the refrigerator I'd been blocking.

" 'Scuse me," she said, in a tone that didn't remotely beg forgiveness. She removed two cans of soda: one for her, the other for Nan. Their metal sides rasped at me as they paraded past.

Flustered, I stooped to pick up the mayonnaise. The jar was plastic.

I was ashamed of this incident afterward. The shame clung to me like a musky secretion that had rubbed off Rhonda and onto me. I resented it, at the same time that I knew I should be beyond it, beyond giving another person that kind of power over me—especially someone who was a common bully, a quarter-century my junior. What was wrong with me? I was either on the brink of an important growth experience or having a deeply regrettable regression.

In bed at night a vague impulse moved me. It caused my fingers to creep to the buttons of my pajama top and undo them and then slide the elastic of my pants below my hips until I separated myself completely, rolling away to leave the pajamas behind like a shed husk on one side of the sheets.

"Oh, Rhonda," I whispered, and then was amazed at myself, and then went right ahead and thought it again anyway.

This emotion was about as welcome, and negotiable, as a piece of flaming debris falling from the sky and into my living room or backyard. I didn't know what to do with it or where to put it. It was a serious problem for me until I realized I could have it all, just as some married men keep mistresses: with nights of indulgence fitting neatly into days of propriety and power. Only I would just go to bed with the idea, not the real thing. The real thing I could ignore, and it would be none the wiser.

So I ignored her. It worked frighteningly well. For nearly a week following the incident at the refrigerator, I didn't recognize Rhonda in any way, didn't allow her to exist. I ignored her every entrance and exit. How did she react to me? I had no idea, I simply turned away.

"How's business, Nancy?" When Rhonda met me now in the kitchen, her text was the same, but her tone had turned querulous, pleading.

And I turned away.

At the end of the week she confronted me at the sink. Her jacket creaked and her rings clashed against the hard tile like an ultimatum. I looked about, but Nan had vanished off the face of the earth.

"Are you avoiding me?" Rhonda demanded.

It was a question that was impossible to ignore without proving. I mopped water off the rim of the sink, stalling. Finally, I decided I could be as frank as her.

"Rhonda, what do you want from me?"

She looked evasive. "What do you want from me?"

I had to smile at this. I had to laugh. *I asked you first. No, you. No, you.* I looked at the chessboard pattern of tiles on the counter, the game we were playing.

"You don't seem to like me very much," I said.

She took the sides of my face and kissed me. It was like a drink of hot coffee: smooth milky liquid with a bitter narcotic finish, nicotine. It wasn't a drink exactly, it was more a flush, an infusion: something sudden and pervasive and completely nonelective. I took her leather hide in my hands.

Her face left me, but her hands remained. She looked at me reasonably.

"I'm just not ready for Nan to know," she said.

"Know what?" I said stupidly.

As if on cue, Nan's steps sounded down the hall. Rhonda frowned me a terse semaphore, then scuttled to the refrigerator: the clever little tugboat, separating from the ponderous berthing ship.

I WAS TAKING A SHOWER one afternoon, and there were no towels. I swore and walked out dripping to the linen closet. But as soon as I entered the hallway I stopped. Rhonda was standing there, though it wasn't lunchtime. Neither of us was supposed to be there. I covered my breasts with my arms.

She stared at me.

"Well," I said impatiently, after a stillborn minute. "Get me a towel."

"Where are they?"

"In the closet." I pointed.

She opened the closet door. The folded towels and linens presented themselves like so many soft stuck-out tongues. She pulled one out and held it up.

"Is this okay?"

"It's fine." I reached out to take it, but she withdrew it against her breast and came toward me.

"No, let me."

She herded me back into the bathroom and closed the door behind us. I wasn't pleased to be herded, and dripping, but as Rhonda began to carefully blot the water off me I became placated by the luxury of having a personal attendant. She sat me on a chair and dried my hair, then laid the towel about my shoulders. I heard drawers being pulled out and pushed in. I turned around beneath my towel.

"What are you looking for?"

"A brush."

"Over the sink," I said. "In the cabinet."

She found it and came back. The teeth of the brush traveled over my scalp in long, slow, deliberate strokes, followed closely by the light pressure of her trailing hand. A part was executed with the same diligence. She appeared again in front of me to evaluate the result. Then she set the brush aside.

"Now I'm going to have to muss it up," she apologized.

Her fingers ran into the wet hair, her mouth lighted on mine. A hand went to my breast. I stopped it. My heart was pounding uncomfortably, demonstratively, just inches from the contact, squirting blood through my body with misapplied zeal.

"Rhonda, I can't do this."

"Do what?"

"This." My fingers closed around her hand. She smiled.

"Why not?"

I was very aware that I hadn't shaved—as in, any time in the past decade. But that wasn't the reason. That wasn't any of the reasons.

"I have herpes," I said. And because she didn't say anything, I started to explain. "It's a sexually transmitted virus that's incurable and highly contagious—"

"I know what it is," she said. "Do you have it in your mouth?"

"No!" I was emphatic.

"Then it's okay to kiss you."

"Yes."

"Can I touch your breasts?"

"Yes…"

"Can I touch your bottom?"

I frowned and blushed. "Well, yes, but—"

"Can I touch your genitals?"

"*No*," I said. "Not while I'm having an outbreak."

"Are you having an outbreak now?"

"No…"

"Okay." She smiled again. "Then it's all okay, right?"

"Rhonda, I think you should be *careful*—"

"I'm just going to touch you with my fingers."

She held up the fingers of one hand and wiggled them. I

watched as she undressed them, twisting off the rings and putting them into her pocket. Then the fingers came to roost on the side of my neck.

"I don't know anything," I said.

That interested her. "Like what, for instance?"

"Anything."

She brought her face back close to mine, to hover by the side of my cheek, her dry hairs touching my damp.

"We could talk about love," she said in my ear, "but I think you just want me to fuck you."

I WOULDN'T LET HER take me to bed for the first orgasm, which I had crazily sitting on the chair with my breast in her mouth. After that I was much more tractable, and willing to overcome my prejudice against the horizontal position. Rhonda was a genie, a wonder, and made miracles out of the simplest things.

"How do you learn how to do that?" I said, after she had finally assembled us into a resting position in the bed like spoons in repose.

"Somebody who knows shows you." Her voice vibrated behind my head. "Somebody really generous."

"Did you meet somebody really generous?"

"Yes."

"Not *Nan*—"

"No, no," she said. "Nan is my best friend."

"I know."

"You're generous…" she offered.

"Me? Generous? About this?" I laughed. "Rhonda, I've never had an orgasm in my life."

"Are you serious?"

"I thought something was wrong with me."

"Jesus." She shifted against me. "I wish I'd known."

"Why? What do you think 'I don't know anything' means?"

"It's a little general. I mean, you have a child."

I turned around to look at her. "So now you're telling me there's a premium package I didn't get? Maybe four or five instead of three?"

"No, I mean I could have been…"

"Nicer? More educational? Somewhere else?"

"Just nicer."

"No, you couldn't," I said.

Rhonda got up first. "I'd better get out of here before I have to go out through the window," she said. I watched her dress.

"Can I ask you a question?" she said, pulling on her jacket. "How long were you married?"

"Six years." My breast was lying out exposed from the retreated tide of the sheet.

"And how often did you have sex?"

"Often."

"Listen, I'm just going to say this once." She was ready to go now, and leaned down suddenly close to me as if sharing a secret. "Your husband was a fucking idiot."

She left but was back a second later. "Guess I'm going out the window," she said. And she did: lifting the sash, squeezing through the frame, and dropping out of sight into the shrubbery below.

A minute later I heard Nan in the house.

Had we agreed not to talk about love? I wasn't sure. All I knew was that in bed now, at night, after I ritually shed beneath the sheet the pajamas I had just ritually put on, my fantasies turned to hearts like sugared Valentine candies.

THE NEXT DAY AT NOON, when the three of us were at home, the doorbell rang. It was a young man in uniform shorts with a florist's arrangement.

"There must be a mistake." But the name and address were mine, so there was no point in arguing. I took the flowers into the kitchen and set them down on the counter.

"What's that?" said Nan from the couch. Rhonda looked merely interested, like the dog.

"I don't know." I slit open the envelope with my name on it. My chemicals began scampering again when I read the note:

I used to think you were distant and sharp and hard. But now that I've touched you, I find you soft beyond belief.

"What is it?" said Nan.

"I don't know," I said.

"Let's see."

"No." I crumpled the card into a tight wad in my hand.

Rhonda and I sat at opposite ends of the sofa, Nan in the middle. When Nan got up to go to the bathroom, I held Rhonda's hand across the vacated cushion.

"So did you like them?" she said.

"Yes," I said. "But dangerous."

"You're not ready to tell her either."

"No." The bathroom door opened down the hall and we separated.

I ABSOLUTELY WASN'T READY to tell Nan. There might have been nothing to lose, since she could hardly become more estranged from me than she was already. But even if she was emotionally unavailable, still she orbited about me physically, materially; and I knew I would be devastated if I lost this last intimacy, like a familiar piece of furniture.

But then her nearness became a logistical problem. If Nan wasn't going to be with Rhonda, then most likely she was going to be with me. And if she wasn't going to be with me, then she was going to be with Rhonda. It was hard to find a time when she wasn't in one of our spheres. And if we manufactured too many such times—Rhonda declining to come to our house for lunch, for instance, and me choosing to stay at the store—then they would become an obvious pattern and advertise our attachment.

So Rhonda and I met at the house during the day when we

could. I left the store in the hands of my assistant. Rhonda, undoubtedly, simply skipped her classes. But it would have been hypocritical of me to protest; I was as happy as she to get anything we could. It just had to be one of the few small things out of place.

I did take up the matter of smoking with her, though—smoking, and the wardrobe.

"Perhaps it's something you don't have to do anymore," I suggested.

"Look, Nancy, let's be realistic about this."

Her voice was shockingly cold. For an awful moment I thought she was breaking up with me. *Oh God, no,* I thought. No realism please.

"Smoking is just too useful to me right now," she said. "The clothes are just too useful."

"Useful…for what?"

"I am a *total* outcast at school. They *despise* me. I have no friends. I am *trash.* It's all not very glamorous, unless I pretend it is."

It hurt me to hear her describe herself in the very same terms I might have used about her, privately, not so long ago.

"You have Nan," I said.

"Yes, I do."

"Why do they despise you?"

She shrugged. "Sex. Money. As in, not having any. Being new. But mostly sex."

She cast about as if she were looking for a cigarette. She *was* looking for a cigarette, going through the pockets of her discarded jacket.

"The crazy thing is," she said, "sex is great. People are stupid. And do you know what the really crazy thing is?"

"No, what?"

"*Their* sex lives are probably crap. The people who are despising me for sex are probably having miserable sex themselves. Either none at all, or with teenage boys. Can you imagine?"

"Rhonda, if I bought you clothes, would you wear them when we're together?"

"What, so I could take them right off again? Like pink lace panties or something?"

I thought of my pajamas.

WE WENT TO MACY'S at lunchtime. I bought Rhonda a pair of khakis. Then I bought her another. Then we chose a couple of shirts. The shirts were trim button-downs that made her look perfectly suave. She posed in front of the mirror, considering. Then we went back to get shoes and a sweater. Then she made me stop.

"This is too much," she said. "This is too expensive. What am I going to tell my grandma?" Rhonda lived with her grandmother.

"I want to," I said imperiously.

"I want to tell you how I got herpes," I said to Rhonda. "Can I tell you?"

"Okay. But I don't have to know."

"It was the stupidest thing I've ever done in my life, bar none."

"Nancy." She laughed. "Stupider than getting married?"

"I adore my daughter. And I thought you weren't going to mention it anymore."

"Stupider than...any stupid thing you ever did in school?"

"Yes. It was right after the divorce. I went to bed with someone I didn't know, didn't care about, and didn't even want. I guess it goes without saying that I didn't even enjoy it. When I found out, I tried to kill myself with pills. Not successfully, of course."

"Yes, Nan told me."

"She did? About what?"

"About your trying to kill yourself. At least she thought. When she was five or something."

"Well, that wasn't stupid, just emotional."

Rhonda considered it, like her shirted reflection in the Macy's mirror.

"So," she finally said, "isn't it a relief to know you've already done the stupidest thing you'll ever do? I'm not really looking forward to that, for myself."

"But Rhonda, how do I even know that?"

"Well, but if you do end up doing something stupider, then this won't be the stupidest thing you've ever done anymore, will it?"

I smiled dubiously.

"Does Nan know?" said Rhonda. "Have you told her?"

"About the stupidity or the herpes?"

"Either."

"No."

She looked askance at me.

"You don't talk about that with a child of five," I said. "And then later it was just too late."

"Too late for what?"

"It's not a conversation I can ever imagine having."

"You're having it with me."

"Yes, I am." It was the miracle. "But you're—"

"A total stranger."

"No." I searched for a word. "Extraordinary."

She shook her head but contradicted the modesty by looking pleased: sun shining through rain. "I'm just a kid," she said. "I didn't even know how to talk to you."

RHONDA WORKED AT DOMINIC'S, a local pizza parlor. Nan and I had often been. When Rhonda and I started scheming about a dinner date, it was what we came up with. We would all go out to Dominic's: Rhonda, Nan, and I. It would be Rhonda's treat, and she got a discount.

Rhonda showed up at our house in her new clothes.

"Jesus," said Nan, "what happened to you?"

Nan and Rhonda sat on one side of a booth, I sat on the

other. Rhonda and I could look into each other's eyes but did so only fleetingly. Rhonda ordered. She knew the server. She ordered us beer too, for which she was underage, but in this parlor her word was law and the server didn't question it. We got a tremendous pizza with everything. We ate and drank, and it was an apotheosis, a vision of earthly paradise: Rhonda trim and dapper in my fleeting glance; Rhonda omnipotently providing, in her own eyes; and the three of us having fun together, breaking pizza crust in perfect harmony.

"Oh, man," said Nan.

"Who is it?" said Rhonda.

I looked up from the olive slices I was carefully picking out and setting aside. Nan and Rhonda were staring at someone behind me.

"It's my dad."

I turned around. Jack was indeed sitting three booths down, with a young female companion. She wasn't young enough to be his child, just his fantasy. With wine glasses dotting the table between them, it was his own vision of earthly paradise.

Rhonda excused herself and left the table. I presumed she was going to the bathroom; she was drinking a lot of beer. Moments later I heard a commotion erupt behind me.

"You freak!"

"Son of a bitch!"

I turned around again. Three booths down, Jack had Rhonda in a chokehold. She swung at his nose and blood flowed. He returned the favor to her eye. Her knee connected with him and he crumpled, bending sharply at the middle. Wine glasses flew across the table, causing his companion in the booth to flinch backward, throw her hands in the air, and stare at her lap in dismay.

The manager arrived on the scene. I paid quickly. Rhonda, Nan, and I hurried out.

THE THREE OF US SAT at home in the living room.

"Is there something somebody wants to tell me?" said Nan. "Or doesn't want to tell me?"

"I'm in love with your mom," said Rhonda. There was a blood spatter on her khakis, or maybe it was just tomato sauce.

"So does she know?"

Rhonda looked at me.

"Sort of... Yes."

"And does this have anything to do with the clothes?"

"I bought them for her," I said.

"So, are you...having sex too?" Nan behaved just like I would, looking accusingly from one of us to the other and holding out the phrase in tongs.

"Yes," said Rhonda.

Nan looked devastated. "Terrific. Terrific. How long?"

"Nan," I broke in, "we wanted to tell you, but we didn't know how."

"*Know*? Correction, you didn't have the *guts* to tell me. Or maybe it was just too much *fun,* keeping me in the dark."

She blurted out a sound, buried her fist in a pillow, burst into tears, and left.

Rhonda and I looked at each other. "Do you want to go after her?" I said, yielding the right of way. "Go ahead."

Rhonda left. She was back after five minutes.

"Did you find her?"

Rhonda made a face, then grimaced doubly from the pain of her eye, which was beginning to swell and color unbeautifully like a gorging tick.

"Not really," she said.

It was reality smeared all over us. We were both suddenly Nan-less. We were both being unfaithful to our respective mates, and they had both just found out and walked out on us, but— confusingly, economically, fortuitously, regrettably—they were both the same person. We sat down on the couch, each at our own end.

"I'm sorry," Rhonda said.

"Sorry for what?"

"For the scene. Big me. Fucking stupid."

The truth was that it was not significantly different than scenes I myself had had with Jack in the distant past: histrionics, mutually blackened eyes. I couldn't decide whether to admit this to Rhonda or not.

"Are you going to lose your job?" I said.

"Nah." And after a minute, "I don't think so. I hope not."

"I could put in a word."

"Sure."

We were silent for a while.

"Well," I said, "if that's the stupidest thing you ever do in your life..."

She turned and smiled at me, the "I'm not really feeling good enough yet to be amused but I'm forcing myself to acknowledge your humor anyway" kind. I waited to see if our hands would find themselves over the middle cushion. They did.

"She'll be back," I said.

"Sure," said Rhonda.

We turned on the TV. I had a vision: In this nest of crazy sticks, we were curled up tight and tiny in the center, spooning happily.

—LIFE AT A GLANCE—

Lesléa Newman

FUNNY HOW THE SMALLEST, most mundane, seemingly unimportant decision can change your life forever. Like deciding to eat soup instead of a sandwich for lunch on a Tuesday afternoon.

Now, this wasn't any Tuesday, mind you. This Tuesday was the first day that really felt like fall, with a sky so blue it almost hurt to look up, and the air so crisp you could practically take a bite of it. A day to pull on your favorite pair of jeans and ratty sweater, lace up your hiking boots and start up a mountain, with a big brown dog wagging her feathered tail as she trots along beside you.

And that's exactly what I would be doing if I didn't have to work for a living. But here I am at the office going through my prework rituals: I hang my leather jacket on the hook behind my door, stash my sandwich in the top drawer of my desk (bologna and cheese on Tuesdays and Thursdays; PB&J on Mondays, Wednesdays, and Fridays), measure out exactly four scoops of coffee grains and brew a pot, lay three sharpened pencils next to the phone on my desk alongside a yellow—not green or orange or, heaven forbid, pink—Post-it pad. I sit down at 8:58 according to the digital clock to my left, slide my hands along the sides of my head to make sure every short dark hair is in its proper place, take off my glasses to polish them with a special cloth I keep in my middle drawer, slip my spectacles back up my nose, and turn on my computer at exactly 9 o'clock. I don't look up until noon, even though I know it's bad for my eyes to stare at a computer screen for more than thirty minutes at a time. But I'm a computer geek, and we don't believe in taking breaks. Most days I even eat lunch at my desk. If it weren't for my bladder, I'd probably stay put the entire afternoon.

But once in a while a day comes along like that Tuesday. It was more like a commercial for a day than an actual day. An advertisement that shows you in living Technicolor how glorious a day can be. A day that makes you feel your life has suddenly grown too small for you. A day that reminds you that you have places to go, people to meet, things to do. Or if you don't, as in my case, you damn well should.

At high noon I did what I do every day: took off my glasses and rubbed my eyes, pulled open my desk drawer, unwrapped my sandwich, and took a bite. My usual Tuesday fare had all the appeal of wet sand on toast. I threw it into the trash and looked out the window. The day simply beckoned; there's no other way to describe it. So at 12:02 I did the unthinkable: shoved my glasses onto my face, grabbed my jacket off its hook, and took myself out to lunch.

As I walked out the front door I imagined an announcement being made: "Laura has left the building." It was that dramatic a departure for me. I'm the type of person who rarely departs from her precise—some would say rigid—schedule. Besides my working 9 to 5 Monday through Friday, my dance card is pretty full. I work out at the gym on Tuesdays, Thursdays, and Saturdays. I read the paper and grocery shop on Sundays. Monday evenings I call my mother; Wednesday evenings I do the laundry. I guess you could call me a low risk-taker; I don't leave much to chance. *Ha, that's an understatement,* I can hear my last girlfriend say.

You see, this is why I don't like to divert from my schedule.

Five minutes out of the office and I start thinking about Nora. Nora was what you'd call a free spirit, and we were always butting heads, since spontaneity is hardly my middle name. Every fight we had—and there were many in the three years we were together—boiled down to the same thing: My lists and schedules made her crazy, and her refusal (my word) or inability (her word) to make concrete plans drove me out of my mind.

"It's only Wednesday, Laura," she'd remind me, as if I, of all people, ever forgot what day it was. "I don't know if I'll feel like eating at the West End Grill on Saturday night."

"Well, do you know when you'll know? I need to make reservations or we'll never get in."

"So if we don't get in, we'll do something else. No big deal."

"Maybe I'll make a reservation anyway, and if you decide you're not in the mood, I'll cancel it."

"Can't you wait and see for once in your life?"

"Would it kill you to make a commitment?"

And so it would go. When things got nasty, Nora brought up sex, always her trump card. "If we did everything your way," she'd shriek, "we'd even schedule our sex life. Let's see," and she'd pick up the phone bill, pretending it was one of my lists. "Things to do: work out at the gym, call the dentist for an appointment, send Aunt Edith a birthday card, fuck Nora's brains out, change smoke-alarm batteries..."

"What's so wrong with that?" I'd yell, my voice grating on my own nerves as it rose in fever and pitch. "A lot of couples don't even have sex after the first year they're together. I don't see anything wrong with scheduling it. Haven't you ever heard of the best *laid* plans?" Nora didn't respond to my attempt at a joke so I continued. "At least if we scheduled sex, you'd know we were going to have it and then there wouldn't be all this pressure..."

"Pressure?" Nora's tone matched mine and bettered it at least forty decibels. "You feel pressure to have sex with me? *Pressure?* It should be something you look forward to, something you enjoy. Something you feel like doing spon-tan-e-ous-ly." She stretched out the word like I was unfamiliar with the English language.

So much for a relaxing stroll about town during my lunch break. As I made my way down the street with leaves crunching underfoot, a chant started up in my head: *Nora and Laura, Laura and Nora.* Christ, other people get pop songs or advertising jingles stuck in their brains. But not me. Everyone, including Nora, thought it was so cute the way our names rhymed. I found it nauseating.

I walked by a shoe repair shop, a women's clothing boutique, a Chinese restaurant, and a bookstore. As I stopped to admire an orange cat sleeping in the bookshop's window on top of a book called (and I'm not making this up) *Feng Shui for You and Your Cat,* my stomach let out a growl that I'm sure the kitty would have taken as a challenge if she could have heard it through the thick glass separating us. I walked half a block farther, trying to figure out what I wanted to eat. Across the street was a restaurant called Soup to Nuts, and I headed right for it. It was definitely a soup kind of day.

A few other customers were ahead of me in line, so I glanced up at the chalkboard of a menu as I waited. Someone had scrawled the words "We Serve" in front of the name of the restaurant, so the chalkboard proclaimed "We Serve SOUP TO NUTS," which made me smile. The place was small and cozy and had no table service; you placed your order at the counter and then received your meal on a tray, which you carried over to one of the few round black tables in the back. It was warmer inside the café than it had been outside, and the words on the blackboard blurred as my glasses fogged up. I removed them, rubbed them against my pant leg, and put them on again.

"What'll it be, love?" I looked up through my now defogged lenses and thought I was dreaming. A young woman didn't stand before me—a *vision* of a young woman stood before me. A vision of loveliness, as the poets say. Maybe it was because everyone else was burdened down with sweaters and scarves and jackets, and she stood there in a tiny tank top with straps thin as dental floss, but I had the feeling she could hide inside a down parka with nothing sticking out but the tip of her perfect nose and still take my breath away.

"Soup," I croaked, and she laughed like I had just made a brilliant, witty remark.

"I know you want soup, love," she went on in a fake British accent I found completely endearing. "But what kind of soup?" And she gestured with a dainty arm that reminded me of the graceful neck of a swan.

I pushed my glasses up my nose even though they hadn't slid down—it's a nervous habit I have, and boy, was I nervous—and read the board: chicken noodle, tomato rice, clam chowder, black bean, cream of cauliflower. "I'll have tomato rice," I said, and the Soup Goddess smiled like I had come up with just the right answer.

"Tomato rice," she said, pronouncing it to-*mah*-toe, making me want to burst into that goofy song about to-may-toes and to-mah-toes and po-tay-toes and po-tah-toes my father used to sing around the house. But I would have been drowned out by the radio, which the other woman behind the counter turned up as "The Girl From Ipanema" came on.

"Here's an oldie but goodie," the woman mumbled to no one in particular.

"I've never heard it," my girl said, as she cocked her head to listen. She shut her eyes for a minute, giving me a chance to study her. All her light brown hair was pulled back from her face except for a few sexy, flyaway wisps, and her features were chiseled and fine: high cheekbones that reminded me of a young Katharine Hepburn, a long straight nose dotted with freckles and a tiny diamond stud above her left nostril, lips that could break your heart with just one kiss or pout. She didn't use much makeup, just a hint of eyeliner, mascara, and lip gloss. A pair of gold hoop earrings, big enough for two small birds to perch on, hung from her ears.

"Da da da, da DA da, da da da." The Soup Goddess opened her eyes and laughed with delight. "It's a little jazzy, isn't it, mate?" She started moving her shoulders, pushing first one forward and then the other in time with the beat. She engaged her upper body with the movement too, then extended her arms and threw her hips into it. I watched in awe, my hand flying up to my chin to make sure my mouth wasn't hanging open. What spirit, what joie de vivre, what—dare I say it—spontaneity! Oh, I was a goner. This girl was just my type. *Opposites attract,* as I'd frequently told Nora when she wondered aloud what she saw in me. Once while grocery shopping, we had seen a headline in a fashion magazine: "Take the Test: Would You Sleep With Yourself?"

"Well?" Nora asked, pointing at the magazine.

"No way." I didn't hesitate. "I'm not my type."

The object of my affection turned her back to me and ladled my soup out of an enormous pot simmering on a stove behind the counter. I imagined leaning over and licking the cashmere nape of her neck, but before I had a chance to (like I ever would do such a thing) she turned back around.

"Anything else, dah-ling?" She smiled at me and the other woman behind the counter rolled her eyes, but I didn't care. I was smitten. *Your phone number,* I wanted to say, but the words were trapped somewhere in the pit of my stomach. I'd never asked a woman for her phone number in my life, and I certainly wasn't going to start now. Especially with someone so out of my league, which would only result in my making a fool of myself. There was no way in hell this super chick would go out with me. First of all, she was maybe twenty, twenty-two at the most, a good ten years my junior. Second, I doubted she was a lesbian, though rumor has it the young ones these days think it's very trendy to call themselves bi. But even if she was some form of queer, I doubted she'd ever be interested in someone like me. She'd want someone young, someone free, someone *alive.* As the word hit my brain like a slap of cold water, I realized that was exactly the problem. I was dead. Oh, I walked, talked, breathed, ate, slept, did all the things human beings do. But on the inside I was a zombie. And it had taken a close encounter of the lustful kind to remind me how much there was to life. For some people, anyway.

"Are you all set?" my lady's grumpy coworker barked, and all of a sudden I realized there was a long line of hungry people behind me.

"Uh, yeah," I mumbled as I fumbled with my wallet. Soup server number two groaned and muttered, "Oh, great," as the bills and change I had managed to extract from my wallet slipped from my hand and spilled all over the counter. The Soup Goddess, who was probably used to having this effect on people, remained unfazed as I hurried to scoop up the money.

"Thanks, old girl," she said as I gave her the cash. Our hands touched for the briefest second, and then she sashayed, still shimmying, to the cash register to ring up my sale. I turned and was halfway to a table before I realized I'd forgotten my soup.

"This yours?" My girl was busy with another lucky customer, so her coworker handed me my tray with a *for chrissake* look in her eye. I could hardly blame her—I was acting like an idiot.

I picked a table where I could watch the goings-on behind the counter without being too obvious. How could I strike up a conversation with such a living doll? I could tell her what I had read in the paper just the other day: A woman who claimed she inspired "The Girl From Ipanema" was being sued by whoever owned the rights to the song because they didn't want her using the title to advertise her clothing boutique—but knowing that kind of factoid is exactly what makes me the nerd I am. I could tell her she was the most exquisite thing I had ever seen and I could happily spend the rest of my life watching her serve soup to nuts like myself, but that would only make me sound...well, nuts. I could do nothing but finish my bowl of tomato rice, go back to work, and return for more soup for dinner, which is exactly what I did.

All afternoon I tried to concentrate on the Web site I was supposed to be designing, but it was no use. All I could think about was dinner. This time I would be prepared. I wouldn't be such a jerk. I would...would what? I had courted Nora with flowers and chocolate, but Nora knew she was being courted and had let me know she was ready, willing, and able. I admit it was very high schoolish, but since I hate to take chances in any aspect of life, let alone in the L-O-V-E department, I had a friend of mine ask a friend of Nora's whether she'd go out with me. Nora told her friend who told my friend who told me she'd jump at the chance, so it was full-speed ahead. But with this wet dream of a girl, I was on my own.

In typical New England fashion, the weather completely changed during the course of the afternoon. By 4:30 the sky was gray and filled with pregnant-looking clouds; even the air in my office felt moist and heavy. At exactly 5 o'clock, I rose from my desk and shrugged on my jacket. Should I take an umbrella? Since I firmly believe in the Boy Scout motto "Be prepared," just the fact that I was considering leaving it in the office was new behavior for me. In my attempt to be more of a free-wheeling type of gal, I asked myself, *What would Nora do?* The answer was obvious: Not only would Nora risk getting wet, she would enjoy it and probably break into song ("Singin' in the Rain") if caught in a downpour. So be it. I left the office umbrella-free.

Soup to Nuts was crowded at this hour, but I wasn't impatient. I could wait in line forever as long as the Babe of Broth was feeding the masses. But she wasn't. Her cohort was alone behind the counter, looking crankier than ever, the black braid that hung halfway down her back coming undone and a big orange splotch of soup decorating the front of her apron. She thrust her hands on her hips and tapped one foot as she waited for a customer to make up his mind. As I watched her, I tried not to panic. Maybe the love of my life was on break; maybe she was in the bathroom. Maybe she had been an illusion? I squeezed my eyes shut, praying that when I opened them she'd appear, and when I did there she was, holding an enormous vat of soup in her slender arms.

"*Pardonnez-moi, s'il vous plaît. Excusez-moi.*" She spoke in an over-the-top French accent for the supper crowd, and wore a black beret. My lips curved up into a huge smile at the sight of her, though she didn't seem to notice. "Took you long enough," Old Sourpuss snapped as Mademoiselle hoisted the big silver pot onto the stove. How could she talk to her like that? Didn't she know just being in her presence was an honor? The nerve!

As the line crept forward, I practiced what I would say to her. *Voulez-vous couchez avec moi ce soir?* is what I wished I had the guts to utter. But leaving my umbrella in the office was one thing—having a total personality change was another. All I could manage to squeak out when I finally stood before her was "Small clam chowder for here," and it was an effort to say even that.

My femme fatale turned from me to scoop my soup and as she did so she dropped something on the floor. I almost fainted as she bent over; her tank top rode up her back and exposed a vine-shaped tattoo crawling up her spine. Oh, to be Jack climbing that beanstalk!

"*Voilà!*" My beret-sporting babe turned back around and presented my soup with a flourish.

"Do you speak English?" I asked, playing along with her game as I counted out my money.

"*Oui, oui,*" she answered.

"Where are you from?"

"Where else but gay Paree?" she said and I almost died. *Gay* Paree? Gay as in I-like-girls-and-you-like-girls-so-let's-get-it-on gay, or gay as in happy, which is what I'd be if she would *couchez avec moi ce soir* or any *soir* for that matter? No one just threw the word "gay" around anymore. She had to know what she was saying, and how that one small word made of those three little letters lifted my heart with hope. If only the beret she was wearing was lavender, or the diamond stud in her nose a pink triangle, then I could be sure.

"*Merci beaucoup.*" *Ma belle amie* handed over my change, and I took my supper over to the same table where I'd sat earlier. God, I was such a creature of habit. Maybe I'd just eat soup here every day for the rest of my life. I'd have tomato rice for lunch and clam chowder for supper. It wouldn't be such a bad way to go. And maybe in a year or two or twenty, I'd work up enough nerve to say more than five words to the Goddess of a Thousand Accents.

I ate my soup and alternated staring at my femme du jour and out the window. It had begun to rain, and damn if I wasn't going to ruin my leather jacket walking to my car. So much for being carefree. Maybe the rain would stop before I had to leave. Or maybe I'd just hang out until the place closed. Why not? Skip the gym and say the hell with everything. Maybe I'd even get coffee and some big gooey dessert. Enjoy myself for once. And besides, that would give me a chance to go up to the counter again. I still remembered a smidgen of high school French. "*Bonjour,*" I could say. "*Comment allez-vous? Vous êtes très jolie. Je vous aime avec tout mon coeur.*" Why not? What did I possibly have to lose?

As I sat there trying to work up the nerve to go back to the counter, the restaurant started filling up. The drizzle outside had turned into a downpour, and soggy folks ducked into the restaurant two and three at a time. I lost my view of the counter and hardly looked up when someone said, "Are you using this chair?"

"No, no, go ahead," I said, waving my hand as if to shoo away a fly. I craned my neck and moved this way and that, but I still couldn't get a good sighting of the hired help and I was starting to worry. How was my damsel in distress going to handle this crowd with no one to help her but the grouchiest coworker east of the Mississippi? Maybe I should leap over the counter and offer my services. Be her knight in shining armor.

But before I could slide back my chair to get up, someone tapped me on the shoulder.

"She doesn't play on our team."

"Huh?" I looked up, and there, standing at my table, was none other than Miss Crab Cakes of 2002, still wearing her tomato-soup-stained apron. Up close, I saw she also wore a gold labyris around her neck.

"Two-four-six-eight. The pretty girl's not gay, she's straight." She flipped a dishrag off her shoulder and started wiping my table with it. "Forget it. She's a thespian, not a lesbian. Thinks she's going to be a big movie star someday." My unwanted guest pretended to stifle a yawn.

At least that explained the accents. "In other words, I don't stand a chance."

"Nope." She folded her arms and grinned like the Cheshire Cat.

That really pissed me off, probably because it was so clear that she was right. "You seem awfully happy about the situation," I said.

She nodded. "Yep."

"Not that I care, but what makes you so goddamn grouchy anyway?" I couldn't believe the words that had just come out of my mouth—normally I'm not a rude person—but I also couldn't believe she had just burst my bubble like that.

"What makes me so grouchy?" She drummed her fingers against her cheek like she was thinking over my question. "Oh, I don't know. Maybe working next to Miss America day in and day out, while every Tom, Dick, and Harriet drools all over themselves at the mere sight of her—maybe that might have something to do with it. Did you ever think of that?" She put her hands on the edge of the table and leaned forward, about to say something, but then apparently changed her mind and straightened up. Then she spoke so softly, I could hardly hear her. "I'd give anything to have a woman as attractive as you look at me the way you look at her." She pointed with disdain toward the counter with the tip of her chin, which had begun to quiver. "I know I'm not exactly eye candy, but hey, I still deserve a chance." And before I could say anything in reply, she turned on her heel and disappeared into the crowd.

Whoa, Nellie, I thought, rearing back as though I'd been slapped. I was stunned. First of all, I was beyond mortified that I'd been that obvious. Second, had a total stranger just called me attractive? And last, I was amazed she'd had the guts to make herself that vulnerable—talk about taking risks!—and say what she'd said. I looked over toward the counter with new respect for the grinch of a soup server. She'd issued me a challenge if I'd ever heard one. Dare I take her up on it? Ask her out and be *her* knight in shining armor?

When the crowd thinned, I made my humble way over to the counter and waited for the dyke to look up. She was making herself awfully busy, trying to crack open a roll of quarters against the edge of the cash register, hitting it with much more force than necessary. I cleared my throat, pushed my glasses up my nose with my index finger, and said all in one breath: "Would-you-please-go-out-with-me-Friday-night?"

"Who, me?" She looked up and splayed her fingers over her heart in mock astonishment. "Why," she said in a pathetic Scarlett O'Hara accent, "I thought you'd never ask."

The beautiful straight girl I knew I'd never have backed off to give us some privacy as my new love interest consulted her red leather date book.

"I have the same life-at-a-glance," I said as she flipped to this week's page.

"What?" She looked up, startled.

"I said, 'I have the same week-at-glance.' "

"No, you didn't. You said, 'I have the same life-at-a-glance.' "

"I did?" Christ, I'd been thinking about Nora so much today, I'd started channeling her. "My last girlfriend called my weekly planner my 'life-at-a-glance.' " I shrugged like I was apologizing. "She was always stealing it from me and writing in things like 'breathe' or 'live in the moment.' It was against her religion to make plans."

"That's wild. My last girlfriend called it my 'life-at-a-glance' too. When she wasn't throwing it out the window." We stared at each other for a split second before we both smiled and looked away. Then she quickly looked down at her date book. "Okay, let's see. Usually on Friday nights I go to a meeting, but I suppose I could skip it."

"Is Saturday better for you?" I asked.

"Saturday, Saturday..." She scanned the page. "Saturday nights I take in a movie..."

"Sunday night?" I asked, beginning to get the picture.

"Sunday nights I always have a hot date at the Laundromat."

I nodded with understanding. "How about Sunday afternoon?" I said.

"Sunday afternoon is perfect."

"Oh, good," I said with relief. "I wouldn't want to disrupt your schedule."

"You wouldn't?" She looked at me again, and I noticed she had pretty blue eyes.

"No way. You know what they say about the best *laid* plans." I gave her the lewdest look I could manage and she laughed with delight.

—EVERY DAY IS A GOOD DAY—

Siobhán Houston

I LAY ON THE RUMPLED BED, watching Christa get ready for sleep. Twirling a strand of hair in my fingers, I smiled as she shed her jeans and sweatshirt and put on her favorite sleeping outfit, a paint-splattered, stretched-out, faded and ripped periwinkle T-shirt. I liked to tease her that this piece of lingerie was the height of butch eroticism, and how aroused this particular costume made me.

"So if she's coming to your opening, do I have to go too?" I sounded like a disgruntled third-grader asked to do an especially onerous task, like copying out times tables or cleaning the guinea pig cage.

Christa turned to look at me and laughed incredulously. "Of course you do, Leigh! I mean, you're my partner, and it's my first solo show. I can't believe you'd even consider not going."

A few minutes ago one of Christa's ex-lovers had phoned to announce that she'd planned a visit to Denver to briefly escape the doldrums of the Midwest. I thought it must be pathetically dull in the Plains if she was coming here for excitement. I still longed for my adopted hometown of Boston and periodically railed against the Fates, who had decreed that I live in this provincial hinterland. Anyway, Lexie, who had lived with Christa for several years at one time, wanted to spend a few days at Christa's house, do some day trips into the mountains, and generally hang out with her former lover and current friend. Christa, whose kindness and generosity I could only hope to attain after arduous austerities and many incarnations, immediately agreed to the visit. She also invited Lexie to her Saturday night opening at a prestigious gallery in LoDo, the chic and happening district of downtown Denver.

Christa expected me to be thrilled with this plan, and she envisioned how all three of us would pal around, hiking in the mountains, bathing in waterfalls, and reminiscing about old times. Since I had never met Lexie, however, I wouldn't be in on the nostalgia part—I'd be a spectator as they relived their common past. In my mind's eye, I saw all three of us sitting around some run-down mountain diner, my eyes glazing over while they told tales of whatever folks did in their native Midwest: fleeing tornadoes, watching the weevils eat the corn, and so forth.

That's not what really bothered me, though. All I had thought about since hearing about Lexie's visit was that this was a woman with whom Christa had *lived* and made *love*. Visions of Lexie and Christa writhing around on their bed, of Christa's head between Lexie's legs, of Christa wearing a harnessed dildo and topping Lexie—my mind went spinning out of control, imagining all the permutations of their sexual congress. Plus, this woman had known my lover for many years and had reams of intimate memories with Christa. Our accumulation of shared remembrances, while growing after a year together, looked slight in comparison.

Christa and I are alike in a lot of ways, but we differ greatly in the way we relate to ex-lovers. She keeps in contact with a number of them—I see their names on the social justice alerts she sends out to her E-mail distribution list. Even though I've been a lesbian for decades, I find certain elements of dyke culture bewildering. To be honest, this compulsion of most lesbians to include their ex-lovers in their close family group completely escapes me. Admittedly, I've never been one of those toe-the-party-line lesbians. In college, the majority of my sisters ostracized me because I refused to wear the regulation denim and cropped hair, flaunting instead a high-femme sensibility coupled with a devotion to Camille Paglia.

In regard to ex-lovers, my motto is "keep the past in the past." I'm sure Dr. Paglia is with me on this one. I pride myself on my ice-queen demeanor toward my former girlfriends. Not only do I not talk to them, I don't talk *about* them. When Christa and I first met, she kept asking me about my past love life. My attempts to evade her questioning didn't go over well, so finally I threw her a few tidbits about previous lovers. Most of these were even true, or at least loosely based on events that may have actually happened.

Although I never inquired about her ex-lovers, she told me about them anyway, and I cringed whenever she mentioned them. I think this visceral reaction is rooted in the idea that if they each could end up as her ex, then so could I, and to consider that possibility is more than I can handle. I know some archaic abandonment complex underlies this attitude, but there it is. It's not that I hadn't been trying to work through this with every relationship book, homo and hetero, that I could get my hands on. It appears, though, that my progress in this area has not been satisfactory to the Powers That Be. They've obviously decided to dramatically increase the learning curve and adjust the intensity of my life curriculum to high.

I've had it especially hard when I've spent time in her house, which is full of mementos of past lovers. Photos and souvenirs of their trips with Christa festooned the walls and decorated the window ledges, and birthday cards and other knickknacks and gewgaws from her past relationships vied for precious space on her bookcases and unexpectedly popped out from drawers and cupboards. Not to mention that she's been baby-sitting a previous mate's dog for the past year and a half, for God's sake. You can see how the prospect of actually *meeting* one of her former flames brought me to my knees emotionally. My body felt hollowed out, as if it had been bombed and strafed and now sat blackened and burning and empty. Nausea assaulted me, and my head throbbed with pain. My psyche felt as devastated as Dresden after the fire-bombing.

"Look, Leigh, if Lexie visiting is so upsetting to you, I'll call her and tell her it's not a good time. I should have talked with you before I agreed to have her come." Christa leaned over and switched on the window fan and then slid under the sheets next to me, her breath smelling sweet with the scent of peppermint toothpaste.

I'd die before I'd admit how distraught I was over this. "No, no," I heard myself say. "I don't mind if she comes and if she stays with you. I just don't want to meet her."

Christa looked at me, irritated and uncomprehending. "What's the big deal? We broke up six years ago, and we're not even that close anymore. I'm not planning to rekindle some flame with her, if that's what you're worried about. Anyway, I want her to meet you and see what an incredible person you are."

"You mean you want her to see that you're doing so much better romantically since you two broke up so she can feel envious," I joked.

Christa laughed. "Exactly." Then she pulled me close to her under the covers and nuzzled my ear. "Leigh, baby, you know you're my main drug, don't you?" she murmured, quoting from my favorite Lucinda Williams song. As she burrowed into the crook of my arm and I stroked the soft skin of her belly, I felt her breath already slowing down. She'd been putting in long hours at the gallery getting ready for this show and seemed tired most of the time. I kissed her forehead and lay back down on my pillow, trying to fall asleep even though my mind whirled with foreboding thoughts of the impending visit.

The next day at work, I moved through the hours like an

unearthed zombie. Unable to concentrate, incapable even of composing the most innocuous E-mail or conversing intelligibly on the phone with my colleagues, I gave up the idea of accomplishing anything productive. I closed the door to my office, pulled out my cell phone, and called a friend in Massachusetts, a woman who is psychically gifted. Her intuitive reading of the situation left me aghast. "Christa is having a hard time right now, with all the stress in her life," she informed me. "There's a good chance she'll leave you to go back to this woman, whom she sees as familiar and comforting. I don't see you staying with her much longer." This was so completely at odds with my sense of our relationship that it momentarily shook me up. Then I remembered that psychics aren't immune from projecting their own issues onto clients' readings, and decided that this was one piece of advice I wouldn't buy into.

I then logged on to the Internet, looking for anything to help me cope with the runaway train of emotions on which I was riding. I didn't find much on difficulties dealing with your lesbian lover's ex; it seemed that the majority of dyke writers assumed you'd welcome these women into your life and home with nary a whimper. One straight psychotherapist sermonized about how her former boyfriend had become a good friend of her current husband and was welcome to stay in their home any time. After a good hour of Web crawling, I still couldn't find a worthwhile reason to maintain my position of avoidance. Damn. I'm sure if I'd visited Dr. Laura's Web site, she would have backed me up and said not to let the ex stay over, but then again, she wouldn't be too keen that we were talking about a girl-on-girl relationship.

I called Christa at work and told her in a conciliatory tone that I'd go to the opening and meet Lexie. And that I would *try* to sleep over at her house while Lexie was there and do some socializing with the two of them. I warned her, though, not to expect me to be my usual vivacious, charming, coquettish, witty self. I'd aim for civility, not charisma.

As soon as I hung up, I galvanized myself. I remembered that I'd been through some difficult and seemingly insurmountable situations in my life. For example, I'd been homeless in San Francisco as a teenager and later spent time (did time?) as an Ivy League grad student—it was a toss-up as to which was more harrowing. I knew from the past that I needed a game plan to successfully navigate through my complicated paranoia about Lexie.

My inbred inclination as a native Californian consisted of turning to my huge collection of spirituality and self-help treatises when under stress. Unfortunately, reading them for pleasure and the illusion of spiritual advancement wouldn't cut it this time—I'd really have to do some substantive inner work. The thought appalled me, but my desire to keep my relationship with Christa on an even keel and extending into infinity egged me on.

I sat on the floor in my living room, surrounded by volumes with titles like *Companions on the Inner Way, The Sacred Magic of Angelic Healing,* and, most apropos, *When Things Fall Apart* strewn all about me. There were dozens more such books on the shelves and packed away in boxes in my basement with alphabetized inventory lists taped to their tops. I picked up an old favorite that had nourished me through my undergraduate years—*Rilke on Love and Other Difficulties.* Whenever I felt depressed over yet another fizzled college romance, I slept clutching various collections of Rilke poetry, especially this one and *Neue Gedichte* (New Poems), which he wrote during his time as Rodin's amanuensis in Paris. I sensed the poet still existed in another realm, protectively watching over his fellow tragic romantics as they blundered from one ruinous affair to the next. I opened it randomly and read a line aloud: "Are not the nights fashioned from the sorrowful space of all the open arms a lover suddenly lost?" No, no, no! I slammed the cover shut and impatiently shoved the book back on the shelf, where it sat crookedly next to a collection of Christina Rossetti poems.

After a few hours of poring through these texts, I still felt, well, destroyed. Nothing seemed to help. I spotted a set of tapes from the library, lectures that Stephen and Ondrea Levine gave in Boulder on "Relationship as a Spiritual Path." I fitted a cassette into the tape deck and lay back on the floor to listen, my head pressed into the Moroccan kilim rug. The mellifluous and measured cadences of the Levines' voices soothed me as they spoke of how suppressing painful thoughts is not wisdom—the courageous path is to observe fear head-on. "The willingness to watch fear builds so much courage," one of them intoned. As I listened, I felt my body become more languorous and my gyrating mind gradually slow down its revolutions, like a top running out of momentum. "Have mercy on yourself. Merciful awareness heals."

Merciful awareness heals. Merciful awareness heals. For some reason, those words resonated at my core, and I sensed an immediate softening of the mind, a quieting within. I remembered another Buddhist aphorism: "Every day is a good day." That is, every day you can use whatever presents itself as grist for the mill of awareness. Yes, yes, I exulted, as an influx of spiritual warrior energy flooded through me. I resolved to prevail over this situation. Not only would I impress Christa with my newly found emotional equanimity, I'd use this experience as an advanced placement class to expanded consciousness. I felt a rush of power, the same sort of force that had sustained me through a multitude of self-induced crises during my crazed and tempestuous life thus far.

By the time Saturday night arrived, I knew I was up to the challenge. After helping Christa hang the last pieces on the gallery walls, I made sure the caterers set up the appetizers and wine in their proper places. Then I rushed to my apartment to get dressed—the owner wanted to do some publicity shots with Christa before the show opened to the public, and I'd agreed to meet her later at the gallery. Lexie planned to come by the show around seven-thirty.

I stood in my bathroom at home, doing my makeup and ruminating that all those years of *Vogue* subscriptions had paid off—I didn't look half bad. I slipped on my black embroidered April Cornell dress and wove my long hair into intricate coils. Noticing a pair of black silk gloves on my dresser (most recently worn for "Catholic Schoolgirls Gone Bad Night" at a local club), I pulled them on and considered the effect. Superb. Just the sort of decadent femme *noir* look I was after. Now, if the men would just leave me alone (they hadn't when I'd dressed up as a fallen parochial student), I'd have a smashing evening.

As I entered the well-lighted gallery, I took in the lustrous hardwood floor and the vases of freshly cut red and white gladioli artfully positioned around the spacious loft. Strains of the Kronos Quartet playing *Spem in alium* by Tallis lifted through the air. (Christa and I, both classical music aficionados, chose their *Black Angels* CD for the opening's background.)

There stood Christa as the triumphant artist, poised and smiling next to the largest painting, talking to a small knot of admirers. She looked, well, great—after a year with her, my breath still caught in my throat every time I saw her. She wore black jeans, an impeccable white T-shirt topped with a black leather vest, and—*merde*—black motorcycle boots. She knew full well that those boots were at the top of my butch-girl fetish list, I thought, along with electric guitars, tattoos, and four-by-four trucks (curiously, SUVs didn't have the same aphrodisiacal effect on me). I only hoped that by choosing this footwear, she meant to signal her interest in a session of private frolicking later on.

She strode over to me, kissed me lightly on the lips, and grinned. "So, uh, where's Lexie?" I asked as I glanced around the crowd, steeling myself by silently chanting "merciful awareness, merciful awareness" as my chest tightened. I couldn't see anyone who looked like the pictures of Lexie that Christa kept taped to her refrigerator.

"She's not coming to Denver at all. I checked my machine a few minutes ago, and she left a message saying she decided not to come. I told you that she's a little, um, flaky sometimes about plans. I half-expected this to happen."

"What?" I fumed. "I spent the last four days doing extreme psychic calisthenics to get ready for her, and she cancels! Damn it!"

"Yeah, I know you're really disappointed," Christa said, a sarcastic edge to her voice. I could tell she was stifling the laughter that threatened to bubble up at any moment.

"Well, since you have numerous ex-lovers with whom you feel compelled to keep in touch, I'm sure this situation is bound to come up again, and I'll be ready for the next time," I countered. I stood facing her, held her hands at my sides, and stepped down hard on the toes of her boots with the tips of my shoes. "So, you think you'll have any energy left after the show?" I said, looking into her luminous eyes with unmistakable longing. I always thought of her eyes as sea-misted, since they shifted color from azure to aqua to emerald and back again like the ocean mirrored the changing hues of the sky. *Los ojos del mar,* eyes of the sea.

"I think the chances are very good, *inamorata*," she said gently as she gazed back at me and tightened her grip on my hands. We stood staring at each other for a minute or an hour, I'm not sure which, as time seemed to expand infinitely. Christa and I did this trancing-out thing often, and even when we were apart, I could close my eyes and summon up a sense of the *eternally full and present moment* that I experienced so frequently with her. *Kairos,* I remembered the ancient Greeks calling this sort of limitless interval. In that all-encompassing instant, her ex-girlfriends and their pictures and paraphernalia and our respective histories and insecurities vanished, and I knew that there was nothing, absolutely nothing, to worry about.

—LIFE JACKETS UNDER SEATS—

Kathryn Ann

FIONA WAS BORN WANTING to consume the things that attracted her, a proclivity that has never left her, though she has learned to discriminate somewhat.

When she was little, just an infant, really, she was partial to pussy willows; she would brush the tips over her eyelids and cheeks, then push them up her nose. They tickled going in, caressed coming out. Other things, things that didn't shed, she put in her mouth: bottle caps, her big brother's Brylcreem, the smooth inner rind of a cracked walnut, a flimsy Dixie cup paddle that she liked to suck on even more than the ice cream in the little paper pot.

Once, her mother interceded just as she was about to pour a bright pearl of mercury from a smashed thermometer out of her palm onto her tongue.

She was a sensitive kid. She couldn't be spanked. The one time her mother tried it, when Fiona wouldn't stay down for her nap, she locked herself in the bathroom and stayed in there (gnawing her toothbrush and reading comics in the empty bathtub) until her father came home and took the door off its hinges and scooped her back to her bedroom, where she clambered out

onto the sloped cedar shakes and almost escaped in a spectacu-
lar flight off the rain gutter before she was snatched back.

There were no more naps, and no more spankings.

GROWN UP, FIONA HAS TENDED to declare herself too soon in
a relationship, upsetting the delicate balance of advance and
retreat with which two people approach intimacy.

Now, at her second meeting with Greta, she wants to say "I
love you," but while honesty is the best policy, she has learned
there is an etiquette to wooing, never served by blunders of
timing. Instead she offers tea: Bengal Spice, Cranberry Cove, or
Earl Grey if caffeine is required.

She wants to say, "I love you. Stay for dinner" but doesn't.
Instead she fills a stainless-steel pot with cold water from the
tap, puts it on a burner, and flips the heat to high. Dinner will
have to wait for some subtle indication of permission before
it is offered. It would be—and here Fiona wonders if Greta
senses this too—a metaphor for what they might do together
in bed.

Fiona likes beautiful foods. A basket filled with fruits and
vegetables in the front hall, piled high with new white potatoes,
clutches of purple-tinged garlic, tomatoes with leaves and a smell
that peppers the air as soon as they are touched, a black avoca-
do, two astringent lemons, and four sweet little limes. Draped
over the side of the basket, a splay of bananas.

In the mornings she grinds her own beans for the coffee—a
blend of Kenyan for smooth and Dark French for bite—and
splashes vanilla into her oversize cup, then adds half-and-half
and a packet of Splenda (sugar makes her teeth ache) and a
scraping of nutmeg. She takes this back to bed, props the pillows, and cradles the cup, inhaling sweet steam, dopey-eyed, not
yet committed. Early morning is her favorite time of day, the
time before she has to start being herself.

And here she is again dying to say, "I love you. Stay to dinner. Stay to breakfast." Instead she pours boiling water into two

mugs and carries them into the living room, sniffing the arch cranberry scent (she sniffs at everything she plans to put into her mouth), and places them on coasters across from each other on the glass-topped coffee table.

"Take the sofa," she tells Greta and her black-and-silver marbled hair. "I like to sit on the floor."

"No. I'd rather be down there where you are," Greta answers, pushing her mug catercornered from Fiona's and levering her long body down to the rug, a shimmer of sound from the gold-plated bracelets on her long-boned wrist.

Fiona thinks of offering one of her big yellow cushions, or maybe a pillow from her bed, and decides there is such a thing as being too solicitous. She sips her tea, blinking at the berry tartness in the back of her nose as she fills her mouth with heat, pressing it against her soft inner cheeks before she swallows.

"Would you like something to eat?" is what she finally says, and feels like kicking herself.

FIONA TAMPS A CIGARETTE out of her pack of Ultra Lights as soon as Greta is out the door. She abstained for the length of the visit because Greta doesn't smoke, and now she briefly considers quitting altogether.

Fiona realizes this is a problem of hers, adopting the good habits of the people she falls in love with. The problem isn't with the good habits—it is with her own nature, which she sees as uncertain, variable, as iffy as a weather report. She pauses to read the warning in block letters across the front: CIGARETTES CAUSE CANCER. Nothing iffy about that. She prefers the French translation on the back: *la cigarette, le cancer.* There is more of a mannerliness about it, less of the bullying truth.

Greta had asked Fiona to be her sponsor after hearing her address the fourth step, the one about delineating one's character defects, at an A.A. meeting the week before.

Being a teacher, Fiona was comfortable standing at the front of the room. She had a little trick of placing herself beside the lectern instead of behind it, which suggested more candor than she really felt. She knew most of the A.A. members had listened to countless drunkalogues, so she always took a moment to consider what she might say, or how she might say it, to keep shuffling feet and glazed-over eyes to a minimum. A little self-deprecating humor, a dash of cayenne in your own eye, tended to perk people up.

"Doing this step the first time," Fiona began, her eyes scanning the room just above everyone's head, "I finally got a good look at myself." She paused, then cracked a grin. "And oh, my God..."

A ripple of laughter through the room.

"It's like—the ladies here will likely relate to this—it's like the last time you checked in the mirror you were twenty-five, Jane Fonda was your guru, salad was your main food group, you know how it is, and you figured, 'Not perfect, but not too shabby either.'

"Ten years later you take another look, not just the frontal view, but from three sides, under bright lights. And from the back too..." Here Fiona paused to pat her rump for effect. "...and well, when I finally did that with the fourth step, it wasn't what I would call the high point of my life."

Greta was the only one in the place who didn't smile. She sat there in the front row leaning forward, legs crossed, her chin propped on her fist, a bemused expression on her olive-skinned face.

She's wondering if it's raining in Nigeria, Fiona thought, and made a point of introducing herself before Greta could escape at the end of the meeting.

FIONA PUTS THE RECEIVER back in its cradle and massages the fine hair on her temples, eyes closed against the green sunlight cascading through her south-facing window, which is obscured by plants. She breathes out tension, breathes in chlorophylled relief. Greta has said yes to lunch. It's progress. One meal closer to supper.

When they discussed where, Greta suggested the Inn Cogneato, a new place midway between their apartments. Convenient. Fair.

"I can't eat at a restaurant with a pun in its name," Fiona had said, and then thought, *I would like to go back to bed now.*

A *huss* of nasal breath through the receiver. Then Greta's voice, smiling. "*Two* puns. You say where."

They agreed on the Bread Garden on Fourteenth, just off Lonsdale. Greta would have farther to come. Fiona pointed this out.

"You're sweet," Greta had said, hanging up.

Tenderness is not as light as a feather, Fiona decides, still massaging her temples. It weighs a ton.

GRAHAM CALLS LATER that day, distraught, his voice flailing with helplessness over his wife's first relapse in almost two years.

Fiona scribbles a red note in the margin of one of her students' physics exams, then pushes the stack to one side.

"What's with this family?" she says, lighting a cigarette and putting her feet up on the filing cabinet, settling in for the long haul. "Either we are an alcoholic or we marry one."

"I can't handle this anymore," Graham says, his voice now sliding into despondency. "How many times is she gonna quit before she quits? She told me she was taking Antabuse."

"They always tell you what you want to hear," Fiona says. "Addicts make excellent mirrors. Anyway, disulfiram is the alcoholic's patch. When you're planning to use, you just take it off."

"She said she wasn't planning it. Clare's been skipping classes again. The stress just…"

"Uh-huh. That's what Mom always said. Us. Dad. The stress."

"The neighbors. The boredom…" Graham is laughing now.

"The doldrums," they finish together, voices deadpan.

"It's true, though. Clare is being a little pissant. She locks herself in her room after school—when she actually goes to school. And nothing but back talk. She sneers. She's Heather Locklear on bad acid."

"She has a lot to be pissanted about, doesn't she? Do they still do acid these days? The children?"

"Black lipstick. Never a smile. And the music! If you can call it that," Graham goes on, ignoring Fiona's question.

"Yep. They're great till they're thirteen and kick you out of the nest."

"You should've been her mother. You would've been a dandy mother."

"Oh, stop. It's bad enough you passing those genes along. I made the only responsible choice."

"Too bad, sis. I love the prototype. Not to mention you're the only grownup she respects."

"Graham, I put Bailey's in her formula when she wouldn't sleep. She does not *respect* me. She recognizes a fellow anarchist, is all. Anyhow, I don't want to be a mother. I *want* a mother."

"So. I'm hoping if I can coax Helen into detox—could you handle Clare for a few days?"

"The word *flight* comes to mind."

FIONA IS MORE NERVOUS than hungry. At least that is how she interprets the clench in her stomach. A vision of straw-colored Chardonnay, moisture beaded on the glass, blossoms in her mind's eye. She blinks and it is gone.

The café is crowded with workers on their lunch breaks. People line up at the long counter, bend over the glass-fronted display case, carry trays of spinach quiche and chicken and sundried tomato sandwiches on focaccia bread to their tables.

Fiona picks at a blueberry scone and wonders if there are any shreds of blueberry skin between her teeth. She swishes coffee around the inside of her mouth and wishes she had selected an apple instead from the bowl of fruit on the countertop right beside the muffins and scones. She decides the placement must be strategic. People think "fruit" and "nutritious" as they reach for an oatmeal-cinnamon fat bomb.

Greta's scent arrives slightly ahead of the rest of her. Vanilla and something citrusy. She nudges a chair with her knee, sits down opposite Fiona, and looks across the table at her. Her gaze is like a stone dropped into a pond. There is a moment before either of them speaks when something like a clatter of wings passes between them.

Less said, Fiona reminds herself.

GRAHAM CALLS A FEW DAYS later to inform Fiona he is waiting for a cab to take Helen to detox and that Clare is making her way over via public transit.

"Why aren't you driving everybody? Did Helen get another DUI? Car impounded?"

"Bad timing. It's in the shop. Something about the carburetor. Hey, sit down! You just had one!" Graham's voice momentarily fades as he muffles the receiver with his hand.

"I told you not to get the Civic. No power in the plant. How bad is she?"

"I had to bring her vodka and milk in bed this morning. She couldn't get up. Now she won't stay down."

"Oh, Christ, Graham. Let her have what she wants. If she's that sick, she needs it. You want her having a seizure?"

"I don't want her totally incoherent and falling down before we get to the clinic."

"Um. Has it occurred to you that's why they call it detox?"

"Clare's aiming to arrive on the six-fifteen Seabus. Can you meet her at the quay?"

"Delighted to. She'll be just in time to make a circus out of my first dinner date with Greta."

FIONA WAITS IN FRONT of the link fence at the quay, smoking a cigarette and watching the Seabus beetle across English Bay.

All day it does that, like a waterbug skimming the surface with its little load of commuters. Inside, there are signs reading LIFE JACKETS UNDER SEATS. There ought to be signs like that and life jackets everywhere, Fiona reflects, the world being what it is.

She rarely rides the Seabus. It makes her uneasy. What if it should capsize? Or be rammed by one of the Alaska cruise ships that steams in and out of the harbor, too vast to see right under its nose? All it is is a floating room, with six sealed pneumatic doors on each side. If it sank, there would be no way to get out. It would slowly fill up with cloudy water and everyone would bob around inside in their life jackets until they drowned.

Suddenly, Clare is kissing her cheek, leaving a warm sticky spot and a whiff of grape bubble gum.

"Hi, Aunty Fee."

She checks an impulse to cluck her tongue at the sight of Clare's pale, oval face. The maroon eye shadow she wears makes her look like she's been socked, twice.

I want to feed and shelter this street urchin, Fiona thinks, hefting the girl's duffel bag and starting back to the car. She heaves the duffel into the trunk of her yellow VW bug, which Clare once described as a lemon on steroids.

Nothing much in the plant there, either, but it looks vaguely edible, which appeals to Fiona.

They drive in mutual silence. Small talk has never worked with Clare, not even when she was a baby being cradled by the big people who cooed and chirruped into her startled little face. At first she'd seemed alarmed by the racket they made, white showing around her watery blue irises. But by the time her eyes darkened to teal she had learned to gaze beyond or through the chattering heads, except when Fiona held her.

She'd seemed interested in Fiona, who spoke to her in complete sentences, her voice lightly emotive as she mused to her about the mechanics of reality, the overarching truths of quantum theory, rehearsing her classroom presentations.

"You can't talk to a baby like that," Helen had said, but she couldn't do anything about it since she relied on her sister-in-law, who mostly managed to keep her drinking to a nightly routine, for impromptu baby-sitting services.

"May the Dancing Wu-Li Masters be with you," she would whisper into Clare's pink shell of an ear before handing her over at the end of a session—which might have lasted a couple of days or a week, depending on the length of Helen's spree.

It was at this time, when Helen's postpartum depression threw off its cowl and revealed itself as just another gaudy addiction, that Fiona started to quit drinking herself. It took her three years, like a car in the wrong gear stuttering down the road. Then she slammed it into first and floored it, and never looked back.

When Graham asked how she'd done it—hoping that whatever it was was something Helen might do as well—all she would say was, "I got religion."

"Uh-huh. The only time you say 'Jesus' is before 'fucking' and 'Christ.' "

"Well, that's true."

"YOU'VE MUTATED INTO A BOBO, Aunty Fee."

Clare has dumped her Walkman into the cornucopia in the front hall, affixed her earphones to a Spanish onion, dragged her duffel through to the bedroom, and is now rooting through the fridge. She hauls out a can of Dr. Pepper and goes into the living room, tosses herself onto the couch, platform sneakers not quite touching its hemp surface.

"Dare I ask?"

"A bourgeois bohemian. Check out your stuff." She cracks open the soda and chugs half the can.

"Don't spill, munchkin. I have company coming."

"Palm plants. Nubby furniture. Brown and white walls. It looks like an IKEA catalog in here. Except for the bottle of booze on the bookcase. Hey, what's with that?"

"In case I ever decide the right choice is suicide."

"Oh."

"And that's not brown and white. It's ecru and butternut."

Fiona looks at the bottle. She's had it there perched on the bookcase for months (a Christmas gift from a friend who didn't know she'd quit) like a raven croaking: *nevermore*. Now it occurs to her to wonder why she didn't just pour it down the sink or leave it on a park bench for someone who could make use of it.

"My point exactly. Tiffany lamps. Pretentious."

"They're faux Tiffany. And much as I'd like to discuss my decor with you, I have to start dinner. Amuse yourself. The remote is within reach of your right arm."

"*Sex and the City* isn't on till nine."

"Tripe. You might as well smoke pot."

"I do. Lots and lots of pot."

"Not here you don't."

"HOW'S SCHOOL?" Fiona is standing in front of the stove stirring sliced almonds and coconut in a copper pan.

Clare has wandered into the kitchen. She leans both elbows on the counter and sticks her finger into a ceramic bowl of hummus, then licks it clean, catlike.

"Gratuitous," she answers, rolling the tip of her tongue around her lips.

Einstein's spawn and Lolita rolled into one, thinks Fiona. *My God.*

"Is it a date?" She pokes at the hummus again.

"Is what a date?"

"This. Tonight. Who's the company?"

"Oh. Greta. She's just someone from my A.A. meetings. I'm her sponsor."

"I thought sponsors weren't supposed to date the rank and file."

"We're not dating. We're having dinner."

"Right. Is she gay?"

"We haven't discussed our affectional orientations," Fiona says dryly.

"Is she nicer than Carly?"

"Carly was nice. What do you care about Carly? She moved out over a year ago."

"She didn't like me."

"Well, she didn't like me either, as it turned out. Perceptive people intimidate her. Take it as a compliment."

The phone warbles and Clare runs to answer it. Fiona hears her say, "No way." Then, "Aunty Fee, Dad wants to talk to you."

Fiona rinses curry powder and turmeric from her fingers and takes the receiver from Clare, who stage whispers: "Mom's escaped."

SHE SUDDENLY CAN'T remember the etiquette of introductions—is the older person presented first, or the younger?—like she can never remember which direction to turn the steering wheel when the car goes into a skid. Not that she's ever needed to know, but she puzzles over it now and then just in case.

Clare is lying on the couch again. She tips her head over her shoulder and raises an arm in salute.

"Hi. I'm the niece." She rolls onto her side and twists her neck to get a better look at Greta, who lifts an eyebrow, smiles.

"Family emergency," Fiona says. "Clare's joining us for dinner. I'm sorry there wasn't time to warn you."

Curtains are drawn, daisies fresh from the park across the street adorn the dining table, candles flicker.

"No. I like surprises," Greta says. "You have a beautiful home." She appraises the room, her eyes catching on the bottle of Maker's Mark on the bookcase. "Everything is so…considered."

Clare snorts with a child's gleeful abandon.

"Spritzer?" Fiona says. "Come on in the kitchen. You can advise me on the garlic-ginger sauce. I tend to overdo it on the spices."

"You got that from Carly," Clare says. "She always said your cooking was bland. Carly was Aunty Fee's last lov-er," she adds helpfully, stretching out the end syllable and casting a sly glance at Greta.

A little tune cycles through Fiona's head. She realizes it's the one the I Screem truck plays without cease when it motors by her apartment on hot afternoons. She figures that even if she wanted an ice cream, she couldn't get outside fast enough to stop the truck. She imagines the driver is so mesmerized by his own jingle that all he can do is stare straight ahead and drive and drive. A kid would have to fall under the wheels to get his attention.

She drops ice cubes into a tall glass, fills it with club soda, and offers it along with a saucer of lime wedges. Her cheeks are hot, and it probably shows.

"I used to do this with Cuervo Gold and a little salt," Greta says, taking the proffered glass and sucking the lime before she plops it into the soda.

Fiona turns away and starts crushing garlic bulbs on a breadboard with the flat of a knife.

THE KNOCKING AT THE DOOR is hesitant, then urgent. After a pause there is a loud thud, possibly from the heel of a hand, possibly from a forehead.

Fiona, who is passing the apple chutney to Greta, freezes.

Clare says, "Fuck! Mom."

Greta reaches out and takes the bowl of chutney, places it back on the dining table, looks from Fiona to Clare.

"Want me to get it?" she asks.

Fiona stares at her, considering the pros and cons. She and Clare could hide in the bathroom. Helen might be drunk enough to believe she's come to the wrong apartment.

"Let's nobody get it," Clare suggests, swallowing the last of her milk and banging her tumbler down on the table.

"It's all right," Greta says, briefly touching the back of Fiona's hand. "We'll deal with it, whatever it is."

Fiona takes a deep breath, pushes her chair back, and stands up. "I don't think Helen likes East Indian cuisine," she says inanely.

"Meet the family emergency," Clare says, wiping at her milk mustache.

A WAVE OF ETHYL ALCOHOL precedes Helen into the front hall.

Fiona sizes her up instantly and concludes she is at that precarious point where a drink too many, or one too few, will topple her either into belligerence on the one hand or a fit of weeping on the other. For the moment, she is neutral.

Fiona takes advantage of Helen's brief passivity to steer her into the bedroom, where she helps her onto the bed, removes her shoes, and snuggles a blanket up to her chin.

Helen has temporarily lost track of her reason for coming here. She permits Fiona's ministrations, then starts to clamber back out of the bed.

"I need a drink," she says.

"Did you bring anything?"

"In my purse."

The purse is on the desk. Fiona riffles through it—lipstick, a vial of pills, a pack of Rothmans, sunglasses with shreds of tobacco on the lenses, a roll of Certs breath mints, a plastic mickey of Smirnoff's full to the shoulders, and, inexplicably, a melon baller. Possibly she had been aiming for the corkscrew in her kitchen drawer and missed.

Fiona goes to the kitchen and comes back with a glass half full of milk, pours two inches of the vodka into it so Helen can see what she's getting, and gives her the glass.

Helen drinks, takes a breath, drinks again. Her hands are trembling, but not too badly yet.

"Take it easy with that," Fiona says, taking the glass away and putting it on the bedside table out of reach. "We just want to keep you topped up until we can get you to detox."

"Topped up. Ha ha. Where's Clare? I have to talk to her," she says, suddenly remembering her mission. "She's doing drugs, the little shit."

"Oh, well. They do," Fiona says vaguely.

She turns her head and sees Clare standing in the doorway, hands stuffed into the pockets of her Mavi jeans. Her expression is a study in contrast: lips squinched into a moue of disgust, eyebrows drawn together, eyes wounded.

Fiona remembers standing just this way as a kid arriving home from school, angry, bewildered, staring at her own mother asleep on a bed or a couch or even in a chair, head lolling as if on hinges, a strand of spittle stretching from her chin.

She had taught herself how to cook reasonably nutritious meals for four by the time she was eleven, wanting more than anything to hold the family together at a time when food seemed to be the only glue at hand.

"Hey," she says softly to Clare. "Call your Dad. Tell him your Mom's okay."

CLARE IS LAUGHING when Fiona comes out of the bedroom.

She has the vodka—now down by half—with her, and tucks it in behind the bottle of Maker's Mark before she sits down at the table. Thinking it's starting to look like a bar in here, Fiona decides to dump the bourbon down the sink at first opportunity.

"He said he'll be right over," Clare says.

Whatever they were talking about has temporarily made Clare forget the woman in the bedroom who is and isn't her mother. Her blue eyes are lighted. There are spots of pink on her pale cheeks.

"I was telling your niece about hearing you speak at A.A.," Greta offers. "You were so composed. I'm told that's your teacher persona."

"Introducing grade twelves to the inadequacies of Newtonian physics requires composure. A lot of composure."

"Much like convincing my kids that history doesn't have to be boring."

"You have kids?" This from Clare.

"I'm a teacher, like your aunt." Greta gives Clare an apologetic smile, as if with this information she has placed herself under suspicion.

"Actually, they grasp quantum theory pretty well when I use the movie *The Matrix* as an analogy."

"Keanu Reeves is extremely passé," Clare says. "Whoa!" she adds in the most moronic voice she can muster.

"I don't bring Keanu into it."

"Aunty Fee manages people," Clare says happily. "Dad says she's the only one who can get me to do something I don't want." She looks at Greta. There is pride in her face.

"Getting you to do something you don't want is like trying to herd grasshoppers."

Clare yelps with laughter picturing this.

"Pipe down," Fiona says, pointing toward the bedroom. "Let's not rouse the lion. She has in mind you need a serious talking to."

"Like, I'd rather die."

"Not an option," says Fiona, stacking plates and heading for the kitchen. She comes back a minute later carrying a clear glass bowl of mango ice cream sprinkled with toasted almonds and coconut.

This time the knock on the door is terse.

"Are we popular or what?" Clare says, helping herself to ice cream.

WHILE GRAHAM IS IN the bedroom, Fiona puts the dishes in the sink to soak and starts a pot of coffee.

When Greta comes back from the bathroom, Fiona is at the table drumming her fingers on her placemat, trying not to think about a cigarette. Now that she's seen Greta three times and hasn't smoked during any of their encounters, she has given the false impression that she is a nonsmoker. She has snared herself in a lie of omission.

The burbling coffeemaker emits a sigh and subsides.

Clare sits cross-legged on the living room floor with one of the yellow cushions clasped against her chest, her face too close to the television screen, watching *Sex and the City*. Even from behind, she looks rapt. Fiona wonders how she can so blithely ignore the drama unfolding around her. Then again, she's had a lot of practice.

Voices drift from the bedroom, Graham's, coaxing, then Helen's, adamant. The words "and God knows what else" emerge, but the rest is indistinct.

Greta slides her hand across the table. Her fingertips come to rest near Fiona's, who stops drumming.

"I'm sorry. What a disaster this…" Fiona starts to say, and stops when Greta's fingers close over hers.

"Oh, I don't know," Greta says. "So much of life is bad theater. This is actually pretty interesting."

Fiona slowly turns her hand until it is palm up inside Greta's. It is warm in there. Possibly even safe. For the moment she forgets about the cigarette.

Helen, suddenly oblivious to everything except a prickling anxiety as her blood alcohol level falters, chooses this moment to come looking for the vodka. When Graham tries to stop her she yells, "Get off, you bastard!"

There is a brief scuffle, a crash, and then Helen emerges from the bedroom and stands swaying at the entrance to the living room, her hand cupped over her nose.

"Who shut the door?" she says, as if the door, or whoever closed it, is responsible for her blunder. Her eyes roam the room, then settle on Fiona.

"I need to be topped up," she says. Her words are slurring. "Top me up," she tries again.

No one moves. Graham comes out of the bedroom and hovers behind his wife. He looks grim, possibly on the verge of tears. He raises his hand and puts it on her shoulder. She shakes it off and, finally spotting the liquor cache, aims herself at the bookcase, arms outstretched like a wind-up toy.

Two things happen at once:

Clare, who has decided to seek refuge in the bathroom, stands up and spins around, accidentally catching her mother in the face with her cushion as she tosses it toward the couch. At the same instant, Graham reaches out to stop Helen and accidentally gives her a shove.

Helen, whose reflexes are sluggish, collides with the bookcase face first.

Everyone freezes while it teeters, barely holds on to its cargo of books, but tips the bottle of bourbon onto the floor, where it shatters. The pungent smell of sour mash whiskey chokes the room.

Helen is first to break the tableau.

She says, "Whoopsie doodle," wipes a smear of blood across her chin, and picks the unjettisoned mickey of vodka—lying on its side—off the shelf. She unscrews the cap, takes a slug, then sinks to the floor, legs splayed.

"Well. I was just thinking of getting rid of that bottle," Fiona says, shading her eyes with her free hand.

Graham clears his throat, strides back to the bedroom, starts collecting Helen's things.

Greta releases Fiona's hand and heads for the bathroom. She comes back with a wet washcloth and kneels in front of Helen, cupping her chin and dabbing at the blood. Helen sprawls passively, like a broken puppet.

CLARE HAS DECLINED FIONA'S offer of Ovaltine and gone to bed. Bourbon and glass shards have been mopped and cleared, but the fumes still drench the air. The candles have long since gone out, and Fiona hasn't thought to light fresh ones.

Greta dries the last bowl and puts it in the cupboard. She folds the tea towel neatly, drapes it over the dish rack.

"Let's go sit on the porch," she says. "It's still a bit fragrant in here. And you probably want a cigarette."

Fiona looks at her, blinks.

"Nope. Not psychic," Greta says. She lifts a clean ashtray from the cupboard and shuts the door. "Come with me."

They sit in pine-green plastic chairs sturdy enough to balance on the back legs, and prop their feet up on the porch rail. They can see all the way up Grouse to the shaved strip of earth and the strings of lights that outline the boundaries of the ski slope on the peak, deserted now, the snow rolled up for summer like a white rug.

"They'll go out at two, precisely," Fiona says. She is holding a smoking cigarette as far from Greta as she can get it.

"What will? Relax. I've been around smokers all my life. You're a pretty considerate one, as they go."

"The lights. I picture a little old man in coveralls up there, the janitor, mopping up. He hits the switch on his way out."

"Whimsy *and* wit. Insomniac?"

"Not really. I just need the quiet time. More as I get older, it seems. Less sleep, more reflection. By the way, thanks for taking charge of Helen. You were heroic."

"She'd worn the rest of you out, is all. Poor Helen."

"Poor Graham."

"That too. Can I ask you something?"

"Depends," Fiona says, stubbing her cigarette. "Will the answer further lower your estimation of me?"

"You judge." Greta smiles in the dark. "Was Carly a sober relationship?"

Fiona watches as a cat slinks from the shadow of a car parked on the street below, hesitates, ears pricked for danger, then hurtles itself across the road into the park. A quivering of daffodils marks its progress through a flower bed.

"Not at first. But it wasn't till I stopped drinking that it stopped working. She was demanding. Critical. Not particularly giving. I don't know how I didn't see that right away."

"You were sedated."

"Well, that. And low expectations. I had the absurd notion that abstinence would equal happiness. But it didn't. She took the furniture. I redecorated. End of sitcom."

"Not drinking only makes you *eligible* to be happy. How are your expectations these days?"

Their conversation is interrupted by a light tap-tap on the sliding door, and Clare steps out onto the porch, trailing a blanket.

"Can't sleep?" Fiona asks.

"Nuh-uh," Clare says.

Greta gets up, puts her hand on Clare's shoulder, guides her into the chair she has vacated. She leans her lower back against the rail, hands tucked into her armpits, and gazes down at the two of them.

Clare hunches forward, clasping the blanket around her throat, peering intently at her bare toes as if she might be considering a pedicure.

Waif, Fiona thinks, glad inside that her niece is here, wrapped in a blanket, safe. Sober, Fiona is a safe person to be with. Her little cup brims with this thought. She can't change the past, but at least she has a say in the present. Though at the moment, words seem to be at a premium.

Graham is probably still at the detox clinic, sitting in an office while a worker asks questions and fills out forms and forms. They'll have given Helen something, phenobarb or Ativan, something to keep her quiet until morning, when they'll force her to get up for a medical assessment—Fiona wonders if the dwarf doctor with the glass eye is still attending—and then there'll be the seventy-two hours of withdrawing in agonizingly slow increments before she can come home and start the real work of sobering up. Or not.

"I didn't mean to butt in," Clare whispers. Fiona almost doesn't hear her.

She reaches over and strokes Clare's back, then slips her hand under the blanket at the nape of the girl's neck and squeezes.

"Ovaltine first. Then bed," she says.

—THE LOCKED DRAWER—
Mary Sharratt

"I am half sick of shadows," said
The Lady of Shalott.

—"The Lady of Shalott," Alfred Lord Tennyson

THERE ARE NIGHTS when she still comes to me. On winter nights or late in fall when the wind is raw and wet, blowing hail or freezing rain, she wakes me from deep sleep. I hear her fists beating on the window, her schoolgirl voice stretched thin and high as she calls to me like Cathy's ghost to Heathcliff.

"Elaine, let me in! It's so cold out here."

When you die young, you are frozen, a photograph behind glass. My hair whitens and goes brittle, my skin mottles and sags, but she will always be seventeen. The girl who once burned my letters. She never had such power as the power she'd had over me. Like a demon lover, she held me by the throat, wholly in her thrall until I was willing to make any promise. Then one day she decided to call it quits. "You knew there would come a time when we'd have to stop this," she told me. When I wept and protested, she said, "Grow up, Elaine. You're embarrassing me." But the same hands that once

270

pushed me away now pound on my window, trying to force their way back in.

She is so close. All I have to do is crawl out from under the covers—carefully as not to wake Ed, who sleeps fitfully these nights, his breath labored and sour, smelling of the medication they make him take for his heart. My feet find the Chinese slippers with the worn-down soles and take me silently across the room. I reach the window, my palms on the sill, my forehead against the cold pane. This is the moment she vanishes, her spell broken. I shiver and cry without making any noise. Only an elm branch is scraping at the window. Elm is the coffin-maker's tree. She is sixty years dead, bones in a box in the earth.

THERE WAS A TIME I WENT to visit her grave every year. I told Ed I was going to see an old school friend. Though her parents had money and though she was their only child, they buried her under a small gray slab and then neglected her. If someone came to tend her grave and leave her flowers, it was me. I used to bring her lilies on her birthday, her favorite flower.

The events surrounding her death were these. After a bitter fight with her father, she drank half a bottle of his cognac and fell off a bridge into the river and drowned. I was fifty miles away when it happened, and yet I cannot blot out the image of the twisting arc of her body plunging off that bridge. How long did she fall before she sliced into the water? And once she broke the surface, how deep did gravity drag her? All the way to the bottom of the river, her face lost in the mud and weeds? How long was she conscious before the darkness swallowed her?

Her parents insisted it was an accident, a dare. Not a suicide. *Vivian Webster: 1922–1939.* They only had her name and the dates of her birth and death carved on the stone. No endearments, no Bible verses, no "Rest in Peace." Maybe that was why her soul took to wandering.

When Ed and I moved to Pennsylvania, even I began to forget about her. Except Vivian would not be forgotten. Each time I thought I had finally gotten over her, she came to me, cold and drenched in river water, crying my name on the other side of the closed window.

NOW MY SLIPPERED FEET turn away and guide me back to bed. Easing my body down beside Ed, I try to take comfort in his warmth, the sound of his breathing. I want more than anything to go back into a dreamless sleep, but it's no use. I keep seeing her on the inside of my eyelids. Her fingers fight their way through the covers, clutching at me. When we were sixteen, she made me promise I would love her forever. She keeps coming back to remind me of my promise. Now it's my turn to push her away.

"Leave me alone, Vivian. I'm too old for this."

But her drowned voice eats away at me relentlessly, waves lashing against a cliff. One day I will crumble, my defenses eroded.

She made me swear I would never marry. Except when it came to her, she wanted me to remain as chaste as those maidens in the medieval romances she read to me. As pure as Elaine the Lily Maid. But even Elaine married Lancelot in the end. Never mind that she had to trick him into it by pretending to be someone else, wearing Guinevere's dress. She got Lancelot and then gave birth to his son, Galahad. The end of their story.

I met Ed when he was on leave from the war. Everyone was astonished that a man like him would see anything in me. My mother said I would be lucky to get any husband at all, considering how I had disgraced myself over you. But life always contrives of a way to punish us for our betrayals. I couldn't have children. My uterus was a cracked vessel; I could conceive but not carry. All those disappointments, Vivian. The lives that were lost inside me, never to be born. Waking up at night to the cramping and the blood, then the doctor gave me pills and I saw angels on the ceiling. When it was over, Ed brought me roses. After the fifth miscarriage, he told me we didn't have to try anymore.

Over the years, he slipped away from me. Maybe he was haunted by his own lost love, a wartime romance, some hungry and adoring French girl he shared his chocolate ration with, who called him a hero. Now that we are both old, we sleep side by side like brother and sister. I can hear you laughing and telling me that I kept my promise to you after all.

Remember how you made me memorize "The Lady of Shalott"? That poem became my life. I spent my years weaving the sights and shadows I saw in the mirror, never daring to look out the window at the world, at the fabled city we created in the stories we told each other—our magic city, many-towered. I knew if I looked toward that place, I would be cursed.

Ed is dying. The doctor hedges and equivocates, but I can see him fading day by day. I try to be a comfort, to make him laugh like he used to, but soon he will lie in the earth like you. I think he, at least, will slumber quietly, leaving me to live out the rest of my days alone in the four-bedroom house we bought for the children we thought we would have.

These are the things that make up a home. The wainscoted walls enclose me like the planks of coffinwood enclose you. They shine like the dark mirror I lived my life inside. My house smells of the beeswax I use to polish the heavy furniture and the cherrywood writing table with the locked drawer where your photograph is hidden. I have not unlocked that drawer in fifty-odd years. Now I can no longer remember where I hid the key.

When I am a widow, my own woman again, I will gather my strength, go to that drawer, break the wood with Ed's old hatchet if I have to. I will take out your picture. Then the mirror will shatter. The web I have spent sixty years weaving will fly apart. I will look toward the magic city we built together stone by stone. I will find an abandoned boat, write my name on the prow, and float down that river, even if it costs me what little life that remains, even if my eyes darken and go blind at the sight of that grandeur, I will go there. I will make the journey down the river that claimed your body. Then the glass will shatter and you will finally step in from out of the cold.

—HEAT—

Betty Blue

for a summer girl

THERE WAS SOMETHING WONDERFUL about the pain of summer asphalt on the soles of her feet. June walked to the mailbox slowly, deliberately, letting it ride her nerves straight up from the ground to her heart. The air was almost tangible, shimmering at a temperature of over 110. The metal box would burn too, and she gripped the handle and let her hand sit a moment, enjoying the sting. If there was nothing inside, it would be an answer, and she wasn't sure she wanted to know, not yet.

This moment in which she stood under the sweltering sun— a pure, glad, hopeful moment full of the scent of hot ground and the white noise of rising cicadas (and desire, for the heat in her hand and her feet to be coming off the body of Claira beneath her own)—this moment was unassailable and she wanted it as much as she wanted Claira, and it crushed her lungs and flushed her skin and made her drip deep rivers of sweat beneath her cotton shirt as much as the thought of Claira did. And in this box was the end of The Moment, and maybe the end of something else, and so she stood still and fused with the seconds and the sun.

Claira had been nothing more than another body in the air-conditioned attic of the Copy House just a month ago. It was a job, and they zoned out in front of the terminals, secretly glad to have to work because it was keeping them cool. June spent her nights at the university, absurdly trying to create a postbaccalaureate premed student out of herself in her thirties, cramming her brain with things a liberal arts student had managed to miss: trig, biology, physics, and chem.

The only med school to integrate traditional healing with holistic was here, at the University of Arizona, and its oncology program was one of the best in the nation. Only in-state students could apply, so she'd stayed here after the death of her Naomi, like the biblical Ruth making Naomi's people her people, and Tucson became home. This crusade to enter medical school was the only way June knew to avenge the loss of Naomi to the monster of cancer.

She hardly noticed the changing landscape of bodies beside her in the data entry room by day; they were arms moving in kinetic rhythm with the chatter of the keys while she recited chemical equations in her head. Claira, who sat beside her, had come from somewhere up north. She had beautiful sienna skin, and dark eyes like new moons, and that was all June knew about her.

The air conditioning quit on a Friday afternoon, the first of July. The upstairs loft was impossible, and they gathered on the mailing floor below. It was an impromptu party; even the boss joined in, actually cracked the beer he kept in his own fridge and passed it around. Claira laughed and smiled an amazing wide, white grin as they chatted and drank, and June had looked at her, really looked. In a hot instant among the grime and clatter of postal machinery, her life was altered.

Claira evidently thought June was a riot with her deadpan humor, laughing and pressing her cool fingers against June's arm when she'd push her mockingly away after a joke. June began to fall.

They went out for drinks with the rest of the crew after "work" blurred into a slow exodus to evening. June had never gone along before, but Monday was a holiday and she could afford to skip studying for just one night. They talked, and June had too much to drink and flirted openly, and Claira thought that was funny, thought she was being teased. She leaned into the table on her elbows and rested her chin in her hands, grinning, forgetting the others, enjoying June, and June devoured her light. There had been no one in the three years since Naomi; she hadn't wanted anyone. And now Claira had woken her.

Friday night became Saturday morning, and they left reluctantly at the closing of the bar. "I don't want the night to end," said Claira, ruby lips turning into a frown on which a full moon painted a pale invitation. June drew her close on the pretext of falling against the door of Claira's truck, and looked again at the light-painted lips. She would be sorry later if necessary; she would do something about this now. She brought her mouth to Claira's and partook. There was a stunned immobility from the mouth against her own, but as her hand slipped up into the nap of Claira's hair to keep the unsober world from tilting, June was thrust back against the pickup door and a body was pressing into hers, an unbelievably soft body, a woman, Claira.

Claira pursued the kisses as though they would float away like butterflies, taking them into her mouth, taking June against her tongue frantically, without breathing. June surrendered, overpowered, overwhelmed, certain she was dreaming. When Claira lifted her head to breathe at last, her eyes stared into June's and melted her, the embodiment of truth. Behind her in the parking lot was an empty space where their coworkers' cars had been. June's car stood alone.

"You're not driving," said Claira in answer to the glance. She brushed June's curls back from her face and flattened her hands against the panel of the truck, one on either side of the auburn head as though studying her. June had not let go of her, and so the arms around Claira's waist still pressed them together. "I'm taking you home."

June stumbled into the passenger seat as Claira steered her inside, head reeling as she tried to decide what that meant. Was she taking her to June's home or to Claira's? She hadn't gotten around the blur in her head to realize Claira had no idea where she lived until the truck was pulling into the drive of a west-side house, not June's, so obviously Claira's.

It was intensely quiet out here beyond the city, nestled in the desert feet of the mountains. Still eighty degrees at two in the morning, it felt good to stand under the unbothered stars. June leaned back with her body against the door as she waited for Claira to lock up the truck. The air was electric with the promise of coming monsoons, picking up the scent of sage and mesquite and lifting the tiny hairs on her arms in a soft almost-breeze. She closed her eyes and listened to the crickets harmonize the night, and heard the crunch of Claira's boots on the gravel before her.

"Come on," said Claira, taking her hand and leading her to the door. It was a small one with a screen, the back of the old house, and their feet drew welcoming creaks from the floors as they slipped silently through the kitchen to a room that smelled like the sage-rubbed wind. "Lie down," said Claira, and June found a wooden bed frame beside her in the dark with the help of her shins.

June sat and watched Claira in the beads of light from the half-covered window, wishing she could say something but finding her tongue as thick and formless as the featherbed she sat on. She wanted to grab Claira, do something, but her nervous drinking had been over the top, and she was beginning to be sorry.

"I'm going to make you some tea," said Claira, turning to the door. "Just lie down."

It hadn't taken long for the spinning bed beneath her to send June staggering for the door that she hoped led to a bathroom. She was sick, with the merciful lack of feeling that too much beer allowed.

"I thought I'd find you here," said Claira, behind her.

June put her head down on the seat of the toilet. "Oh, God, Claira," she moaned. "I'm sorry. I'm sorry. God, I'm an asshole."

"Actually, I'm flattered," Claira replied, and though June didn't look up she could hear the devilish smile that delivered the words. "I assume you drank all that to give you bravado. I've never inspired the need for bravado before."

June laughed weakly and Claira held out her hand to help her up, but she shook her head. "Leave me *some* dignity," said June ruefully.

The protest of a kettle whistled at the other end of the house. "There's tea," Claira said, and disappeared, leaving June to drag herself up to the porcelain pedestal of the sink and flood her face with water and her mouth with toothpaste. She looked in the mirror and tried to give some order to her disorganized curls, then sighed. It didn't matter now. She'd be sleeping on a couch.

In the kitchen, Claira was standing by the window with her mug, looking out, and June felt an ache in her stomach that had nothing to do with the queasiness of alcohol. The smooth lines of Claira's bare arms made June want to step up behind her and run her hands along them, down the outsides and up the insides to meet the dip of her breasts and hold Claira against her, hands over the rise in the tempo of her heart and the quickening of breath beneath them. June had fucked up. She picked up her tea from the table and breathed in the unusual scent. She tested it and Claira turned from the window.

"Raspberry leaves and alfalfa," said Claira. "Good for the stomach."

"Folk wisdom," said June, with a smile. "That's what I'm planning to specialize in."

"UA med?" asked Claira, and June nodded as she sipped. "I thought about that," said Claira. "Thinking of vet science now. Oncology."

Oncology. June watched Claira's strong and slender hand trace the border of her cup, unable to speak for a moment at the utterance of that word. "Sometimes I think animals are more civilized than people," Clara said after a moment. She smiled over her cup and went out of the kitchen toward the living room, and June followed.

It was more of a parlor, June thought as she came into the room from the narrow hall. A house like this would have a parlor, from an era of genteel ranch simplicity. At first glance, it appeared to be decorated in southwestern chic, which didn't seem like Claira's thing. June looked more closely at the pottery and jewelry arranged inside the built-in armoire and saw that these weren't the fashionable things that even bohemian Fourth Avenue Street Fair vendors sold now for a grotesque profit. These were made by someone's hand. They were real, and she had seen this sort of work before.

"They're mine," Claira said when June looked up at her. "I used to make them for tourists at Window Rock, but these were my favorites and I kept them for me."

"Window Rock?" asked June. It hugged the Arizona–New Mexico border, and that, June knew, was reservation land.

"I'm Navajo," said Claira, and June paused, surprised, in the act of bringing the mug to her lips. Claira laughed. "Half," she added. "A lot of people mistake me for Mexican. But my mother's Anglo; she fell in love with my dad and moved to the reservation with him—and here I am."

"Really?" said June, feeling the room tilt around her. Something moved in her that was beyond longing. Naomi was Navajo. It seemed absurd, but she felt suddenly that this was her "Boaz" standing before her; Naomi had sent June to her: *her people.* She looked once more at Claira's understanding smile, wishing she could belong to it.

Behind Claira, the room was welcoming and warm, with woven blankets draped among antique leather lampshades and dark wooden beams. Crimson cushions in a tribal pattern augmented an old striped ranch-house couch. June sighed. At least she'd sleep comfortably. She sat down on the cushions weakly, grateful for someplace to light.

"You okay?" asked Claira, sitting down beside her.

"Oh, feelin' no pain," she said and leaned back, closing her eyes. "How 'bout you?"

"Me?" asked Claira. "I don't drink."

June opened one eye and looked suspiciously at Claira. "What do you mean, you don't drink? You were having something—Long Island iced tea?"

"Just tea," said Claira with a grin that knocked June in the gut. "So I'll be up for a while." She reached over June's head and cranked the window open and a beneficent breeze wended in. A flash of heat lightning lit the mountains for a moment. Thunder was beginning to rumble closer. "I'm an alcoholic," said Claira. "Don't do it anymore."

June sat up. "Oh. God. Why didn't you tell me? I could've gone without—"

"No, forget it, June." Claira reached over and surprised her by twirling her finger in a loose curl. "I wouldn't go out to a bar if I couldn't handle people drinking." She leaned her head against the couch and let it touch June's barely. "I quit after the miscarriage, and I haven't had a drop since."

June looked down at her tea, which she had somehow finished. "I'm sorry, Claira. I didn't know."

Claira laughed softly. "Of course you didn't. That's why I'm telling you." She took June's cup and traded her for the one she hadn't touched yet. "That's when I learned about raspberry leaf and alfalfa," Claira said. "Morning sickness. And it works, doesn't it? You're feeling better."

June realized she was. She set the cup down on the kidney-shaped table before them and brought her arm up over the couch back, looking at Claira. The kiss had been an impulse; like Claira said: drinking bravada. Claira was straight. She had a boyfriend who was off working rodeos. June knew all that from their conversation at the Cactus Club. But there was something in the reflective black of her eyes and the wise set of her rock-carved jaw—*something*. June rested her head against her arm and looked out at the trees whipping up in the storm-coming wind. "God, I love that," she murmured. "It's like the world's about to—" She stopped and Claira laughed.

"To come," she said, and it was June's turn to grin. "I know what you mean," said Claira, following her gaze. "Anything could happen. Potential energy." The pattering hiss of the first drops broke the silence of the barren night and the smell of irrigation rushed up from the dust.

Claira closed her eyes, and June watched her wistfully, envious of him, whoever he was, that would touch that skin and feel the storm in it. She lifted Claira's straight, midnight hair and placed it over her shoulder and Claira turned her head and looked up at her. "God, June," she whispered, "I don't know what it is," and she was kissing June once more—startled and amazed beneath Claira's esurient mouth.

June wrapped her arms around Claira and drew her across her lap, holding her tightly, afraid to breathe and dissipate this ghost. She smelled like home, and June was unaware that she was crying. Their jeans rubbed together as Claira settled over her, covetously grasping at her tongue, and June gasped at the touch of insistent fingers inside the placket of her shirt. "Claira," June breathed, afraid this wild monsoon would come to her senses and pull away from her in embarrassment, but Claira had finished unbuttoning her, and the dark head dipped. June moaned at the touch of those lips against her breast. She let her own hands slide up beneath Claira's shirt, and here she found a bra impeding her intentions. Claira was rocking against her, enveloping each nipple in turn with an eager benediction, and June arched back and let her fingers follow instinct, tearing the barrier of cloth and lace away from what she wanted. Shit, she'd buy Claira another one. Claira let out a sharp sound, almost a squeal, and June feared she'd gone too far, but the warm cups of the freed breasts pressed into her hands insistently.

June held on to the solid strength of those breasts, closing her hands tightly over them, more than a handful, and urged Claira's body upward until they came within tongue's reach and she was able to taste. Claira swelled into her mouth, tight and hard against her tongue, and June was lost for a long moment in the bliss of sucking, pressing Claira against her as hard as she could. Claira's rising cries drew June from her distraction. She looked up at Claira with her prize still in her mouth and saw the rain reflected from a window across the room on the upstretched neck and stone cheek. It was the nearest June had come to God.

She let go of the breast she held in her mouth and drew Claira up farther still, *en pointe* on her knees, and slid down against the couch as Claira went up. With a crack of thunder that shook the house, Claira fell forward against the back of the couch, her feet still raised behind her. She was almost wailing under the din of the storm as June deftly unlooped the button fly and pulled the rough denim down to reveal her. Claira wore pale pink panties, and June sank her mouth into them.

"Oh, God!" Claira breathed, and June took this as a sign of approval. Claira was already wet in the center of this cotton pink, but June made certain it was saturated from without and within. Claira was jerking silently against her now, and June gave a cry of her own into the humid depths as she realized that Claira was coming without quite yet being touched. There was only the pale sound of attenuated breath and the smattering of hot rain on the patio behind them as Claira rose into June's mouth like the rolling hills beneath the mountain. June rolled the pantie down as Claira stilled, and pressed her tongue against the inflamed skin of her cunt. Claira stiffened, her body arching against the couch in agreement, and marked the drop between one orgasm and the next with the renewal of unbridled sound. June, in heaven, let the corners of her mouth turn up beneath the deluge of Claira as she saw the feet swaying before her cross at the ankles. She had ferreted out Claira's weakest point and she went in for the kill.

The sudden silence that allowed the shattering of rain to brace the air told June she had hit the jackpot. Though she was silent, nearly holding her breath, Claira's trembling cunt released its own storm and thunder, and as invigorating a scent as the pummeled body of the earth. June nearly fell into a bliss of her own beneath her, returning fully to herself only as Claira slipped away from her and rested damp breasts against June's.

The wildness of the rain had settled into a steady shirring, like shaken beads. Claira's heart thumped against her. Somewhere June heard a clock tick against the pull of a weighted pendulum, and it was these sounds that she would hear always with this moment in her head; these sounds that made The Moment, with the wet heat of Claira's skin melting into hers, and the scent of sex and the earth.

They had slipped away from the couch after a bit, and into Claira's room, and there were hours yet before the rain would end.

THE BOX OPENED under June's hand. She had to find out what was inside—if it held Claira or emptiness. Claira had gone home to Window Rock after the Fourth of July, quiet and without a word to June. It took June a month to track her down. She had sent Claira a letter with a simple question: *Are you gone for good?* She had asked Claira not to write at all if the answer was yes, to just count this as goodbye, with no hard feelings.

June, eyes still closed against the contents of the box, laughed with a painful catch in her chest at this. She was a fool. She had fallen deep and hard before Claira's body had ever brushed against her on the warm metal of a pickup, under the buzzing glow of a neon cactus. She had dissected herself and laid the center open, bare and susceptible, for Claira—Claira, who had never even kissed a woman before that night. Claira, who was engaged to a rodeo king.

June took an angry breath against her own stupidity and returned her attention to the box. It had been ten days; this was the last. She had said, "If I don't hear from you by then..." She put her hand in slowly and let it slide tentatively over the warm metal interior, painfully reminiscent of another trepid exploration. There was something...a bill with a plastic front, a flier for something, another bill...and then a smooth, firm square that could only be personal. June's fingers shook as she pulled it out and turned it over, and saw the postmark from Gallup. She wiped her nervous palms on the sides of her jeans and took one last look at the heavy cumulus clouds that were forming overhead, making a white umbrella of the sun. She opened it.

It was a card, blank on the outside except for a stencil-like ghost of an Ansel Adams tree. Inside was another question: *Does a fish need a bicycle?*

—MRS. HOUDINI'S WIFE—

Orly Brownstein

HARRY HOUDINI DIDN'T KNOW A THING.

Sure, he knew how to produce a flower out of thin air. And he could pull a tape through his neck before an audience of gaping, cork-faced men at curio halls. And it was no problem for him to sprint five miles along the Hudson River in one stretch, and later that day backstroke three more and barely lose his breath. But when it came to his wife Bess, he didn't know a damn thing.

It was 1895, and as twenty-year-old Bess lay in bed next to Harry that sticky August night, a stew of odors wafted through the open window and kept her awake: beer, cigar smoke, various colognes and perfumes, sex, possibility. Their small, cluttered apartment sat at the corner of Sixth Avenue and West 29th, smack in the heart of what New York City clergy had taken to calling "Satan's Circus." In the afternoons, Bess often strolled along Sixth Avenue, otherwise known as Ladies' Mile, which attracted armies of elegantly dressed female shoppers with its enormous cast-iron and brick department stores like Altman's, W. and J. Sloane, and the 200-foot-wide, seven-story Stern Brothers, which Harry scornfully called "That Monster." Bess was especially fond of R.H. Macy's, with its elaborate Christmas displays; she'd stare with delight at the flickering green-and-white lights and rosy-cheeked mechanical Santa. But at night, Ladies' Mile transformed itself into a boisterous, brightly lit whores' promenade, where rowdy johns filled horse-drawn landaus, broughams, and coupes, reeking of liquor and sweat. Perfumed prostitutes lined the avenue like dolls at Coney Island game booths, waiting to be picked. Not all of them were pretty, but all were good at what they did. And the men didn't mind. "A hole's a hole," Bess had heard more than one loaded john exclaim, when she and her husband ventured out at night, arm in arm, Harry always on the lookout for trouble. A block west of that blighted strip, swarms of black prostitutes choked Seventh Avenue, which residents and visitors alike flatly called "African Broadway."

"Satan's Circus, indeed," Bess muttered as she wrapped one of Harry's thick black curls around her slender index finger, careful not to wake him. But something besides busy Sixth Avenue kept Bess awake that night, and it had nothing to do with the devil.

In just two days, Bess and Harry would be leaving the city, to tour their act in small Pennsylvania towns. How would she—could she—say goodbye to Tom? She closed her eyes, recalling the May afternoon when they had met.

Twenty-one-year-old Harry—a mere babe in the magic world—had been working small-time theaters and circuses, dragging an exhausted Bess in tow, barely making ends meet. He supplemented their income with what he called "The Graft": magic and how-to booklets he penned himself and hawked outside their venues for ten cents a pop. That day, Bess had been standing in the lobby of Huber's Palace Museum in Union Square, reading one of Houdini's pamphlets, a poorly cut-and-pasted tract called *Dogs and How to Keep and Train Them*. Harry had dashed out a few minutes before to round up some lunch for the two, when a gentleman approached her. His first words upon greeting the five-foot, ninety-pound woman were: "Like a bird, you are. So small, such a *bisel freyd*!" His voice was like honey, thick with a Yiddish accent.

"A *bisel freyd*?" a wide-eyed Bess replied.

"A little joy!" the man said, grinning devilishly and tossing his hands into the air.

He was perhaps a head taller than Bess, with a handsome olive-skinned face that was rugged but not hard. He was around thirty years old and dressed to the nines, Bess thought, in a freshly pressed black suit, with a gold watch fob running from a vest button to a pocket. A shiny top hat was perched on his head, and his brown eyes gleamed—nearly laughed, Bess now mused—in the mid-afternoon sun that streamed through a window in the shabby dime-museum lobby.

When the man removed his hat, masses of dark-brown curls tumbled out. "Berta Thomashefsky," the man—now woman—said, placing a firm hand at the small of Bess's back, in a manner that was not so much forward as fatherly. "But everyone knows me as Tom," she went on. "And you?"

"Bess Houdini," the other woman replied, perplexed and very curious. In fact, she felt more than a little intimidated; she was practically frozen in her spot. Why in heaven's name was this woman dressed in such a way?

"Your face is very sweet," Tom said, brushing her hand against Bess's cheek. "And look at those eyes. So big! You'd think I was the King of Egypt!" She grinned again. "Loosen up, *khaver*. You're stiff as a board. My outfit?" she said, reading Bess's mind. "It's part of the act," she whispered, and poked Bess playfully with her elbow.

Bess felt a little more at ease now. How could she not? Tom was an absolute charmer. And never before had she met a woman so forthright and sure of herself. Bess was envious.

"You're waiting for someone?" asked Tom.

"My husband and I have a magic act," Bess explained. "We started here today, a three-month run."

"How nice," she replied, but Bess noticed a change in Tom's expression when she mentioned Harry. Still, she didn't think much of it, at least not then. "I've been here five years," Tom continued. "*Meshugeneh* work but it pays the rent."

Bess laughed softly, and Tom explained her post at the dime museum: She ran an animal act, one in which she repeatedly allowed rattlesnakes to bite her on the arm.

"But before they dig their fangs in," Tom told her, "I show the crowd how deadly the venom is."

"How?" Bess asked.

"I take a long needle and inject it into a rabbit. And those bunnies don't like it a bit! Their eyes pop out of their heads. *Oy*, they writhe. At home I have a heap of rabbit skins knee-high. Someday I'll make a lady a nice fur coat. Maybe for you, even!"

Bess was aghast. "You watch those animals die day after day?"

"It's not so bad, really." Tom smiled. "There are worse things a woman could do for a living, *nu*?"

"And how do you get the venom out of the snakes?"

"What *tsuris* that would be!" Tom chuckled. "It's not real venom, *khaver*. I use kerosene!" She doubled over in laughter, and Bess smiled faintly, horrified by Tom's story but taken with her strong cheekbones and thick lips. She saw a long scar running from Tom's left ear to her chin.

"How on earth do you survive the bites?" Bess asked.

"You're a magician, yes?" Tom smirked. "You should know better than to ask a girl for her secrets."

When Tom offered her a tour of the museum, Bess protested—"My husband will be back soon," she said—but Tom would have none of it. "Just a few minutes, dear. It's not so big a place." And they walked arm in arm through the empty, musty corridors; paying customers were few and far between in the warm late-spring and summer months. As they strolled, Bess noticed a slight limp in Tom's gait.

The place was crammed with oddities, anything that might

draw in the river of East 14th Street pedestrians: shrunken heads, wax figures of African pygmies, a model of Niagara Falls with running water, biblical dioramas, stuffed and preserved creatures that were painstakingly patched together: a half-dog, half-fish, for example. Even after P.T. Barnum's death several years before, humbug was alive and well in New York City.

"There's so much more here. This place is a world of its own," Tom said, her eyes lighting up again. "And you'll make friends, I'm sure of it. William, the human windowpane? You can practically see his heart beating, the poor thing. And my buddy Gillian? God bless her. Forearms as big as a boxer's! She can lift fifty pounds with her pinky finger! Some call them freaks, but I call them my tribe, good people. I'll introduce you to them."

"I would like that." Bess smiled, enchanted by Tom's enthusiasm.

No matter how many dime museums she and Harry worked, these sorts of places always fascinated her; she was just a nice Catholic girl from Brooklyn, and while she'd grown tired of performing over the months, the museums' wonders continued to surprise and delight her. Now she stood silently before an expertly crafted wax dummy of Napoleon, admiring the artistry of its furrowed brow and serious expression. When the mannequin winked at her, she jumped back and covered her mouth with her tiny hands. "Oh, my!" she squealed.

"Frank, you should know better!" Tom chided the man through a quiet laugh, then put her arm around a clearly shaken Bess. "It's called living statuary, *shayna maidel*. Relax."

"What's *shayna maidel*?" Bess asked, a little calmer now.

"Pretty girl," Tom said, and Bess blushed.

OVER THE NEXT FEW WEEKS, Bess stole away from her act with Harry whenever possible to spend time with Tom. Although her husband got along with the "freaks" employed by the museum, he showed disdain for Bess's new friend. "Too manly," he'd tell her. "I don't know what's wrong with her, but she gives good Jewish women a bad name." And then he'd bury his broad handsome face in his hands.

Bess didn't know what Harry meant. "And you give good Jewish *men* a bad name. Talking like that!" she'd say.

Many times she'd join Tom and the other performers out back when they'd slip away for a cigarette or swig of whiskey. Her favorites were Nell—a humorless, rail-thin, bearded woman—and Jerome, a midget with Chiclet teeth who performed in a variety act with trained chimpanzees. One afternoon he brought one of the chimps outside and put on a show especially for Bess. "Watch this," he said, and lit a cigarette. When the monkey squawked raucously, Jerome handed him the cigarette and the creature started puffing away. "How about that!" Jerome chuckled, and when he did, his face screwed up into a twisted little walnut. When Bess kneeled down to pet the animal, the chimp reached out and grabbed her left breast, squeezing it hard; Tom quickly slapped the paw away. "He's as bad as I am!" Tom said with a wink, and everyone laughed except Bess, who didn't understand the joke until later that night. And when she did, a slow smile spread across her face.

AFTER THAT AFTERNOON, Bess thought a lot about Tom, and a lot about Harry too. Even though they'd been married less than a year, she felt a divide in their relationship. Many nights after dinner, Harry would leave the house, walking along the river-front for hours, creating new and better acts in his head. "The Metamorphosis...it isn't right," he'd say, referring to an act in which he'd enter a large cabinet and Bess would secure him in a black sack. She'd then draw the curtain shut, come around the back, and in a matter of moments, Harry would appear, pull open the curtain, and there Bess would be, bound in the same bag. "We're taking too long. We've got to shave off a few seconds," he'd say, and off he'd go along the Hudson.

This isn't to say Harry Houdini wasn't a decent man. Surely

he protected Bess. He made certain she was taken care of and well fed. He loved to have her by his side, with her silky dark hair, cherub face, and big hazel eyes. And he sweetly referred to her as his "large wife." But even more, he treasured the adulation of the crowds, the thrill of performing. He loved the way ladies looked at him when he pulled Buffalo nickels from behind their ears, loved the way gentlemen envied him with Bess on his arm.

And Bess was certain she didn't want to be loved like this, knew that love could be more than self-fulfillment. And then one night, when Tom invited her over for Shabbos dinner, she began to think her curiosity might be love in disguise.

They had taken the Culver Line from the Bowery to Coney Island, where Tom lived in a hotel by the ocean. Even though Tom was wearing her suit and top hat, no one had given the couple a second glance; they looked for all the world like man and wife. In fact, Tom had told Bess that no one ever gave her trouble when she dressed like a man; it was her form of self-protection, and she felt more comfortable in men's clothing anyway. Tom lived in what was called "The Elephant"; shaped like a giant pachyderm, the hotel was a wood-framed, tin-skinned building—more than a hundred feet long and a hundred feet wide—that housed dozens of rooms in its head, stomach, and feet, and various shops in its trunk and one of its forelegs. Outside the hotel, the smells of clam roasts, ice cream, and lager hung in the warm air. The area was just as seedy as Bess's corner of Sixth Avenue, but it had a prettier, more festive appeal.

Bess had told Harry she was visiting her mother overnight in Brooklyn, certain he wouldn't approve of her plans. "Send Mama my love," he had said, a bit sarcastically, since Bess's mother continued to object to the marriage simply because Harry was Jewish.

"Why do you live in such a strange place? There are plenty of apartments in Manhattan," Bess said, as they rode a cramped elevator up to Tom's room.

"That kind of life is so ordinary," Tom replied, trying to manage the two bags of food she and Bess had picked up from a delicatessen along the way. "And I'm not an ordinary girl, *shayna*. You know that. Sure, it costs a little more, but the worthwhile things in life always do."

When the couple entered Tom's room, Bess's eyes grew wide. Yiddish theater posters plastered almost every inch of her walls, a red-velvet-covered bed took up a great deal of the small room, and the sweet smell of jasmine floated in the air. "What are all these?" Bess said, pointing to the posters.

"*Oy*," said Tom. "Those are from my previous life."

"Were you an actress?"

"For a time." She placed her bags on a small oak table in the corner of the room. "Before the trouble."

"The trouble?" Bess asked, her eyebrows raised.

"Let's put it this way: I was a damn good actress—and a looker. *King Solomon*, I was in, at the Thalia Theater. Goneril in *The Jewish King Lear*...at the National Theater. The lead in Jacob Gordin's *Sappho*, even."

"Sappho?" Bess asked.

"Sort of a Greek princess," Tom mumbled.

"What happened?"

Tom and Bess sat on the bed, and Bess summoned the courage to place her arm around Tom. Her back felt strong and firm.

"I had just finished up a melodrama at the Bowery Garden," Tom sighed. "You know, the kind where poor *shlubs* win out over rich villains, and sweet, pure shopgirls escape their advances? And you know how the Bowery is, *nu*?"

Bess nodded. Harry had taken her to a production of *Thomas Edison, Amazing Electrician*, and even though the play was purported to be "educational," she could barely make out the actors' lines over the spectators' drunken hollering and hooting.

"After the show," Tom went on, "my boss says, 'There's some men who want your autograph.' And I thought nothing of it.

People always wanted my autograph. With a face like this, why not?" She let out a small laugh, but Bess could tell it was laced with sadness. "So I went out back, behind the theater, where actors gather, and there they were."

"There who were?" Bess said, her hand now slightly rubbing Tom's back.

"Three men. *Shmutsiks*. Greasy, they were. And I wanted to run, but instead I said, 'You want my autograph?' What did I know from anything? I was young, you know, like you. And they said, 'Yes.' And I said to them, 'You've got something to write on?' And one of them said, 'Write on this.' And then they grabbed me...and they had their way with me. *Gotenyu*, so much pain I was in afterward."

"Is that what this is from?" Bess ran her hand down the scar on Tom's cheek.

"And the limp. You're sweet for not asking before. And then I quit. '*Dayenu*. Enough,' I said. I needed it for nothing. Like they would want a cripple onstage anyway."

"Thank you for telling me," Bess said.

"I never told anyone before," Tom answered, looking at the floor. "But enough about me. Let's celebrate! It's Shabbos!" She jumped to her feet and raced to the bags in the corner of the room. "What's this, a roasted chicken? Oh, my! And a bottle of good red wine! And sweet little green beans and a cherry cheese-cake! But first we will light the Shabbos candles, *mein shayna*!"

Tom placed the food on the oak table, along with dinnerware and glasses, and then retrieved two brass candlesticks from a closet. "Do you and Harry light the candles together?"

"Oh, no," Bess said. "I mean, my husband was raised religious. His father was a rabbi. But Harry turned away from all that when he left home. I'm not Jewish, but it makes me sad that he doesn't follow his tradition."

"What about you? Do you go to church?"

"Not since Harry and I married. But don't get me wrong—I do believe in God."

"Well, sweet girl, you're going to believe in God a little more in a moment."

Bess raised her eyebrows, unsure of Tom's remark.

"Here, I've written out the blessing. We can say it together. But first you light the candles."

"It looks so foreign. What if I mess up the words?"

"God won't mind. Go ahead, *shayna*."

Bess tentatively struck a match and lit the tapered white candles, and the two read the blessing together: *Baruch atah Adonai, eloheynu melech haolam, asher kidshanu bmitzvotav vetzivanu lehadlik ner shel Shabbat*. Blessed are You, O Lord our God, Master of the universe, who has sanctified us with your commandments and commanded us to light the Shabbat candles.

When Bess looked up and saw the glow of flames, she understood what Tom had said about believing in God. "They're so lovely!" she exclaimed. "Not like other candles. It's like seeing God before my eyes."

"And if you close your eyes, you can almost hear God," Tom whispered in Bess's ear. And as she did, Bess let her head drop back, and Tom kissed her lightly on the neck. Bess turned toward her and stared into her soft eyes. She took Tom's hand in hers and silently led her to the bed.

One by one, their articles of clothing slowly came off and were tossed to the floor. First Bess's button-up boots, then her petticoats, her bustle, her knickers and corset. Tom's polished black shoes, trousers and suspenders, crisp white dress shirt and tie, her undershirt. Wordlessly, the two lay side by side on the bed, naked, wanting. Bess leaned over Tom's lithe, muscular body and began kissing her from head to toe. Gentle kisses, tiny licks, butterfly kisses, starting at her forehead, running down the slope of her nose. Dotting her cheekbones, resting on the long scar on her face, lingering on her chin. Down her smooth neck and breastbone. She ran her tongue lightly along Tom's clavicle, which was lovely and defined; like a Rodin sculpture, Bess thought. Tom's eyes were open, her body calm and receiving, her chest slowly rising and falling. Bess focused on Tom's arms, which were badly scarred with snakebites; with each kiss, she healed Tom's body, transformed her wounds into something beautiful. When every section of Tom's front side was kissed, Bess whispered, "Turn over. I don't want to miss a spot."

Tom did as told, and Bess began all over again, until she had finished her work. "No one's ever kissed me like that before," Tom said.

"No one's ever *let me* before," Bess smiled.

So it went all evening, the two making love in the bright light of the Shabbos candles, stopping occasionally to eat and drink, to whisper words that lovers do. And it was that night that Bess first noticed how Tom's voice changed when the two were alone together, how her tone grew softer, more urgent, tinged with what can only be described as prayer, as if she were saying, "I love you" every time she opened her mouth.

"You make love like a Jewish woman," Tom said, as the two were curled in each other's arms, Tom's hand on Bess's soft belly.

"What's that supposed to mean?" Bess asked through a quiet laugh.

"You know what you want and don't stop until you get it." She lowered her voice a bit. "Maybe you're a *gilgul*."

"A *gilgul*?"

"Legend claims there are those who are born in a *goyishe* body but have a Jewish soul. They say Jewish souls always come home."

Bess just smiled and closed her eyes.

"My sweet *gilgul*," Tom whispered in Bess's ear. "Welcome home." And they drifted off to sleep as the last flickers of the candles died out.

EVERY OTHER FRIDAY for nearly two months, Bess spent Shabbos evening with Tom, each time telling Harry she was visiting her mother in Brooklyn, each time surprised he believed her. But now, as she lay in bed next to her husband on this hot August night, knowing she'd be saying goodbye to Tom the following evening, it wasn't her lying to Harry that bothered her; it was her lying to Tom: her sin of omission. Even though they'd been spending the night together, lighting the candles in joy and wonder, speaking to each other from their hearts, she hadn't told Tom she loved her. But was that necessary? Did Tom not know? *Of course she knows*, Bess thought. *But she also knows I can't leave Harry. It would kill him. And what kind of life could I live with her?* Still, she made up her mind to tell Tom how she felt. That's the worst sin of all, Bess thought, to keep your heart locked up, to not say the words you need to say, because you're too proud and maybe afraid.

The following night, both Bess and Tom knew, would be their last together. The Pennsylvania tour would be followed by a Midwest run through Milwaukee, Chicago, and St. Louis, and who knew where the husband-and-wife team would go from there. The sky was the limit, especially since Harry had been receiving so many favorable notices in the city papers.

That Friday morning, Tom had asked Bess to bring her bathing suit; she had a surprise in store for her. Bess would have to ride the Culver Line alone, since Tom had taken the afternoon off from Huber's. "I've got something special planned," she'd said, and Bess had something in mind as well. When Bess knocked on Tom's hotel room door that evening, she was taken aback by the sight before her: Tom's hair was shorn into a stylish men's cut. "Oh, my!" Bess said. "How handsome you look! But why?"

"Just for you, *shayna*," Tom replied. She was wearing a striped one-piece men's swimsuit, and Bess stood there admiring her toned physique, thought for a moment that Tom really might be a man, with her flat chest and tight biceps. But to Bess, she was unmistakably a woman. "You'll see," Tom said. "You brought your suit, *nu*?"

"It's in my bag." Bess gestured toward a small valise at her side, then entered Tom's room, where she quickly changed into her bathing suit. She didn't know what Tom had up her sleeve, but she was willing to play along.

"All done?" Tom said, and Bess nodded. "We're going Electric Bathing, my sweetness."

Bess had heard about Electric Bathing, although Harry had refused to take her on more than one occasion. "Lovebirds swooning in the ocean!" he'd say. "Makes a mockery out of a decent sport like swimming. No wonder they call it Sodom by the Sea." Coney Island retailers had pitched in a few years before and installed arc lighting at the beach, and for the first time, people could swim at night and actually see where they were headed. Of course, more often than not—especially in the past few years, when men and women no longer adhered to separate swim schedules—couples took advantage of Electric Bathing to become intimate with each other, away from prying eyes, albeit in public.

Now Tom's new haircut and outfit made sense, Bess thought. If they were going Electric Bathing—which meant only one thing—they couldn't go in as two women, now could they? At this moment, Bess loved Tom more than ever.

When they got to the beach, Tom asked Bess to sit down for a moment, and Tom wrapped her arm around her lover. "I've got something to tell you," she said, reaching into a paper bag she'd brought along.

"No," Bess interrupted. "Let me go first."

Tom smiled and waited for Bess to speak.

"I just want to say…" Bess paused, trying to find the words. "I love you."

"Is that all? I know, *shayna*," Tom said, and placed a kiss on Bess's forehead. "Now, *sha*. Listen. Remember how I told you about the *gilgul*?" Bess nodded. "Well, here's another story. And maybe it's true and maybe it's not. What do I know? They say certain people meet for a reason, they're soul mates. You've heard this, yes?"

Again Bess nodded, and smiled a little, seeing Tom's sad eyes shine in the electric lights.

"Some say that two *neshemahs*—two souls—who come together in this life were standing side by side at Sinai when the Israelites received the Ten Commandments. Maybe it's *shmaltzy*, a *bobe meyse*—you know, a tall tale—but maybe there's a little truth there. So I'm giving you this, just in case." Tom reached into the paper bag and withdrew two silver rings. "Nothing much. But something. I picked them up at the drugstore." She placed one of the rings on Bess's pinky finger and the other on her own. "So when we're apart, you just look at this, and there I'll be, always with you. And when I get sad, and maybe a little lonely even, there'll you be with me."

"Like your wife?"

"*Mein khosen.* My chosen. And me yours."

When Bess reached out to wipe a tear from Tom's cheek, Tom just smiled and said, "So you want to go swimming or what?"

Hand in hand they waded into the ocean, surrounded by a multitude of couples. They walked out as far as they could until the water reached Bess's shoulders. She looked up at the dark sky speckled with dozens of bright white stars, and then at the shoreline, where she saw hundreds of blinking lights—blue and green, red and yellow—and the Loop-the-Loop and the towering Coney Island Roller Coaster and the massive trunk of The Elephant in which Tom, her tender lover, lived. And as Tom's hands made their way down the curves of Bess's body and she whispered, "My sweet *gilgul*" in her ear, Bess knew, at least for the moment, she was where she was supposed to be.

—CONTRIBUTORS—

Kathryn Ann lives, walks the dog, and plays a lot of Unreal Tournament in Vancouver, Canada. Her book *Snakes and Ladders,* a collection of stories about lesbian relationships, is available from Amazon.com or directly from the author at kat@lynx.bc.ca.

Julie Auer's short fiction and essays have appeared in Lesléa Newman's *Bedroom Eyes*, Jess Wells's *Love Shook My Heart 2*, and other anthologies and periodicals. Alyson Books will publish her first novel in 2004.

Sally Bellerose received an NEA fellowship to write a novel, *The GirlsClub*. Her prose has been chosen as a finalist for the Thomas Wolf Fiction Prize in 1998, the James Jones First Novel Fellowship in 1999, and the Bellwether Prize in 2000. She is currently working on a novel titled *Legs*.

Betty Blue is a transplanted desert girl currently shivering in San Francisco. Her fiction has appeared in *Best Bisexual Erotica, Anything That Moves* magazine, *Tough Girls,* and *Best Lesbian Erotica 2002*.

Orly Brownstein, a lifelong Harry Houdini fan, and a more recent devotee of his wife, lives in West Hollywood, Calif., where she is an editor and writer. In third grade she dressed up as Houdini for an oral book report, the only one in her class to cross the gender line.

Emily Chávez was born and raised in Cincinnati. She is currently a student at Swarthmore College, where she is special-majoring in education and sociology/anthropology with a concentration in women's studies. "This Girl" is her first published story.

Jill Dolan is the author of *The Feminist Spectator as Critic* (University of Michigan Press, 1991), *Presence and Desire: Essays on Gender, Sexuality, Performance* (Michigan, 1993), and *Geographies of Learning: Theory and Practice, Activism and Performance* (Wesleyan, 2001). She is the former Executive Director of the Center for Lesbian and Gay Studies at the Graduate Center of the City University of New York, and now holds the Zachary T. Scott Family Chair in Drama at the University of Texas at Austin, where she heads the MA/Ph.D. program in performance studies.

Elana Dykewomon has been a cultural worker and radical activist since the 1970s. She has published five books of fiction and poetry, most recently *Nothing Will Be as Sweet as the Taste—Selected Poems,* and the Jewish lesbian historical novel *Beyond the Pale,* which won both the Lambda Literary and Gay and Lesbian Publishers' awards for lesbian fiction in 1998, and hopes to have a new short story collection out in 2003. She brought the international lesbian feminist journal of arts and politics *Sinister Wisdom,* to the San Francisco Bay area, serving as an editor between 1987 and 1995. She teaches creative writing (see www.dykewomon.org), lives happily with her partner among friends, and tries to make trouble whenever she can.

Zsa Zsa Gershick is associate director of the University of Southern California News Service and the author of *Gay Old Girls* (Alyson Publications, 1998), honored as *ForeWord* magazine's Best Gay and Lesbian Book of the Year. E-mail her at gayoldgirls@hotmail.com.

Katherine Granfield was born in Wilmington, Del., and lives in Northern California with her partner of sixteen years. She has written a novel and other stories.

Carol Guess lives in Seattle. She is the author of four books: *Seeing Dell, Switch, Gaslight,* and *Love Is a Map I Must Not Set on Fire* (forthcoming). "Martin Bebartin" is dedicated to Esther and Alex, and all the women who worked at Aquarius Books in Bloomington, Ind.

Renee Hawkins, a disc jockey, has recently moved from Albuquerque, N.M., to Atlanta. Although not quite used to Southern cuisine, she will eat grits—as long as green chile is served with the meal. Her story "Burning Zozobra" appears in *Pillow Talk II.*

Siobhán Houston holds degrees in religious studies from California State University, Chico and Harvard Divinity School. Her work has appeared in numerous publications, including *Parabola Magazine, GNOSIS: A Journal of the Western Inner Traditions, Intuition Magazine,* and *Weird Sisters.* A native of the California coast, she now lives near Boulder, Colo., with her spouse, musician and artist Rachel Miller.

Abbe Ireland has previously published two stories in Alyson anthologies, *The Ghost of Carmen Miranda and Other Spooky Gay and Lesbian Tales* and *Skin Deep.* She has also published articles and short stories in national children's magazines. Abbe currently hangs out with a herd of neutered tomcats in the Arizona desert, an odd life dynamic for writing lesbian stories, but it seems to work.

Lesléa Newman is an author and editor whose forty books include *Girls Will Be Girls; Out of the Closet and Nothing to Wear; Pillow Talk; Bedroom Eyes; She Loves Me, She Loves*

Me Not; and *Best Short Stories of Lesléa Newman* (forthcoming from Alyson Books). Visit www.lesleanewman.com to learn more about her work.

Shelly Rafferty is a writer, editor, and Ph.D. student. Her work has appeared in *Wilma Loves Betty, Close Calls,* and *Best American Erotica 2002.* A parent and activist, she has interests in public policy, epistemology, medical anthropology, and all things arctic.

Gina Ranalli has contributed stories and essays to many anthologies, including *Pillow Talk II, Dykes With Baggage, Set in Stone, Body Check, The Moment of Truth,* and *Bedroom Eyes.* A native of Massachusetts, she now lives in Oregon.

Vittoria repetto is the hardest working guinea dyke poet on NYC's lower east side. She has been published in *Mudfish, The Paterson Literary Review, Voices in Italian Americana, Harrington Lesbian Fiction Quarterly, Lips, Unsettling America: An Anthology of Contemporary Multicultural Poetry,* and *Curaggia: Writing by Women of Italian Descent,* among other places. She is also the vice president of the Italian American Writers Association and hosts a women's poetry jam at Bluestockings Bookstore.

Ruthann Robson is the award-winning author of the short story collections *Cecile, Eye of a Hurricane,* and *The Struggle for Happiness;* the novels *a/k/a* and *Another Mother;* and the non-fiction books *Legal Issues for Lesbians and Gay Men, Lesbian (Out)Law: Survival Under the Rule of Law,* and *Sappho Goes to Law School: Fragments in Lesbian Legal Theory.*

Sylvia Rose has ridden on lots of roads, including many less traveled, but this is her first trip as a fiction writer. Right now she's pulled over in San Francisco.

Anne Seale is a creator of lesbian songs, stories, and plays who has performed on gay stages singing tunes from her tape *Sex for Breakfast*. More of her work can be found in *Dykes With Baggage, Lip Service, Set in Stone, Pillow Talk,* and other lesbian anthologies and periodicals.

Mary Sharratt's short fiction and essays have been published in *Puerto del Sol, Bookwomon, Iris: A Journal for Women, Hurricane Alice,* and elsewhere. A Pushcart Prize nominee, she is the author of the novel *Summit Avenue* (Coffee House Press, 2000). She lives in Manchester, England.

Sarah Pemberton Strong, author of the critically acclaimed novel *Burning the Sea,* was born in California in 1967. She now lives outside of Boston.

Terry Wolverton is the author of the novel *Bailey's Beads;* two collections of poetry, *Black Slip* and *Mystery Bruise;* and a memoir about her years in the feminist art movement, *Insurgent Muse. Embers,* a novel-in-poem, will be published by Red Hen Press this year. She has also edited numerous literary compilations, among them *Circa 2000: Lesbian Fiction at the Millennium* and *Circa 2000: Gay Fiction at the Millennium.*